OLD BONES

OLD BONES

TRUDY NAN BOYCE

G. P. PUTNAM'S SONS / NEW YORK

G. P. PUTNAM'S SONS
Publishers Since 1838
An imprint of Penguin Random House LLC
375 Hudson Street
New York, New York 10014

Library of Congress Cataloging-in-Publication Data

Names: Boyce, Trudy Nan, author.
Title: Old bones / Trudy Nan Boyce.
Description: New York : G. P. Putnam's Sons, 2017.
Identifiers: LCCN 2016036562 | ISBN 9780399167270 (hardback)
Subjects:
BISAC: FICTION / Mystery & Detective / General. | FICTION /
    Mystery & Detective / Police Procedural. | FICTION / Crime.
GSAFD: Mystery fiction.
Classification: LCC PS3602.O927 O43 2017 | DDC 813/.6—dc23
LC record available at https://lccn.loc.gov/2016036562
p.   cm.

Printed in the United States of America
10 9 8 7 6 5 4 3 2 1

BOOK DESIGN BY MEIGHAN CAVANAUGH

In memory of Jan Dotson Provencial

There are years that ask questions and years that answer.

—Zora Neale Hurston

OLD BONES

ATLANTA

THE CALL CAME AT THREE MINUTES AFTER MIDNIGHT. DETECTIVE
Sarah Alt's shift was over.

"Detective radio raising any Homicide Unit." Dispatch sounded out of breath.

"4132, go ahead," answered Detective "Cochise" Chatterjee, the midnights detective who'd just walked in the door of the Homicide office.

"Zone Five is requesting Homicide to respond to Peachtree Street and Auburn Avenue, Woodruff Park, eleven people shot, one dead on the scene. Witnesses report that the victims are Spelman College students who were participating in the Take Back the Night vigil."

"Radio, copy. Show myself and 4137 en route," said Chatterjee, walking toward Huff's office.

Alt, known to most as Salt, stood up in her cubicle at the far end of the aisle. Wills, Gardner, and Felton stepped into the aisle as Sergeant

Huff came out of his office, radio in hand. He nodded at Chatterjee, then responded to radio. "4110 to radio. Show myself and"—he looked down the aisle at the detectives who hadn't yet left for the night—"4125, 4120, 4144, 4133, and 4139 also en route."

As the familiar adrenaline rush began, Salt's scalp tightened around the scar barely visible at the top of her forehead; no longer tired from the previous eight hours, she lifted the long coat from the peg above her desk, the coat she'd just begun wearing as the weather turned colder.

Sergeant Huff and the detectives looked at one another, acknowledging the oncoming storm that an incident of this kind would generate, a high-profile case like this, a red ball: Spelman College was the historically black women's college in the heart of Atlanta; Woodruff Park at the intersection of Peachtree Street and Auburn Avenue was the crossroads of Atlanta commerce and the cradle of the civil rights movement. The red ball was rolling.

"Fuck me!" Huff said, turning to get his coat. "Radio, notify Unit One."

The burning-oil smell inside the unmarked Taurus was worse with the windows up; she could taste the smell in the back of her throat. The coat, on the passenger seat beside her, once belonged to her father. She'd gone looking for it when she'd been promoted to detective last year. Detectives with the least seniority got the shit cars. At this time of night, traffic on five-lane, one-way, southbound Courtland was light. Sirens echoed off the downtown buildings, helicopter lights washed over the streets, and the Handie-Talkie on the car seat beside her crackled with units responding and arriving at the scene of the shooting. Huff had assigned her to report to the city hospital in order to interview the victims as they arrived, those conscious and able to talk.

Police reform had been the unifying message of the recent demonstrations and tonight's vigil. In silence they'd carried posters, blow-up pictures of injuries to local victims, an unsolved rape and a bungled domestic violence investigation, and photos of Trayvon Martin, Michael Brown, Eric Garner, and Tamir Rice. The students wore midnight-blue T-shirts. "No Justice, No Peace," was chanted mournfully rather than angrily.

Salt was a few blocks from the hospital ready to make the turn when an insistent dispatcher broke through the radio chatter. "Units in the vicinity of Peachtree and Memorial, a witness to the Woodruff Park incident reports that she is following the vehicle occupied by the shooter."

Salt picked up the handheld and turned the volume knob. "4133, en route," she responded. "Peachtree and Memorial. I'm two away." It was a straight shot and possible for her to intercept the perp vehicle. "Description, radio?"

"4133, be advised caller is in a silver-blue Jaguar, Georgia license BR 951. Suspect vehicle is a black Chevy Blazer." Dispatch's voice was hurried but firm.

"I'm southbound on Courtland, radio." She switched on the emergency lights and flipped on the siren, but both were weak and unconvincing; lights only in the back window, the siren sounded like a squawk.

"4133, caller reports they are now eastbound on Memorial."

"Damn," Salt said, slowing and burping the siren through a red light. "Copy, radio, eastbound." She stepped on the gas hard, eased off when she got to Memorial. Holding the wheel tight, she took a hard left, then accelerated out of it. At the top of the hill at Capitol and

Memorial she saw the Jag a quarter of a mile in front of her and two lights farther, the black Blazer. "Radio, I have a visual." She barely slowed through another red light, gaining on the target vehicles.

"4110 to 4133, hold your distance. Do not approach. Radio, advise the witness to back off," Huff ordered.

"Beat cars are en route. The zone has been notified," radio reported.

"Radio, I'm at Hill Street." Salt was one light behind the Blazer as the Jag pulled off.

"4110 to 33, back off. Hold your distance. Repeat. Do not approach. Zone units will make the stop." Huff was loud.

"Copy," Salt said as the Blazer, one block ahead, turned right on Cherokee. "They're southbound on Cherokee," she reported, taking the turn.

The Blazer, idling, exhaust clouding the air, had stopped in the middle of the street ten yards in front of her. Sirens sounded in the distance, closing. A rifle extended from the passenger-side window. "Radio . . ." Her windshield shattered, glass spraying inward as she ducked. A tire blew, sending the Taurus across the sidewalk and into a low brick wall. The gunfire ceased, replaced by the sound of squealing tires.

It was the smell of Homicide tripled, pungent. More detectives, body odor, overripe clothes: morning-watch detectives held over, day watch just in waiting for assignments, and Salt and the rest of evening watch dragging butt after being up all night after the shooting and chase. The coffeepot and microwave going all night; the smell of burnt grounds and popcorn permeated the air.

Huff, wearing the same clothes he had worn the night before, came out of his office pulling on his "good" jacket, a nubby brown number, over a straining Harley belt buckle. Walking through the aisle of detectives on his way out, he said, "I've been ordered to the fucking press conference upstairs."

Rosie was at Salt's desk as soon as Huff left. The six-three transgender cop, a former uniformed officer, placed a large hand on the back of Salt's head. "Anything hurting? Sometimes whiplash doesn't show up until later."

"Sore knee, not anything much. That's about it. Aikido helps. You on your way to the break room?" She and Rosie joined the others as they pulled molded plastic tables and chairs around the TV in the crowded, too-bright room. On the screen a reporter for a national news station was saying, "Press conference about to begin . . ." The mayor, the chief, the deputy chief, two majors, three sergeants—including Huff—Detective Chatterjee, and representatives from the FBI filled the area in front of and below the city's phoenix-rising seal. Community leaders and prominent civil rights figures stood in front of the officials.

The mayor stepped up to the podium. "Not since the Atlanta Child Murders in the late seventies has Atlanta experienced this degree of horror and . . ."

Detectives, some dead on their feet, dragged chairs close enough to the TV in order to hear and gauge the amount of pressure the case would generate.

The FBI assistant special agent in charge was mercifully brief. "The attorney general has asked me to . . . contribute whatever resources . . ."

Eyes rolled all over the break room. "Yeah, they'll be more busy tryin' to squirrel our informants," said a day-watch veteran.

A senior civil rights leader took the podium and began an homage to the movement interspersed with demands that suspects be quickly identified and brought to justice.

"I think I heard him make that same speech in the seventies," said Marshall Daniels from Salt's crew. He and Steve Barney, both prone to antics, had been partners for so long they were known as the Wild Things, One and Two. Street smart and good investigators, they were not great with the paperwork, but they solved cases.

The chief was at the mic for Q and A. First question from the reporters: "Is the officer who chased the suspects here?" The chief turned to the major, who turned to Huff, who shook his head. "She's not available right now."

The break room audience turned to Salt, who smiled tightly and waved like a prom queen.

"Why were no other officers able to assist with apprehending the suspects?" was the next question.

"I've been informed that the chase developed so quickly that no other cars were able to arrive before the suspects fired on Detective Salt . . . Alt. The first officer to arrive attended to Detective Alt to determine the extent of her injuries. Two other beat cars arrived within two minutes and began searching the area. Be-On-the-Lookouts were immediately broadcast to all zones and other jurisdictions. Unfortunately that location is close to both the east/west and the north/south interstates and the suspects were not located."

"Was the detective injured? Why didn't she return fire?" another reporter shouted.

"Yeah, Salt, where was your Wonder Woman bullet deflector?" shouted Barney from across the break room.

Another voice from the press: "Can you give us the name of the witness? Will the witness be able to identify the suspects? What about a license tag number?"

"The investigation is ongoing. The witness will not be identified for safety reasons. The witness saw the shots coming from the truck and followed them while trying to call 911. The witness was not able to obtain a tag number because it was obscured."

"Obscured? How?"

"Mud, dirt, we don't know."

"Are the suspects white? Did race play a role in Detective Alt's decision not to return fire?"

The Public Affairs officer stepped up to end the press conference: ". . . providing daily updates . . ."

A COLD DAY

AS SALT PULLED NEXT TO THE CURB BEHIND THE PATROL CAR, its blue lights flashing, she was already composing the report in her head: *Intermittent clouds, temperature in the mid-forties. Low-income residential neighborhood.* Tightening the belt on her coat and securing her fedora in the rearview mirror, she saw Felton's Taurus pulling up behind her.

The two of them stood looking down at the yellow tape wavering from a bank of brown waist-high blackberry brambles midfield. Felton's presence on crime scenes was welcome by most cops and by every Homicide detective; he had a one hundred percent clear-up rate on his cases. He was one of the few out gay detectives on the PD, and for that reason, it was assumed, he had not been offered a partner. Truth was he'd declined all offers for partnering. Lately he'd been assisting Salt, helping to process her scenes and talking her through cases.

"This sucks," he said. "We've got our hands full." He pulled down the black fedora he always wore. Atlanta Homicide was known as the Hat Squad for the fedoras they earned once they solved their first case.

"People will still get murdered. Somebody has to work the new cases; they didn't ask me to be on the task force."

"That makes no sense. You saw the perps. Did you go home at all last night?" he asked.

Silently they began walking single file down a narrow footpath worn through the weedy, vacant urban lot. "I napped at Wills' house for an hour," she said. Briars caught at their pant legs and brown-seed tagalongs attached themselves to their clothes from the knee down.

"You gave us a scare, you know?"

"Bit of a shock to me, too, when I took the turn and there they were."

"How's Wills?"

Salt shrugged. She and Wills had been lovers for close to two years. They'd met over dead bodies while Salt was still in patrol and he was already a veteran Homicide detective.

"He's still shaken, I take it?"

The low four o'clock winter sun shone on the tips of the taller grasses and just barely lit the top of the bank, underneath which the body lay. The rest of the field and surrounding crumbling neighborhood was cast into lavenders and mauves. They stopped five yards from where a uniformed officer stood protecting the crime scene. "Officer Greenberg," the young woman officer introduced herself and semi-saluted as they approached. "I was chasing a perp from that code 19." She pointed to a car, exhaust billowing, driver's-side door open, idling in front of the patrol car on the street above. "I lost sight of him on the other side." She nodded to the opposite street. "So coming back through here, breathing heavy—I guess the smell caught my attention—I looked and saw a bit of pink, her shirt, then the skull here." She lifted a long, thorny stem.

The overly sweet smell had lost most of the cloying heaviness of the newly decomposed. Instead there was just enough of an organic lump in the air around the bones to halt one's breath. The officer called the remains "her." Salt wouldn't assume a gender but noted the small shirt grayed by weather and dirt holding a rib cage, bones outlined beneath the fabric, in spots its original pink slightly visible. "I got it." Salt nodded. Officer Greenberg stepped back. Clumps of matted hair were entwined with dried foliage beneath the mostly denuded facial and cranial bones. Bits of connective tissue had loosened their hold, causing the left arm and hand to lie separated some two feet beyond where they originally came to rest. Denim shorts covered the small pelvis.

The day suddenly darkened. A low, gray cloud overcame what was left of the sun and lowered the "feels like" by ten degrees. Felton slipped an actual pocket watch from his vest.

"How gay." Salt winked at him.

"If you're happy and you know it . . ." he sang and hummed. "We've got at best an hour or so before we won't be able to see anything. I'll notify the ME. Techs are on the way." He started back up to the street, his attention on his mobile phone.

"Meanwhile . . ." Salt bent over, parting the brambles and weeds, and drew close to the remains. Just then the rain began, splattering drops that sounded full and fat as they landed on Salt's shoulders and the brim of her hat. She lifted out of her crouch, told Greenberg she could stand by in the patrol car, then bent back to the victim. Rain began to form in little streams on either side of the skull, beside one wrist joint, and below the pelvis. As water gathered, a bit of hair further separated from the matted mess under the head. Salt tucked her notepad in an inside pocket and stood. Entwined among the thorny vines and briars was a pokeberry bush, its gray stalks no longer lively summer crimson, but still holding dried berry clusters, a few tiny withered fruits just above the skull.

"Right beside the path." Felton was back from his car with two large black umbrellas, one he held out to her. "A well-used path. No way she's not been noticed before today," he added, voice sagging.

Cold weather, the nearest residence at least thirty yards away; still, onlookers and street kids were unusually absent. Salt and Felton turned to a clattering from the street, a "Bubbles" with his shopping cart piled high with bags of cans. "I'll ask him." Felton shrugged and strode up the hill after the can man, who began to push faster.

"Sorrowful," she said to herself. "Body has been here and no one called—left like a rotting animal." Salt crossed one arm over her chest, tugging the coat closed.

Rosie's mouth and eyes formed O's when Salt and Felton opened the outer doors to the Homicide office. Ignoring the ringing phone, she pushed herself from behind the receptionist's desk. "You are absolutely soaked through. Get out of that coat. I'll heat water for tea."

They'd waited at the scene for the medical examiner's investigator and directed the processing of the scene by the techs, who photographed, measured, and collected what little evidence there was. The rain had continued through the bagging and removal.

People of various stripes filled the chairs lining the reception area. Someone was knocking on the double doors asking to be buzzed in.

Felton held out his arms and hands in futile expectancy of the same sympathy Rosie gave Salt. Ignoring him and the rest of the chaos entirely, Rosie followed on Salt's heels. She'd shown an affinity for and a devotion to Salt since her arrival in the squad a year ago.

"Chopped liver," Felton mumbled as they threaded their way through the gray cubicles. Small, round Day-Glo-orange stickers were affixed to everything of value in the Homicide office. The last city personnel to inhabit the old building, the squad had been scheduled to move to the new headquarters downtown, but now with the assault on the Spelman students the consensus was that the move would be delayed. Federal agents, in navy golf shirts, khaki pants, and navy windbreakers, their eyes following Salt, were coming and going and sat at the previously empty cubicles. A task force was being formed.

Sergeant Huff met them at Salt's desk. "Well?"

"Sorry, Sarge," Felton said. "We won't know until the autopsy. It's hard to tell either way—decomp too far advanced, small pink teen or woman's shirt and shorts. Of course, nothing to identify her, no ID, nothing."

"Shit. Don't call me Sarge."

"Sorry, Sarge."

As Felton left, Salt sat down at her desk and touched the keyboard. The monitor lit while she stood to hang the dripping coat. She sat back down and tapped the mouse to select the first report template. Sticking his head around the partition, Huff reappeared. "See me before you leave."

"Report's done. ME says the autopsy will be tomorrow. We'll at least have some idea about her after that."

Murder books of every color, always stacked all over Huff's small glass-front office—on his desk, the two chairs, the floor—gave the space a kaleidoscope feel opposite the stark, cavernous empty spaces of the barren building. Salt stood in his doorway. Huff, forty-five going on sixty, was on his second marriage, to a New Age wife who had him on sequential, sometimes concurrent, self-improvement regimens in keeping with whatever ideas were floating around in the social media. He'd been on diets and spiritual retreats. Lately he'd enrolled at some gym owned by a mystic, and before that he'd been doing hip-hop aerobics, which he'd tried to keep secret until someone saw him in the class rhythmically clutching his crotch. But he was still a white guy with a paunch and a receding buzz cut. The only constant in his life seemed to be his love for his wife and an affinity for solving murders.

"How're you holding up, Sarge?"

"Sit," he said, pointing to a surprisingly empty chair in front of his desk while uncharacteristically straightening some of the stacks of case files and aligning one pile with the edge. Wary, Salt inched toward the seat. Huff picked up some files from the floor and swiveled his chair to restack them on the shelves behind him. With his back to her he mumbled something.

"I didn't hear you, Sarge."

He turned. "You've been ordered for a fitness-for-duty." Avoiding eye contact, he picked up a sheet of paper, unfolded it, and handed it to her. "Don't kill the messenger."

"Is this about last night? I had no idea they were waiting for me."

"No, it's not that, although you scared the shit outta us. Read," he said.

It was from the personnel department through the chain of command. "Detective Sarah D. Alt, having met threshold criteria specified by S.O.P. 05-1432 Fitness for Duty and having been involved in two use-of-lethal-force incidents, meeting criteria number 4, is hereby ordered to report to the Psychological Services Unit for referral for evaluation within five days of receipt of this notice."

"Sarge, those shoots were justified." Her throat tightened, voice rising to a slightly childlike timbre.

"Christ, I hate this shit. Salt, just make the appointment. What can it hurt? You're not gonna cry on me!"

"I'm not crying. Jesus, what are you doing?"

He'd been chewing nicotine gum recently and now had five pieces from the foil packet in front of him. Rolling his head around on his neck, he popped one after the other in his mouth. "This is the kind of shit that stresses me—girl talk, psychological bullshit, *feelings*," he sneered. "Give me a good old dead body. I just want to work murders and what do I get? *Feelings*."

"Sarge, I'll go."

"What?"

"I'll go. I'll make the appointment. Don't get your panties in a twist. You're right. It isn't personal." She laid the order on his desk, picked up a pen, and signed on the line showing receipt of the order. "You got my copy?"

"It's completely confidential." Huff flipped his chair upright and handed Salt her copy. "Uh, thanks."

"See, you got yourself all worked up for nothing." Salt stood.

"I did?"

"I'm good, Sarge. I'm good." She turned to go.

"Don't call me Sarge," he mumbled.

Salt dropped the order on Wills' desk as she passed him. He was at her cubicle within seconds. "What the fuck?"

Felton came over. "Sarge said you got ordered to see the shrink."

"Oh, Salt, you shouldn't worry. I'm sure the doctor will say you're sane." Rosie rushed up, brushing past Felton, and grabbed Salt in a dramatic, consoling embrace.

"I got sent once." The group turned, surprised to see the normally taciturn Gardner, Wills' partner, approaching. They waited for him to elaborate. He did not.

"Maybe they should just put a notice in the daily bulletin. So much for confidentiality." Water dripped from the hem of her soaked coat.

"Can we testify or something on your behalf?" Rosie fiddled big fingers along the pearls at her thick neck.

The Things, ever curious, joined them. "Are we having a meeting?" Barney asked.

"Salt's being sent to the shrink," Rosie announced with a deep sigh.

The legs of the chair Felton was pulling scraped gratingly on the beat-up linoleum tiles. He sat down next to Salt. "Here's the list for the task force," he said, handing her the memo. Of course there was Chatterjee as lead, another morning-watch detective, Wills, Gardner, and Huff from Salt's watch, and they split the day-watch partners Best and Hamm, with Best going to the task force, plus their lieutenant. There were five agents from the FBI and two from the ATF, all of whom it seemed now stood along the walls of the break room, having declined offers of chairs.

Ten or more detectives shambled in for the late news. Scraping the sorry plastic chairs again, they gathered around the TV. The lead story. Screen filling with the young women holding candles that cast an upward glow on their faces. Their jackets and coats open over their T-shirts, they sang "This Little Light of Mine" with lots of harmony and call and response. Then the moment they fell on the pavement in front of the fountain's wall of water, the camera view falling and shaking with them, the lens recording the bodies of the prone women.

The taste of burning oil returned to the back of Salt's throat.

THE MORNING OF

SALT LEFT WILLS IN HER BED STILL ASLEEP. SIPPING ON A FIRST cup of coffee, she walked out into the early morning with the dogs, Wills' two Rottweilers and her border collie mix, Wonder. Both she and Wills were catching cases and there were nights or days when Salt stayed at Wills' house in the city closer to the job. But when they had time Wills brought the dogs down to her house. Wonder was exuberant, enjoying his Rottie girlfriends, racing them through the defrosting pasture and leaving silvery trails in the glittering grasses.

The new white fence around the front half acre made the old house look impressive, gave it an estate-like aura, implying large harvests, money crops, orchards, and colonial relationships. But Salt loved the fence she and her friends and a neighbor, Mr. Gooden, had built. She loved the ability it gave her to let her five sheep keep the grass cropped. Built shortly after the Civil War, the house had belonged to her family for generations. The addition of the fence implied a history grander than her experience of it. Now the front of the square box-like house begged for a railed wraparound covered porch and portico to soften its appearance and to make the front entrance inviting.

Having walked to the roadside border fence farthest from the front of the house, Salt propped one foot against the low rail, drank from the steaming mug, and watched the dogs tear through the field. The autopsy would begin right about now. *That pink shirt.* Salt pulled her quilted-wool shirt close, hugging herself against the cold morning.

Wonder suddenly halted mid-chase, his black fur shimmering in the sun. He assumed the typical border collie stance of attention, ears on alert and trained toward the house. Wills appeared from around the south corner. The dog scampered with his pack to gather around Wills, who waved and beckoned to Salt. "Biscuits in the oven," he called.

The air in the kitchen was fragrant with the cold smells from outside brought in by Salt and the dogs and the warm smells from the oven. The old house was typical of many nineteenth-century Southern homes, little insulation and drafty doors and windows; homes built more to conserve cool rather than heat. North Georgia and Atlanta, at the foothills of the Appalachians, could and did turn cold at times during the winter, even getting a little dusting of snow once a year or so.

Post breakfast, she asked, "Are we having a tree this year?" They sat at the paint-chipped table over second cups of coffee, dogs sprawled around the kitchen floor.

"No talk of Christmas before Thanksgiving, right? Besides, that's a can-o-worms." He reached for the honey pot, garnishing the last biscuit.

"Worms? Christmas? Neither one of us is observant, but that's a little harsh, don't you think?" She raised her eyebrows, smiling, happy he was here, this morning after.

"Would we have a tree at both our houses, Salt? Or just here? One at my place?"

Salt leaned over, frowning into her cup. "Worm can. You're right."

Salt lifted her eyes to meet his. "Biscuits were perfect."

He was staring at his plate.

"I'm sorry about the other night," she said.

Wills raised his steady brown eyes. "Rationally I know it's not your fault." He stopped and looked up at the ceiling as if petitioning a higher power.

"But?" she prompted.

"I do not understand why it keeps happening—you getting into tight situations, time after time. Maybe the psychological eval is a good idea," he said.

It was her turn to be quiet, to look away. Wills had been supportive through the aftermaths of the lethal-force encounters for which she was now under scrutiny.

Already dressed for work in a short-sleeve white shirt, a tie with a crime scene motif, and cotton slacks, he untied the white baker's apron from around his thick chest, hung it on the pantry door, came around to her, stepping carefully between dogs, and encircled her in his arms. "Okay, Blue Eyes, we've both got a lot on our plates right now, what with the task force, our other cases, and now this fitness-for-duty evaluation. Are you worried about the shrink thing?" he asked into her hair.

"Yes."

"Your dad?"

"I know what a psychiatrist will make of that. He'll wonder how I was ever hired in the first place—daughter of a cop who committed suicide."

"If he's any good, he'll understand how sometimes people get stronger at their broken places. If he doesn't, then maybe he's not fit for duty."

"What if my broken places are still bleeding?" Wills pulled her to standing, holding her tight. His chest smelled warm and of baking flour. "Where will we celebrate the holidays, Wills?" She leaned back in his embrace, close to his five-ten height, their eyes almost level.

"That's the thing. I want us to think about what are we doing here. I'm renovating my house in town. You're making improvements to this place. You've got the sheep. It's almost an hour's drive between our homes," he said. Wills lifted the gold St. Michael's pendant he'd given her by its chain from between her breasts. "You do hoodoo, mang," he said, imitating Howlin' Wolf, blew on the saint for luck, kissed Salt, and called his dogs to follow him to his car out back.

Wonder stood at the door watching and listening as his adopted pack left, then turned his gold eyes inquiringly to her—his old eyes amber, the color of fossilized resin produced by trees to clot their wounds.

She'd taken the dog for a five-mile run along the rural two-lane that fronted her property and led from the expressway to the one-traffic-light town of Cloud. They'd done the gathering, feeding, and watering of the five sheep. She was showering when her phone rang.

When she called Wills back, he sounded as though he was walking, his breath jerky. "Turn on your TV." He panted.

"Hold on. I'm drying off."

"Huff has me calling the entire watch. They want everyone in ASAP. Day watch and morning are being called in, too."

"What?"

"Spelman students, students from the Atlanta University Center, the other Atlanta colleges and universities joined in a spontaneous march last night to show solidarity or defiance of the assault on the Spelman women."

Salt wrapped the towel around herself and padded to the kitchen, where she switched on her small TV, fitted into an old side cabinet. A local anchor was reporting, "Students from all over Atlanta— Morehouse, Emory, Georgia State, Georgia Tech—came to stand with the Spelman students." The screen images were hard to make out. The flashing lights of emergency vehicles cast the surrounding scene into contrasting dark. Figures could be seen, hurried and frantic, waving arms back and forth, running silhouettes backed by news lights behind or beside them. "Video has surfaced showing a white man, a passenger in a black truck, aiming and shooting the Spelman women . . ." the scroll beneath the news footage read.

"The students are angry," Wills said. "National press, cable channels, social media are already on the story. And the feds got word from one of their informants in an Aryan Nation group, the one with their headquarters west of the city. The informant says that group's all stirred up: meetings, training. There's a worry for the students demonstrating."

"Did the informant have anything about who did the shooting? When does Sarge want us in?"

"No, nothing on the shooters. We're due in now."

"I've got the psychiatrist appointment."

"Call Sarge. Oh, and in case I forgot to tell you. I love you." Wills hung up.

"You, too," she replied to the dimming phone in her hand. She left the TV on, went to get dressed, and then called Huff.

"Shit. Shit. Shit. Salt, I've got two other calls holding." He inhaled deeply, as if drawing smoke into his lungs.

"Wills called but I've got that psychiatrist evaluation at noon."

"I need you here. I need girls to represent. The brass said they wanted all female personnel front and center on this."

"I'm happy to cancel the shrink."

"Wait, wait, wait. Let me think." He exhaled.

"Are you back smoking, Sarge?"

"Jesus. Go to the appointment and then get here ASAP."

"Let me remind you that I just caught the body yesterday—" she was saying, but Huff had hung up.

"In other news . . ." The scene changed behind the TV anchor, then zoomed to a full-screen shot of the mayor and rap producer "Flash Daddy" Jones standing behind a wide ribbon, each with their hands on large, oversized scissors.

APPOINTMENT

SALT THOUGHT ABOUT STOPPING SOMEWHERE TO BUY A SCARF or some accessory that might soften her appearance, minimize her height, brighten the outfit she now saw as austere—black jacket, gray slacks, white shirt, and black leather athletic shoes. She'd kept her curly, almost black hair short since the shooting two years ago that had left a scar under one ringlet on her forehead and parted her hair halfway, visible only when it was wet. She wanted to appear normal, sympathetic, wanted to signal to the psychiatrist that there was more to her than being just a cop.

The address was a small bungalow on a side street lined with magnolias, their dark, waxy leaves shining and reflecting the distant noon sun. The mostly brick Craftsman homes along the short street had been converted to boutique businesses: accountants, attorneys, a chiropractor, a couple of high-end clothing shops, and The Wellness Center, the name of Dr. Ian Marshall's practice. She followed arrows pointing to parking in back and took a path of awkwardly paced paving stones to the arched front door.

As she entered, a bell chimed and a scowling, lank-haired young woman came from a doorway in back of the chest-high receptionist counter. "I have an appointment—" Before Salt finished introducing herself, the girl handed her a clipboard with multiple forms. "You need to complete these." She pointed to the waiting area.

Salt chose a corner in the otherwise empty room. A gurgling fountain powered by an electric motor plugged in below the table beside the chair kept drawing her attention, distracting her. She wondered if that was the intended effect.

"Sarah Alt?" At her elbow a barrel-chested man of about fifty and close to Salt's height stood with his hand extended.

Salt wiped her sweaty palm on her slacks, got up, and shook his offered hand.

"I'm Ian Marshall. Come on back." He led her down a short hall to a room that had most likely once been the dining room off a small kitchen farther down the hall. An overstuffed sofa sat along one wall. Dr. Marshall's desk faced the opposite wall of shelves so that his chair swiveled to a conversation area of two matching easy chairs and a coffee table, on which lay a box of tissues, a carafe of water and glasses, and a crystal bowl of hard candies.

"Water? Coffee, tea?" He nodded to a counter on the shelves where there was a coffeemaker.

"I'm good," Salt said, standing beside one of the chairs and taking off her jacket in the overly warm room.

"Sorry," Marshall said, coming to his desk. "They must have forgotten to tell you. You can't have your gun here." He nodded at the weapon in the leather shoulder holster under her left arm.

"They didn't tell me." She halted halfway to sitting, feeling this was a bad start.

"Can you take it to your car?" he asked.

"Not really. I'm not that kind of cop." She sank into the chair.

"No?"

"Careless, I mean. It could get stolen if my car was broken into."

Marshall sat down facing her. "Could you leave it with our receptionist?"

"You're kidding, right? Is this part of the evaluation? She looks, um, depressed."

"My daughter. But I see your point. I guess for this first session we can let it go, but next time I'd appreciate it if you'd leave the gun somewhere?" He raised his hands and eyebrows, gentling the request.

Salt rubbed her palms on her thighs again. "Next time? How many times will I have to come here?"

Marshall's eyes took on a gleam. The corners of his mouth turned up as if trying to suppress a smile. He leaned back in his chair, thumbing through the forms she'd filled out. His mustache seemed to be fading from some color of red to an orange-and-white bristle. A tweed jacket hung on the back of his chair, but he was tieless. He ran his hand through iron-gray hair as he flipped through the forms. "You understand I'm to make a determination of your psychological fitness?"

She nodded.

"The procedure states that when an officer is involved in more than one lethal use-of-force incident within five years, they are required to undergo a fitness-for-duty evaluation.

"You should also know that otherwise what you tell me is confidential. I only report fit or not fit."

"Okay," she responded. "Have you evaluated many cops? Do you treat cops?"

"Yes and no. But we should get started talking about you." He put the clipboard down and sat upright. "You're here because of regulations that require evaluations for officers who have experienced specific events or conditions that might stress them to the point that they may have difficulties doing their jobs. Do you think that applies to you in any way?"

"Doc, those incidents, the two shootings were a year ago and two years ago."

"Okay, so let's talk about now." He brought the clipboard back to his lap. "I see you've checked 'yes' to sometimes having vivid dreams."

"I was being honest. Doesn't everyone have vivid dreams? People wouldn't remember them if they weren't, would they?" she asked, on guard now. She definitely wasn't going to get into the dreams she'd had after the shootings. She wondered if he knew about her father.

Dr. Marshall waited.

She tried to breathe quietly.

Nothing about the fifty minutes made Salt less stressed. She wasn't able to figure out if Dr. Marshall was judging her one way or the other.

News trucks lined Ponce de Leon Avenue in front of the massive nine-floor former Sears, Roebuck building—brick, art deco brass, and rust-meets-seventies' cheap renovations and peeling paint, spread over an entire city block. It had been temporary office space for some city government departments, police headquarters, and detective units, including the Homicide squad. Now mostly vacant, it had once been the largest retail distribution center in the Southeast, its two million square feet a grand time capsule from the early 1900s. The vast un-inhabited areas were littered with old black-and-white wall clocks and flimsy furniture, side by side with solid-wood sorting cabinets. Tempting wood-handled circuit breakers, disconnected control panels, vacuum tube conveyers, tangles of wire, mangled metal and exposed ductwork, all sorts of fantastic accoutrements contributed to

Salt's romance with the building and the ghosts of its former workers. She imagined their shoes, the cigarette smoke, clingy dresses, and pleated pants.

Once again, the "new" elevators installed in the '80s weren't in service. She took the stairwell that echoed with the curses and disgruntled voices of other employees.

In the Homicide Unit's waiting area it was standing room only, filled with people wanting—needing—a word with some official who had information about the assault on the Spelman students. Rosie and the day-watch receptionist were tag-teaming, barely controlling the chaos.

"Miss, can I talk to you?" One man beckoned as she passed through to the inner door.

"Sorry," Salt said through the closing door.

Inside, the office teemed: detectives from all three watches, supervisors and commanders, people wanting, demanding, ordering, and directing action. Salt shouldered through. "I'm here," she said, standing at the open door to Huff's office.

Huff, on the phone, held up a finger for her to wait. He covered the mouthpiece. "I need you to go to Grady. Hamm is already there. She'll fill you in."

"Sarge, I caught a body yesterday. I need to get on that."

"Fuck it. Those bones are so cold nobody's gonna give a shit. Now we got neo-Nazi nut jobs coming out of the woodwork, one dead Spelman girl rapidly becoming the social media's newest Joan of Arc, and eleven of her sister saints in three city hospitals. I need you to go hold their families' hands." Huff waved her off and returned to his call.

Wills tugged at her elbow, beckoning her to follow him to the break room, where there was only slightly less chaos. "How did it go with the shrink?"

She shrugged. The break room counters had begun to fill with food containers, empty take-out boxes, and disposable cups. Paper plates, Styrofoam, all manner of litter covered the surfaces. "So much for the city's recycling program." She scanned the waste.

"Salt." Wills squared his body with hers.

"I don't know. It doesn't make sense to worry about it."

"But you are, aren't you?" There was no touching in the office, as their relationship had to be kept strictly professional while they were on duty. And they had to be careful who knew. Romantic relationships were officially discouraged between employees on the same shift. They could both be transferred out of Homicide if word got out.

"I'm on my way to the hospital. I gotta go."

"This is not good. You just caught a case yesterday."

"Wills." She stood with him eye to eye. "All of us, you included, have our shoulders to the wheel."

"Just so you share the load. Okay? None of that Lone Ranger stuff."

She chuckled. "Nobody knows who the Lone Ranger is anymore, Wills." She turned to the door. "See you when we get there, Kemosabe."

Days like this leading to longer nights kept them apart. They had murders to investigate. Wills was renovating his house. Salt had sheep to herd. And they both had their dogs, the commonality that had brought them together initially; over dead bodies they'd met, talking about their dogs, the dogs that now required their separate attentions. Wills was right; maintaining separate homes was wasting their energies.

Salt pulled into the cop lot beside the massive city hospital called the Gradys by some older Atlantans, a reference to the era of segregation when black and white patients were cared for in separate buildings. Although familiar to Salt from bedside interviews with victims and witnesses, as well as having personally benefited from its emergency care, she still got lost in the labyrinthine halls. Directional signs illustrated with Christian crosses, somewhat disquietingly ubiquitous, guided her to the chapel. She wondered where the Muslims, Hindus, Jews, and Buddhists went to be comforted.

Church-like double doors paid homage to the room's intended religious use and opening them was like unsealing a vacuum, the sounds in the rest of the hospital sharp and harsh while in the chapel everything was muffled. Dim light from wall sconces focused soft glows up the beige walls of the small sanctuary. Wiping their eyes, family members of the injured students quietly slid along the polished oak pews as they came and went. And Charissa Hamm, day-watch detective and the only other woman in Homicide, attended them; going from group to group or person to person, she settled her considerable bulk in the row in front of each and turned around to speak quietly to them. Hamm raised her eyes briefly, touched the hands of a man and woman with bowed heads who were tightly grasping the pew in front of them, then stood and walked to Salt at the doors of the chapel. "This is not good. I'm glad you're here. Maybe some of them will be reassured by a white face."

"Why do you say that? You're the veteran. Looks to me like you know what you're doing."

"Yeah, but for some of these old-school folks, white people still have the power to make things happen."

"What am I supposed to do? We don't have anything to tell them yet. Can't give them what they want right now, which is an arrest."

"Give them the Homicide all-hands-on-deck, pulling-out-all-the-stops routine. Explain the task force, the FBI. Give them your card.

The hospital has been on top of keeping them updated on their daughters. Two have regained consciousness and we'll need to interview them when they're stable."

Salt reached for the phone vibrating in her jacket pocket. "You know I just caught a body yesterday?"

Hamm shrugged, pulling on a what-can-I-say face.

"Probably the ME with the autopsy findings." Salt held up the phone.

"Take the call. I'll wait." Hamm turned back to the families.

The corridor outside the chapel was lined with gurneys, some empty, some with patients triaged to the hallway because their illnesses or injuries were less serious. "Hold on," she said to the ME's office. "I'm in Grady." She moved along the hallway trying to get a clear connection—reception in the bowels of the hospital being notoriously poor—as well as a spot where she wouldn't be overheard. She stopped across from a sign that read TURN OFF ALL PHONES. Her back to a nearby occupied gurney, she faced the green tile wall. "Hi, Marc. Sorry. It is crazy." She leaned her forehead against the wall. There was an inviting empty gurney to her left. "Yeah, I thought that was probably the case. Body left to decompose outside like that. What caliber?" She sat down on the clean sheet, reconsidered, and instead leaned against the wall. "How long had she . . . The body was female? Marc?" Salt had to turn again to regain the signal. "I'll start the search right away. A girl that age will likely be a flyer by now." There was more dead air and static. "Thanks. I appreciate the quick work, Marc."

Turning the phone off, Salt lowered her chin and closed her eyes. Strong, slightly sour disinfectant fumes triggered something between déjà vu and a flashback that muted the echoing voices in the corridor. Two blurred silhouettes, backlit and with a haze, spoke indistinctly to each other. By their tones she recognized her father and mother. Her first memories of this hospital were from when she was a child and had been brought there by her mother to see her father.

She felt a sudden blow along at her waist, not so much painful as startling.

"I said wake up," said a vaguely familiar voice. The man on the gurney to her right propped up on his elbows was wielding an aluminum cuff crutch. He growled, "You that girly detective hangs around with the HOPE Team."

"Did you just hit me?"

"So what?" Thin as he was, he would have been easily unnoticeable lying under the sheet.

"You're Mr. Makepeace. We talked to you last year when we were looking for Pearl."

"What's wrong with you? Why you lookin' all hangdog?"

"It's already been a long day, Mr. Makepeace, and it's about to get longer." Salt pushed off the wall.

"Yeah, well, I don't feel sorry for you one bit. I don't feel sorry for nobody got two good legs under 'em." He slapped the crutch against the tile wall.

"What are you here for?"

"Goddamn infection." He pointed with the crutch to his right foot under the sheet.

"You know, you might think about getting off the street."

"You should shut your goddamn mouth. You don't know shit 'bout me or being on the street." He fell back on the skimpy, thin pillow.

"Oh, brother." With the heel of her hand Salt pushed on the scar at her hairline and turned toward the chapel doors. "You did help us find Pearl. Thanks," she said to the now-silent Makepeace.

"Gimme your card." Eyes closed, he held out his dark, cracked, and weathered hand, turning up the softer pink palm on which Salt placed without further comment her card, one of the ones that had her mobile number, not just the office line. He enclosed the card with his fingers and tucked his hand beneath the hospital sheet.

BREAK ROOM

THE BURNT-COFFEE SMELL OF THE BREAK ROOM WAS STRONGER than usual. Salt sat with Huff at one of the patio tables, one with a hole for an umbrella in the center. There were no orange stickers to move anything in the break room. The appliances, every piece of furniture—all were to be junked.

"It's being ruled a homicide," Salt said. "The shirt held a bullet and a bone fragment. There was corresponding damage to her spinal column; front to back, indicating she'd been shot through the chest, probably got her heart. Holes in the shirt confirmed the trajectory. She was between twelve and fourteen years old, black female. And, Sarge, her body'd been lying there for about three months. Nobody called it in."

Huff, scooping hummus with a celery stick from a compartmentalized lunch container, squinted at the old bulky TV on a stand against the wall. The news was on, sound muted. "Nothing human beings do to each other shocks me anymore." With a loud crunch he broke off a piece of celery between his teeth. The TV brightened with orange flickerings. "Oh, shit, here we go. Turn it up." Fire flamed behind dark images moving around the scene.

Barney and Daniels rounded the corner into the room. "Sarge, are you watching?"

The volume crescendoed as Salt pressed the button. "Students have joined from other campuses, other colleges and universities throughout the city, in what had been a peaceful march. But, Steve, as you can see behind me the situation has escalated," a blond reporter said to the camera. "Someone torched one of the businesses, a copy center and paper supply shop here at the corner of Peachtree and Decatur Street." Demonstrators, most of whom were college-age women, passed behind her. Some held signs: NO JUSTICE, NO PEACE. Some shouted at the camera, "No justice, no peace."

Huff looked down at his phone vibrating on the tabletop, took a breath, and picked it up, answering, "LT. Got it. Tomorrow." He put the phone in his shirt pocket. "Get everybody in here. Rosie, too," he told the Things.

"I got the girl's description to Missing Persons," said Salt, trying to get Huff's attention. "And Sergeant Fellows has her people checking reports for runaway girls her age. I need to call the counties." On the TV black smoke began to obliterate the orange as the fire department's hoses flushed water through a now glassless storefront. Although she rarely smoked, Salt felt a sudden craving for a cigarette.

"Whatever you need to do, do it now. You are reporting to the academy at eight a.m. tomorrow for a refresher on 'crowd management.'" He wiggled his fingers with the air quotes familiar to his detectives. "That's what they're calling it nowadays."

The reporter was jostled by some young male teens who came running gleefully alongside the placard-carrying marchers. The boys mugged for the camera, fingers in gang signs, acting out, taking advantage of what had been a peaceful event.

"Jesus Christ," said Huff.

"Sarge, what about my case?"

"On hold." He looked at his ringing phone again but didn't answer. Wills, Gardner, and the others came in the room.

"We're now receiving reports that police have arrested some of the student marchers," said the reporter, who was becoming obscured by people passing between her and the camera. "Back to you, Steve. We're relocating to . . ." The picture on the screen wobbled.

Salt's phone lit up. The caller ID, "Mother." She held up the phone, indicating to Huff that she was taking a call.

"Academy at eight tomorrow," he said. "The rest of you jackasses are on twelve-hour shifts."

Walking to her desk, holding the phone to her ear, she answered. "Hi, Mom." She got a pack of cigarettes from a drawer and headed for the unauthorized smoking area. "Just going to someplace quiet." No PERSONNEL BEYOND THIS DOOR read the sign on the double doors. "Yep, at work." Salt lit the smoke as soon as she was through the doors. "Kinda. Probably just looks worse on TV than it is," Salt said, getting a word in. It was as if her mother talked to avoid conversation. She responded. "The city's not so bad. People are just upset right now . . ." "They have a right . . ." "I'm glad John and the family don't have to worry, either . . ." "Tell Susan thank you for asking . . ." "I call but it's never at a good time for you, Mom." Salt sat down beneath an open lever window at an old upended wooden cable spool that served as a table. Drink cans used for ashtrays reeked of wet butts. The cavernous space was cold but Salt's ear began to sweat. They'd never been close. Charlotte Alt was traditional and held certain ideals about propriety. Living one state away with Jake, her second husband, was probably good for everyone, and there she was closer to Salt's brother,

John, and his wife and children. "I won't have the holidays off, Mom. Just Thanksgiving. One day. I'm still a rookie detective . . ." "One year is not long for detectives . . ."

"You, too, Mom." She hung up and stood to look out the window. The eighth-floor view was of construction, or more accurately, pre-liminary deconstruction around the old building: a crane with a wrecking ball, a high boom excavator, loaders, and bulldozers. The demolition had begun.

She rubbed up under the curl on her forehead where the scar began. With her mother's call the blurred images at the hospital yesterday now felt like a conjuring. She lit a second smoke. "Just a kid," Salt said to the vast empty space. "She was just a kid."

REFRESHER

COPS GOT OUT OF THEIR CARS IN THE PARKING LOT OF THE MAIN
academy building, once an elementary school. They carried to-go
cups, their mumbled greetings to one another accompanied by puffs
of condensation in the cold, bright air. Guys on midnights blinked
like they'd never seen sunlight.

Leaning against the east-facing brick wall of the building, Salt,
eyes closed, warmed her face in the sun as she waited to go in for the
eight a.m. classroom roll call.

"More than twelve years now since I first saw you in that exact
pose."

"Ah, the warmth of another sun." She smiled, opening her eyes.

The morning light reflected off Pepper's dark forehead. "My hero,"
he said, adopting the pose, hands clasped at his heart, batting his eyes
down at her.

"You're smooth." She rubbed her palm on her friend and former shift mate's clean-shaven cheek, opposite the long scar that ran from his forehead to his chin.

"Shit." He felt both sides of his face. "Just when I had my beard perfect." They'd been ordered to shave for the gas masks to fit. Many of the plainclothes resented having to cut long-cultivated hair and beards grown so they would blend into a scene. "What about you? I'm surprised they sent anyone from Homicide what with all you guys have going on."

"Apparently the brass sent word that all detective units are required to contribute bodies to the training. Most of the units have half their people assigned to attend. Their one concession to Homicide was that they only had to send one body. I'm not on the task force. I've got the least time in the unit. So here I am. Besides, it's just training, half a day. I don't mind."

In a flash his hands went from touching his face to tightly grabbing her upper left arm, an invitation for her to come back with a countermove or throw. They'd begun playing like this as rookies in the academy, practicing newly learned come-along holds and restraint techniques. They had worked adjacent beats for ten years and had both been promoted to detective at the same time last year, he to Narcotics and she to Homicide. Now he brought his boys to her house about once a week so the four of them could practice aikido in the space she'd converted into a small dojo. Pepper had achieved his black belt and continued his practice by studying with an esteemed local sensei and by passing on what he was learning to his boys and Salt. It was one arena of his life in which he limited his penchant for mischief.

Pep had been the first to call her "Salt," during their rookie training, after they'd gotten their name tags and he'd read hers, "S. Alt."

His smile and sense of joy rivaled the morning's brilliance. Instead of a throw, Salt pulled Pepper to walk arm in arm with her into the academy entrance.

Although the day was still crisp, layers of outerwear lay in clumps on the periphery of the training field. The cops, clustered in groups for drill formations and tactical maneuvers, were loaded, each of them with a helmet, a four-foot polycarbon riot shield, and a long baton. Gas masks dangled in pouches from their waists.

Pepper had forged his name on her squad's list so that the two of them could be on the same team of twelve. Now, just as the squad sergeant shouted them to attention and issued a command for a formation, Pepper flipped up the visor on his helmet, revealing the fake mustache he'd painted on his upper lip with shoeblack from the kit she'd seen him with earlier. The training was like play, especially for Salt, who enjoyed the physical workout. They'd all been through basic crowd-control training as rookies, and every third year or so they'd be retrained with new masks when the technology changed. Long-baton commands and techniques were second nature and similar enough to the collapsible batons they carried for daily use that most of them easily fell into the correct stances and positions for deployment. The veterans among them, some of whom had been in the last major disturbance a decade ago, rolled their eyes at the commands, their movements lethargic, expressions cynical.

Two hundred cops in teams of twelve were spread across the grounds. Sergeants barked commands and practiced nonverbal signals for situations in which they might not be able to be heard over noise from crowds or explosions. Salt thought the preparations might be seen as excessive for an event whose participants would be mostly women students. The FBI had no further news from their informant with the supremacists. Of course there were always some, usually boys, teens, high on testosterone and sometimes other substances—those who could turn a peaceful event into something else. Still, Salt thought gearing up for the current unrest might appear extreme, unless the department revealed their concerns about the supremacist group.

Pepper mugged at her. "Where we going for lunch?"

OLD BONES

SALT, BACK FROM THE MORNING TRAINING, STUCK HER HEAD into the sergeant's closet-size office. "Caught," she said.

Sergeant Laurel Fellows raised her head from the desk and a stack of reports on which she'd been resting her forehead. She wiped her nose with the back of her hand. "Sorry," she said. Keeping her head lowered, she fumbled around in a desk drawer and tore off a piece of brown paper towel. The Special Victims Unit handled crimes against children, elder abuse, domestic cases, and juveniles who'd been reported missing. Fellows supervised the juvenile and children's detectives.

"Are you crying?" Salt came fully into the office and sat in the only chair.

Fellows blew her nose. "I knew this was a mistake. I knew it. I should never have agreed to this assignment." A small speck of paper towel stuck to her upper lip.

"I couldn't do it," Salt said.

On Fellows' desk were files and stacks of reports, each describing in detail abuse or suspicions of abuse of a child, or reports of runaways and missing children. The files were neatly stacked in five piles, an investigator's name scrawled in red in the top right corner. "Every day I read these. Forty or more waiting for me every fucking morning. Now I've got to report to the academy this afternoon for training. And if we get assigned to the protest detail, who's going to follow up on these?" Fellows flipped the corners of the reports in front of her. "Our first report forms, blue, the color blue. They got that right. I get the blues every morning reading them. You ever consider that the detectives that work in this unit are outcasts? Other cops avoid SVU detectives for fear they'll hear something about these cases, these children."

"I'm sorry." Salt tried to think of something else to say.

"I do have a possible match for you." The sergeant reached for a manila folder on the shelf behind her. "I almost didn't consider this one." She opened the file. "Reason was because she was reported as a runaway only a month ago. Your girl has been dead, what? Three months?" Fellows read from the top report in the file. "'Mary Marie McCloud,' beautiful name." She handed the report to Salt, who was suddenly weak with the exertion it took to reach for the file.

More than two years had passed since Salt had last seen Mary Marie, when she'd been taken into the state juvenile system. She was twelve years old at the time. Shannell, her mother, a street whore and crack addict, had been known to Salt from Salt's first days as a beat cop. Mary's father was an old-school car thief. Mary's brother, Lil D, had been a street dealer in The Homes gang, and Mary had been living with her grandmother. It seemed to Salt as if she'd been predestined to witness every one of Mary's family's traumas. Otherwise, what were the possibilities that she would now be investigating the girl's murder? But in The Homes, Salt's old beat and home to Mary's family, Salt had stopped being surprised at the connections. Her instincts now told her the bones would be determined to be Mary's. Salt had arrested her for murder. Twelve years old. Murder. Taken her from her punishing grandmother. Salt had testified for Mary at the hearing, advocating for her to receive treatment as a juvenile rather than be tried as an adult.

"Do you think she might be your body?" Fellows sounded almost hopeful. Salt understood it meant one less case for SVU.

"I knew her. Mary Marie." Salt closed the file and smoothed her hand over the cover. "I thought she was safe, in custody. How could she have been released?"

"I'm sorry," said Fellows.

As Salt came into the Homicide entrance, Rosie looked up from the log she kept on a yellow legal tablet. "Sarge is at the academy for the afternoon training session," she said. Rosie tracked all of the detectives' comings and goings in hieroglyphics doodled beside their names on the tablet. "You're dressed perfect in those fatigues to meet Hamm and Best. They caught some old bones out at the river on Marietta Boulevard. They went out thinking it would be an animal, but they've been out all morning and I heard them call for the GBI. So I guess it's turning into a case. Anyway, they asked for an assist, first available evening-watch detective not on the task force, and that, my dear, appears to be you."

"Damn, Rosie." Salt slumped into one of the upholstered waiting-room chairs along the wall. "I worked last night, got up this morning early for the training. I caught my own case a day ago that I need to work."

"Oh, and off days are cancelled." With a flourish Rosie made a check mark on the tablet. The phone rang. "Homicide. Yep. Salt just walked in." She silently mouthed to Salt, "Charissa," and handed her the receiver.

"I'm on my way." Salt was tired from the exercises of the morning, but the call from Hamm meant her shift wouldn't be over for another ten hours.

Salt made her way from the gravel parking area surrounded by woods and along a walkway. A bridge of wood planks that led partway around the lakes struck a pose on the tallest spear of a gray-weathered stump along the shore of the wetlands. Geese and crows took to the air across the shallow waters of the preserve. Turtles waddled between the trail and the mucky banks, plopping themselves into reedy water. Beyond reflections of trees at the water's edge, out where the sky and clouds were mirrored, fish jumped, appearing to rise from heaven. Though copperhead and cottonmouth snakes were more likely to be dormant in the cold months, Salt was watchful as she left the end of the plank walkway and followed the dirt path.

At a fork in the dirt path a three-foot-by-two-foot white eraser board was nailed to a tree and green Magic Marker arrows pointed the way to "Doll's Head Trail." On the trail, mobiles, found-object art made into wind chimes, and other curiosities began to appear on the lower limbs of trees. Close by the trail old bottles were held aloft by dolls' arms sticking out of the ground. Broken terra-cotta tiles arrayed like puzzle pieces displayed the odd quote. Neil Young: "A greedy man never knows what he's done." Muhammad Ali: "I'm so bad I hospitalized a brick." The lakes had formed when a brick factory had been abandoned in the early twentieth century, its clay pits then flooded by the nearby river. Just off the trail, coils from an old box spring hung in a leafless tree. Preserve rules were displayed along the path on hand-painted signs. "Only pieces found in the preserve may be used to make art."

Salt trekked past a round thigh-high, four-foot-diameter abandoned well, the north side of the brick and mortar soft with green moss, its original depth slowly rising, filling with discarded debris both from man and nature. It was a remnant of the home of a black family that had been burned out by whites in the 1960s. The family had run a fishing camp and now old lures hung in the trees like ossified insects. A marker next to the trail identified an enormous willow oak, taller than any of its neighbors, as a heritage tree, verified as the second largest willow oak in the Atlanta area.

Salt breathed a sigh of pleasure. The preserve and wetlands were only a few miles from the absolute business center of the city: pieces of porcelain, bits of machinery, toy parts, and broken brick tiles, all of which had been employed in the creation of an evocative jungle that hinted at some essence of the past.

A hawk flew above the dense canopy of trees and into a reddening sky in the west. Salt increased her vigilance of the roots and ruts, mindful that snakes were more likely to be active at dusk. Lights began to flicker among the foliage, bushes, and wagging tree limbs.

A vaporous mist rose between the banks of a sandy creek bed. On the other side an expanse of hill rose, slashed to its red clay core by two dozers now sitting quietly on the slant. Beneath a high train trestle made of hundreds of grayed-wood crossbeams that held the tracks seventy feet above a tributary of the river, the beams of a front loader illuminated Hamm, a cluster of detectives, and a construction crew.

Salt and Charissa stood fifteen feet from a wall of red clay and a five-foot mosaic of streaked beige—long bones near two partially unearthed brown-white skulls. "I just caught a case. I need to work it, Charissa. I was at the academy all morning." Mary's file was locked in the trunk of Salt's Taurus back in the parking lot.

"Girl, every other evening-watch detective is either on the task force or on something else. You're it until midnight. I'll get a uniform to bring you something to eat. You don't have to do nothin' but be here. See those femurs?" She pointed at the bones. "We count at least a dozen or more pairs that were uncovered by the construction workers. No telling how many more we'll find. All we know now is that the bones are old; all the clothes have rotted away."

"Cemetery?"

"No caskets or space for caskets. Could have been paupers, but we'll know more tomorrow when the ME's anthropologist gets here."

"Seems like I'm always saying how much I appreciate your help, Mr. Gooden. You, too. Bye now. See you in the morning." She pushed the end-call button. Her neighbor, a field of several acres between them, had agreed with what sounded like genuine elation to let Wonder out to gather the sheep, as well as promising to keep company with the dog until bedtime. Mr. Gooden had helped build her new fence. He regularly shared produce from his garden and fresh eggs. In his eighties now, he'd known three generations of her family.

She called Wills. "Wills, I'm afraid we have a match on the girl's bones," she told him.

"That should be a good thing."

"I think it is probably Mary Marie."

"What? She was in for murder."

"I called the Hampton Youth Center. She was released four months ago. She'd been released to the grandmother, who she was living with when we took her into custody. She had reported Mary missing a month ago," Salt told him. "I knew as soon as I saw the missing-runaway report. You know how Mary always wore pink when she wasn't in her school clothes?"

"But the body was there what? Three months?"

"I called the grandmother. She didn't report her missing for two months, she said because she didn't want Mary to go back into custody."

A staging area was being assembled there in the deep woods. Salt and an investigator from the ME's office were the only personnel remaining on the scene. Techs had brought in a generator and klieg lights on the back of an ATV.

Wills was silent, then sighed. "Salt, please don't let this get to you. You testified for her at the hearing. You've been advocating for her, first to get her into the treatment program at Hampton and then to get her into a community program."

"The worst possible outcome was for her to go back to that grandmother, one of the most judgmental, punitive people I've ever met. It's no wonder her daughter, Mary's mother, was an addict."

"How long are you going to be at the river?"

"At least until one a.m. when morning watch can relieve me. I'll call you, Wills. Don't worry," Salt said.

There was a long pause from Wills, then he said, "I miss you," and hung up.

But the long day was getting to Salt; cold setting in made worse by a penetrating damp seeping up from the creek nearby. She walked up the hill, then down to the edge of the water and back, moving to keep warm. Fatigue began its ache under the cold. The beam of her flashlight flared across the bare branches and limbs of leafless hardwoods swaying in the night wind high above. Evergreens, loblolly, and slash pines wailed in unison with groans from the weathered timbers of the trestle above, until it increased to grumbling at the distant approach of a train. The ground beneath Salt's feet began to tremble. Then the train, a slow freight of mostly sand cars, rumbled and clacked overhead, sending bits of debris raining into the creek.

HEAT

THE UNIT WAS FULL OF UNIFORM-WEARING DETECTIVES AND
supervisors in their blues. Commanders in white-shirt uniforms
came and went. Violence had attached to the demonstrations; everyone had been ordered to suit up for a show of force, a presence. Salt's
uniform felt irritatingly tight, especially the pants, which edged into
sensitive crevices and seemed to no longer fit right. She did have on
thermals beneath the navy gabardine, but still she hadn't remembered the uniform being this uncomfortable.

"Do these pants make my butt look big?" In an unusual display
of affection Felton stood in the aisle beside Salt's desk poised with
his hands on his hips looking back over one shoulder, eyelashes
fluttering.

"Perhaps this will devastate you, but I hadn't previously considered the size of your posterior." Salt dumped her gear belt and vest in

the chair. "But as you now have brought your butt to my attention, yes."

"Really?" Felton's eyes widened as did his gleeful grin.

"Is it hot in here?"

"Steam's on the fritz again." Felton, sans uniform shirt, pulled at the neck of his V-neck white tee.

Now the old building was all but empty, just the squad left and city workers tasked with sorting what was worth the city's effort to keep and what to dump. Repairs were therefore not going to be done and nothing worked consistently: water, lights, heat, or AC. It was certain that the vast unoccupied floors and vacant warehouse spaces of the behemoth were being wastefully heated, some areas overheated, as was the case in the Homicide office.

"Jesus fucking Christ." Huff walked spraddle-legged toward them, tugging at his shirt neck with one hand while pulling at the seat of his pants with the other. He wiped his forehead with the clip-on uniform tie hanging from his unbuttoned collar. "You," he pointed at Salt, "report to the academy at eight a.m. and stand by to stand by. They're gearing up for a detail for the demonstrations."

"Sarge."

"Don't call me Sarge." He waddled on, delivering bad news to the rest of the squad.

The Things slumped by. "Why wouldn't someone have recognized the truck by now? I don't get it. It's been all over the news." Thing One, Daniels, asked the question everyone was asking. Over and over the media played the video of the suspect's truck, repeating the plea from the PD for someone to come forward. The Confederate flag and the gun rights bumper sticker revealed in the video should have made the truck easily recognizable.

"God knows they're heating this entire building." Felton sat down at the empty desk across from her. "I heard you got a possible ID on your bones from the other day." He nodded at the new file on her desk.

"Yep, and now I need your help. I need a quick interview with the probable victim's grandmother. I have a history with this family. I knew the girl." Mary had also been the reporting party on her mother, dead in a closet, having bled out from a gunshot through the heart. Mary's pink shirt and tight braids were distinct in Salt's memory of that day.

"You usually like to do your own interviews."

"This grandmother and I also have a history. She'll be a whole lot more likely to talk to you."

On the corner of the block just north of Mrs. McCloud's house affixed to the street sign was a makeshift memorial of plastic carnations and a molting teddy bear beneath a crude cross. RIP Peanut was printed in marker on the horizontal bar. The Homes, the 306, Atlanta's most densely populated housing project, was Salt's beat for ten years prior to her promotion to detective. Most of the beat was The Homes plus some areas of low-income apartments and single-family houses on the project's periphery, crumbling three-story Victorians and shabby post-bellum cottages that dotted the streets and sat adjacent to vacant lots grown high with trash, weeds, and nuisance trees. Corrugated twelve-foot-high security fences topped with razor wire surrounded some small, legitimate industries, the profitability of which was hard to determine partly because of the fences.

Mrs. McCloud lived in one of the older houses, wood frame painted white with matte-black shutters. Along with the houses on either side, it sat on a bank above the street, each house having ten or so steps to a small yard and more steps to a concrete front porch.

Felton parked across the street so that from the front door Mary's grandmother could not see the passenger side of the car where Salt waited. Felton got out. She canted her head to look up when she heard his voice and caught a glimpse of Mrs. McCloud's dress at the door, the same purple-black dress she'd worn the last time Salt had been here. She pressed her fingers into her knees, remembering the feel of the old woman's hard corset when she'd placed her hand out to stop her advance on Mary, daughter of her daughter. *How could Juvenile have released Mary back to that?*

Ten minutes later, Felton opened the driver's door and sank behind the wheel. "Whew!" He puffed out his cheeks and exhaled. "That woman is a piece of work!"

"Why did it take her so long to report Mary missing? If it is Mary."

"Oh, I think it's Mary," Felton said. "Something is very wrong with that woman. She didn't seem to either care or be very shocked about the possibility that her granddaughter might be dead."

"Will she do the DNA?"

"Eager, she seemed eager, asking for the details and how soon could she go to the lab. Tomorrow is what she said."

"DNA is good, given that she tried to deny that Big D was Mary's father. It can't hurt to confirm that Mary and Lil D are siblings by the same father and mother. She have any recent photos?"

"Said she'd look. That was also odd. Most families, even ones in this neighborhood, have boxes and albums they grab immediately and go through while you're there. They cry." He looked down at his hands gripping the wheel, knuckles white. "She said it serves you right. That Mary's death is your fault. That must be some history."

Salt's cheeks began to heat. Jaws tight, she said, "She's one to call the kettle black. Good at offering her own daughter and granddaughter judgment without hope of forgiveness."

"And that house—she's some kind of neat freak, control freak. Plastic covering everything. Not a speck of dust."

"She make you take your shoes off?"

"She didn't invite me farther than the hall." Felton looked up at the house. "That's it, then." He turned back to Salt. "You gotta go quell a riot, dear." Felton turned the wheel and headed them back to the office. Tomorrow she reported for twelve-hour street assignments.

A DAY LIKE ANY OTHER

LIL D WOKE IN THE DARK TO THE WARM FUNK, YEASTY AND
sweet, of their three bodies. Danny T, his and Latonya's three-year-
old, had wedged himself between them. Lil D always woke up wanting Latonya's skinny body, but he never broke her sleep, especially not
with the boy there. Instead he rolled over and tried to think about
some way to make her happy. But his thinking got tangled in all the
twists to their problems: how they would manage being together
after she was forced to move, the housing authority sending her to the
east side, his business being here, not that he was making any kind of
money, his car a shitty beater, The Homes and everything they knew
being torn down.

He faced the bedroom wall of painted concrete on which Latonya
had taped a poster about books, a stack of them. "Climb up," it said.
The only books Danny T had left were dirty and torn ABC baby

books, and Lil D was tired of reading the same ones to him over and over.

The boy woke crying. Lil D turned to find the bed wet where the boy's diaper had soaked through and leaked onto sheets already overdue for the laundromat. *I could do that.* Latonya's curled lashes fluttered open. She rolled out of bed in one smooth move, bent to slip into her sneakers, and stood straightening her sweats. The empty box of disposable diapers tumbled to the floor as she grabbed the last one and flipped Danny T on his back to change him. She was quiet in the mornings, sniffing and staying to herself, easing into their struggles. She picked the boy up and shuffled, sneakers untied, out of the bedroom. She could do with some new sneaks. Sometimes she'd get that slanted smile when she opened a present. He couldn't think how he was going to fix getting a place for them all three to live. He went back to thinking of her opening a box of bright shoes, maybe neon green or blue glow.

KINDLING

WHEN SHE'D ARRIVED, DR. MARSHALL'S DAUGHTER DIDN'T SEEM to recognize her. "You've got the wrong address, Officer. Nobody here called the police. You can't even come in without a warrant. I know my rights." She came from behind the receptionist's desk, her body rigid, arms stiff by her sides, fists balled.

"Um, I have an appointment. Sarah Alt? I was here last week?"

"Oh." The young woman frowned. "You look different," she'd said, her tone accusatory.

Half an hour late, Dr. Marshall came out of his office. "Aha! Sarah, you're here."

"In all my glory." Salt spread her hands down and out from her attire.

"So I see. Come on back. I apologize for the delay. The client before you was in crisis. It happens."

"I didn't recognize her with the uniform," said his daughter.

"It's okay," he said quietly to the girl as he waved Salt down the hall in front of him.

Sitting down, Salt said, "Sorry about the gun again, but you know our off days have been cancelled and we're on twelve-hour shifts. I'm on my way to a long day."

"Terrible about what happened to those students. Is there any progress on the case?" Marshall asked.

Salt thought back to the hospital chapel, the strained voices of the victims' families, Hamm shifting from side to side in shoes split on the sides to accommodate her wide, swelling feet. And to Mary. She felt a tightening in her throat but managed to answer. "No. Not really." Out of Marshall's window an earthmover rolled across the parking lot at the rear of a business.

"Is that the scar?"

Salt dropped her hand from the rippled-silk ribbon of skin at her hairline.

"Last time you said the dreams began soon after you received that injury." He motioned a finger at her head.

"Look," Salt leaned forward, rested her forearms on her thighs, and clasped her hands. "I don't mind the dreams. Well, I do mind them, but in a different way. They've helped."

"How's that?"

"You're going to think this is crazy. Uh-oh." She winced.

"Go on," he said, mocking the trope, smiling, hands clasped under his chin.

"A couple of those dreams, it was like they removed a veil, took down some barrier. I'm not sure what's the right way to describe what they do . . . did."

"Go on," he said. They both smiled, acknowledging his clichéd response.

"Connections. I dreamed about connections in both those cases."

"Your unconscious."

"What do you mean? I was a psych major. I know about our unconscious, dreams theoretically revealing what we've forgotten. But these gave me answers to how to find a perp—" She stopped short.

"You majored in psychology, yet you became a cop?"

"My father, you know."

"Yes. I guess the sooner we get to that, his suicide, the better? Hmm?"

"It's not complicated or a mystery. He had depression. I understand that now; the books he read on it line a shelf in our library. He had the classic symptoms. I've done a lot of reading about it."

Marshall leaned back in his swivel chair, fingers meshed together, pointer fingers steepled. "Yeah, but how about your experience? You were what? Ten?"

"My tenth birthday."

An old steam radiator under Marshall's window popped. Mourning doves cooed just outside from the eaves. Out of view, from down the block, some kind of machinery roared.

"Do you think about that? Why on your birthday?"

The radiator pinged and clanked.

Salt checked her watch. "You're good, Doc. I'll give you that." She tapped the watch face. "But speaking of crises, I've got a riot to go to. You hit on the big question, though, the one that I kept avoiding for a long time, to be truthful. Now it's the one I think about most. Not why anymore, but why on my birthday?" She quickly stood and straightened her pant legs, pulling at the front creases.

Marshall got up from behind his desk, his face somber. "You come to these sessions armed in more ways than one."

"Locked and loaded." She grinned, relieved to have an excuse to get out of there. "Kidding. See you next time."

. . .

"**Stand by to stand by**," said one of the nearby cops, leaning against the cinder-block gym wall.

"Quoting Tolstoy again, are we?" Pepper replied. He pushed off the wall, sat down on one of the wrestling mats they'd finally brought out, and began pulling at the laces on his boots.

They were lousy with inaction, especially the young cops and the ones like Salt, used to daily workouts, street action, and adrenaline highs. Their bodies reacted with lethargy to being on hold. All around the gym floor wrestling mats had been pulled out, on which the cops, in their undershirts and navy uniform pants, now sprawled, bored and grumbling. Reminders of the coming deployment, a phalanx of gear stood like sentinels in careful rows and precise order on the bleachers and against the wall: batons leaning against shields draped with navy uniform shirts, behind which were helmets and visors and the officers' vests, gear belts, and gas mask packs.

Salt sat down beside Pep on a mat.

He leaned close. "You cannot have kept track of all the kids we took into custody. In the Homes we took kids into custody at least once a month, more likely once a week. At the minimum that would be over a hundred kids."

"Yeah, but Mary . . ." She began jerking at her laces.

"**Listen up, people.**" The major shouted from the podium at the front of the gym. "We're being deployed as a precaution only. We do not expect to engage in any confrontations." He adjusted the neck of the microphone. "We've got the press, national and local, watching every breath we take. Keep your language clean and your opinions to yourself."

One of the old guys sitting in front of Salt said, "Oh, shit," adjusting the Velcro on his vest. "Same thing they said before the last riot I was in."

"Our mission," continued the major, "is to"—he looked down and began to read—"prevent the destruction of property and to protect citizens. Spelman College lost a member of their community. Eleven more young women are in the hospital, several critical. There's a legitimate concern for the safety of those marching, most of whom are peacefully exercising their rights. The suspects were white and had a Confederate flag sticker on their truck. There've been rumblings from at least one of the supremacist groups headquartered near the city. And some of the supremacists are trying to get their fifteen minutes, claiming they're being harassed, their rights violated. Only in Atlanta." He shook his head. "Lieutenant . . ." and stepped aside.

"Gear up," said the lieutenant.

"What's up with the 'up'?" asked one of the guys as they began moving. "Why do we always gear *up*, listen *up*? We do stand by, but never do we—"

"We stand down," interrupted another.

"I never was told to stand down." They mumbled back and forth, heading for the bleachers, strapping vests over T-shirts, buttoning and tucking the dark shirts in, buckling belts, and loading themselves with the rest of their gear, and then they tromped out to the PAL van. The sky was beginning to darken over the city as Pepper drove the squad of twelve, taking the expressway toward downtown. They pulled into the parking lot of a church that had been conscripted as a staging area and where other police vehicles, department buses, patrol cars, and PD motorcycles, engines revving, were also arriving.

Sergeant Fellows from SVU trotted to their packed van, squad still inside, grabbing up gear. She opened the side door. "Hey, guys," she said panting slightly. "I was just told to meet you. I'll be your squad sergeant for this, ah, disturbance. Your original sergeant was reassigned. They"—she tapped the radio mic on her shoulder—"gave me the order and I'm supposed to make sure we're where we're supposed to be." She unfolded a sheet of paper, checking it as they alighted from the van. "As far as I'm concerned my job will be to try to make sure we stay together, that we're safe, and that we try to keep other folks safe." She folded the paper and put it in her jacket pocket. The older guys leaned against the van looking at the ground. "I've never done this before," Fellows said, twirling a ring on her right hand. "I'm new at this. Some of you were in the Rodney King disturbances and know more than I do. But, like I said"—she lifted the mic—"somebody has to be the point of contact. We'll be on frequency three, channel four. Radio check."

They pulled the radios from their belts and began turning the knobs to the assigned frequency. "Send an ambulance to Peachtree..." "Block south..." "Unit Forty to all units, stand by, you're stepping on each other..." "Hold radio traffic unless you have an emergency..." Unit Forty, the detail commander, sounded harried. Radio traffic filled the frequency. The squad looked at one another, silent.

"Good luck with those radio instructions, Sarge." The old guy shook his head. "Just like last time. They'll send us someplace and then won't know where we are. You'll try to get confirmations and you'll get nothing."

Next to Salt, Pepper said, "I think it was Tolstoy, 'Stand by to stand by.'"

To the west the sun had just gone down, giving its last light to some low blue-gray clouds. They didn't see smoke but caught wafts of something burning.

With her ear to her radio Sergeant Fellows walked away from the group so she could hear the transmissions. She came back to them. "We'll just stay together. I haven't been told where they want us yet."

The radio crackled with constant traffic, officers reporting crowd movements, damage to property, injuries to marchers and bystanders, and requests for the fire department.

"Oh, hell, no!" Suddenly Pepper began squeezing his eyes open and shut. "Shit. Shit. Shit!"

Then she smelled it. "CS." *SWAT was probably only blocks away. Things must be getting dicey.*

Pepper wasn't just sensitive to the capsicum gas but was strongly reactive, always had been. The faintest molecule sent him into fits of watering eyes and sneezing. "You got any tissues, napkins?" He bent over, wiping his eyes.

"Eyewash." Fellows handed him a bottled water and a package of baby wipes. "I'm with you all the way, dude." She carried a large packed-full gear bag.

Salt's phone vibrated again. Ann, Pepper's wife, said, "He forgot the first-aid kit I put together for him, including the eyewash. I am not going to watch TV or get on the Internet. You'll be my only source, Salt. Call me."

"So far we're just on standby. If they deploy us—" A car alarm sounded close by but out of sight on the other side of the church. Salt plugged one ear and held the phone close. "Nothing, Ann. Just a car alarm. Listen, if we're deployed we probably won't be able to use our phones, noise and all."

"Squad! Form up!" Fellows shouted.

A large plume of black smoke snaked above the lower buildings to the southwest in a valley of streets. The smell of burning rubber combined with the peppery CS odor.

"I'll call, Ann." Salt couldn't hear anything more. She tucked the phone away, secured the straps on her helmet, gathered up her shield, and fell in beside the others.

"Okay, folks." Fellows raised her voice so she could be heard over the other sergeants nearby also giving assignments to their squads. "We've drawn City Hall, the main entrance on Mitchell Street. All we have to do is stand there and look formidable. They don't know what the crowds will do so they're assigning us to strategic locations. Squad . . ." Fellows paused. "Forward. March. Whatever." She led them to the sidewalk and then fell back and walked beside Salt. It wasn't like they didn't know the way. "I don't know what the fuck I'm doing," she told Salt out of the side of her mouth.

"I suspect that as long as you know that, you'll be fine." Salt grinned. "We got your back, Sarge."

In the distance came the sound of breaking glass, as though large shards were falling to the pavement from high up. As they turned the corner onto Mitchell Street, less than a block away, a burning car flared, then exploded, shooting flames up, down, and sideways. "Holy shit," Fellows said, stepping to the front of their group, halted at the sight. She began talking into the radio.

Salt fell back beside Pepper as they walked half a block to the bottom of the two-level steps that led up to the filigree brass doors of City Hall. He sniffed and wiped his eyes. "Your eyes clearing?" she asked. There was another *boom* from blocks away and another explosion from the burning car. They all instinctively ducked. "They better be," Pepper said, adjusting his grip on his shield, the surface of which flashed with reflections of flames. The intersection west of them, half a block below, began to flow with people walking mostly south. In the flow were currents, peaceful marchers carrying signs and chanting. Then there were partyers and pranksters, and groups of young males. The squad stood at ease, shields in the at-rest position. They grouped around Salt and Pepper, some of them former academy mates. Jackson Thornton, her friend from the HOPE Team, and a couple of other uniforms from the downtown precinct, two detectives and a brand-new rookie, twenty-two years old and fresh from graduation, made up the rest of the squad waiting there together, protecting the city government's entrance.

The crowd below continued south. "They want us literally at the front doors," said Fellows, leading them up the steps where their backs would be against the glass and brass filigree of the locked and chained doors. Standing along the top step, which seemed too narrow for good purchase, the toes of their boots hanging over the next step, they watched the crowd below move by. "No justice, no peace." Some of the participants turned their heads toward them. "Fuck the police," as they passed less than a block away.

"Stand by. Stand by," a commander repeated over and over, emphatically, amidst other radio traffic: "Looting Pryor and Wall . . ." "Stand by . . ." "Ambulance . . ."

"At ease," Fellows said.

It was getting cold, but on the side of Pepper's face a single drop of sweat slid along the scar that ran from his temple to his jaw. As if he wouldn't anyway, Salt knew Wills would have asked him to watch out for her. Instinctively she was comforted by Pep's presence, that he would be the more likely target just because of his size. Then almost simultaneously she felt ashamed of the feeling. He turned his face to her, eyes moist, twinkling. "Don't be standin' next to me, white girl. You got a target on you." He made a show of backing away, his infectious laugh spreading to the rest.

Many of them had started the day earlier than their usual shift times, later for some, all of them tired from the tension of waiting, and now being on post was getting to them. They sat on the steps. Pepper, flexible from his aikido practice, easily folded his long legs crosswise. He was wearing his uniform boots, the sole of one separated at the toe. Fellows sat down next to Salt. "You find out why that grandmother waited so long to report the girl missing?"

"We just barely got a preliminary interview with her before this detail. She said she didn't want Mary to go back into custody."

"It occur to you that this"— Fellows nodded at the marchers— "began all in the name of, as a demand and a call to action for, women and the right to be safe? And here you are not solving the case of a murdered girl."

"People want their voices heard," Salt said, shrugging.

Pepper leaned over. "You two gonna solve the world's problems or get me something to eat?"

"Eat!" Fellows got on her phone.

The marchers dwindled to a few stragglers. Fire trucks pulled up to the car down the street and began hosing it down, steam rising from the scalding spray. A paddy wagon delivered bags of cold burgers, wilting fries, and boxes of watery coffee. The granite steps grew hard and chilling as the night wore on.

THE HOMES

ACROSS THE SHORT, QUIET STREET FROM SISTER CONNELLY'S old house, two surveyors in orange vests were taking readings, positioning their tripods at various locations around two dilapidated apartment buildings, most of the units boarded up. Sister was sitting on one of the bottom steps to her front porch, eyes closed, face turned up to the early morning sun. Her waist-length white hair, loosened from its usual braid, was spread over a towel around her shoulders. Salt stood at the gate admiring her winter garden. "I'm glad I brought pecans and not some of Mr. Gooden's greens. Looks like I'd be bringing coals to Newcastle." She held up the bag she'd brought.

"Mornin' Sarah. Come on in. I don't want to miss the best of the sun."

Sister, the an informal neighborhood historian, was old as in no-one-knew-how-old. Nothing much happened around The Homes that Sister didn't know about or at least know who the people involved were, and who they were related to.

There was little activity on the street, no cars, no pedestrians, no one out except for the men across the street now taking photos of the apartment property. One of the top apartments was where Mary's mother, Shannell, had been found shot through the chest, a crime scene photo capturing forever the sprigs of wisteria from Sister's garden, blooms and petals strewn on the grimy kitchen floor.

Salt sat down on the steps and stretched her legs. She was already tired, and the sun turned her body to sludge. A warm coconut fragrance radiated from Sister's hair. "You look like one of those picture-book fantasy goddesses with your hair down. I've never seen it unbraided."

"Well, my magical power tells me that right now you ain't stoppin' by just to bring me nuts."

"No way to put this but to come right out and say it, Sister. We found a body, a young girl, shot to death. We believe it's Mary Marie."

Sister didn't move a hair, a muscle or even seem to breathe. Then, without looking at Salt, she straightened, pulled the towel from her shoulders, gathered her hair in one hand, and asked, "What do you mean, 'believe it's Mary Marie'?"

"The body was decomposed. We're testing for a DNA match with Mrs. McCloud and Lil D."

"I ain't got to hear no more." Sister stood and shook the towel. "I guess you didn't have to come tell me in person. Thank you for the pecans." She started up the steps.

"I thought you'd blame me." Salt stood.

Sister, up on the porch, turned to Salt. "I should never have told you what I saw—Mary and her mother."

"I knew anyway and kept after you. You helped me find out how Mary's mother died."

"You still houndin' me—always comin' 'round asking *your* questions. Just like your daddy when he policed 'round here."

Salt picked up the brown bag and put it on the top step in easier reach for Sister. "I'm sorry," she told her, and turned to go. Fastening the gate, looking around the garden at faded stalks and stems composting around the winter vegetables, Salt remembered Sister telling how Shannell would come sneaking into her yard, picking any old bloom for bouquets to give Mary. "We're both hounded, Sister." But the old woman had left the porch and gone inside.

The Homes had been built on rolling hills, its many buildings at varying elevations. Salt drove in from Pryor Street looking up at the blocks and blocks of what once was the most densely populated housing development in the city. In the distance Shaw Street ran along the highest hill, where now only three buildings still stood, their stripped windows and doors like dark eye sockets and mouth holes, a Golgotha. Most of the residences along the winding avenues had been reduced to hill-size mounds of brick rubble, but here and there some still stood and were inhabited.

Latonya lived on one of the small side streets that had not yet become part of the teardown. Salt rapped on the rackety screen door. After repeated knocking, the inner metal door opened a crack. Latonya, toddler on her hip, peered out and then yelled back into the dark apartment. "D!" The kid screeched in reaction to his mother's loud voice and Latonya abruptly shut the door. Salt waited. Lil D opened the door and came out rubbing his face and holding the towel he always wore around his neck to cover the wine-colored birthmark shaped like a continent.

"You got a reason for showing yourself here?" he said, but his tone was mild.

"Word will be out, D," she said. "I've got bad news."

"What could be bad news? All's I care 'bout here and they cool." He jerked his head toward the apartment.

"We found a body, a girl. She's been dead some months, shot. Your grandmother had reported your sister missing. I believe it's Mary Marie."

Lil D looked off. He made a fed-up clicking sound with his mouth.

"I'm sorry," she said.

He swiped at his face.

"We'd like to get a DNA sample from you and your grandmother to make the final identification."

"That ol' bitch been told?"

"Yes. I didn't even know Mary was out, much less back in her custody."

"Mary out but she ain't stay there. Damn." He released a long breath, sighing.

"Did you see her after she got out? I didn't get the idea you were close."

"Naw, but she still my sister, only kin I count now 'sides my boy."

Salt held out her card. "On the back I've written the address for the DNA lab. It won't take five minutes. They just swab your mouth."

"I know. I seen that shit on *CSI*." He pocketed the card and stood looking down at the concrete stoop, shifting his weight from side to side. "You gone find who killed her?"

They stood there on the stoop, a history between them but without day-to-day touchstones. Salt had seen him grow up in The Homes. His family. Their tragedies. He'd probably saved her life while she'd been trying to save his.

"I'm sorry for your loss," Salt said again. "I'll do my best."

Lil D, first lieutenant of The Homes gang, drug dealer, now

entrepreneur in a strip club business, working for Man, the local source for everything black market—drugs, guns, prostitution.

"You still got my mobile number?" she asked him.

"I can find it."

"Here"—she held out her hand—"gimme the card." He handed it back. "Just in case." She wrote her number on the card. "What about you? You got a number where I can reach you?"

"No, man, Latonya got to move out. She ain't found no place yet, and I ain't gone have no poleese in my phone."

She handed the card back, tapping the address. "It's that blue building at Five Points. If you lose the card, Man has my number."

"That Man's bidness who he talk to." He looked at the card, turning it over, back and forth, a couple of times.

"How are things for you these days? Since I've been in Detectives I feel like I'm behind on the news. Looks like The Homes will be gone before long."

The door squeaked and tiny fat fingers squirmed through the opening at the level of Lil D's knees. One bright eye peeked out from the dark inside. "Get your ass back in there, Danny T," Lil D said, harsher than needed, to the child.

Dantavious seemed to find some playfulness in his daddy's tone. He cackled, shut the door, and pried it right back open.

"They love hide-and-seek, don't they?" Salt leaned down and made wide eyes at the boy.

"I gotta help Latonya pack." Lil D shifted his weight from one foot to the other. He adjusted the towel, holding the ends with both hands, ducked his head, and turned to the door.

HISTORY

"ANN'S BEEN READING MORE AND MORE OF THE CITY'S HIS-tory." Pepper unwrapped a sandwich from the carryout box on his knees. They were again stationed at the doors to City Hall.

"She knows more about this city now than any of the natives." Salt peered over at his sandwich. "Trade you my ham for your turkey."

"No thanks." He took a big bite. "Okay," he said, handing it to her and taking her still-unwrapped sandwich.

"Gosh, Pep. Thanks."

A young white woman, peacock-blue streaks in her unnaturally black hair, on her way to join the ongoing protest forming up the street walked past hoisting a sign: MANDATORY DIVERSITY TRAINING FOR COPS. Skirt swinging above Doc Martens, she cut her eyes briefly at the squad eating on the steps. Pepper, cheeks fat with food, smiled and waved his sandwich. She averted her eyes and kept going.

"You know 'bout the riot in 1906?" Pepper asked Salt but looked in the direction of the other cops on the steps, including them in the question.

Salt chewed and swallowed a bite of the dry sandwich. "Not much. Just that there was one."

"Same old story. Black men reported to be raping fair flowers of the South. White men running for governor trying to out-redneck each other for the benefit of newspaper coverage. Black people killed, arrested, and one police shot. No white citizens were harmed in the making of the riot."

Salt nodded in the direction of the woman with the sign. "We're easy and obvious targets for their impatience—they want justice right now. We represent the status quo."

"Like canaries in a mine, that's what we are." Pepper chewed his sandwich. "Like those pathetic redneck supremacists. They're just another group of have-nots. If the haves can just keep the have-nots focused on the police or another group of have-nots, then they get to keep us all in the mines."

"Yeah, well, keeping us on this detail sure keeps me from finding justice for one little have-not." Salt started to close her lunch.

"You gonna eat the rest of that cookie?"

"Trade." Salt helped herself to Pep's apple.

Dr. Marshall had one of those desk toys, a rack of small hanging steel balls that demonstrate some law of physics about the transfer of energy. Salt plucked one of the balls as she sat down. "You from Atlanta, Doc?"

"All my life except for college and grad school. Why do you ask?"

"Just that once you start to learn about the city's history, you see how one event"—she lifted one of the balls again—"impacts on something else you might not expect it to." She let the ball drop.

"It was Faulkner I think who said, 'History isn't dead. It isn't even past.'"

"True dat." Salt slumped back in the cushioned chair.

"Are you thinking of some event in particular, Sarah . . . Salt? Which do you prefer I call you?"

"Either's fine. I guess 'Salt.'"

"I'm curious how you got the name. But let's come back to that. What was it made you say that about the past?"

"It's just the way I think about my job—that I work around a lot of desperate people."

"Cops?" Marshall laughed. "Kidding."

Salt smiled back. "I like that. That's something we'd say when no citizens are around."

"So, desperate people?"

"They do desperate things. An act of violence"—she leaned forward and started the balls again—"has consequences you might not expect. The balls stay in motion."

"Are you talking about your father, Salt? Is he the main reason you became a cop?"

Salt raised a brow and drew back her chin. "Actually, I was thinking about a young girl, murdered—my new case."

"A young girl?" Marshall pushed back in his chair, hands tightening on the armrests. "You always carry this much tragedy around with you? You're in the middle of a riot, trying to solve the murder of a girl, consoling families of a multiple-victim shooting, and didn't you tell me you spent the other night standing watch over some kind of mass grave?"

"In my free time I bend steel with my bare hands." She laughed, a bubble of hysteria loosening.

Marshall wasn't returning the humor.

"Really, Doc. It's no more than most cops have on their plates."

"I don't know most cops. I've been asked to evaluate you." He leaned forward, one arm stretched along his desk.

Salt turned her head toward the window and focused on something blurry in the light. "Pepper gave me the name." She lowered her head and looked at her hands in her lap.

"Pepper? Your friend?"

"Yeah, although 'friend' hardly covers it."

"Why so?"

"Oh, he's saved my life. I've saved his. That kind of thing."

The room was quiet. The motion toy stilled. "Salt, this is our third session and I appreciate your honesty. You're dealing with incident after incident, any one of which would, quite frankly, necessitate therapy for anyone. I'm not saying you're crazy or unfit for the job, but this isn't TV or the movies. You're not Superman or Superwoman. You're not Dirty Harry. You have a past. You are a person who can be wounded, might be wounded. Last time we'd almost gotten to your father's suicide."

"My history not being past and all." She lifted one of the pendulum balls again. "You want me to tell you about your daughter?"

Dr. Marshall didn't respond, blink, or flinch. All he said was "Go on," concentrating on her.

"I think she needs help." Salt felt almost giddy. "She's trouble waiting to happen. She shouldn't be working here."

"Is that how you operate, Salt? All mild mannered and compliant, then wham! You blindside an opponent?"

"Opponent? I thought you were on my side."

Marshall broke eye contact, looking over to his right at the shelves of books, a muscle at his jawline drawing taut.

STAND DOWN

THE PROTEST ORGANIZERS HAD ASKED THAT INSTEAD OF PUB-
lic marches, participants observe "Days of Silence" during the wake
and funeral of their sister student. No planned demonstrations had
been announced. Though still on twelve-hour shifts, officers and detectives had been told to report back to their regular assigned duties.
But they were to keep wearing the uniform.

The task force to find the perpetrators of the shooting of the Spelman women met in the Homicide Unit's conference room, most of
the meetings at two p.m., before Salt came on at four. She wouldn't be
asked to participate, though they had debriefed her again about the
pursuit of the truck and being fired on by one of the suspects. The
federal agents, two men and one woman almost always in identical
blue padded jackets, seemed most disappointed that she'd "lost the
perps," as if they had now tired of not having someone to blame for

the lack of progress. The motive for the shooting was unknown, a seemingly random assault. Daily, Chatterjee's clothing hung looser, the circles under his eyes growing darker and darker. Wills, Gardner, and Huff represented evening watch on the task force. Day watch contributed the unit's lieutenant and Detective Best. Even with all that personnel, other detectives were called on for assistance, including Salt, who was told to go out before the end of each shift, around midnight, to the park to search for witnesses, people who habituated the area during those hours. So far she, like the task force and everyone else, had come up with nothing.

But unlike most of the others, Salt was not unhappy about the extended shifts or the uniform. People in The Homes were used to seeing her in uniform and she could use the extra hours trying to find anyone who might know something of Mary's last days. It was just after noon, early for Man, but she knew the hour would likely find him at Sam's in the back room, an adjoining cinder-block juke joint called the Blue Room. Man, aka James Simmons, had quit school in the seventh grade, when his entrepreneurial endeavors in the drug trade increasingly took more of his time and rewarded his efforts far more powerfully than the inner-city school curriculum ever could.

She and Man had long had a symbiotic and relatively friendly relationship. He depended on her to keep a certain amount of chaos at bay and she relied on him for information and to uphold certain aspects of the social contract. Over more than ten years now they'd kept up a conversation about current events and their cultural implications. He claimed he was going straight and had moved from street dealing to doing business in and with strip clubs; his legal status with clubs like Toy Dolls was ambiguous.

From his usual spot, a lone single table in the center of the floor, a can of high-caffeine power drink at his elbow, an ever-present book open in front of him, Man lifted his head as Salt entered. "Have a seat." He smiled and nudged a molded-plastic chair from the table with his sneakered foot. In addition to the large academic-looking book he was reading, there was a stack of children's books on the table.

"Book group selection for the month of November, Man?" She looked over his shoulder and tapped the book he'd been reading.

"Book group. You kill me." He laughed and closed the book, enabling her to read the title, *Understanding Schizophrenia*. Not exactly surprised, she was curious. His smile widened over his perfect white teeth. He wore the simple white T-shirt she was used to seeing on him, every day always new, over long athletic shorts. In concession to the cold he'd added runners' leggings under the shorts. A sports team hoodie, also new looking, hung on the back of his chair and a Braves cap hung on another chair. "How come you back to the uniform? You get busted out of Detectives?"

"The situation downtown, demonstrations, there's been some looting. We have to be ready in case something flares up again."

"Yeah, folks easy to upset when they already on they last nerve."

Already uncomfortable with her back to the door, Salt flinched when what sounded like a metal pot fell and rolled around the floor of the kitchen that separated the take-out chicken place from the Blue Room. She slid her chair to Man's right in order to have a better view of who came in.

"Chocolate city like this, there's lots of folks uneasy. How come you wanna poleese here in the city anyway? You live in the country, don't you? You could be one of them sheriffs or somethin'."

"Trying to get rid of me again, huh, Man?" She gave him a crooked grin. "I've always thought of it as home." She saw that the stack of books were mostly for toddler-age kids. "You mind?" She shifted through them, *Thomas the Tank Engine, Sesame Street, Clifford the Big Red Dog.* "For your kids?" she asked him.

"Naw, mine outgrew them. I brung 'em for Danny T."

"Book club, book exchange—what's next, Oprah?"

"Readin's important. I been checkin' out books at The Homes library since I left school. I get a bigger picture and it makes me wanna move up that socio ladder."

"Broaden your worldview?"

"Yeah, that's it." Man thumbed the book. "Stone back in The Homes. He paroled out." He held a steady gaze on her.

Salt shifted the chair again, slightly, so that she had almost as good a view of the door as did Man. More rattling came from the kitchen. The smell of chicken frying grew thick. "Lil D here?" She nodded toward the banging. Leaning over the table, she drew a finger under the title on the cover. "*Schizophrenia.* I get it now—the book." *Stone,* she thought, *always Stone.* She became aware of the blood pumping through her veins.

"They got him on medication. He go down to the mental health center every day so they can keep track of him, test his blood and all."

"How long has he been out?"

"Couple of months. I thought they'd tell you. You poleese don't talk to each other? He stay right next door at that store-church, God's World. The preacher there let him use the back room."

"Right under your feet? No wonder you're trying to figure out what's up with him," Salt said, tapping the schizophrenia book with her trigger finger.

"Naw, I ain't studyin' him. He different now."

"How different?"

"I don't know." Man frowned. "Maybe it's the medicine. His head more mixed up in some ways. I read people first get schizophrenia when they young, like Stone's age. But it's like now he's a zombie or something, not all there."

Salt sat up and took a breath. "Look, the reason I came by—"

"Oh, here it comes. You all the time come 'round makin' my life hard, complicatin' shit."

"This should be easy for you, Man. Communicating, that's all this is about. Lil D tell you about his sister?"

BACK TO MARY

BOXES WERE STACKED IN DETECTIVES' CUBICLES THROUGHOUT the office. They'd taken down and packed up personal touches. Gone were the mug shots, crime-scene photos, BOLOs, mementos, and commendations that had been displayed along with photos of their families, pets, or fishing trips. Wills' framed picture of Pansy and Violet, his dogs, was gone from his desk. The pastel planting-season chart was down from Gardner's cubicle wall. But as Salt walked through the aisles to her far-corner desk she began to notice identical memos newly pushpinned to the stained, ripped walls of each cubicle. And on her desk she found an envelope and inside the identical letter of "Accommodation" that Deputy Chief "Malaprop" had sent to all of them commending their sacrifice during the recent detail that had required extended shifts and cancellation of off days.

"Where will you be taking your accommodation? I'm thinking the Keys, myself. I am so ready for some sunshine." Felton dropped into the chair opposite her desk, where he could be found with increasing frequency when he wasn't on the street or at his own desk.

"You guys are so wrong. So what if the deputy chief mangles a few phrases or words. It's the effort and spirit of his recognition." She tacked her memo up, dug in a drawer, and came up with a "Get Away to the Islands" advertisement, which she promptly pinned beside the "Accommodation."

"Hey, mon. I need to be accommodated," he said, leaning back in the chair, hands behind his head, legs extended, feet up on the desktop. "By the way, I'm single again." He smirked matter-of-factly.

"Oh, no! You had such hopes for this one."

"Dumped me for a fireman."

The phone on her desk began to crackle, its ring sounding more and more like an electrical short circuit with every call.

"That sounds dangerous," Felton said, nodding at the phone as she picked up the receiver.

"Be right out, Rosie," she said and hung up. "Mrs. McCloud is here. Rosie said she brought in a photo of Mary."

"How do you want to work it?"

"Maybe you should get her back to the conference room and then I'll see how she reacts to me."

"You got it." Felton swung his feet to the floor.

Salt opened Mary's file and lifted the pages to the recent BOLO on her that Missing Persons had distributed. It was a school picture several years old with some kind of blue tint to it that in light of her death seemed morbid. Felton had asked her grandmother to bring in a more recent one partly as a reason to get her to the office.

Felton came back escorting Mrs. McCloud. Every hair of her blond bun slicked into place, the heavyset woman stiffly surveyed the room. Giving Felton time to get settled, Salt waited until he came out to get two coffees, then followed him back into the conference room. Mrs. McCloud sat on the far side of the long table with her hands folded on top of a satchel-size black-patent handbag. She looked up from under lowered lids as Salt came in behind Felton. She didn't blink.

"Mrs. McCloud?" Salt said, offering her a coffee.

Mary's grandmother gave no acknowledgment of Salt.

"You know Detective Alt?" Felton prompted.

"I do," she replied. "But what has she to do with Mary's case? She is one of the reasons that Mary's dead."

Salt came to the side of the conference table where Mrs. McCloud sat. She pushed one of the chairs to the wall, where it hit with a thud, and sat down, turning to square her body with the old woman's. "I know you're a true Bible Christian, Mrs. McCloud." Salt knew the one subject the grandmother could not resist flaunting her knowledge of. "You must be here today partly to render to Caesar? Right? Did you give your DNA at the lab? Bring us a newer photo?"

Mrs. McCloud bristled, straightening her shoulders and lifting her chin. "I want you to bring whoever was involved in killing Mary to judgment. I don't need Caesar as a reason to cooperate." She unsnapped the handbag, reached in, and came out with an eight-by-ten picture of her granddaughter that appeared to be printed off a computer on cheap photocopy paper. "Somebody in my church saw this picture of Mary on their computer and gave it to me." She put the picture on the table.

Salt slid the photo over. It was a blurry Mary standing between two larger girls, girls who were wearing jeans strategically ripped at the thighs and cut-off T-shirts with barely recognizable logos of the Toy Dolls strip club. She'd be seeing Man again for sure. He ran Toy Dolls now.

"Who gave you the photo?" Felton asked.

"They got nothing to do with it. They got it off their son's phone.

He got it from some other kid's phone—neighborhood kids who know Mary. They all know how she is now." She snapped the purse shut.

"Why did it take you so long to file a missing person on her?" Felton asked, switching to bad cop. "She'd likely been dead at least a month when you made the report."

"I already told you that twice." She turned her head, facing Felton. "Mary would still be alive if Miss Alt hadn't interfered and if you police did your job—kept girls out of strip clubs and whoring instead of locking girls up with other whores."

"Did Mary talk to you about Hampton, who she hung out with there?" Salt asked.

Eyes narrowed, Mrs. McCloud turned and stared at Salt. "I don't talk about evil now and I didn't want Mary telling me about evil."

"You were ashamed—the neighborhood knowing," Salt said, picking up the photo, her focus drifting. *Mary had had a habit of pulling, pulling at her fingers, one by one. She'd stood in the hall at the door to the bedroom pointing to where her mother crouched dead in the closet, blood congealing in her lap, flies laying their eggs.*

"Ashamed? Mary did this on her own!" Mrs. McCloud leaned from the waist like an old listing tree trunk, tapping the photo that Salt had laid back down on the table between them, *thunk-thunk*. "No, I didn't report her. I didn't want her to go back to Juvenile. You see what kind of trash she took up with?" She shoved the photo across the table.

Felton picked it up. "This the best photo you have? It would help if we had a good close-up of her face."

The grandmother raised her chin and looked down her nose. "Detective, you can get her mug shot from Juvenile." She rose from the chair and stood over Salt, whose focus had remained with the image of Mary in that hall. "I gave my DNA."

"As the hart panteth after the water . . ." Salt quoted from the psalm. "You know when I was a kid"—she rose to face Mrs. McCloud—"I used to think the word was 'heart,' h-e-a-r-t, since I'd never heard of an animal called a hart. I was comforted that somebody felt their heart panted like mine did." Salt reached out to move Mrs. McCloud, to turn her toward the door, remembering the feel of the old woman's hard corset the day she took Mary into custody.

Mrs. McCloud slowly looked down at Salt's hand, snatched up her bag, turned, and strode to the door, Felton following her out. At the conference room doorway he looked back over his shoulder, eyes and mouth screwed up in a question mark. Salt watched them go out, but her mind's eye lingered still in that hallway with Mary.

Salt found Felton seated in the reception area after he had seen Mrs. McCloud out. Except for Rosie, the area was for once quiet and otherwise empty.

"What was that in there? You said you had a history with her, but that—what was that about?" Felton looked over at Rosie filing her nails like some gal in an old noir detective movie. He fidgeted and stuck his hands in his pockets.

"What?" Salt said.

He shrugged. "You know—some kind of witchy-woman thing—feminine energy? It was spooky. I don't pay any attention when some of the guys say things, but I don't know, Salt—you are sometimes, well, odd."

Rosie looked up from her nails.

"What do they say?" Salt put her hands on her hips.

Rosie put the file down and turned her chair to face Felton.

Felton sighed. "They say you've got some kind of mojo, hoodoo, that you're tuned to another channel. Don't look at me like that. I'm not the one saying it. Still . . ."

"Dude, Sherlock, Mister-One-Hundred-Percent-Clear-Up, you told me when I first came that each detective here brings their own way of working cases, point of view, story, to this murder work."

"Maybe it's a woman thing. It just looks different. You pay attention to things others don't." Felton straightened his vest and tugged at his cuffs. "I realize I'm not the one to talk about what's different."

Rosie propped her elbows on her crossed legs and focused on them with chin in her hands.

"She uses religion to bully people, that's all. She used it on her daughter and then her granddaughter," Salt said. "I don't like it that people get away with that kind of hurt." She had a flashback to the hospital and her father in a bed, in restraints.

Huff blew in carrying the cold in his clothes and glanced at the three of them. "All three of my favorite dicks, right when I come in the door. Jesus Christ," he said, stomping his feet, blowing on his hands, and rubbing them together.

Rosie quickly slipped the manicure kit in a drawer. "Would you like some fresh java, Charlie?"

He looked up at the ceiling and sighed. "I guess there are perks to putting up with you freaks. *Perks. Perks.* Get it?"

They stared at him.

"Rosie is going to make me coffee. Perks?"

Salt and Felton rolled their eyes.

"Perks. That's funny, Charlie." Rosie stood. "Let me get you out of that coat," she said, reaching toward the sergeant's shoulders as he sidestepped, punched the keypad, and darted through the inner door. Rosie, undeterred, followed on his heels.

She needed to get to the Youth Detention Center, but before she could get out the door, the FBI agents came to her with a book of photos of rifles and asked Salt to try to identify the weapon that had been pointed at her from the truck. Impossible. She'd been ducking glass and bullets. The task force seemed desperate.

Salt began to pay attention to her breath as soon as she drove in sight of the Hampton YDC. It was to steel herself. The facility represented the system's massive failure to intervene and care for kids before they were housed there. Behind fences topped with razor wire, behind metal doors and concrete walls were the most vulnerable, those most in need of a soft place to land. She was able to find a front-row parking space, the lot being large and only partly utilized. At the entrance her admittance was accompanied by a loud, obnoxious electronic-door buzzer operated by staff behind hard Plexiglas. Showing her badge and ID, she handed her 9mm through the retractable tray and leaned close to the round metal speaker. "I have an appointment with Ms. Shannon."

"Keep your arms by your side and go through the metal detector," said the uniformed corrections officer behind the glass. "I'll call her."

Down the hall from a cross corridor walked a line of juveniles, holding their arms crossed at the wrists as if handcuffed. They wore, both girls and boys, dark blue cotton elastic-waist pants and shirts stenciled with the letters "HYDC." There was one hollow-cheeked white-faced boy in a line of fifteen dark faces. She stared, remembering the day she'd seen Mary getting off the school bus with the other kids, her socks slipping down into her shoes as she walked, and Salt's fantasy at that moment for Wonder to herd Mary to a safe place.

"Detective?" A striking woman of six feet or more came from around the corner. "I'm Natalie Shannon," she said, holding her hand out to Salt. "Let's go back to my office," she said and turned, leading down the hall.

Skylights and wire-mesh windows at the end of the hall added to the glare from a plethora of industrial fixtures that threw a harsh light against the highly polished white-and-blue-tile floors and white walls. Salt felt an urgent need to get home to her dog, to touch his downy undercoat, remembered the soft feel of the heated cloth her mother would put against her chest when she had a cold.

Ms. Shannon swiped a card attached to the lanyard around her neck across a sensor next to the office door. "Have a seat." She waved Salt toward a faux-leather couch between two chairs in a conversation arrangement. A tower of stacking chairs took up one corner of the room. "You look ready to bolt," she said to Salt, still standing hat in hand at the door.

"Mary Marie McCloud." Salt walked to the couch and sat down. The armrests were worn from the original dark blue to a lighter hue.

Shannon went to her desk across the small room and picked up a file. "She was released May fifteenth. She was in the trauma group that I run and I also treated her in individual therapy." Shannon came over and sat down in a chair across from Salt. She ran her hand over her hair, which was pulled back in a flawless chignon. "This place was inappropriate for her. She was too soft. Also, she was owning up to what she'd done and why. I was shocked when her case worker called me and said she'd gone missing."

Salt tried to shake the image of Mary's hair entwined in the brambles. "Who made the decision she could go back to her grandmother?"

"Mary was here only because of the seriousness of her crime. The record shows that the detectives that arrested her even advocated for her. Because she had no previous record, because she was making progress in therapy, she qualified for community treatment."

"Did you meet the grandmother?"

Shannon stood and walked to her desk. "Mary told me she wanted to go back to her. I warned her—told her that Mrs. McCloud would be the same. Yes, I met her."

"I was the one who arrested her."

Both Salt and Shannon sat in silence until finally Salt stood and came over to the desk where Shannon now sat. "Help me. Was there someone here she was close to—made friends with?"

Shannon opened the file and flipped through, tracing down the pages with her finger. "No." More flipping. "Maybe." Almost to the back of the folder she stopped and read silently. "This is an incident report from when she was first admitted. She was discovered in bed with another girl."

"Name?"

Shannon looked down. "Josephina Jones, aka . . ."

"JoJo."

"This says," Shannon continued to read from the file, "both girls were fully clothed." She looked up. "I remember now. JoJo was also in my trauma group." She tapped the keyboard in front of the monitor on her desk, typed, and reading from the screen, said, "Released almost exactly a month from the day Mary arrived."

"What was JoJo in for?"

"Habitual," she read, "theft, shoplifting, early and often." Shannon copied to a notepad, tore off the paper, and handed it to Salt. "JoJo's guardian, her auntie's address."

SALT AND FELTON
TAKE A RIDE

"YOU GOT TIME TO TAKE A RIDE WITH ME?" SALT ASKED FELTON, who was at his desk, a half-full packing box on the floor beside him. He blinked up at her from a framed photo of him and another man on a beach, the sun setting behind them, their arms entwined. He threw it, frame and all, into his wastebasket. "Sure," he said, standing and grabbing his fedora and coat.

In the elevator on their way down Salt said, "It's just that I have a history with the people in The Homes, most of it positive, but I made some enemies, too. I worked that beat for ten years. I need to stop by there on the way to Toy Dolls."

"I hear they're tearing The Homes down. Lot of those folks won't be there for long."

"I'm sure the first ones to go were the ones easiest to place, those who had clean records, the fewest complaints, ones without troubled relatives." The elevator opened to the parking deck level. "There is this one guy—Stone, Curtis Stone."

"I thought he was in prison. Isn't he the one that tried to kill you? Wasn't he also convicted on gun charges?" Felton asked as they wandered around the poorly lit detective parking lot looking for Salt's Taurus among all the other Tauruses.

"Yeah, and he's out now, on medication for some pretty serious mental health issues." They found the car and Salt got behind the wheel. "I used to believe he was just violent, an enforcer for the gang but unpredictable. He had a childhood of more abuse and neglect than usual, one that would turn a healthy mind sick. But as his illness has gotten worse, I actually think I understand him better. But . . . Wills." She shrugged.

"Oh, I get it. Sure. What I wouldn't do for somebody who cared about me like that." He turned his head to look out the passenger window.

"I don't want to be an albatross."

"Come on." He shrugged. "It'll be good. Pepper must have liked having you back him up all the time. You and he are still close. Everybody loves Pepper."

"He's a good guy, my brother from another mother."

"And who knows, maybe your lucky-in-love karma will rub off on me." He let out a long breath.

They passed The Homes and Sam's Chicken Shack and the Blue Room, Sam's and the Blue Room sharing a parking lot with the adjacent run-down former retail strip where God's World Ministries occupied one storefront, from which light now shone. Salt took the next left and circled back into the lot in front of the church, the door opening and closing as people came and went. "Man said Stone was staying in a back room of the ministry." She pointed to God's World.

"You think it's a good idea to stir him up? Maybe Wills has good reason to be worried. Why take a chance that you'll be the cause of Stone going off the deep end?"

"Maybe," she said. A stirring drumbeat could be heard each time the church door opened. "I don't know."

Felton unbuckled his seat belt. "What does he look like?"

"What are you doing?"

"I'll just talk to the preacher—see what he says about Stone."

"They're having a service."

"Then I'll give one of the deacons my card and ask him to have the preacher call me. Be right back."

It was becoming clear to Salt why Felton had been so successful clearing his cases—he worked the opportunities. A tambourine rattle accompanied the drums when he opened the storefront door. As the door closed behind him, suddenly, from above her head came a loud metal-bending sound. The car roof caved inward over her head. She ducked, slid to the passenger side, got the door open, and crawled out. Stone was perched cross-legged on top of the Taurus, his long, talon-like fingers grasping a Bible. "Behold the angel of the Lord." His eyes rolled upward, light from a nearby pole shining directly on his face. Then he looked down at her and smiled, the whiteness of his new teeth gleaming in the streetlight and in contrast with the red-brown skin of his too small, round face and head.

"I heard you got parole," she said, making sure both his hands were on the Bible and evening her breath.

"Born again. I been saved. Washed in blood." Stone cocked his head, narrowing a one-eyed gaze on her, a glimmering in his focus.

Salt was facing Stone and had her back to the door of the church, where the sound of the drums from inside briefly intensified. She turned sideways to see Felton coming out.

The roof unbuckled with a heavy pop as Stone slid down the windshield onto the hood and off the Taurus, landing with a jump.

Felton came up beside her. "Detective Felton, this is Curtis Stone," she said.

Stone had begun thumbing through the Bible, his motions jerky and frenetic, ignoring Felton and Salt's introduction. "What's the sign? What's the sign?" he repeated over and over as he flipped the pages. He pounded a finger to a page, pointing and reading, "There, 'Suffer the children . . .' In red, in red." He hit the Bible with his fist and it fell from his hands to the dusty gravel parking lot. His eyelids dropped like hoods covering the mad light from his eyes. His shoulders folded inward, curving to their familiar vulture-like shape.

Felton touched her arm. "We should go. Keys?"

Salt handed him the keys. "Curtis?" she said.

He'd become inert, head bowed, slumped, arms hanging at his side.

"Curtis? Can I pick it up for you?" She waited but he didn't respond. Keeping her eyes on him, she walked closer, bent down, picked up the Bible, and held it out. Muffled shouts from the minister exhorted responses from the congregation inside God's World. Stone slowly opened his eyes to the Bible in Salt's extended hand. He took it and walked toward the corner of the building and out of sight.

"No wonder Wills is worried. That guy is very scary. He is unpredictable, ready to explode. He's big and wiry at the same time," Felton said as they drove down Pryor toward Toy Dolls.

"Yeah, but I've known him since he was about twelve," Salt said. "The way he was raised, left to fend for himself, would have been enough to make anyone crazy, especially someone so young and already predisposed to mental illness. He's always been a ticking bomb."

"That is not just a product of poor parenting. He's got misfiring circuits for sure." Felton tapped his temple.

"And nobody to care or take care of him," she said.

"A monster. Hold on. I'm as compassionate as the next guy, but when you look at him, you know there's nothing that can save that guy."

"He's already lived his life in hell—born into hell. He's never had a chance. There but for the grace of God or the Universe and all that."

Felton turned off the car and looked up at the derrick-like steel tower that rose above the Toy Dolls Club, on which a silhouette of a reclining curvy woman in pink neon lit up the night. "I've got my own cross to carry," he said.

The last time Salt had been to Toy Dolls she'd been part of a team serving a warrant. It hadn't ended well.

They got out and went through the double doors. An interior wall blocked the view from the entrance to the main room and created an alcove in which a doorman sat behind a chest-high counter. The walls of the club were painted flat black, off of which disco lights reflected, winking and swirling to the deafening beat of the music. Leaning over the counter in order to be heard over the pounding bass, she showed her badge. "Man. We're here to see Man." He held up a finger and picked up an old-fashioned cord phone from under the counter. "Tell him Salt is here," she shouted. "Office," he mouthed, replacing the receiver, pointing his finger toward the ceiling. As they passed through the room, a young woman onstage wearing angel wings, back to the audience, bent from her waist and bared her genitals, exposing them to the men at the tables in front of the stage. Felton held up a hand shielding his eyes. Salt led the way up the stairs to an office with a long, wide window overlooking the stage and tables. Man was standing at the window when they opened the door.

"This is Detective Felton. Detective, meet Man-Man, aka James Simmons."

He pointed his chin in Felton's direction. "You got backup now?" he said, then smiled, teeth glowing blue-white in the low fluorescent light of the office. He was wearing what for him was unusually flashy athletic gear, shiny red shirt and long shorts that obscured the slight bow of his legs.

She took the photo of Mary and the two females from an inside pocket of her coat and handed it to him.

"I see what you're gettin' at—girls wearing my club shirts, looking all girl-friendly with Lil D's sister," he said, brow furrowing as he looked at the picture.

"How did she know them? Both of those girls, by the way, look too young to strip."

"Yeah, they do look fresh." Man smiled. "But they legal. That one, with the ponytail"—he tapped the image with a manicured nail—"she call herself JoJo. She from The Homes, used to live not far from where Mary's daddy used to stay. Mary come in here one night with her and I made JoJo take her home, use my car. I'm not gonna let Lil D's sister start here."

"You got their permits?"

"Right here, all legal." He went over, opened one of the file cabinets against the back wall, thumbed through, and retrieved paperwork on Josephina Jones, aka JoJo, and Gloria Glover, aka Glory. The permits showed both to be just past their twenty-first birthdays.

A couple of times Man glanced at Felton, who had stayed silent but kept his eyes on Man. "You top or bottom, Detective?"

Felton, about the same height, came close to Man, up in his face. "I realize you want me to think of that as rhetorical, Mr. Man. But I don't take it as such. I'm out-and-out top. How 'bout you?" Almost nose to nose he eyed him feet to head.

"Are either of them working tonight?" she asked, interrupting the showdown.

The phone rang and Man snatched it. "How soon?" he asked into the receiver, then hung up. "You got to go. Now. You got the addresses. I'll ask around. You got to leave right now." He opened the office door, followed them down the stairs and through the room, pounding music accompanying them out the doors.

Outside Salt said, "You've got my number, Man."

Already inside the door he gave a backward wave.

Back in the Taurus, Salt looked at Felton. "That was kinda weird," she said.

He turned on the ignition. "Where should we wait?" he asked.

"The whole lot is wide open. We should just stay right here, lights off. What was that between you and Man? I've seen guys beat their chests at each other but that was a different vibe, speaking of different!"

He turned the car and lights off. "You mean sexual?"

"I guess."

"He was trying to sell me wolf tickets and I challenged him."

"See, that's why—"

"No different. Straight or gay we beat our chests, guys do. You think it impedes communication?"

Not wanting to appear ungrateful for his help, she said, "I don't know."

Felton looked out over the cars in the lot. "He's beautiful, your Mr. Man-Man. He swings both ways in case you didn't know. Trust me, I can smell it. If I'm going to hang with you and if I see him again, he has to know I'm not gonna pull punches, either. I'll be straight with him, so to speak." Felton grinned.

A long black Bentley with tinted windows glided into the parking lot and stopped at the entrance of the club. The driver went around and opened the rear passenger door. Flash Daddy Jones, Atlanta's most powerful music mogul, got out holding a phone to his ear as he went through the club's front door. Jones lived in that world between worlds, where street met legit, where the search was always on for ways to wash dirty money. On paper he sometimes owned Magic Girls. If he needed something from the city or the city needed something from him, the mayor was the go-between. All that club money was rain that made rap music grow in Atlanta. And rap music was now giving birth to a fresh new industry in Atlanta—moviemaking.

"Whoa," Salt exclaimed.

"I'll say."

"No wonder Man was anxious for us to leave."

ORPHANS AND OUTLAWS

SALT DROVE THROUGH THE HOMES, JUST AS SHE'D DONE WHEN IT was her beat, and went by Sister Connelly's. She needed Sister's understanding about Mary. Sister, out in the middle of her front-yard garden stooped over her plants, straightened and waved when she saw Salt drive by. Halfway down the block Salt stepped on the brake, backed up, stopped, got out, and went to Sister's gate. "What are you doing for Thanksgiving?"

Sister held a small pair of pruning shears. "Probably going to a cousin's. Why?"

"Because I'd like to invite you to my place. We call it the Orphans and Outlaws Thanksgiving. Please. I'd love for you to come. I've told you about my old place and I'd like you to see it. And Mr. Gooden, my next-door neighbor, next field over, has the most amazing garden, not as pretty as yours, but he grows terrific vegetables. You and he are about the same age. Please say you will."

Sister dropped the shears into a bucket and dusted her hands. She looked off into the distance as if considering Salt's invitation.

Hopeful that Sister hadn't immediately rejected the idea, Salt hurriedly said, "For once I'm off on a holiday, only the one day, but Detective Wills, you've met him, lives close to here and you're on his way. I'd bring you home."

"Who else will be there?" Sister tilted her head. "Would I be an orphan or an outlaw? Any other black folks coming?"

"Pepper and his family. You know Officer Greer. He's a detective now. Ann, his boys." Salt balanced on her toes. "I was afraid to ask. I didn't think you would."

"Only if I can bring something, something special," Sister said.

"We love coming down to Salt's, for a lot of reasons," said Pepper's wife, Ann, sitting across from Sister Connelly at the kitchen table. Salt and Wills came and went carrying dishes to the dining room, putting the finishing touches on the Thanksgiving table. "The boys love the sheep, the dogs, the trees, everything about this place." Ann tilted her head toward the back door. "Listen to them." Out back the dogs were barking, the boys whooping and laughing.

"All this space." Sister lifted her eyes to the high ceiling where an ornate plaster medallion surrounded a single hanging bulb and over to the white cupboards and the wide window over the deep porcelain sink.

Wills peeled plastic wrap from the crystal bowl that Sister had brought. "What do we have here?"

"Needs to heat in a pan a few minutes right before we sit down," Sister said.

Salt took the lid off the big cast-iron pot and emptied the bowl into it. "Greens?"

Sister opened the brown bag in her lap. "Can you fry this up quick?" She handed Salt wax-paper-wrapped sliced bacon. "I see you got a good skillet."

"Both the skillet and the pot have been part of the kitchen since before I can remember," Salt said.

"I'd never used cast iron before, but using Salt's has made me a believer," said Wills, taking the bacon and aligning the slices in the pan.

Sister turned back to Ann. "You don't sound like you're from here, either."

"Just another transplant. My husband is the Southerner," Ann said.

"Ann teaches fifth grade and she's been reading up on Atlanta's history. She probably knows more about the city than the rest of us natives put together." Salt picked up a dish of green beans with one hand and a bowl of baked yams with the other. "Y'all grab something." She nodded at the food-laden serving dishes and bowls that crowded the kitchen counter. The smell of bacon frying combined with the other Thanksgiving fragrances filling the house—sage, cinnamon, and baking turkey. Without being called, the men and boys came up on the porch, their voices boisterous, feet heavy on the board floors. Mr. Gooden took charge of the dogs, settling them on the porch. Pepper ordered the boys to quiet down and mind their manners.

Mr. Gooden came in the dining room. "Table fits perfect." He'd been storing the oak table in an outdoor shed and it was weathered and stained, but Salt had found several old lace and linen tablecloths, tattered and in different shades of white, stored in the same trunk where she'd found her father's coat. The cloths lay nicely on the table, layered and soft. The chairs were mismatched, as were the plates and silverware Salt had picked up from time to time at flea markets and yard sales.

They came to the table, Sister last, bearing her crystal dish of greens garnished with crumbles of bacon. Mr. Gooden's eyes widened as he leaned to the center of the table, sniffing Sister's dish. "Is that what I think? Poke salad? How can that be?"

Sister Connelly pursed her lips, suppressing a smile. "I freeze some every spring so I have them for Thanksgiving."

"Oh, Lord," Mr. Gooden said. "I think I've died and gone to heaven. I haven't had poke greens since before my wife passed."

"I've never had them at all," Salt said. "Heard all my life about poke salad, but this is a first for me." Salt lifted a serving to her plate.

"Mama, is that the same as pokeberries?" Ten-year-old Miles' eyes widened. "You said they were poison."

"Your mother is right," Mr. Gooden said, looking down to the boy beside him. "It is the same plant." He forked a heap of the greens onto his plate. "But if you get the leaves young, in the spring like Sister Connelly said, and boil them three times, they aren't poison and are some of the best eating ever." He scooped a bite into his mouth, closing his eyes and chewing. "Umm, umm."

"Compliments also to our head chef." Salt lifted her glass, toasting Wills at the opposite end of the table. "Let's hear it for turkey and tofurkey."

"You forgot the blessing," Theo, Pepper's youngest, complained.

"Bow your heads, you heathens." Pepper folded his hands for the prayer. "Lord, bring peace to our city. Comfort those in pain. Thank you for our blessings. Amen."

"Amen," echoed the guests.

Miles kept his fascination with the possibility that they were eating poisonous pokeberry. "How do you know the poison is gone?" He had put one little piece of the greens on his plate, staring at it.

"I learned from my mother," Sister told him. "Our family ate poke greens every spring and as often as we could get them."

"Seems like a lot of trouble to prepare," Ann said. "I admit they are delicious."

"Back in those days poor folks got food where they could. Sometimes the best food came from people who had to find ways to make what they had taste good." Sister pushed back from the table.

"Were you poor?" Theo asked incredulously.

"My grandmother was born a slave. Yes, we were very poor."

"A slave! No way!" Theo stiffened his arms, holding himself off his chair and swiveling his head to the others at the table.

"Settle down," his mother admonished.

"Are you still poor?" he asked.

"That's enough, young man." Pepper frowned at his son.

"Oh, that's all right. I like to tell young people. They need to hear how it was." Sister smiled at Theo. "It's good to be curious. But listen to your parents. What they want you to learn is good manners. Sometimes people don't want to talk about certain things and it's not polite to ask them to. Your mother and father just want you to learn when to ask."

"I grew up eating poke salad, too." Mr. Gooden slid his empty plate toward the yams.

"Wasn't just black folks poor in Georgia." Sister nodded at him.

There was hardly a breath to catch between words and mouthfuls, much less lags in conversation. They kept to the unspoken rule of no talking about the job. The kids and the elders kept it lively until they were sated. They bused their own dishes to soak in the sudsy sink. Then while the others went for a walk in the orchard, Salt showed Sister the rest of the house.

"I might have been here before—when I was a real little girl, maybe Theo's age," Sister said as they walked down the hall.

"That's right. I remember. You had family that lived in Cloud," Salt said, standing in the hallway between the library and the living room.

"Maybe it was just a house like this." Sister ran her hand over the oak trim of the library doors.

"You were kind to answer the kids' questions." Salt pushed back the pocket doors. "I don't have a lot of furniture." She went in and Sister followed.

"That's cedar I smell." Sister inhaled slowly.

"The shelves. You can smell them all through the house when there's nothing to compete, like a turkey dinner."

"What happened to the furniture? House like this probably was filled with antiques."

"My mother took a lot of it when she remarried and went to live with her new husband in North Carolina. Come on, I'll show you upstairs. I've made some changes."

Sister stood in the center of the room, turning to take in the four walls of books.

Salt motioned her toward the living room and the stairs to the second floor. At the top of the landing Salt waited for the old woman. As Salt looked down the second-floor hall, the now-familiar blurred image edged into her vision. She touched the tip of the scar at her hairline, then sat down suddenly, her back against the wall. "Sorry. I lost my breath there for a second," she told Sister when she got to the top step. Salt blinked several times, trying to clear the jagged crimson outlines. "Must have eaten too much."

Sister sat down, leaning her back against the banister facing Salt. She just sat quietly without saying a word. Salt became hyperaware of the voices from out back, the dogs barking, the baas of the sheep. She smelled Sister's tobacco and coconut aura. "Whew, it's been a while since I had one of those. They pass pretty quick." She closed her eyes, then opened them. "I'm fine." She stood and offered her hand to help Sister stand.

Sister took up the conversation like there'd been nothing unusual. "Somehow I got the notion you didn't have no mother."

They went into the first bedroom on the right, through the bath between it and the second bedroom, then back out to the end of the hall, where Salt opened the door to the screened sleeping porch. She and Sister stood there looking down at the paddock and over the orchard, where the other guests were walking among the almost bare trees, the boys and dogs running ahead. "Come, let me show you the renovation." Salt closed the door to the porch and led Sister to the dojo. She slipped off her shoes, put them on the little wooden rack, and opened the door.

Watching, Sister looked down at her low-heel strap shoes. "Why don't I just peek in."

Salt turned the warm recessed lights up and stepped onto the white floor mat. Daylight from the chest-high windows slanted across the room and up the bamboo and weathered-wood walls. Salt knelt before the low altar on the wall opposite the door. "We call it a 'practice.'" Hands in prayer pose, she bowed to the altar.

"Feels like church almost." Sister unstrapped her shoes and entered in stocking feet. "I've seen pictures of rooms like this. You fight in here." Sister's knobby feet, encased in opaque stockings, whispered as she walked over to one of the windows and turned to face Salt. "I'm too stiff to be kneelin'. I see you got your father on that altar." She motioned to the shelf.

Salt sat seiza. "His picture is in the place where traditionally the picture of a sensei, a teacher, is placed. He died here, in this space. It was my parents' bedroom before I redid it."

"Why you want me to come here?" Sister turned her back to Salt and spoke while she looked out the window toward Mr. Gooden's.

"You don't got some idea I'm one of them hoodoo Negroes, can weave some spell and make wishes come true or somethin'?"

"We've had some things in common. From all the talk at the table I'd say we have more, maybe." Salt looked up at Sister's back, stood and joined her at the window. They looked out at the field between Salt's place and Mr. Gooden's. "Poke salad, the history lessons." She turned to Sister.

"What I think—your mama makes herself known by what's not here and you got your daddy's picture on a altar." Sister pointed toward Mr. Gooden's. "That ol' man got chickens?"

"You feel like some jazz?" Wills sat on the living room sofa and sorted through the CDs he'd brought.

Salt, in the nearby armchair, said, "We should probably talk first."

"Yeah?" He went to the CD player and put in three of the discs.

"I stopped in at the Blue Room today. I wanted to talk to Man about Mary."

"And . . ." He sat down, leaned back, and used the remote to start the music at a low volume.

"He was his usual self—'I'm movin' on up' and all that. But he also said Stone is out. They paroled him."

Wills sat up, silenced the music, and turned to face her. "I knew it was coming, his release, but somehow I thought he would be in a halfway house or something. He's been fixated on you in the past. He believed that you were a threat to Man and came after you. I don't understand why they wouldn't have warned you and why they just let him out."

"According to Man, he's being monitored down at the mental health clinic on Hilltop. He's on medication and Man says he's okay."

Wills listened, elbows on his knees, head hung between his shoulders, quiet. Then he sat back. "And now with Mary's murder, you'll be going back to The Homes, crossing his path, him crossing yours."

"I'm sorry, Wills. It seems like all I do is cause you to worry. Felton and I already ran into Stone. He's still very sick, even on the meds."

He patted the sofa beside him, reached over, and pulled her next to him. "We'll think of something." He thumbed the volume up.

Miles Davis held a wavy note, echoing light, his longing horn calling across the ocher hills of Spain in *Concierto de Aranjuez*. Miles with his sneers and stares.

"Ha! Listen to that," Wills exclaimed with a breathless whisper.

Salt had pulled to her lap an old earth-tone velvet quilt with red satin trim, and in the dim light any movement she made, even the slightest, made the lamplight catch the color differently, from crimson to dark scarlet.

"Last night I dreamed of an apartment building." Salt spoke quietly below the music, between sections. "I wandered around, able to enter rooms with diaphanous walls. I could see into places. One of the apartment bedrooms had dark gray walls, a bed canopied with a sheer lavender drape, nothing else except opposite the bed there was some kind of wall sculpture, metal and light, distressed silver over black dull steel, backlit with a white and lavender glow. Drifting along halls, through walled rooms, I was trying to discover a way to rid myself of some feeling, to find a basket or a bowl to hold something sorrowful. Then I woke up this morning, sun filling the bedroom, the trees outside with a few small leaves left twirling in the wind, and I just let myself remember."

The tambourine rattled like the jangle of silver spurs, evoking horses, battle ready with beribboned reins. The drummer executed press rolls, building the tension. They listened to Miles until the track ended and went to the next CD.

"What were you remembering?" Wills asked. His old sweatshirt, freshly laundered, still smelled like him, like sautéing garlic and lead pencils, warm smells.

"Are you sniffing me?" He looked down at her face.

"You smell good, like you."

As the next CD started, Wayne Shorter made music with sounds like plums and stars, blue notes out of a tunnel from Africa. A piano trickled notes, falling, looking for a place to rest, tinkling down keys. Salt imagined a bar before a fight is ready to break out, beer bottles, an old upright piano, pieces of ebony and ivory missing.

Wills leaned back on the armrest, facing her. "Any more discussions with Huff about a partner?"

They listened to the music. Salt held on to an image—a tan, barefoot woman, skin like new moist silk, wearing a brilliant grass-green and blue cotton blouse embroidered with red-thread vines and green roses, and a skirt the yellow and red of parrots, her gait in time with the music.

She leaned against the other end of the sofa. "Kinda obvious, don't you think? Felton is the only other detective without a partner and he's never partnered. If he wants to, he'll have to be the one to ask. He's senior. And don't you go meddling."

Miles was back on. Enormous strength holding the notes tenderly, respectful, the sounds of other cultures, other nations, nuanced and evocative of places and times. Blowing colors against the soft, high frequency sizzle of the brush circling the cymbals. Miles Davis played riffs that rained sheets of sound.

Salt got up and lit two candles. The sky was now all black. The candle near her chair flickered in a beaded glass, flame blinking in tempo, now a tango rhythm. The music seemed to embroider the room, trumpet a bright orange skein on a blue so blue, it seemed to expand and fill every space, under the rug, behind the mantel clock, up to the high ceiling.

"You and Felton already work a lot together."

"We do. And we get along. But still he'll have to be the one that wants to make it official."

Wills smiled. "That's the kind of talk people do when they're talking about maybe getting married." He looked at her and winked. Then he sat up. "Could you ask him along? Just when you go near The Homes?"

The folds of the white cotton curtains that were pushed back from the front window were shadowed where the fabric doubled over, shades of white, soft uneven lines like the angles of a woman's body, hanging curves. Between the cotton panels were old lace ones. The room was suffused with music and rich layers of light and dark. The music . . . themes and variations, Salt raised her hands and held her breath. The musicians unconstrained, uncontained, breaking through.

She exhaled. "Wills, people like Man and Lil D know me. They don't know Felton. I'll look weak to them if I start showing up all the time with Felton, like I need protection."

Wills paused the music. "Can we compromise? How 'bout you ask Felton to come along with you when he can, when you're gonna be out in The Homes? And you ask him to hang back?"

She thought about it. "I already do that some and I told him some of the backstory with Stone. Deal." They shook hands. "We're getting better at this," she said.

"It made me crazy when you'd go off on your own, never telling anyone what you were up to."

"There is one other thing."

"Uh-oh."

"No, really, it's not life-threatening."

"Okay."

"I got smart with Dr. Marshall."

"How so?"

"He was pushing me about my dad. I insulted his parenting—his daughter."

"Oh."

"Next appointment I'll apologize, but I don't want to lose it talking about my dad."

"So tell him." Wills turned on the music.

The spaces between notes, notes on a blues scale, gritty, greasy, created a longing for a return to funk. Herbie Hancock and Wayne Shorter introduced a theme, rhythms, and inflections forming tense line questions. Some notes were like destinations; some, certain pitches, signaled the melody to have the questions answered. They held the theme. The harmony grew richer, thick and more complex. "Come on. Now. Just listen," Wills said, pulling her to lie close beside him.

BAD NEWS

SALT WAS WALKING BY HAMM'S DESK AS THE VETERAN DETEC-
tive punched at the computer keyboard. "I don't give a shit," she said
to the supervisor standing over her shoulder. "I got murders to solve."

"The city will take the hit. On paper our murders, and probably our solve rate, will look horrific—up fifty percent," her lieutenant said.

The bold one-inch newspaper headlines were scattered throughout
the office—break room, conference room, wherever Salt went, even
the ladies' room, the black type catching her eye: NO PROGRESS, NO
ARRESTS.

Again the office roiled with activity. Phones rang with calls from
the press, politicians at every level, council members, and candidates
for office who sought information so they could report back to folks
who wanted to be the first to express outrage.

Salt stopped in the doorway of Huff's office and waited for him to finish his phone call. He smiled, mobile phone to his ear, rocking back and forth in his swivel chair. "They were delicious, sweetie." He waved an expansive welcome for Salt to come in, stood and vigorously swiped several green murder books off the chair to the floor in front of his desk. "Gotta go now. Workie, workie. You, too." He tapped the phone. "Hold on," he said to Salt. Humming, he fumbled at his phone and then tapped its screen several times. Sitar music began playing.

"Sarge? I was just gonna give you a quick update."

"Sarge, Sarge, Sarge. I love the sound of Sarge."

"You taking medication?" she asked.

"Close the door," he said. "Want a brownie?" He brought a Tupperware container from under his desk. "Best brownies ever." He scooped up some chocolate gooey paste with his fingers.

"Uh, Sarge—brownies? Really?"

Huff looked at the chocolate on his fingers, then back at Salt. "Brownies," he repeated. "She only gave me two, said I could have just one, and save one for later. She wants me to watch my calories."

"Brownies, Sarge."

His eyes widened in realization. "What was she thinking?" Quickly scraping his fingers on the edge of the plastic container, he shook his head. "My God! I could be fired. How fucked up am I?" he said, blinding his bloodshot eyes.

"Just keep your door closed for a couple of hours or three. I'm sure your wife had the best intentions, probably worried about all the stress you're under. Besides, who's going to know? Give me the evidence." She grinned. "Uh, brownie. I'll get rid of it." Salt slid the Tupperware from beneath his hand. Closing the door behind her, she left him, head hanging between his hands, sitar still thrumming.

"They were able to date the bodies. Nineteen ten—around then. I don't know—belt buckles, buttons or something . . ." Pieces of conversation floated up like captions.

At her desk Salt got a small plastic evidence bag, scooped in the remaining THC-laced chocolate, and took the container to the break room to wash it.

"Yeah, family still here, old money," Thing One was saying to Thing Two as they sat sipping coffee at one of the tables.

"I don't know, man." Lil D stood looking from the office window out to the stage of Toy Dolls.

Man, smoking a blunt, crossed his feet on the top of the small round table in the middle of the rectangular space. "You have your ride. East Lake's not that far."

"She don't know nobody over there. It's bad. Them Blood wannabes frontin'. I don't want Danny T growin' up in no gang." Lil D tugged at the towel around his neck, staring out without seeming to see the dancers onstage.

"Salt be back about your sister." Man took a puff, watching the smoke filter through bands of light coming from the stage, streaking the dark office with blue and pink.

"Why she come to you 'bout Mary?" Lil D turned his back to the window and faced Man. "'Cause Stone out?"

"Naw, man, that ain't it." Man uncrossed his feet and sat up. "Chill, bro. She had a picture of Mary with JoJo and Glory. She want to talk to them 'bout her."

"You holdin' out on me? Mary come 'round here?" Lil D swiveled his head to one side, making a disturbed click with his mouth.

"I ain't got to explain nothin' to you but yeah, she come 'round, once. I run her off. Got JoJo to take her home even."

"You know who killed my sister, Man? You ain't tellin' me?"

"Naw, Lil D. Your sister out of it. She weren't no problem."

Lil D tilted his head down, then looked up at Man sideways. "How come Salt always mixed up in our shit? You ever think about that?"

"She all right. She straight."

"We gangsta, Man. Don't no other gangsta got no one cop hangin' 'round all the time."

"Check it out." Man pointed the blunt at Lil D. "We gettin' out that illegal shit anyway. We be gangsta when we got to, but we be gettin' out a that. You never put your hand on no dope ever again. Soon as Johnny C ready, he be the one makin' the deals."

"How come C be stayin' in?"

"My brother like thug life. He don't have no ambition. You and me"—Man stood up and went over to beside Lil D at the window—"we got families, mouths to feed." They both watched two dancers come to the stage.

"That's what I'm sayin'." Lil D nodded. "I don't want Danny T and Latonya livin' next to some shit I don't know 'bout. But I don't know nothin' but The Homes."

"Just go on get Latonya moved. She be all right."

For a while they watched the dancers, the young JoJo and maybe younger Glory. "Flash Daddy like him some fresh pussy, huh?" Lil D asked Man.

"Yeah."

"Salt be back."

"Yeah."

DAUGHTERS

SALT PUT THE OLD BALL GLASS JAR WITH THE THREE PINK CA-
mellias on the counter. "For you," she said to Dr. Marshall's daughter.

"We can't accept gifts." The girl frowned, fingering the twine bow around the neck of the jar.

"Then it's for the office, for the other patients, clients, whatever we're called."

Marshall came out. "Come on back," he said to Salt.

Standing in his office, still holding her coat, Salt said, "I owe you an apology."

"I doubt it but go ahead. What for?"

"I was angry. I didn't like you pushing about my dad. So I used your daughter's, um, issues to get back at you. I'm sorry." She sat down.

"You brought flowers for her?"

"Just because I acted badly doesn't mean I was wrong about her needing some cheering up."

"You got angry—yes. But why, Sarah?" Marshall sat.

The same wash of emotion came over her, though this time she was prepared and took a breath. "I am protecting myself." Salt bowed her head, pressing a fist to the place that felt hollow, the center of her chest where her mother had once laid her hand and pressed a warm cloth to soothe her when she'd been ill. "She must have been so afraid."

"Who, Sarah? Who was afraid?"

Salt looked up. "Mary, Mary Marie."

Marshall sat back. "Your body in the weeds?"

"Pokeberry . . ." Salt's gaze drifted to the window. "She was left in a patch of pokeberry."

They sat on a large exposed root of the oak tree, its hard veins creasing the back of her skinny legs. Sarah and her dad, heads bent toward each other, dipped their index fingers into a green chipped bowl, in which they'd mashed pokeberries to a vivid purple paste.

Below the hem of her shorts, on the front of her thighs and on her shins, she'd drawn squiggles, jagged Z's, half-moons, and radiant lines—magic berry juice marks.

"Now I'm a Cherokee princess," she declared, standing up, arms out from her sides and looking down at her decorated legs.

"What about your arms?" Her dad grinned.

"And my face," she added.

He shook his head, "You're not gonna get it on your face this time. Tomorrow's Sunday. Your mama will give me heck if I bring you home with marks that won't wash off."

Sarah stuck her finger in the bowl and started a line of large purple freckles on her left forearm. "It's poison if you drink it, you know." She hummed while she drew charm bracelets on both wrists. "When school starts back I'm not going." She sat down in the grass and dirt in front of her dad. "I'm not going into fifth grade at all. Lean forward."

"You are too." He kept his eyes wide while she put an S on his right cheek.

"Nope, I've decided to get a job," Sarah said, dipping her finger again.

"You're just a kid. Kids don't get jobs, and besides, your mama and daddy won't let you quit school."

"I'll be invisible so you won't know. There, now put some stars on my face." She pushed the bowl toward him and swept her hair back from her forehead.

"What kind of job?"

"I'm going to be a spy or a secret agent." His finger felt like a bug's feather tracing the points of the stars. Sarah inhaled her father's self smell.

He leaned back from her to admire the stars he'd drawn. "Ta-da!"

Sarah jumped up and spun around three times. "Do I look magical?"

He squinted at her. The sun through the branches of the big oak spangled one of her arms.

Salt turned back to Dr. Marshall, who'd sat sharing the silence. "She bled out in those weeds—fourteen years old. I blame myself. I should have been more vigilant," she said.

"I imagine there are quite a few children you've come to know who needed more taking care of than they were getting."

Salt lowered her head, eyes on her hands in her lap.

"It must be hard to constantly empathize with all the kids you come in contact with, their abandonment."

Head still bowed, "Fuck you," she croaked weakly.

"Salt, just because someone else is in pain doesn't mean you don't hurt. You can't push your tragedy away or cover it by focusing on others. As you may be starting to realize, it surfaces, breaks through anyway—in dreams, memories, images." He raised his hands, palms up.

JoJo and Glory had given their address on the permits as Marvin's, a whore motel on Metropolitan. Although she was sure they'd never lived there, Salt wanted to check with the women that tricked out of the place to see if they might have some bit of information. At the top of the hill overlooking Metropolitan Avenue, the motel consisted of freestanding units that reminded Salt of slave cabins. When she drove up, a cold, white moon shone down directly over six women gathered around a fire barrel in the median of the circular drive. Bright orange fragments floated from the barrel, illuminating the women's faces and cleavage.

Rocksand put a hand above her eyes, shielding them from the firelight. Peering in Salt's direction, she was the first to recognize her. "Salt!" she called in a voice somewhere between a greeting and a warning to the others. But all of them, except one older woman Salt didn't know, came over to the Taurus and got in, like a clown car in reverse, sharing the warmth of the car. Before she got in, Peaches, the youngest, tucked something into her cleavage.

"Where you been?"

"She got promoted, didn't you, Salt?"

"Ooh, you stink, Peach."

They talked over each other.

"Ya'll be quiet," Glenda said. "Maybe Salt wants to say something."

"I've missed you," Salt told them. "What are you hiding, Peach?"

Glenda in the front seat smiled a missing-teeth, gummy grin. "Peach got a sweet tooth, always trying to hide some Snickers."

"I do not," said the young whore. But the smell of chocolate from the backseat was unmistakable.

Salt handed Glenda the photo of Mary and the two strippers. "Do you all know these girls?"

One of the women in the backseat snatched the photo. "That . . ."

"No, it ain't."

"Give it to me."

"Who's that?" Salt pointed to the woman by the fire, who now stood alone except for a dog beside her.

"She go by 'La Luna,'" Glenda said.

"She Mesican," added Peaches. "But she speak English okay. She just live here. She don't work. She got ostiosis and cartridge in her legs."

Salt let them stay in the Taurus while she went to talk to La Luna. The dog, a medium-size collie mix, trotted out to her, his tail wagging behind him. At the fire he lay down with his snout pointing at her shoes.

"He do that when he want get sheep," said La Luna. "He come here with my niece from sheep country. He think you have sheep."

"My secret is out." Salt tried the hand signal for the dog to come to her side. With a slightly skeptical look, white showing at the corners of his eyes, he got up and came to her left hand.

"You know the language," said the woman, dressed in an off-the-shoulder white blouse and a colorful full skirt, with a long black braid down her back, the stereotype of a peasant señora.

"You're new out here?" Salt said.

"Mi marido está muerto." La Luna drew the braid from her back, holding it at her heart. *"Mi sobrina, su propietaria, ha sido deportada."* She squatted and cupped the dog's muzzle in her palms.

Salt handed her the photo. "You ever see any of these girls?"

La Luna took her time, holding the picture of the girls close to the fire. "These two"—she pointed at the strippers who'd given Marvin's as their address on the permits—"no. But this one in the middle, I see her at church."

"Church?"

"The one across from The Homes, God's World. Priest of the Streets, he have mass there Sunday mornings early, for us who just getting finish work. He hear confession. He have mass. The girl, she come to the rock 'n' roll preaching they have there, after mass."

"Was she ever with anyone? Did she talk to you or did you see her talk to anyone?" The dog watched Salt's hands, jerking his head and shoulders one way or the other when she'd gesture. She crossed her arms and the dog lay down. "How often did you see her?"

"I doan know, maybe tree, four times. Reason I remember is she stand at the door like she waiting. She look, what is word? Eyes wild? She do her fingers like this"—La Luna pulled at each of her fingers, one hand, then the other, as Salt had seen Mary do.

A red minivan crammed with men drove around the corner and stopped. The girls got out of Salt's car, hurried to the idling van, and began bantering and gesturing. Rocksand, the only white non-Hispanic of the group, laughed loudly and came over from the johns. "There's one a those guys wants to know how much for you to take him 'round the world, Salt. You got to go. He thinks your uniform is a costume." The girls at the car of johns looked her way, laughing. "He wants to be handcuffed."

"Okay. Okay." She waved and held up a finger. She turned to La Luna. "Most of the women here know how to get in touch with me. Just in case, here's my card. If you think of something else, about the girl especially, call."

La Luna took the card.

"Or if you want help, a better situation, you and the dog." Salt leaned down and patted the mostly white dog's dusty flank.

"Undocumented?" La Luna asked.

"Undocumented. Dogs, too," Salt replied. "Adios, La Luna."

The Taurus smelled like five kinds of cheap cologne. She watched the girls pair up with the men from the van. Face glowing, La Luna tended the fire, adding a broken stick of furniture to the barrel.

The lights on the fountain in the park changed colors, alternating Christmas red and green. White lights outlining the fountains, trees, and pavilion turned Woodruff Park into a fairyland. Salt, doing her end-of-shift check, looking for witnesses, belted her coat and was leaning against the Taurus when she heard the crutches.

"Gimme a ride," Makepeace said, pointing a crutch at the Taurus.

"Happy holidays to you as well, Mr. Makepeace."

"Bullshit. I just come from Grady. Now, you tell me how I'm supposed to stay off this leg. I'm homeless and the doctors say stay off the leg."

She went to the passenger side and opened the door. "Your chariot awaits."

"Don't get smart with me." He swung his legs between the aluminum cuff crutches, coming to the car door she held and closed after he'd gotten in.

Behind the wheel she asked, "Where to? Where are you staying nowdays?"

"Your old stomping ground. I've got a cat hole in one a them buildings they fixin' to tear down in The Homes."

"Really?" She put the car in gear, drove south, and took him to the stripped-out building on Shaw Street he directed her to. He opened the car door himself, and before he got out, she asked, "You didn't happen to come by the fountain the night the Spelman girls were shot?"

"No. Why, you all can't get the ones did that?" Under the car dome light his scowl deepened, his mouth grew thin, and his eyes narrowed.

"No one coming forward about the truck," she answered. "They've had it all over the news."

"You know some white folks seen that truck," he said.

"You'd think," she agreed.

He didn't get out, just sat there looking out the front windshield.

"You know the Gateway Center has medical recovery rooms? You could stay there while they hook you up with the VA."

He looked at her, again scowling, got out, and slammed the door.

"You're welcome," she said to the departing Makepeace.

The next day when Salt and Felton came into the Blue Room, Man drew aside the newspaper, yesterday's, the one with the NO ARRESTS headline. "You all in some deep ol' shit now, boy." He spread the paper, tapping the headline while he watched Felton, who was checking out the room, looking up and down the walls and at the back of the sign in the barred window. Felton flipped the cord switch for the blue neon BLUES sign; its light blinked a reflection on the linoleum floor.

"We ain't open," Man said loudly. "What's dude's problem?" he asked Salt, who sat down beside him at the table.

"You'll get to know him. He's a good guy. We're kinda like partners, like on TV, you know."

"You always been a loner. How come now you got somebody with you?"

"Compromise," she said, letting her eyes wander, then settle. "Remember last year when I was working that case and the guy was shot in here?"

"Yeah, you got Stone time cut around all that." Man nodded.

"It started with Stone and his statement to the FBI about having been pimped when he was a kid—when you first started watching out for him."

"You say so. Me 'n' him don't talk 'bout that shit." Man kept his eyes on Felton, following his movements, now at the counter between the kitchen and the room.

"So what's up with you and Flash Daddy? Is he your ticket?"

"Don't go messin' with my business now, Miss Dee Tec Tiv." Man turned to her, eyes gone hard, lips drawn tight. "We ain't had no hard feelings between you and me lately."

Felton leaned back against the bar, elbows propped, jacket falling away from the black .40-caliber on his right hip. He winked when Man looked his way.

Man gathered up the paper. "Anyway, seems like you might have your hands full." He folded the paper so that just the bold print showed.

Salt and Man had a long history of conversations that were wide-ranging. From economics to social justice to history, he held unique perspectives.

"Man, we got another case the other day. You might have read about it—mass grave? We think the bones are those of convicts sold into labor, like slaves."

"You and macho man over there"—he tipped his head toward Felton—"didn't come by to give me a history lesson."

"You know what they say about the past not being over—it's not even past."

"Why you here?" he asked, leaning forward.

"You wasted my time, Man. You knew JoJo and Glory wouldn't be at Marvin's. How come you don't want me talking to them? I'm trying to find out if they know anything about who could have been involved with Lil D's sister."

He leaned back. "You can talk to them. I don't give a shit." He scowled, crossing his arms over his chest.

"They teach us in cop school how to read body language, you know." She pointed at his arms.

"You gettin' on my last nerve now," he said.

"Where can I find JoJo and Glory?"

"They dancers. Where you think you find them?"

"What is your problem, Man?"

"You. You the problem. You always up in my business. I'm trying to go legit, trying to get out of gangsta life. An' you all up in my shit."

"Prostituting young women, girls, is your legitimate business?"

"Who said anything about my girls prostitutin'? They dancers." He spread his hands in a leave-it-to-fate gesture.

"So none of your girls turn tricks?"

"What they do on they own time is their business. But they don't trick out of my club."

"Stripping is just another way of selling their bodies. It's not much of a stretch to go on to straight-out prostitution. And selling bodies is just another kind of slavery."

He pinched up his face, eyes narrowed, mouth twisted. "They free to go. They got beautiful bodies. Why shouldn't they get the money?"

"I think it troubles you, Man. I do."

They sat. Felton leaned.

"Where do JoJo and Glory stay?" she asked again.

"You ax them."

"All right, Man." She sat back. "But you're just calling my attention by being obvious that you don't want to help me get in touch with them. Makes me even more determined, you know?"

The door to the Blue Room opened and Stone came in. He went behind the bar, got a glass of water, and threw back a handful of pills, Adam's apple bobbing up and down his long neck.

"Hey, Curtis." Salt stood and went to the bar, exchanging positions with Felton, who walked over to where Man was seated, keeping both Man and Stone in his line of sight. "I heard that Mary Marie, Lil D's sister, about three or four months ago—it would have been right around the time you got released—that she was seen at the church." Salt pointed in the direction of God's World next door.

Stone rolled his head around on his shoulders and closed his eyes.

"He don't wanna talk when the hallucinations are bad," said Man as he stood and went to Stone. "You good, dude? You need to eat something with them pills." Man walked to the passageway between the bar and the kitchen, told Sam to hand him a two-piece meal, which Man then gave to Stone, who left without speaking a word. Watching him leave, Man said, "The doctors give crazy people scripts and expect them to take them right—what time, with water or food. He don't know a lot of times if it's night or day. How he gonna keep track of takin' pills three times a day with water or food? Sheeite."

"You ever see Mary next door?"

"Naw."

"She might have been here some early mornings."

"You know I don't do mornings."

"You think Stone could have had anything to do with her? He and Lil D never got along too good. And like you said, it's hard to make sure Stone's taking his meds like he's supposed to."

"Stone ain't no problem." Man looked at the door.

Salt walked to the center of the room, where she was able to barely detect a faint stain on the floor from where the blues guitar man's blood had pooled. The taste of his mouth as she gave him CPR, the feel of his ribs as she pushed on his chest, counting the breaths into his mouth—the scene rushed back to her.

"Salt? Salt." Felton was kneeling beside her while Man stood above looking down. Felton unhooked the Handie-Talkie from her belt and brought it close to his mouth.

"No." Salt put her hand to his. "I'm all right."

"You're on the floor, Salt. You passed out or something."

"I'm okay. I was just light-headed for a second. Please don't make this be a thing. I'm already . . ." She looked at Man. "Well, you know, the fit-for-duty eval."

Man pulled a chair close and helped Felton get her up. He went to get some bottled water and gave it to her.

"Thanks. Maybe I just need to eat."

"You want some of Sam's chicken?" Man asked.

"Probably I need something a little easier on the stomach," she said, getting up. "Really, let's go get some of Mai's pho," she said as Felton gave her his arm.

A BARE TREE

BY THE WEEK BEFORE CHRISTMAS SALT HAD GROWN FRUSTRATED waiting for Felton to be available every time she needed to go to The Homes. They were both tracking leads on separate cases. Wills and Gardner and the Things all had caught fresh bodies and everyone was playing catch-up after having investigations delayed by the deployment to the task force. She needed to speak to the minister at the storefront church, and she'd yet to find JoJo or Glory; their schedules at the club were "not available." And the protest organizers were revving up for one last demonstration before the Christmas break— another of the critically injured students had died, and there was no progress on locating the truck or any suspects. Hamm's partner, Best, worked his new case while Hamm waited for analyses from the forensic scientists of the mass-grave bodies. Members of the media were stomping their feet at the politicians, who stomped on the commanders, who begged for something, anything, from the detectives, all of whom were likely to be diverted at any moment by new cases.

Christmas Eve morning Salt came in early, determined to get to God's World in time to catch the morning service, the one Mary might have attended. In the parking lot of the almost vacant strip mall were three vehicles: an old passenger van, a beater with elaborate rims and spotted with Bondo, and a dented red compact. She parked parallel to the sidewalk in front of the church window with its amateurish globe painting, flaked and disappearing, Florida almost gone. There were no signs of Christmas on the exterior of the storefront church. Entering, Salt took off her fedora. At the front of the room a T-shirt-clad man, his back to her, was decorating a needleless scrub pine, hanging white origami birds on its flimsy bare limbs. The room looked as if the furnishings—plastic stacking chairs, drum kit, and keyboard—might have been borrowed from the Blue Room next door.

Salt raised her voice. "I'm looking for the minister."

The man turned, cigarette pinched in a corner of his mouth, eye squinched to the smoke, a dove dangling from his right hand.

"Reverend Gray," she said.

"Ah, the good detective," Gray said in that way he had of making it sound as if he were identifying her as the protagonist in a parable.

"That's actually quite beautiful, Rev," Salt said, coming forward, nodding at the tree planted in a five-gallon paint bucket of dirt. "The doves add the magic."

"It's supposed to be a live tree. The Homes' elementary school gave it to us when school let out for the holiday break. They made the birds in art class—nondenominational and all. Here . . ." He held the dove out to her. Forty-five, heavy in the belly, he wore his usual T-shirt, this one somewhat white, with "God Is My Copilot" lettered over the outline of a plane, cigarette burn holes dotting the shirt's front like strafing from enemy fire.

The front door opened and an elderly man and woman followed by a bandanna-wearing, saggy-pantsed teen came in. The man, whom she knew from her patrol days, raised his hand in greeting to both Salt and Reverend Gray. From a door at the front of the room, on the other side of the lectern, Stone came out. Keeping her eyes on Stone, she asked the reverend, "This your regular gig?"

Gray was also watching Stone. "Don't let him bother you. He's harmless. Lives in back. I've been doing services here almost since the last time I saw you. If I didn't know better, I'd say I was under suspicion, the way you keep turning up."

"I do seem to keep coming to you for help. At the shelter when you helped me find Lil D's father, and then last year when I was investigating the abuse of young men at the shelter. Maybe God's trying to tell me something."

"I'm gonna need to get this service going, such as it is." Only a few other congregants had arrived. "It won't take long, maybe twenty minutes. Can you stay?"

"Yes. I got up early to be here. You're not going to make me confess or anything?" Salt hung a dove on a top twig.

"We'd be here all day if I was in the confession business." Gray picked up a single sheet of paper, a photocopied hymn, and handed it to her.

She took a chair at the back of the room.

Stone went about the room unstacking chairs, placing Bibles in the seats, glancing at her, then jerking his head away. When Gray went to the lectern, Stone sat down against the wall at the front of the room.

"Let us pray." The reverend raised his arms heavenward. "Oh, God!" His eyes closed as he fervently shook his head. "Today we celebrate the birth of one who came to deliver us from the slavery of shame, to free us and deliver us into our own personal glory."

"Amen," replied the congregants.

"Curtis will now read from the Scripture." Gray sat down.

Stone stood, opened his Bible to the back, and began reading: "And white robes were given unto every one of them; . . . until their fellow servants also and their brethren, that should be killed as they were, should be fulfilled." Stone struggled with the more archaic words. Gray listened with a look of growing curiosity, his brows raised.

"And I beheld when he had opened the sixth seal, and, lo, there was a great earthquake; and the sun became black as sackcloth of hair, and the moon became as blood," Stone read, pausing to wipe his slack mouth with the back of his hand, but he persisted, stumbling over more of the words.

The first memory Salt had of Stone was the Christmas Day she came across him, twelve years old, exposing himself as small children nearby were riding their new Big Wheels and tricycles. Rather than take him to Juvenile, she'd tried to find his guardian, someone to ensure his appearance in court. All she'd found were indifferent relatives who didn't want to be bothered. He'd smeared the window of her patrol car by sucking and plastering his open lips on the glass.

"And the stars of heaven fell unto the earth; . . . she is shaken of a mighty wind." It was painful to watch the drooling drowsiness overtaking Stone. He rocked on his feet, sweat running down his temples. "And the kings of the earth, and the great men, and the rich men, and the chief captains, and the mighty men, and every bondman, and every free man, hid themselves—"

Gray finally stood, interrupting Stone. "Thank you, Curtis," and held up the hymn sheet. "Everyone rise and join me in singing 'Leaning on the Everlasting Arms.' I know it's not a Christmas song, but it's what got copied." Gray began heartily and on key. Here and there

Stone barked out a word or two of the hymn. Salt remembered the harmony.

"I've chosen two texts from Isaiah," Gray said at the end of the hymn: ". . . thou shalt cry, and he shall say, Here I am. If thou take away from the midst of thee the yoke, the putting forth of the finger . . . satisfy the afflicted soul . . . they . . . shall build the old waste places: thou shalt raise up the foundations of many generations; and thou shalt be called, The repairer of the breach."

He continued. "For thou hast broken the yoke of his burden . . . And garments rolled in blood; but this shall be with burning and fuel of fire . . . For unto us a child is born . . ."

He closed the Bible and took up a black journal. "All of us here today need something. Sometimes what we think we need is not what we really need. Sometimes it is, but most of us keep trying to get what might not be good for us. What we want for Christmas we rarely get. We want magic. We want Santa to deliver—to bring us gifts so wonderful our lives will be changed. I'd like to quit smoking, to quit drinking, to lose weight. I guess while we're at it, maybe Santa could drop us all off at an uptown church and we'd be wearing uptown clothes."

"Amen," shouted the old man.

Stone's head shook. "No."

"But instead we wear the clothes we wear in our everyday lives. Our everyday lives."

"Amen," said the old woman without much enthusiasm.

"Where we feel bloodied and often defeated."

"Amen."

"And our everyday clothes are stained in blood."

Salt folded the hem of her coat across her lap and ran her fingers around the inner band of her hat.

"Amen."

"But Isaiah tells us those everyday clothes are fuel for the transformative fire, that our afflicted souls will be satisfied."

"Yes, Lord."

"Our burdens will be lifted and we will be relieved of shame."

"Tell it, brother!"

"This is the magic, the miracle, of Christmas, that each of us has it in us to build and raise up and be a foundation for each other and to be a repairer of the broken places in our worlds, our relations with each other, with our earth, with other nations and within our homes and communities—that we, you and I, may be called a repairer. 'For unto us a child is born.' We have a chance, a new beginning—to be reborn and repaired. Merry Christmas, brothers and sisters! Let us pray."

Gray gave the benediction, arms upraised, short sleeves of his T-shirt revealing sagging triceps. The worshippers stood and Stone began gathering Bibles. Salt waited, and as the man and woman with the teen went to the front to speak to Gray, she went to Stone and handed him the Bible from her chair. "I was blessed by your reading," she said, having thought about the word "blessed" and deciding that, while it wasn't a word she'd ordinarily use, it might be the best for conveying what she wanted to say to him.

". . . the great men, the rich men and the chief captains . . ." His recitations were as if he were chanting spells to ward off demons while continuing to gather Bibles from the chairs.

"Curtis?" She followed along. "Curtis?"

"Repair, repair, repair. I am broke." At last he stood still. He turned toward her, wiped at his mouth, his eyes focused above her head.

"You knew Mary, Lil D's sister. Did you know she was killed?"

". . . the moon became as blood . . ."

"Someone said that Mary had been seen here at the church not long before she was murdered. Do you remember seeing her? It would have been around the time when you were released."

". . . every free man, hid themselves . . . Repair, repair, repair." He rocked side to side, still focusing on the space above Salt's head.

"It would help if I could talk to anyone who might have been with her or knew if she was in some kind of trouble."

". . . the wrath of the Lamb . . ."

"Here's my card. Man knows how to get in touch with me, too. And I'll give Reverend Gray my phone numbers."

Stone took the card without looking and went back to gathering Bibles.

Reverend Gray came over. "I need a smoke. Outside?"

On the sidewalk in front of God's World, under the ragged aluminum awning that fronted the strip mall, Gray shook out a cigarette and lit it with a gimme-lighter. Salt settled the fedora on her head; the overcast day had yet to warm up. From a pocket of her coat Salt took out and unfolded the photo of Mary with the two other girls. "About four months ago maybe," she said, handing Gray the photo, "she was seen early mornings here outside the door of God's World." She pointed to Mary. Gray squinted at the photo through the cigarette smoke.

"You have a relationship with Curtis?" she asked.

"He kinda came with the territory." He looked up from the photo. "Her name is Mary."

"You knew her? The girl in the middle?"

"Knew?"

"Her body was found before Thanksgiving."

He handed the photo back and drew on the smoke, his eyes watering. "Damn."

"Did you talk to her? How often was she here? Ever see her with anyone else? Did you ever see her talking to Stone?"

"I should have called 911, Juvenile, DFACS—anybody," he said, shaking his head.

"That had been done. She'd been in custody, released, and was supposed to be in the care of her grandmother. I should have known she was out, but I didn't."

"She was always alone—always dressed flashy, new clothes that I thought looked too suggestive. But what do I know about how girls dress these days? How old was she?"

"Fourteen."

Gray hung his head. "The only time I ever saw her with anyone was one morning I got here earlier than usual and saw her dropped off from some kind of big black car." He dropped the butt and ground it with the toe of his shoe.

"Could you see who else was in the car? The driver?" She drew her coat close, tightening the belt.

"No, but I remember thinking that the car was way, way too fancy for this neighborhood. So I asked her about it. She said it was just her friends. I knew something was wrong but didn't know what or who to report it to. You see so much around here that is clearly a 911 call—but that's no excuse. I should have—she'd come to the services and just sit. I figured when she was ready to talk she would." He rubbed his bare arms against the chill.

"Did she talk to Curtis?"

"I'm not sure they overlapped—if he was here when she was. It seems she stopped coming around the time he showed up."

"What about him? What's your relationship?"

"Even though he's pretty scary, so far he's been predictable. The guy at the Blue Room?"

"Man?"

"Young guy comes in around noon. Yeah, I think that's the name I've heard people say. He asked me to monitor Curtis' medication, make sure he's takin' his morning pills. He got one of those daily pillboxes and I just make sure he takes the ones for that morning.

Man? He makes a contribution to the ministry." Gray hunched his shoulders, shivering.

"You must be cold. Want to go back in?"

"I'm okay."

"What about Curtis' probation officer? Or his therapist? Doctor? At the clinic?"

"Sad, isn't it? They put all these folks with a mental disability out on the street. I never see anyone official."

Across the parking lot at Sam's take-out window, a few people came and left with boxes of chicken. Atop the hills on the other side of Pryor Street, where The Homes was being demolished, a line of old water oaks that had been left standing spread dark limbs against the cloudy sky. "So, you and Man are Stone's community mental health providers, his monitors," she said.

Although it was early for Man, he drove the big black shiny SUV up to the curb in front of the Blue Room, parked, and went inside. "Exactly what does he do?" Gray asked.

"You could say he's an entrepreneur. He started out street dealing. By the time he was beginning high school he'd already graduated to distributing weight—you know, running larger amounts of drugs, and guns. He ran the gang around The Homes for as long as I've known him, twelve or more years."

"Now?"

"He says he's trying to go straight, legit, in the strip club and rap music business." Salt shrugged.

"Why is it whenever I see you you're always alone? I thought cops, especially homicide detectives, were supposed to have partners. And around here?" He nodded toward The Homes, across the street.

"I'm working on the partner thing, Rev. Last time I saw you, you helped me with a couple of cases that involved the shelter. You'd just left there. What are you doing now?"

"I don't know." He brushed ashes off his shirt. "I'm still trying to figure it out. In spite of the graduate degree from an excellent seminary, I've become practically a street preacher. First, all those years in the hell of that shelter, and now here." He turned to peer in the window to the sanctuary. "I try not to worry about what's next. I'm still learning. I'm sorry about Mary."

Salt handed him a card. "My contact numbers and e-mail. How can I reach you?"

"Just come by. If I'm not here, leave a note under the door—old school. I'm without technology."

"Thanks for the sermon. It's been a long time." She walked to the Taurus and turned back to Gray still standing in the cold. "Merry Christmas!" she called, tipping her fedora.

That night late, right before the shift ended, she was called out on what turned out to be a natural death—homeless guy in his cat hole, a vacant boarded-up house not far from where Mary had been found. His pills for high blood pressure and heart disease were lined up on some bricks, a makeshift nightstand, beside his mattress on the floor.

CHRISTMAS SURPRISE

"MERRY CHRISTMAS! I HAVE A SURPRISE," SALT SAID.

"Well then we both do. Merry Christmas to you." Wills lay on his side facing her, both of them beneath several layers of faded quilts. "You first."

"It means we have to get out of bed," she told him.

"No."

"Come on." Salt swung her legs to the floor, feeling for her slippers, then pulled on an old wool robe. "I'll put the water on."

Wonder met her in the hall, asking to be let out for his morning toilet. "I smell something green," Wills said, coming into the kitchen, sniffing the air.

"Here." She handed him a cup of Cuban drip coffee and took his other hand, leading him down the hall to her living room. "You asked me if and where we were going to have a tree this year. Ta-da!" She swept her arm toward the far corner, where a potted blue cedar, decorated with tiny white lights, sat twinkling. "It's a live tree for your place. Merry Christmas."

Wills went over to the tree. "Blue cedar—does it grow in Georgia?" He touched the prickly stems.

"It's a dwarf cedar. It won't take up too much space in your yard. I checked for the climate range and Georgia is perfect. We can watch it grow—together." She looked at him closely.

He came back to her and led her to the sofa. "Sarah . . ." He put his coffee on the side table.

"Uh-oh," she said. "You only use 'Sarah' when you're reading me the riot act."

"We've had a couple of rough years." Wills sat down beside her. "You've had to adjust to thinking about how your recklessness—"

"Hold on there." Salt sat up, not liking the way Christmas was starting to shape up.

"Sorry. That was a poor choice of words. Maybe independence is a better word. Anyway we've both had to adjust. And then we've had to keep our relationship under wraps because of the job."

I said we can watch it grow together, Salt thought, worried she'd made assumptions without sufficient evidence.

"We certainly can watch that tree grow together," he said as if reading her thoughts. Then, reaching into the pocket of his sweatpants, he brought out a small blue box and got on his knees in front of her. "If I'm going to beg I might as well do it right. In spite of all those difficulties, we've prevailed, and that's a better test than running through a field of daisies." He opened the little hinged box and extended it to Salt.

Inside was a ring of art deco sterling filigree surrounding a dark blue sapphire. Salt raised her eyes to his questioningly.

"Sarah Diana Alt, I'm asking you to marry me. Put it on, please." He took it from the box and slipped it on the ring finger of her left hand. "Say yes. Say, 'Yes, Bernard Wills, I will marry you.'"

"It's breathtaking." She held her hand out, lights and live Christmas tree in the background. Then she inhaled and knew she'd always associate the fragrance of cedar, underscored by the old cedar aroma from the library, with this moment.

Wills, still on his knees, said, "This is painful." He tried to smile, shifting his weight.

"Here." Salt pulled him beside her on the couch. "Yes. Yes, I will marry you, Bernard Wills."

"Really?" He leaned back to look at her.

"I don't know how we'll manage it," she said, looking again at the ring. "I guess if I want to keep it, the marriage thing comes with it, huh?" She elbowed him in the ribs.

"So you like the sapphire?"

"Do they call this color 'police blue'?" She centered the ring on her finger.

"Does it fit? I just had to guess."

"Perfect. But Wills, all I got you was a tree."

"Your having said yes is the best gift of my life, girl. I love you and I will always have your back." He kissed the corners of her mouth, then full on. "The tree is perfect."

She returned his kisses until it was time for her to get up and prepare to go back to the city and work.

SAPPHIRE

THE ELEVATOR CHUGGED, ITS MECHANICAL GROANS ECHOING throughout the floors. Maybe Robbery had someone on call, but other than the 911 call center floors below, as far as Salt knew she was the only other human being in the million-square-foot structure. In the mostly deserted building, even the offices still occupied were empty Christmas Day evening. Huff had said to call him if she needed anything. She smiled while pressing the code lock for admittance to the office, admiring the silver and blue ring that seemed to her to feminize her hand. Rosie's receptionist's desk was neat, bare, and unmanned. Back in her cubicle she switched on the computer and monitor and notified dispatch of her on-duty status: "4133 to radio, radio check."

"Merry Christmas," answered dispatch.

The websites for Toy Dolls and Magic Girls advertised "Christmas Day Specials." Salt took the original photo given by Mrs. McCloud showing Mary with JoJo and Glory from the murder book. Mary was smiling, a grin like her mother's, Shannell's. Her eyes were like her father's, and she wore her hair in two fat braids on either side of her cheeks. "Merry Christmas, Mary." Salt took a breath, reminding herself not to let the sentimentality of the holiday distract her. She held out her left hand again and turned the ring to catch the light.

Judging from the parking lot, quite a few people had decided to avail themselves of the holiday festivities at Toy Dolls. Salt's Christmas spirit took a direct hit going through the heavy front door, where she was blasted by a disco version of "Jingle Bells." The doorman wore a Santa hat and white beard, which he lowered, snapping its elastic under his chin. "Meerry-fucking-Christmas, Detective."

She took off her fedora. "What's the 'special,' Johnny C?"

Man's little brother had the wide family smile, white teeth and dimpled cheeks. But he was shorter and thinner, a small-boned version of Man, and came off as more childlike than charming. "We made the lights Christmassy and the music . . ." He looked up, pursing his mouth, self-congratulatory. Indeed, the pin lights bouncing off the black matte walls were red and green.

"What can I do you for?" he asked.

She felt an inner groan transferring to her face, eyes and brows knitting. "Nothing really. I know my way around." She tapped the countertop and walked on through to the main room. She stood there for a minute letting her eyes adjust to the dark room and stage lights. Onstage a girl wearing something vaguely Santa-like slid down the strippers' pole. Salt skirted the perimeter of the room to the right of the stage and went in a door to an alcove that was lined with racks of costumes and separated from the dressing room by a heavy curtain.

The laughter of the women inside met Salt as she parted the curtain and entered.

"Ladies." Salt stood before the women, fingering the band of her fedora.

Both Glory and JoJo were among the seven women whose smiles halted, their glasses of brown liquid raised in mid-toast. A joint hung between the lips of one freckled girl wearing a pair of antlers.

"Merry Christmas," Salt said, a little shyly.

"I seen you before. You the poleese," said one girl, a little older, maybe in her early thirties.

The girl with the joint ate it.

Salt unfolded the badge case again. "Sorry to break in on your holiday. I just need to talk to JoJo." She nodded at the girl. "And Glory. Is there some place we can talk, private?"

The clash of too much and too many perfumes rose as the women stood, grabbed flimsy cover-ups, and tottered out on high heels.

"Glory, I'd like to talk to you alone. Would you mind if I talk to JoJo first?"

Glory shrugged, wiggled a Minnie Mouse T-shirt over her Christmas pasties, and followed the others out. JoJo lit a cigarette as Salt pulled a chair from one of the illuminated vanity stations; half its mirror's bulbs were missing or replaced by fluorescent coiled bulbs that cast an odd shadow over Salt's reflection.

"You get used to it," JoJo said, looking into the adjacent mirror. She was short, five two, but none of the rest of JoJo would be considered little: tits, ass, hips, waist small in comparison.

Salt handed her the photo. "When's the last time you saw her?"

She glanced at it, then quickly looked back at Salt. "She missing?" she asked, her eyes squinting as if she'd had a sudden pain. "Or something?"

"I'm a homicide detective, Josephina." Salt purposely used her given name.

"She dead?" Her eyes filled with fat tears. She tore tissues from a box on the vanity and tried to minimize the damage, creamy tracks running down her heavily made-up cheeks.

"I'm sorry."

JoJo went to the mirror to repair her face, but her nose kept dripping and she continuously sniffed.

"Did you know her well?"

"She from my skreet," she said, reverting to her Homes accent and dabbing under her eyes with the tissues.

"So you know The Homes?"

"I know you, too. I seen you all my life, much as I remember. You on nights, drivin' the poleese car. 'Salt' they call you and your frien' Pepper. They say you skrate."

"Tell me about Mary." Salt put her finger on the photo.

"How 'bout you get your shit"—JoJo looked up quickly over Salt's shoulder; Salt turned to Johnny C advancing toward them—"and get." He pulled JoJo up by one arm.

"How 'bout you let her go." Salt stood taller than Johnny. "You're interfering with an investigation and I know you and Man wouldn't want your business permit yanked. Let her go."

Johnny dropped the girl's arm, but the damage was done. JoJo fled the room.

"How come suddenly Man doesn't want me talking to them? You were okay with me when I came in and I know you didn't change your own mind."

"That's up to you and him to work out. You do what you gotta do." Johnny C walked back from her, palming his crotch.

"You got an itch?" She nodded at his hand.

"You crazy." He turned to walk out, pants below his tighty-whitie-clad butt cheeks.

"That was the wrong thing to say to get rid of me, Johnny C." She took off her coat in anticipation of spending the rest of her Christmas in the Toy Dolls Club.

Of course it got her nowhere—except for the cold satisfaction of revenge messing with Man's business. Maybe it served as a warning. But the girls had left the club, and Salt knew that unless Man wanted them found, they likely wouldn't be. Whoever had said that revenge was sweet hadn't spent Christmas, the day of one's engagement, toasting the holiday with a cup of stale coffee from a thermos in the parking lot of a strip club. She kept trying on the idea of marriage, living in her house, his? Dogs? Sheep?

Then she tried not to kick herself over Mary but wondered about what would become of the girl's remains.

The blue stone in the ring on her hand reflected a glint of light from the neon overhead.

ABYSS

"THANKS FOR INDULGING ME, COMING TO MAI'S AGAIN." IN A booth at Mai's Vietnamese, Salt spooned broth from a bowl of pho with her left hand and lifted noodles with the chopsticks in her right. "I haven't had any more fainting since the other day; it was probably some small ding from the expressway thing two years ago." She put the spoon to her mouth. "I've had some minor stuff, vision problems mostly, comes and goes. No big deal. I'd appreciate if you wouldn't mention it, especially to Wills. He already worries." She glanced at Felton before taking another spoonful of the hot soup, delicious, curative; cilantro, Thai basil, and mint infusing the broth with freshness.

Felton tore the herbs and scattered them in his soup. "Every detail of that shooting has been told over and over. But I'd never heard how bad your injury was."

"Mild concussion, the doctors said. Most likely from hitting my head on the pavement when I went down." She added hoisin to the bowl. "Anything new from the task force?"

"Zip. Nothing. The ballistics don't match any previous submissions. They've enhanced the video, but there's just so much detail they can get. The truck, a black Blazer, is about as common in Georgia as chickens." Felton snatched his Handie-Talkie off the table in front of his bowl. "4144, go ahead," he said, snarling into the mic.

Salt turned the volume knob on her radio, monitoring the call.

"4144, Zone One is calling for Homicide on a body found in Bellwood Quarry."

"Bellwood," Felton confirmed to dispatch. To Salt he said, "'Bellwood' sounds so idyllic. Want me to drop you at the office? A few minutes won't make any difference to the deceased." He took two quick sips of his newly herbed pho.

"Really, I'm fine." Salt stood and picked up her check stub. They left tips for their barely touched meal. Outside two of Mai's staff were taking down Christmas lights from around the big windows of the noodle shop.

The uniformed officer stationed at the entrance gate to the property pointed southward. "Just follow the road. Can't miss them. Bates is standing by with the guy who found her."

As they drove the rough road through a field of brown weeds, tall grasses slapped at the undercarriage of the Taurus. A patrol car was parked next to a Jeep inside the fenced-off quarry. The officer stood talking with a white guy about fifty years old. Before Felton was out of the car, the man strode up to the Taurus window and held his hand out. "Wow. I've never met real live detectives before." Felton shook his hand. The guy nodded at Salt. "Women—just like on TV. Times change. I'm Jim Britton."

Officer Bates had little to tell them, just that he'd responded when Britton called, gone down and seen that there was a body, and come back up to wait for them. The property, some three hundred acres in which the forty-acre pit was located, had been reclaimed by the city after a hundred years of granite mining. It was used occasionally as a site for movie shoots and a zombie and vampire TV series, and was soon to be developed into a water reservoir and park.

"I can take you down," Britton said. "You need a four-wheel drive to negotiate the road." While Felton went to the passenger door of the mud-splattered high-fender Jeep with the BeltLine logo on the doors, Britton opened the driver's-side door and pulled the seat forward for Salt to get in the back. Thin and agile, Britton hopped into the driver's seat. "Buckle up," Britton said. "Wouldn't want to get a ticket." He seemed nervous fumbling with the seat belt. "Whew." He put the Jeep in gear.

The Jeep's headlights limited their view to the narrow gravel road cut into the sides of the granite and partway up the darker gray walls. However, looking out to the middle of the quarry, the reflection of a half-moon shimmered. The degree of the decline had been lessened by cutting the road to circle the entire mine and then cutting it again so that it snaked around the wall and down to the water. Britton adjusted the gears as the gradient steepened. Raising his voice over the noises from the engine, transmission, and suspension, he said, "The city owns the quarry itself and the BeltLine owns the hundreds of acres around it. I'm with the environmental study group. This is going to be a great asset for the city's water system."

"Any record kept of people who have keys to the gates?" Felton asked.

"Not that I know of. It's actually a punch-code lock. Besides, someone on foot wouldn't need to go through the gate if they were familiar with the property. There are holes everywhere in the fencing around the property and holes in the fence around the quarry itself."

The suspension swayed, rocking Salt on the hard backseat.

"You okay back there?" Britton turned his head briefly.

"What brought you out here?" she asked. "This late?"

Britton stopped the Jeep on a leveled area where a dump truck was parked and where there was room enough for other equipment to maneuver. "I'd been out earlier today looking at drainage from the quarry basin to Proctor Creek, which is a tributary of the Chattahoochee. It took me longer than I expected, but still, after taking my measurements, I wanted to come down just to check on the progress of the reservoir."

Dust stirred up by the Jeep rose and settled around them as they got out. Britton pointed to a small point at the water's edge but stayed at the Jeep door while Felton and Salt walked, their flashlights illuminating the rutted dirt and small dusty clumps of grasses.

Eight feet from the lip of the water a body floated. Clad in a puffy, buoyant-looking quilted green jacket, one arm stretched toward shore, its dark extended hand pointing like God to Adam—or was it Adam pointing to God in Michelangelo's painting? *I'll look that up*, Salt thought.

"Radio, start the techs and ME to this location," Felton said into his Handie-Talkie. "I'd say that's a body," he said to Salt or himself.

"What do you suppose she's reaching for?" Salt said.

"What?"

"Her hand, the fingers."

"Her?"

"Maybe. The coat. Looks like the hair might be longer, overdue for a touch-up." Salt shone her light out across the water.

Good of you to let us keep your vehicle." Salt was driving Felton's Taurus, taking Britton to his home in the Druid Hills neighborhood on the other side of the city from Bellwood Quarry. Older brick and

Tudor homes and classical Georgian revivals sat up hilly landscaped lawns. "Is your family from Atlanta? There was a mayor named Britton, if I'm remembering right."

"My great-grandfather. Left here." He pointed out the next street. As they passed, he looked out at his neighbors' homes. "Next house. There," he said. The big Tudor sat thirty yards from the street, a bank of ivy ending at precisely cut fescue. The bases of three bare hardwoods were mulched and circled with monkey grass.

"Nice," Salt said.

"You don't have to go up the drive. It's a bit tricky. Just let me out here." He grabbed his leather satchel. "I would say it's been a pleasure . . ."

"We've got your contact information. Thank you again for your help, especially with the transportation."

Britton looked forward out at the night, as if he might say something more, then he reached for the door.

LAST DAYS OF THE YEAR

"YOU SMELL GOOD, LIKE ROSES AND COCONUT OR SOMETHING."
Thornton, her friend from the Homeless Outreach and Proactive Enforcement Team, nudged her. He smelled faintly of the all-natural repellent Salt had given the HOPE Team last year. It was dark inside the white unmarked van, the seats of which had been removed and replaced with hard benches along the side walls so that they sat facing each other, six along each side. Again Pepper drove. Fellows sat behind him, Salt across from her.

It probably seemed like a good idea to the organizers—honoring their martyred sister students with a New Year's Eve concert to raise money for a women's shelter. But once again there was concern about counterprotests and violence from the neo-Nazi group. Student leaders had seen and heard on TV the rantings of one of its leaders, so they'd sent an e-mail blast and texts encouraging their fellow students to return to school early, to come back to Atlanta in a show of force for the benefit concert. The performers were mostly local rap artists, including Flash Daddy and some of his protégés. Use of Philips Arena had been made possible through a discount on the part of the facility and donations from national and local celebrities. They'd kept the ticket prices affordable for the students, and the after-party at the annual Peach Drop at Underground Atlanta was free, as it was every year. Juveniles flocked to the annual event, especially those who had few celebratory opportunities the rest of the year. With live music and fireworks, it drew a mix of Atlanta's population.

The van smelled like most used police vehicles—stale French fries, cheap air freshener, and some vague dust-dirt odor. One of their crew had on too much cologne. Someone hadn't showered. "I see that look. If you fart in this van, I swear I will beat you like a rented mule." "No! Sarge, he's lifting his butt." "Aw, come on, man."

Behind the benches on each side were long rectangular tinted windows that while obstructing the view from outside allowed those inside an only slightly dimmed view of the passing scenery. Young people danced in the street holding aloft cans and bottles. Fires burned wherever materials had been found, in trash cans and newspaper boxes. They watched from the darkness of the van; in the foreground the whites of one another's eyes stood out, luminescent.

A bit of skin at Salt's waist, between where her vest met the top of her leather gear belt, was pinching. "For now we see through a glass, darkly." She tugged at her vest and tried to remember the rest of the verse, from one of St. Paul's letters to the Corinthians. Sirens sounded from every direction, the wail of ambulances, the heavy honking of the fire truck horns, the *whoop whoop* of police vehicles cutting through traffic. Building alarms chirped and screamed. Overhead came the *whap whap* of news and law-enforcement helicopters, their floodlights washing over the scenes below, streets lit by high-intensity

streetlights in contrast with darkened alleys. As they drove north on
Spring Street approaching Martin Luther King Jr. Drive, they passed
a smoldering trash receptacle, glowing red behind the iron mesh. Inside the confines of the van, their faces had begun to glisten with
sweat, bullet-resistant vests and stifling winter jackets. Their shields
and helmets were stacked at the rear door. They passed a newspaper
box, opened like a stove, full of bright flames. The fires became more
numerous; at every corner, at bus stops, every trash barrel or paper
box had been set on fire. A fire truck crew hosed a steaming pickup
while a TV news crew disembarked, camerawoman shooting even as
she stepped out. Salt didn't for a second believe the fires were set by
college students. Setting fires was more like the KKK and juveniles.

Storefront retailers had been asked to clear displays of tempting
items. According to Sergeant Fellows, politicians and police command hoped that, as long as the fires were small and confined to
trash bins and paper boxes, the miscreants would be satisfied and not
escalate to looting and destroying businesses.

Salt's mouth tasted stale. She unscrewed her water bottle for just a
sip, not wanting to anger the bladder goddess. "Anybody got gum?"
she asked.

"Mint?" Thornton offered, opening a tin. They each took one and
passed it to the next person.

Salt reached inside her shirt, feeling for the chain with the St. Michael's pendant. Fellows fingered the gold band on her ring finger.
Thornton threw back some pills with a gulp of water. He'd had a
heart attack last year. "You okay?" she asked.

"Just a precaution. Doc gave me the fit-for-duty all clear," he said.
She was reminded of her own precarious status. It would be bad if she
had another use-of-force incident.

Once again their squad was being deployed to City Hall; this time

the difference was they would be closer to the vortex of activity because of their proximity to Underground. Fire department vehicles
and equipment lined both sides of the streets the closer they got to
their assigned area, fire crews watching the scene from inside their
cabs. The largest part of the crowd danced gleefully toward Underground, where the Big Peach had yet to drop. With midnight fast
approaching, the pace of the crowd increased. From the shadows a
group of males fled from a car, the interior of which exploded in
flames. Inside the van was quiet. The eyes of the rookie sitting across
from her were wide. Behind him the window glowed brighter and
brighter.

The sky overhead bloomed with fireworks flowers shedding themselves, replaced by blooms within blooms erupting within one another,
accompanied by the tap-dancing sound of automatic-weapons fire.

"Oh, boy. Not good," said one of the downtown officers in their
group.

"What goes up will come down," said Thornton.

Fire hoses crisscrossed the street in front of the underground precinct, so they left the van parked across the street and hoofed it down
alongside the flowing crowd, down to Mitchell and up to City Hall,
where they found the steps already occupied by members of the media
and ID-lanyard-wearing members of the mayor's staff. Lights were
being positioned, backdrops unfurled, microphones tested.

Up the block, cars had stopped and a circle of headlights surrounded a dancing scrum of bodies that gyrated and bounced to the
blast-out bass from a lowrider. Traffic was backing up behind the
impromptu party. The blaring horns became deafening. Their sergeant looked up the steps of City Hall, their assigned post and where
the media were now convening, safely, then up at the blocked street.
A siren screamed and the driver honked, trying to get the emergency vehicle through the jam. "Fuck," said Fellows, her choice being

to either stay where they'd been assigned, at the steps, protecting the bureaucrats, or lead them into a situation in order to, well, restore order by clearing a way for emergency vehicles.

"Sarge—"

Fellows held up her hand for silence. "Shit doesn't go the way you plan. Stay together." She began walking briskly toward the corner and the dancing New Year's celebrants. Without hesitation, from years of being part of a team and having one another's backs, they followed.

Laurel Fellows might be a new sergeant but she wasn't a kid. She'd worked the streets. About the same age as Salt, she was medium almost everything: height, five five; weight, about 135; medium-brown hair; average looks; neither beautiful nor unattractive. She even had an even disposition. "Happy New Year," she said, raising her voice above the music and her hand in greeting to the partyers in the headlights.

"Oh, shit. Here it comes," said a tall guy, beer in hand, leaning against the vibrating hood of the vehicle from which the music blared. A dozen men and teens stood around five young women in the center of the lights from a couple of beaters, the lowrider, and an SUV.

"I see from the front tags on your cars that some of you might be from out of state. Welcome to Atlanta," Fellows said. "We want you to enjoy your stay and dance the night away. However, we'd appreciate it if you'd take your party to the parking lots—the Braves stadium lots are just a mile that way." She pointed south. "We need to clear this intersection. As you can hear, emergency vehicles are trying to get through."

Some unseen person inside the lowrider turned up the music. The guy in front of the car pushed off the front bumper, raising his beer. One of the girls turned her back to the cops and began twerking, bobbing her butt and looking over her shoulder at Fellows.

Fellows smiled, raising then circling her hand, signaling to the squad, which was bunched behind her, shields lowered, batons at their sides, to stand by for an order. Pepper and Thornton were on either side and just behind the sergeant. A blast from below in the direction of City Hall sounded like a shotgun or a car backfiring. Salt and the rest quickly drew their weapons, holding them barrel down at their sides, and turned their heads in the direction of the boom, which came from a car repeating the backfire. The young women and their admirers dove for either the cars or the pavement. Salt whipped her head, refocusing on a shiny refraction from her peripheral vision, the glint off a pistol barrel in a hand stuck out of one of the beaters. Two shots. Flashes from the car's window.

"Hands where we can see them," Salt yelled, pointing her .9 mm from behind her shield.

A helicopter descended and hovered overhead, lights flooding the scene, rotating blades and engine impairing their hearing. Fellows, washed in the copter's light, her voice drowned by the *chop-flap-chop* of the whirling blades and the blaring horn of the fire truck that had finally broken through the snarled street, mouthed commands, accompanying them with hand and arm signals.

A dreadlocked young man on the ground raised his torso, hands inches off the ground, mouth moving, his voice also lost in the noise. Arm circling above her head, Fellows then stretched her arms in a V down by her sides. The squad responded, forming a wedge and moving in formation, weapons drawn, shields in position, toward the people on the ground, halting at each person in order to pat down for weapons, systematically and tactically making their way to the semicircle of cars. Four of the squad took control of those searched, lining them up, hands behind their heads on the curb. The helicopter continued to hover.

Salt and Fellows, out front, advanced, shields raised, then lowered, then raised again, as they approached the cars. Salt was first at the beater out of which she thought the shots had been fired, approaching from the rear of the car, Pepper and the rookie following. She quickly peeked into the rear compartment. Nothing but a baby seat. "Backseat clear," she shouted, moving forward to the inch of frame between the back and the front doors. "In the car, don't move," she shouted, gun pointed at the back of a person who lay facedown across the front seat. Pepper opened the car door while Salt covered. He nudged one leg and the young man turned a side of his face up. "Stay cool," Pepper said. "Let me see your hands." Barely audible above the ambient noise, he shouted again, "Keep your hands up and sit up." The man complied, sitting upright, hands touching the ceiling of the car. Pepper, covered by Salt and Fellows, holstered and began a pat-down, waistband, torso, down the guy's legs to his high-top shoes. "Move one muscle and you're gone, dude," Pepper said, nodding at Fellows' pistol and backing out of the car with a silver-tone gun in his hand. He tucked the gun in his waistband, leaned back in the car, cuffs in hand. "Turn your back to me, hands in back, too." He cuffed the man, lifted him from the car, and led him to sit with the others, who inched away, staring at him wide-eyed.

Fellows looked up at the news copter, took out her phone, and, finger in her other ear, began trying to talk over the noise above, ducking her head and wincing in frustration.

The group, all of whom now sat on the curb, seemed a happenstance coming together of two separate parties, one local bunch from The Bluff, Atlanta's most blighted neighborhood, the other from an out-of-state college in town to support the march. The girls, who were with the out-of-towners, knew nothing of the locals, including the guy with the gun, who had stopped to admire the dancing girls.

The helicopter finally swirled off, its lights sweeping the gold dome of the state capitol building. The press conferees, oblivious to the close call on the corner above and recovering from the backfire, began their presentation on the City Hall steps, cables and news trucks lining both sides of the street, which left only a single lane open for traffic, along which now crept a single vehicle driven by a young white woman leaning on the car's horn. Heads turned from the spokesperson behind the bouquet of microphones. Mouth twisted in this-has-gotten-on-my-last-nerve disgust, Fellows nodded Salt toward the motorist. Stepping into the street next to the young woman's now blocked car, Salt tapped on the driver's window with her knuckles. "Ma'am?"

The window slid down, driver in midsentence. ". . . instead of harassing black people, how about clearing the streets so people can drive. I've been sitting in traffic for over an hour," said the girl, the familiar odor of alcohol rising with every slurred word from her mouth.

"On your way home?" Salt asked, rolling some of the tension of the prior moments off her shoulders.

"I would be. What's going on? There are fire hoses blocking the street back there." She pointed to the block below.

"May I see your driver's license?" Salt's flight-or-fight breaths returning to normal; relief from the threat, quick decision making, and muscle-memory reactions kicking in.

"What?"

"Your license."

"I'm on my way home." The woman reached down and the window began to scroll up. Salt stuck the baton in the window and it automatically retreated. "Ma'am, please turn your car off and step out."

"I will not. I'm tired and ready to go home. You don't have any reason to stop me."

"I can smell alcohol on your breath from here and your speech is slurred. I'd like to make sure you're safe to drive."

The woman began to cry. Salt opened the door and hoisted her by her elbow. "Why can't I go through?" She fumbled with a tiny clutch bag from which she retrieved her license. "Janine Sanders" was twenty-two years old and had an address that explained the current year's Lexus she was driving.

"As you can see"—Salt nodded to the squad and the former partyers now in custody—"we have what we call a 'situation' and our resources are limited. Do you have someone who can come get you and your car?"

"My car?"

"I can't let you drive, suspecting as I do that you've had too much to drink."

The girl sniffed and turned her mascara-smudged face up to look at Salt. "I went to a shitty party." She began to cry harder. "Now you are completely ruining my night."

"Park your car there." Salt pointed to the yellow curb.

Janine did as she was instructed, crying and wiping her nose on her sparkly T-shirt. Once she was parked, Salt took the keys to the Lexus, made her put on the coat she had in the backseat, and called the girl's father, to whom she gave instructions on how to avoid most of the melee to get to them. "He's on his way," Salt told her.

"He's a bastard, too," Janine said.

"Stay strong, Janine," Salt said. "Stay strong."

Pepper and Salt sat together in the back of the van at four a.m. There was little conversation; all of them were so tired, the constant state of alert catching up to them, their bodies exhausted. "Those shots—we were lucky." Pepper leaned back against the wall of the van. "Dude." Salt patted his knee.

LIL D

"WHY YOU AIN'T EVER GOT NO MONEY?" LATONYA PUNCHED clothes down into one of the black plastic garbage bags. "Man be payin' you."

Lil D was sure she was in a bad mood because she hadn't eaten. He was hungry, too. Danny T was sitting on one of the bags eating potato chips. Lil D looked for a towel for around his neck, to cover the mark, trying to stay cool. "We ain't makin' no street money now. We be goin' straight. He still get a cut but he don't want no dirty money. And he still got all his kids and they mamas."

"You got a child, too, Lil D. And me."

Most of the lightbulbs in the apartment were burned out and since they were moving nobody bothered to replace them. The bags with their clothes, sheets, and towels were everywhere waiting to be stumbled on or to suffocate Danny T, running from bag to bag, climbing on or trying to crawl into them, their contents spilling.

"Just go to the new place for now." He jerked a towel from the bottom of a pile. "Man say we savin' money for the business. An' I ain't wearin' no old clothes, neither. He say we got to maintain a image."

"What kind of playa you be, D? You work three jobs, Sam's, at the club, and you still slingin' a little dope."

Danny T ran and flopped across Lil D's lap, spilling his bag of chips. "Damn, T." The toddler looked up at his dad, laughed, and started scooping the chips into his mouth and smearing some on the floor. Lil D picked up one of the books Man had given him for Danny, one about trains. "Come on, boy." He picked him up to get him out of Latonya's way and opened the book. The card fell out, Salt's card. He'd put it in the book when he'd found it in his pants, the ones he'd been wearing when she'd come by to tell him about Mary. "I got to go downtown to do the DNA test," he said to Latonya.

"You ain't care 'bout Mary."

He knew right where the building for the DNA lab was, near the MARTA on Peachtree. Sometimes he'd called Mary M 'n' M, the times they'd be together like brother and sister, like family. "Wasn't like me and her had no kind of regular life."

SHAME

"SO YOU THINK YOU UNDERSTAND THE REASON HE COMMITTED suicide, just not why on that day, on your birthday?" The old wooden office chair creaked as Dr. Marshall, arms crossed, leaned back.

"I think it was pain and shame—depression and stigma. So much so that he had to give up, his kids, me and my brother, to rid himself of it. Maybe he lost track of what day it was, or maybe—I just don't know." Salt stiffened her arms on the seat cushion of her chair across from Marshall and looked down at her uniform. She'd taken off the gear belt and set it beside her on the floor.

"Why do you think he didn't get help? Why didn't your mother insist?"

"My mother? She would have fought against it. Going to a shrink?

Sorry, psychiatrist. She believed in church healing but wouldn't even do that because she was ashamed."

"Lot of shame in your family."

"I know that's right."

"What about you? How do you feel about your father having killed himself on your birthday? Could it be that you feel shame?"

She was hyperaware of the belt, holster, and gun on the floor at her right side. Her throat closed up so tight she felt she might pass out trying to keep the tears at bay.

"There have been some who theorize that our childhoods end or start to end with the first experience of shame. I'm wondering if, in all your attempts at saving, you aren't trying to save childhoods?"

She rose up, grateful to be off the issue of her personal pain. "This city might find peace if it didn't keep shaming itself. Murders show the city for what it is, has done, or has failed to do. Murders point fingers. Murders are shaming. Peace is what I want for them. Peace."

From the top deck of the parking garage where she and Wills sat in her car they had a view of the black night and diamond-starred city. "As soon as I wear it to work, it will get out and either you or I will get transferred," Salt said. "You've worked Homicide for years. It's what you love. It makes sense that I'd be the one to go, to another assignment or another shift, and then we'd never see each other." She kept her eyes on the city, afraid of ruining the feelings between them, of ruining how they felt about the engagement. "We also need to discuss where we're going to live—whose house. This seems too hard, harder than getting engaged should be."

"'The course of true love . . .' and all. I've been around the block.

We'll work it out." He reached over for her hand, holding it down on the seat between them.

"Wills, I want to tell everyone, to announce our relationship, but we need to decide at least where I should ask to be transferred." She felt ready to cry again. In little more than a few hours she was becoming a weeper.

OFFICE CALLS

THERE WERE NO FURTHER PLANNED PROTESTS, BUT THE CITY was on edge. Any incident could reignite smoldering frustrations. So for now detectives were still in uniform and on twelve-hour shifts, but Salt was back to Homicide.

Flanked by the Things, Huff stopped beside her desk. He'd seemed a little stiff and standoffish since the brownies. "Guy keeps calling me. Wants me to get you to call him. I figure you wanted to talk to him you'd have given him your mobile."

"Thanks, Sar . . . , uh, Huff."

"What's that supposed to mean? Huff?" Behind him the Things mimicked his quizzical hands-on-hips posture.

"It's your name?"

He laid a pink callback note on her desk. "Jim Britton. Says he talked to you at the quarry, on Felton's case."

She looked at the note. "Why's he calling me?"

"He didn't say. I asked him if he wanted to speak to Felton. He said you." Huff turned and caught the Things miming him. "You clowns got nothing to do? I'm sure some of those files need packing." He nodded toward the back. Barney and Daniels did a Road Runner exit, ducking down the nearest row of cubicles.

Salt leaned into the aisle watching Huff scan the tops of the cubicles for the two detectives. Her desk phone rang its broken-short-circuit-sounding ring.

"You owe me," said an angry voice.

"Mr. Makepeace."

"I'm makin' this call anonymously."

"Suits me." She leaned back and propped the phone with her shoulder.

"There is no honor among thieves."

"Say again." She pressed the buzzing earpiece closer.

"You dug up your family's silver yet, white girl?"

"Any day now."

"That's all you got to say?"

"How can I help you, Sugar Pie?"

"That's what I like about you, Snow. You listen more than you talk. What I'm callin' about is 'cause a them college girls got shot."

Salt sat up.

"See, 'cause I'm crippled and homeless, none a these boys out here in the street care if I hear their business. So here's the deal, the ones sellin' flex in the trap at Sam's, they sell to them white boys in the truck they showin' all over TV."

"The truck? The one with the guys that gunned down the Spelman girls?" She slid a pad over and picked up a pen. "They were selling fake?"

"They showin' some other truck on TV? Yeah, fake, flex."

"Why would the dealers not give up the truck?"

"They flexin', man. They don't want word out they sell fake shit to white folks. Damn! I got to explain everything."

"Who was in the trap? Who sold them the flex?"

"Man's brother. The one they call 'Johnny C.' It was his little runners."

"Was it a drive-through or a to-go order? They got a phone number?"

"You the detective! Expect me to do all your work?"

"I will owe you if this pans out."

"How 'bout some silver, knives and forks, or a silver platter? Yeah, that's it, a silver serving tray."

"Or maybe you'll just have to be at peace knowing you've done the right thing."

"Shut up, whitey. They called ahead for an eight-ball." He hung up.

Salt held the phone, thinking how to go about verifying Makepeace's information and what she should do with it. Unconsciously, she'd been sliding Britton's callback note with her fingers. She dialed the number. "Maybe lightning will strike twice," she said to herself.

"Britton." He answered on the first ring, his voice sharp-tempered, irritated, not at all like the meek man who'd helped them at the quarry.

"This is Detective Alt. You left a message for me to call."

"Oh. Thank you." He paused, switching gears before continuing. "This isn't about the case."

"Oh?"

"At least not that case."

"Okay."

"You don't say much."

"Someone just told me that was a good thing."

"Detective, the reason I'm calling is my two children—two very good children."

"I'm sorry, Mr. Britton. I'm not following you."

"The brickworks."

"What? The mass grave?"

"It's going to come out about my great-grandfather, the mayor, the conditions, the abuses."

She didn't know what to say.

"Detective?"

"We can't control what the media reports, Mr. Britton."

"I've spent my life learning how to clean up waste, taking care of the environment, cleaning up land. My father was a good man." His voice was fading. "We inherited a deplorable legacy."

"Why me? How can I help?" She swiveled her chair, a little frustrated trying to figure out what Britton's call was all about.

"I know—first-world angst, right?"

"I'm not sure what to tell you."

"Couldn't you blather some cant about how I shouldn't feel guilty for something that happened a long time ago?"

She'd turned to her coat hanging on the peg behind her desk. "Mr. Britton, I was born and still live in the rural South. The ghosts never seem to rest. They're always rising."

It was Britton's turn at silence.

She took a long breath, then exhaled. "You do good work, the environmental thing. That's good."

"Good luck, Detective."

They sat around a table in the break room. Detective Chatterjee looked beleaguered, exhausted. The dark semicircles under his eyes had deepened, giving him a hangdog look. Huff had stayed after their shift so they could meet with the midnight-shift sergeant, Sergeant White, Chatterjee's supervisor, about the information from Makepeace. Chatterjee's jacket hung more loosely than ever, his white shirt puckering around his waist. Sergeant White was in uniform, having come directly from working his extra job at the Fox Theatre. Midnights for a sergeant could be a good gig to catch up on sleep.

"Couple ways to work this. 'Course it's your call. Salt can stay over or Chatterjee can come in early, go out with her. Maybe you guys want to work it on your own?" Huff said.

"I'm already having to coordinate with the feds," Chatterjee said.

"If it were me, I'd let Salt do her thing. She knows that beat. If there's anything to this guy's story, she can suss it out," Huff said.

"You don't talk much," Sergeant White said, looking at her. "You still got head problems?"

Salt, realizing she'd been fingering the wave of hair over the scar on her forehead, gave the coil of hair a quick tug and dropped her hand. "I'm just tired, I guess."

"I could use the help, Sarge," Chatterjee said to his sergeant.

"Do this. Go ahead and work it on your own, Salt. See what you can find and get back to us as soon as you know something one way or the other," White said to her, looking at Huff for confirmation.

Huff stood. "We're all tired from the long hours. But Salt's a trooper." He slapped her on her shoulder.

WILLS AND WONDER

THE BURNING PECAN WOOD POPPED AND CRACKLED, BITS OF ash rising from the flames of their bonfire. St. Michael glittered between her bare breasts as she lay beside Wills on a pallet of quilts. *"The Owl and the Pussy-cat went to sea in a beautiful pea-green boat,"* he recited, then lifted a flask in a toast toward the fire.

"Are you tipsy?" She gently poked a finger into his naked thigh.

"'Tipsy.' You use all these old-fashioned words. It's charming."

"Let me have a taste of that." She reached for the flask. "I can't believe you raked the ground." They lay beneath the bare limbs of the orchard, the sky above a black-velvet backdrop for brilliant stars and a moon full and bright white, its craters charcoal smudges of the man. Ten feet out, the dogs lounged around them unperturbed and at ease with their loving noises and ways. Their clothes were in a pile on another blanket nearby.

"Can't have lumpy love now, can we." He rolled to her side, whispering more lines from Edward Lear's poem "The Owl and the Pussy-Cat." "*They dined on mince and slices of quince, which they ate with a runcible spoon.*" Wills grabbed up two more quilts at their feet, covered her, and buried his head between her legs.

A sparking flush ran through her body. She opened her eyes to stars that in her altered state appeared to be swirling while she gave herself over to ecstasy. Entering her, Wills threw off the covers in his own euphoria, loudly moaning.

Under the quilts their body heat warmed the aromas of fresh sex that mingled with each of their own scents. Salt inhaled deeply.

"You're at it again, you." He lifted her chin so that her face was out from under the cover.

"I love the way we smell," she said.

"You are a carnal fiend," he said, rubbing noses with her and laughing. "I'm marrying a fiend!" he yelled at the night. The dogs lifted their heads but didn't move, just plunked their snouts back on their paws as if to say, "Oh, it's just their usual people foolishness."

"*Oh! let us be married; too long we have tarried . . .*" Wills orated.

"*They danced by the light of the moon.*"

"**Even in winter I spend** more time out of the house than inside." She fingered the scarred split in Wonder's right ear as he sat beside her chair at the kitchen table. Wills stirred oatmeal on the stove. "I'm either at work, with the sheep and Wonder, out for a run, working around the property, at your place. About the only time I'm in the house is either to sleep or when you or Pepper and the boys are here. I do an hour or so every other day in the dojo but that's about it."

"Are you trying to talk yourself out of this house?" He ladled oatmeal into grass-green bowls and drizzled honey over it.

"It's a big house."

"Maybe we'll have children?"

"Are you trying to talk me into keeping this place? If we're going to get married, we need to decide where we're going to live—your place or mine."

"This property has belonged to your family for generations. I don't want you to have regrets associated with marrying me."

"Yum." Wild clover honey had been her father's favorite.

He'd sat across from her, a tangle of green and lavender between them. He'd taught her how to make this world. Vines of passion-flowers spilled out of the brown paper grocery bag. "I've got enough maypops here for two families." She emptied the rest: green leaves, wide lavender and white blooms, green fruit pods, buds of various sizes, some beginning to open, showing lavender-white between the green petals, onto the soft, flattened pine needles. "So you have." His tan face shone in the summer light slanting through the trees from the west, highlighting the undersides of leaves on the hardwoods.

They sat cross-legged in the center of what she called her fort, a twelve-by-twelve clearing, marked off with bark-covered thin pine logs. She pinched off one of the full blooms and stuck it in a buttonhole on her red shirt, then picked up one of the fruits and broke it in half. "I'll make the beds." She scooped seeds and pulp out of the pod halves, finished the first two maypop beds, and reached for another of the green fruits. Then she went back to pulling the corona away from the inner column of a flower, creating a tiny human-like figure with stamens for arms and legs. "Four big ones and four little ones. I'll make the dresses for the girl ones." She began carefully peeling the feathery skirt-like flower away from its center. She lined up the May people on the pine needles. "There. I've got them all done."

They worked in silence, and when all the May people were defined, the girls and women with lavender skirts, the men and boys only naked stamens, the little ones in the pod beds, Sarah began to hum a lullaby. Her father lay with his hands behind his head looking up through the trees. She lay on her side, curled around the passionflower families. Her voice drifted up and away to the canopy of dense shimmering green overhead while the May people were safe in their still, small world.

"Honey?"

"Sorry. I was remembering. The clover honey reminded me of my dad. Now *he* was tied to the property—knew all about every flower, tree, flora and fauna. It was his passion. I wonder if he was also shamed by an inheritance."

"Shamed?"

"Like me, he didn't do anything to deserve this." She looked up at the tall ceiling and out toward the orchard. "Cops see so many people who are born into so much less."

"This place does haunt you. Maybe with more than just the ghost of your father."

Wonder got to his feet at her side. She automatically reached for his ear, split when he'd been beaten and clubbed while he'd tried to protect the house. The ridged notch had healed in a Y shape, black as the silky fur surrounding it. It would be hard to see unless you knew it was there.

"Don't we have a tree to plant?" she asked.

Slapping his hands on his knees, Wills stood. "Yes, yes we do."

MARSHALL AND SISTER

"CONGRATULATIONS, BY THE WAY, EVEN THOUGH FOR SOME REA-
son you weren't going to tell me about your engagement. That's a
pretty big step. 'Congratulations,' however, is what one is supposed to
say to the guy—Wills?" Dr. Marshall's brow wrinkled. "With all
that's going on, the cases, the unrest, and this." He tapped his desk.
"Where's the ring?" He peered over at her hands.

Salt held them up. "If we made it public, it would get complicated.
He proposed Christmas Day."

"Ah." He nodded. "The birth, a new beginning." He clasped his
hands, smiling behind them, eyebrows arched, pleased with his as-
sociation. "But with complications, this new beginning? You didn't
discuss it before he got the ring?"

"He's a romantic—wanted to surprise me."

"Did he?"

"Yes."

"A good surprise?"

"Yes. Like I said, there are things we need to work out. Do you have to analyze everything?"

Marshall raised his arms, grinning, gesturing to the books and diplomas on the walls.

She laughed. "Well, there is that."

"Seriously, I'm interested. What do cops have to consider when they decide to take these big steps?"

"First, for us there's the shift issue."

"Oh, you mean how to work the same hours?"

"There are rules that we can't work the same hours on the same assignment."

"So you or Wills will have to transfer or work different hours?"

She nodded.

"What else?"

"What else what?"

"Complicates your engagement."

"We each have homes." Salt stood and went over to the window. "It's snowing."

Marshall came over. It happened maybe a couple of times during Atlanta winters, usually no more than a dusting, but the first flakes were always met with excitement. "Always seems like magic," he said.

"I feel the same way," she said. "Even though it means longer work hours for us and not much of a chance to play in it."

"Aspects of police work the public doesn't think about—that we take for granted." Marshall went back to his chair.

"Those parts don't make good TV—long hours, cold, hot, paperwork."

"Family life, shifts." Marshall widened his eyes with a question. "You were saying that you and Wills would have to decide which house to live in?"

"His place is closer to work. He's been renovating it. Put a lot of work into it."

"And your place?"

"The ghosts of generations." She slapped the armrests, punctuating her determination. "I've given it thought. I realize that it's a big step, letting go of all that—my father's death, the legacy. But what's got me stumped is what to do with it."

"Really, you're letting go just like that? Selling it?"

"I don't want to sell."

"So you wouldn't be letting it go. You'd keep it and live in the city?"

"I don't know. That's where I'm stuck. What's best? What will free me and the haints."

"Haints?"

"What country folks call ghosts."

"Do you believe in actual ghosts?"

"Of course not. What do you think, I'm crazy? Don't answer that. Call it karma or bad memories, guilt, shame, the unconscious, whatever."

"You're making my job pretty easy here." He laughed.

"Another stereotype—the psychologically unsophisticated cop. We come to the job with our histories, some of us aware of our moods, our private pressures."

"I was referring to your personal demons, Salt. What ghosts do you most want to leave behind when you start your new life? What shame?"

"Shame? You said that last time. I meant that my father felt that way—about himself, his illness, his family."

"Isn't that at the core of how you feel about his death? I think your risking yourself repeatedly is somehow connected."

She sat there not responding, asking herself if it was shame that she felt. "I'll think on that," she whispered, feeling a familiar brittleness.

. . .

It was late afternoon and the snow had stopped by the time she got home. On her way in, she paused on the porch steps, her eye caught by movement from across the field in Mr. Gooden's backyard. At first she thought she was seeing double again. It looked as though there were two of him in his garden. Wonder woofed from inside the kitchen. When she turned from unlocking the inside door and letting the dog out, the two figures had separated and gone down different rows, and she recognized that one of him was wearing a dress and was darker—Sister Connelly, who to Salt's amazement was helping Mr. Gooden cover his winter greens. She waved, but they didn't seem to notice, or if they did, they weren't responding. She was reminded of how unsettling Sister could be, how it felt like being pulled into another dimension or alternate reality to be with her sometimes. And here she'd appeared incongruously in Salt's neighbor's garden, covering his plants with white sheets. Wonder came out and stood beside her, also watching, alert at the unusual blanketing of the dark green plants.

Before going inside, she called the dog to heel and walked to the paddock, opened the gate, and went in. "Away, away," she commanded. Within seconds Wonder had disappeared and quickly reappeared with the flock trotting from the back of the orchard. He weaved back and forth, gathering and flanking. "Stand." She opened the gate for the pen and kept the dog on hold until the sheep were all in the enclosure. Under Wonder's stare she fed the sheep, freshened the trough water, and laid down fresh hay. "That'll do," she told him, leaving the paddock. She picked up her gear bag from the steps. There was no sign of Mr. Gooden or Sister next door. The garden was now square after square covered with white cotton weighted at the corners.

"That field"—he'd pointed across to the Goodens'—"and the ones on the other side of the road in front were once upon a time all planted in cotton. I remember. I couldn't have been more than three or four years old, but I remember climbing some drawers, a chest of drawers, and looking out the front where some workers, they were called 'field hands' back then, were walking home. At that time the road was still dirt. And I remember they were singing. Which was probably what had drawn my attention. Dust clouded around their bare feet. The heat was like the haze of a dream."

Wonder sat at her feet, watching, waiting. Salt turned and opened the screen door. The dog, shaking off, went ahead of her into the bedroom, where he watched while she changed into sweats and old sneakers, then followed her up the stairs to the second-floor hall. She glanced briefly into the dojo before continuing on down the hall and grabbing hold of the cord for the retractable ladder to the attic. "Stay. You're not coming," she said sternly to the dog. He seemed to have a penchant for high places and had had to be rescued several times from the roof dormers.

Climbing into the attic, at the top of the ladder she found the pull for the single bulb light and sat for a minute surveying the bare beams and rafters. *If I'm leaving, I need to know what's in there,* she thought. The space was mostly shadows, the lone bulb lending only partial light within its weak glow. Even in the cold air it smelled of dry dust. Under the eaves toward the front of the house were two racks of old, misshapen clothes, several boxes, and an old trunk the same size as the one beside her downstairs bed, the one in which she'd found her father's coat, bought for him but never worn until Salt became a detective. There wasn't much else; like the rest of the house, it had been mostly emptied. She walked a beam balancing her way to the trunk. It was too large for her to have gotten down the ladder. There must have been some other access to the attic at some time—Wonder had found some secret passage for himself. She could hear his scratching at the bottom rung of the ladder below.

She propped the flashlight in a triangle of two rafters. The latch of the trunk was locked. She tugged at a cardboard box nearby and the flap tore. Inside the box were palm-size leather-bound books, some in Latin, some slightly larger volumes in English, a frayed book of postcards depicting life in Korea circa 1914, a book of quotations copyright 1942, and a small pocket ledger, the first entry dated 1889. Tiny fragments of the pages fell when she opened the books. The ledger was inscribed with a name she recognized, that of her great-great-grandfather. The other box held a jumble of old, cracked shoes. None of the boxes would hold up to being moved.

The locked trunk—yet another mystery. The books, the inscribed owners, the collection made little sense to her—Korea, Latin, English. Her mother might know a little more. The phone in her pocket buzzed. On hearing her hello, Wonder sent up a whine from below.

"Salt?" Huff asked. "Where are you?"

"In my attic."

"Your attic? You got a problem?"

"You called, Sarge. What's up?"

"Be that way, then. They want you in at noon tomorrow to go find out what you can from The Homes, about the truck and the guys who got flexed. The protests are heating up again and the politicians are breathing down the chief's neck. I can come in early and go with you if you want me to."

She imagined a conversation between Huff and Man. "I got it, Sarge," she said.

THE TRAP

SALT PARKED ON THE STREET ABOVE THE DEMOLITION EQUIP-
ment. Below, a huge excavator sat atop a hill of rubble next to a building long since abandoned; the windows and doors from which she had
frequently concealed herself in order to surveil the "trap," the drug
corner across the street at Sam's Chicken Shack, were now stripped.
She hooked the Handie-Talkie to her belt, took the binoculars, and
leaving her coat and fedora on the floor of the backseat, got out of the
Taurus and made her way down the rutted hill.

Salt pulled herself up on the excavator, climbing on tracks clotted
with packed red clay, to the door of the machine. Apparently the
construction crew had learned the high-crime neighborhood lesson
of leaving vehicles unlocked rather than paying for the broken-
window damage. She swung the door open and lowered herself into
the cracked faux-leather operator seat. The view couldn't have been
better—floor-to-roof Plexiglas. The cab was crowded with lever bars,

joysticks, dials, and the steering wheel, and smelled of gear grease and spilled coffee. Salt felt giddy putting her feet on the big pedals. Tall as she was, it was still a reach for what she guessed was the claw-bucket control.

She sat back and raised the binoculars and adjusted the focus of the powerful, sensitive lenses. Across the street, in the chilly early afternoon, activity was just beginning to pick up. Without her coat and hat, Salt felt the cold but was not uncomfortable. She didn't plan on being there long. The day was still and gray, a dreary overcast without wind. Lil D behind the wheel, Man's SUV pulled into the joint parking lot of Sam's and the Blue Room. Several people were getting to-go boxes from the order window. A beater with three guys arrived and set the trap; Johnny C sat behind the steering wheel of the car supervising the setup. Although she recognized them from The Homes, Salt had not seen these young kids running dope before. One lounged against the Chicken Shack wall, ready to meet the junkies and take their walk-up and drive-up orders. The other kid stood at the back corner of the Blue Room guarding the stash that was likely concealed and camouflaged in the trash on the ground somewhere close.

Stone came out of God's World and got in the front seat of the beater with Johnny. The kid on the wall took more orders than Sam did at the to-go window; one car then another was waited on. No lines formed. Service was good.

She lowered the heavy binoculars and rubbed her eyes, then quickly raised them back, the image jittering, in time to follow Flash Daddy's Bentley pulling in. She watched him get out and go into the Blue Room. The door handle of the excavator door squealed. Startled as the door was pulled open, she leaned back and put her hand on the 9mm at her waist.

"What the—" the man said, stopping mid-sentence when he saw

where her hand had settled. Heavyset and dressed in an orange quilted jumpsuit with the pocket logo of an Asian construction company, he looked like he belonged with the excavator.

She showed her badge and ID. "I work Homicide."

"Ain't no murders been done with this hoe."

"I believe you, sir." She swung her legs toward the door. "This is an innocent hoe."

"I get it—hoe, innocent." He offered his hand as she stepped out. "Billy Williams, they call me . . ."

"Let me guess . . ."

"Williams." He grinned big. "Gotcha. Naw, 'course it's 'Billy Bob.' I see you got your spy glasses there." He nodded to the binoculars hanging from her neck.

"Thanks for the use of your cab, Billy Bob." Salt smiled, shook his hand, and headed up the hill to her car.

The action dwindled quickly when she drove up and parked beside Man's vehicle. The runner kid halted mid-stride when he recognized her. She made a show of speaking into the Handie-Talkie before clipping it to her waist, letting them know she'd reported something to dispatch.

Johnny C got out of the beater. "Yo, wass up there, Detective?" He nodded his chin at her.

She straightened the fedora, tipping the brim down slightly over her forehead. "Hello, Johnny. I'm just taking a trip down memory lane—reminiscing." She looked at each of Johnny's crew. "You know, I don't take this War on Drugs personal. I've always kind of understood that you and I are both a part of the ninety-nine percent."

Stone got out and stood stiffly beside Johnny.

"Really? This is getting to be like old times." She stepped back with her right foot, turning her gun side away from them just as Man and Flash Daddy came out of the Blue Room. Although she hadn't asked dispatch for them, both a patrol unit and the Things roared into the parking lot, their tires loudly churning and crunching the gravel. The beat officer got out of his car, dust clouds swirling around his knees. Barney and Daniels exited their vehicles. They all converged, no one with anything to say. Billy Bob's hoe clanked and rumbled on the bank across the road.

Barney broke the ice. "We heard you pull out with radio and thought we'd come by."

"I saw a chick and all these dudes," said the uniform.

Sam and Lil D appeared in the doorway between the shack and the Blue Room. A city bus stopped at the corner and remained there idling, exhaust fouling the air. Salt asked the uniform if the exterior mic in his car worked. She went to his patrol car, sat down, and picked up the mic. "Testing. One. Two. Three." Amplified, her voice carried for blocks; people on the corner and nearby turned their heads toward the sound. "Someone sells flex around here." She paused. "This is Officer Salt." The Homes residents knew she didn't lie.

Dust blowing, settling, on his suit and the shiny surface of his vehicle, Flash Daddy stood at the door of his car, arms crossed, watching the unfolding drama. Man looked on from the doorway.

Johnny C came over to the open door of the patrol car. "This ain't right."

The young patrol officer joined him. "I heard of you," he said to Salt. "This used to be your beat."

Salt depressed the mic button again. "Sometimes flex is sold from this corner. You take a chance now if you buy from here." She let up on the mic. "Do I lie, Johnny?"

The runners folded shop, drifting back to the beater, as the Things strolled to the chicken window. Stone, arms hanging, lifted his face toward the sky.

"Johnny, remember what I said about cooperation? And here I am again, asking nicely." She settled the mic back in its bracket. "I'd like a private word with you and your brother." She nodded toward Man. "Thank you, Officer . . . ?" She tried to read his silver-tone name tag.

"Nguyen."

"Win?" she repeated.

"Close enough. You got balls, I'll say that for you."

"Not really."

In the Blue Room, Man was agitated, pacing beside the table where she sat. Johnny seemed to have disappeared, evidently deferring to Man in regard to their relationship with her. The Things had stayed, making themselves at home, eating their boxes of chicken in a corner. Any gravitas they'd brought to the scene had dissipated, perhaps because of their seeming lack of interest in anything other than the contents of the loaded Styrofoam clamshells. She began to suspect that Man's agitation was a result not so much of her public accusations but of Flash Daddy's witness of the drama. She sat quietly, waiting for him to vent and come to the conclusion that it was in his best interest to deal with her. She was willing to listen, for a while. It was the truck, the cheated white boys, she was after.

"Fuckin' with my business . . ." At the bar he peeled the wrapper off a blunt, lit it with a tall flame from a Zippo, and filled the air with one furious puff after another. He slammed the lighter on the counter and went to the window, where he stood stiffly staring out, his back to her. "The fuck . . ." he muttered, then abruptly turned to face her. "Why you couldn't just call me? Ask me private? I'm tryin' to negotiate a deal here."

She looked at him, tights under black basketball shorts, loose-tongued athletic shoes, quilted hoodie, and thought she understood his position. She sat forward. "Part of my problem, Man, is that to say to you 'I'm sorry' is to run the risk of having you take that as weakness, especially coming from a woman. Am I right?"

Barney and Daniels held their wings mid-bite.

Man turned his back on her again, grinding the cigar under his heel. He stomped over to where she sat and pointed his finger in her face. "You, you and all the police like the plantation overseer—the hand of the man. You know that?" He bit his words between pinched lips, eyes squinting, forehead in tight wrinkled folds.

The Things wiped their fingers and pushed back from the table.

"Yes," she said. "And we still have someone running around free who shot those young Spelman women and another someone who shot Lil D's sister."

He picked up her hat from the table, her Homicide fedora, the one given her by the squad on the occasion of solving her first murder. Man held the crown in his left palm and ran his fingers over the inner brim.

"Don't push it, Man."

He handed the hat to her, drew up another chair, and sat down. "We ain't on the same side."

"You're so binary." She winked and took out the cigarettes she always carried but rarely smoked.

"I never seen you smoke." He looked over at the Things. "Them goons gotta be in this?"

"It makes the bosses happy to know I've got backup. Lighter?" she asked, opening the pack.

Man went in his pocket and handed her the Zippo.

"I see Johnny's running the trap now," she said, lighting the smoke.

"I told you I'm gettin' out of the street business." He leaned back. "I'm tryin' but you hurtin' my chances, all this frontin'."

"Here's the problem—word is somebody in your, make that Johnny's, trap sold flex to the yahoos who shot those Spelman girls. The video of the truck has been all over the TV and somebody recognized it. Those boys fired into the demonstrators right after being flexed in your and Johnny's trap."

Man crossed his arms on his chest and lowered his chin.

"You don't seem surprised," she said.

"I ain't," he mumbled without raising his head.

"Also, it wasn't a random drive-up, according to the people talking about it. The rubes had called ahead to make the deal, no weight but also not just for their personal use, either. Their number is in somebody's phone."

"Sheeite." Man cursed between his teeth.

"I need that number and I need it now. The city is on the edge of another meltdown." It was her turn to be emphatic, voice rising, stabbing her finger toward Man.

"It was your boys in the trap that duped the guys in the truck and that's the truck on the news."

"How they know it's the same one?" he asked, as if knowing but wanting her to prove how she knew.

"Come on, Man. There's nothing that happens out there you don't know, but here's what we know—same time frame, two white boys, an old black Blazer, Confederate flag in the back window, what looks like a gun-rights bumper sticker—the lab is still working on enhancing the tag. People saw the truck here, same as the truck in the video."

"I told C he need to keep on them young boys—they try to get over, flexin' soon as you round the corner." Man shook his head.

"But this would have to be a contact, somebody they'd have done business with before or they knew somehow."

"Naw, not now days. They drive up, order, give their phone number and get a time to come back. Them meth-head white boys get short, they come lookin' to score in the 'hood."

"So who has the number, Man?"

"Probably one a the kids. He gonna get jacked up on this?"

"We can find a way around it, especially if he's a juvenile."

"Your word?"

"I don't control some things but, yes, I'll do what I can."

Man stood, fished his phone from his pants, walked out of ear-shot, then came back to the table. "He's talkin' to them boys now. You gone owe me on this."

"How about you also tell me where I can find JoJo and Glory and we'll call it even?"

"You crazy. You just used up any owe, and you ain't had none to begin with."

"What's the deal, Man? As long as we're at the table, why is it that you don't want me talking to those girls?"

"You gettin' on my nerves now." He stood, picked up the phone again, and answered as he walked away from the table, "Yo."

Salt took the cigarette butt to the door, threw it out, took a small notepad and pen from her coat, and set them on the table. Man came over and wrote down a phone number. "They got the tag, too," he said, writing it as well, pushing the pad back to her. "Don't be comin' back fuckin' me up again."

As soon as she was back in the car, the Things in theirs, she phoned Huff and read him the phone and tag numbers. "I told them I'd try to keep the flex kid out of it. He's probably a juvenile anyway."

"Fuck 'em, they're assholes."

"Maybe, Sarge, but they're my assholes."

She was identified—Our Lady of the Quarry." Felton stood beside her desk. "It's your girl, Glory."

The chill ran up from her feet.

"Salt?"

"I was looking for her and JoJo. I put the word out."

"Come on."

"No, Felton. Sometimes this job stinks."

"Salt, whoever killed her—"

"Cause? What was the cause, Felton?"

"Gunshot."

"Head?"

"Yes."

Salt reached for her coat.

THE FIRE NEXT TIME

ANOTHER OF THE SPELMAN GIRLS HAD DIED, AND ANOTHER
had taken a critical turn. More protests were planned. The truck
from which the shots had been fired was located, its owner having
belatedly reported it stolen. Negotiations were ongoing to get him in
for an interview and to be in the lineup for the as-yet-to-be-identified
drug boys to view. Unconfirmed, none of this could be released to
the media.

Salt was anxious about JoJo, but she'd been ordered again to report for the demonstration detail. "Sarge, please."

"No can do," Huff said, sucking in his stomach and buckling his
own gear belt. "All the detective units have cases that need personnel
ASAP. But they've had to assign bodies to the 'occupation,'" he said,
pausing to swipe the air with finger quotes.

. . .

"What she doin' here, La?" Lil D dropped plastic bags of groceries on the counter between the kitchenette and the living room/dining room where Latonya sat in one beanbag chair and JoJo in the other, the two of them sharing a pint of ice cream with Danny T.

"She helpin' me, D. I ain't know nobody over here and JoJo say she need to stay away from The Homes for a minute."

JoJo sat up. "I got some money, D. I ain't seen Glory in a week. I think she in trouble. Man done told us both to stay hid, but Glory, she can't stay still. She go to the Gold String on the north side thinking nobody there will know her. I ain't seen her since. That ain't like her." JoJo wiped the back of her hand under her nose. "I think she dead." She lifted the hem of her T-shirt to her eyes. "Please, D. I'm scared."

"Damn." Lil D hung his head. "This some fucked-up shit."

"Who after us, D? Why Man say we gotta stay hid? I don't even know who to be scared of. Even you?"

Lil D started taking groceries out of the bags and setting them on the counter. "Where you want these at, La?"

"I don't know. You cook much as me. Wherever you want." She was going to be mad, Lil D knew, until he said JoJo could stay. People from projects being torn down all over the city had gotten vouchers for apartments in their east-side complex. But no one they knew from The Homes. Latonya didn't have one other kin or play kin or friend here to keep her company or help with Danny T. And she'd been working on her GED, her books still in one of the black plastic garbage bags spilled around the apartment.

Lil D measured out the rice, enough for four.

IN THE ATTIC

"I FEEL LIKE I'M FINALLY BEING ADMITTED TO THE INNER SANC-
tum," Wills said, standing next to Salt and looking up as she pulled
the rope for the retractable ladder to the attic. He ducked as dirt and
insulation fell from the opening when the ladder descended.

"Not terribly mysterious, mostly dust, very little phantasmagoria."
Salt brushed debris from his shoulders. "You're a good sport to help
me with this, especially now that we're going to the twelve-hour shifts
again, maybe as soon as tomorrow."

Picking up the crowbar and shaking it, "Yeah, but I get to do my
manly duty," he said, voice lowered an octave. "Plus it's not often a
Yankee is privy to an excavation of the old gothic South." He poked
her playfully in the ribs with his elbow.

"All right, Rhett, follow me." They climbed up and through the
opening, Salt tugging the cord for the bulb. She carried a small fluorescent lantern by which she led them across the beams to the corner

and the trunk. "Careful." Balancing on one of the beams, they squatted in front of the old steamer trunk. "I could probably have done this myself," she said, "but it would have been tough going. This way I can hold it while you leverage the hasp." She hung the lantern on a nail sticking out of an overhead beam.

Wills wedged the chisel end of the bar into the lock. "Ready?"

"Hold on," she said, bracing the trunk with her feet and legs. "Ready."

Wills levered the wedge end of the bar into the mechanism, which immediately gave way, the entire latch tearing from the trunk and lid. "Well, that did it," he said. "I hope it's not badly damaged."

"It's not the trunk that's of interest to me. There are probably thousands of these old things in attics all over the South." They turned their faces from the flying dust as she lifted the lid.

Letters in their envelopes were packed in a tray that separated the top from a deeper bottom compartment. About half of the letters were addressed to James Alt, Salt's grandfather, during World War II, and half were from him to family, his parents and wife, the grandmother Salt knew little about.

They lifted the tray. Indeed, there was a wood chest in which Salt found the clichéd hidden silver, a badly tarnished full service for twelve, intricately patterned with roses and leaves, that Mr. Makepeace had alleged to be in her possession. There were also ledgers, old photo albums, portraits in frames with glass yellowed by dirt. Salt coughed. "Well, this will take a while." She opened the silverware chest.

"It will take a couple of trips," Wills said.

"Let's just bring some of it down. Now that it's open, I can get the rest when we're not pushed for time."

"Okay. What do you want me to bring down?"

"I'll come back with a bag for the letters." She handed Wills an album, picked out a couple of ledgers to take down herself, replaced the tray, and closed the lid.

"We're pretty sure now that the perps belong to or attended meetings of the White Is Right Citizens, otherwise known as WIRC." Wills took a sip of whiskey. "Informant says the head of the group, Lincoln Sugarman, knows the truck."

"Why not pull Sugarman in?"

"They don't want to burn the informant, so I called and asked him to come in as a good citizen." Wills leaned back, stretched his legs out, and crossed his ankles.

"So they are depending on your legendary interviewing skills," she said. Wills had solidified some big and many not-so-big cases partly based on interviews in which suspects or witnesses gave up important information or disclosed damaging details.

"I don't know." He threw back the last of his whiskey. "These guys, these hick Hitlers—I'd sooner interview an outright murderer."

BLACK AND RED

"UNBELIEVABLE." SALT EXAGGERATED THE WORD UNDER HER breath. "A picket fence, an actual white picket fence." She was sitting in the Taurus, parked in front of the house Man shared part time with the mother of two of his daughters. She'd known about his house in the suburbs and a couple of days ago had asked the county cops to keep their eyes out for him and to let her know when he was home. The call came and this morning she'd been there. His SUV, as reported, in the driveway. Two little girls, both bearing a strong resemblance to Man, ran out the door to catch the school bus, their cartoon character backpacks strapped around their shoulders.

She punched his number in her phone. "Out front," she said when he answered.

The cul-de-sac street of middle-class homes was quiet, a few cars leaving for the morning's commute. Man strode from the house, his bowlegs giving him a bit of side-to-side gait. Warm-up jacket unzipped and flapping against his bare chest, he grabbed the handle of the passenger-side door, opened it, and stuck half his body in. "What the fuck?"

"Latte or plain, light or dark roast?" She offered him one of the two coffees she'd bought from the coffee chain store around the corner.

"What?"

"Have a seat, Man. Or would you rather invite me in?" She smiled.

"Latte," he said, slipping into the passenger seat, closing the door, and zipping his jacket. "You want to tell me why you violating my personal space by coming here?" He took a sip of the coffee and looked at the logo on the take-out cup.

"Good?" she asked.

"I ax you a question," he said, turning to face her.

She looked past him to the fence. "A picket fence, Man? Come on. I don't believe you," she said, still grinning.

His lips tightened in a crooked smile. "You love it, huh?"

"Those little girls—pretty cute. They look like you."

The smile disappeared. "Don't go there, Salt."

"I had no intention of intruding, but you didn't hold up your end of our agreement. I need those boys to come in for a lineup, to ID the white guys in the truck. Downtown looks like Beirut. There's been looting. Traffic's a nightmare. People want arrests for those girls' deaths."

"I been busy."

Salt took a breath, closed her eyes, slowly exhaled, and turned to look out the window. "You've been busy."

"All right, all right. It was Rodderick and Orphan. I'll bring them to you myself."

"Orphan? How old are they?"

"They at least sixteen. Yeah, Orphan."

"Still starting them young," she said, thinking of how young Man and Lil D and Stone had been when she first saw them working the trap. She said, "They found Glory."

Took him a beat but then Man shrugged and stared straight ahead, out to the suburban street. "What you mean 'they'? Who else lookin' for her 'sides you?"

"Somebody else was. She was shot and dumped in Bellwood Quarry." When he didn't say anything, she added, "Just another dead stripper?"

"Naw. She all right," he said quietly in a low tone.

"Comes with the job, huh? And being female?"

"What you want me to say, Glory be a ho. Hos be gettin' they-selves kilt."

"Getting themselves killed? She wasn't that much older than your girls, Man. How is it you don't feel some responsibility? They worked for you."

"I told you not to bring my kids in this. Glory and JoJo, they part of the game—they hos. Game fixed. Ain't no hos gone win. I play the cards I been given and I'm stackin' the deck for my kids."

It was her turn to look off to the distant horizon. "I think that's what all parents want, Man. But the fathers' sins keep coming back on the children."

"You out of line comin' out here talkin' 'bout my sins on my children."

Then she asked him, "You have any idea where JoJo is?"

Man shook his head. "No, I do not. You need to take what I'm givin'. I'm already bringin' them boys to you."

"Tomorrow. Six-thirty. I do not want to bother you again by coming here."

"Best not." Man got out, taking the latte and slamming the car door.

EVERYMAN

SHE AND THE MAN WERE THE ONLY TWO ON THE SLOW-MOVING elevator. He smiled, nodding politely at her as they moved to the back corners. She saw that he'd punched the floor number for Homicide and, except for the whiff of gun oil, had considered that he might be there to fix the printer or take care of some mid-level management issue regarding the move. Stocky, brown eyes, a bit more hair than Wills but otherwise could have been his brother, and was dressed a little better: blue chambray shirt, khaki work pants, red plaid padded work shirt worn as a jacket. When the elevator doors opened, he motioned for her to precede him and followed her to the Homicide entrance, watching as she punched the code for admittance.

"Hey, Salt." Rosie raised a lacquered nail. "May I help you, sir?"

"I didn't expect to encounter so many beautiful women today." He held out his hand to Rosie. "Lincoln Sugarman to see Detective Wills."

"I'll let Wills know, Rosie." Salt went through the inner door, leaving Sugarman still holding Rosie's hand. She found Wills and Huff at Wills' desk. "He's here. I rode the elevator with him not realizing who he was."

Wills rolled his chair back. "Impression?" he asked, gathering a notepad and pen.

"I'll get the others," Huff said but looking at her to hear her response.

"Kind of an everyman." She shrugged. "Making an effort to be pleasant."

Huff made the sign of the cross at Wills. "I don't need to tell you how much is riding on this interview," he said, turning to go get the rest of the task force.

"Thanks, Sarge," Wills said to his back.

Huff gave him a backward wave.

Wills winked at Salt. "Wish me luck."

She pulled the St. Michael's pendant from her shirt and kissed it.

She'd waited until Wills had escorted Sugarman to the interview room and until Huff, the feds, and a few other detectives from the task force had settled before going down the hall and standing in the doorway of the observation room. There was a slightly disturbing odor of heated dust coming from the monitoring equipment. The setup was a combination of low- and hi-tech: an old-school two-way mirror on the wall between the rooms that gave people a bit of an underwater tint; a monitor for the cameras in the corners of the interview room; and speakers for the slightly fuzzy audio that gave voices a bit of a lisp.

One of the agents gave her a look when she appeared in the doorway, then turned to Huff, his mouth and brows in a question mark.

"She's good," Huff said, turning his back to the agent.

Wills was wearing almost the same clothing as Sugarman, khaki pants and a blue short-sleeve shirt, but also one of his Homicide ties on which were little deerstalker caps and magnifying glasses.

". . . just like in the movies," Sugarman was saying, nodding at the two-way.

Wills, just as affable, said, "We're trying to move toward the twenty-first century." He smiled across the table and leaned back in his chair. "But I guess we should get to it, Mr. Sugarman." He sat up. "Maybe to start you could give me a brief summary about your organization. I'd like to hear it from you firsthand; you know how the media can distort things these days."

Sugarman smiled politely but his eyes lacked warmth. "I appreciate that. Yes, there's a lot about us out there." He leaned forward trying to match Wills' hail-fellow-well-met tone. "Our organization from the start has been primarily concerned about individual rights." He continued with what seemed a well-rehearsed spiel, building a case for the basis of their fears of oppression and trampled rights, never once identifying particular sources of that oppression.

Finally, Wills interrupted. "You make some valid points. But what's this I hear about guns being sold at some of your meetings?"

Sugarman smiled coyly and held up his hands, as if showing them to be clean. He wore no wedding band, only a pinky ring on his left hand and on the ring finger of his right what looked to be a ruby. He tipped his head. "You can't expect me to know what all goes on between my members, Detective?"

Wills lost his smile and leaned across the table, hands clasped, staring Sugarman in the eye. "My dad used to tell me, 'Son, if you're in charge of something, you're responsible.' Now, I get the individual rights you want to uphold, but along with rights come responsibilities. We received information that you were present the night guns were sold to an individual whose vehicle matches the description of the truck used in the shooting of the Spelman college students."

Sugarman's mouth turned downward, lips pursed. His brow furrowed and he narrowed his eyes. "I don't know . . ." he began.

"Your organization, your responsibility. If you don't know now, I'm sure you can find out. Our information is reliable." Wills leaned back, done engaging.

Sugarman looked over to the two-way mirror. "You work for the City of Atlanta. I guess you got diversity," he said, twisting the last word and nodding his chin toward the glass.

Wills kept his silence.

"What if I'm not able to find out?" He addressed the mirror rather than Wills, then looked up at the cameras in the corners of the room.

"We have faith, Mr. Sugarman—faith that you understand the meaning of the word 'conspiracy,' what it means legally, not to mention morally. One way to demonstrate that you personally didn't conspire to kill those students is to help us find who did."

"You mean give up the names of my members."

"Someone in your organization sold a gun that is likely a murder weapon, and you know or can find out to whom that weapon was sold."

"Oh, I see now how this works. But you don't have a warrant, do you? Can I go now?"

"You've always been free to go. You are not under arrest, yet." Wills waited as Sugarman stood, then opened the door to lead him out.

CONFLAGRATION

MAN DIDN'T BRING THE BOYS IN FOR THE LINEUP. HE CALLED
and said they'd ducked and he was looking for them. So once again
queuing up for roll call in the academy gym, Salt widened her eyes,
trying to get rid of the heavy-lidded feeling. Pepper, rubbing lotion
into his hands and along his arms from a bottle held under his arm,
asked, "You and Wills up late?"

Slow getting rid of the fuzzy feeling, she swiped her hands over her
eyes. "Not really. He's helping me with the attic. I'm purging."

Noon, four hours earlier than her regular shift, but not so much
earlier that she shouldn't be able to shake it off. They were all coming
in at times other than their normal hours.

In an effort to minimize the appearance of militarization, the
brass had declared that the cops on the inner perimeter would not
deploy with shields and helmets, a mixed blessing. Their batons were

to remain holstered unless there was an immediate threat. Salt was just as happy to shed the cumbersome equipment.

"Want some?" Pep asked, holding up the lotion.

She brightened a bit. "I'm good," she said, giving the response that had been her daily answer when they'd worked their beats and stood roll call together every day. Now that they'd both gone to separate units, he missed their day-to-day camaraderie. "We haven't rolled in a while, you know," she said, referring to their weekly aikido practice with his boys.

"Atten-hut!" the Special Ops major shouted.

She and Pepper stood with their squad of twelve while Sergeant Fellows reviewed them, walking down the line and giving them the head-to-toe inspection. Fellows didn't seem to notice dusty shoes, facial stubble, a faded uniform shirt or a frayed pants knee. It became clear that she cared little for appearances; the only part of the ritual not pro forma being the light tap on each of their backs as she passed behind their line, making sure a protective vest was under each uniform.

The commander announced squad assignments. This time they were being deployed to a location closer to the center of the expected demonstration, the site of the assault on the students. "Fall out," yelled the commander.

"Stand by," Fellows said to her twelve. They gathered around. "It's going to be a long day. The forecast is for cold. Once we're on our posts we'll be pretty much stuck there for the duration. So why don't we stop somewhere first and get a good meal? Somewhere warm, a sit-down."

"Busy Bee," several of them said.

"Can I get gluten-free fried chicken?"

"You ain't eat no gluten-free shit."

Pushing, shoving, and grumbling, they went out to the van, all the while arguing the argument of cops everywhere—where to eat. Not having considered its proximity to the AU Center, as the campuses of the historically black colleges—Spelman, Morehouse, and Clark College—were collectively called, they found the Busy Bee packed, almost every table in the small café taken. But all of them had begun to salivate in response to the aroma of the best fried chicken, they agreed, any of them had ever eaten—even "they mamas' Sunday chicken." Eyes and heads turned as they were shown to two tables in the back where they split six to a table. Along with iced tea, the waitress brought them heaping baskets of hot biscuits and corn muffins. Jackets were shed as they dug in, buttering the warm breads while inhaling the smell of chicken that had been marinated overnight, hand-breaded, and fried in peanut oil.

Pepper was seated across from Salt with his back to the room. Their table included Fellows, the rookie, one of the detectives, and the uniformed officer from the downtown precinct. "You the token field hand at the white poleese table, bro?" A young dreadlocked light-skinned man at the table of college-age students behind Pepper said, leaning over and clasping Pepper's shoulder with a meaty hand. His friends, some of them, laughed nervously.

No one else would notice but Salt. The scar along the side of Pepper's face whitened. But also none of them said anything, taking their cue from Pepper, who raised and turned his head to look at the hand on his shoulder. Then the kid moved his hand to Pepper's neat-cut head. "You protectin' these here white cops, bro?"

Pepper smiled over his shoulder while gracefully sliding his hand to the young man's. Gently but firmly Pepper took two of the kid's fingers and pressed them back to the kid's wrist, simultaneously standing and leveraging the guy up and over so that the young man was now seated in the chair Pepper had just vacated, facing Salt at the cops' table. "I'd like to take this opportunity to invite you to be my guest," he told him as the kid tried in vain to break Pepper's hold.

The waitress came by, head high, ignoring anything that might be amiss. Other diners looked at their food. The kid's friends all looked on, silent. "He'll rejoin you gentlemen after he done eat a big mess a crow." Pepper smiled, dragged up a chair, and sat beside the young man. "Let me begin by introducing you to Officer Salt there across the table directly in front of you. She was my partner for ten years or so, and last year she saved my life and in doing so risked her own. May I order something for you?"

The young man shook his head no.

"Okay, next beside Salt is Sergeant Fellows. Yes, I know she's white, but let's give her a break, shall we? She normally spends her days trying to save neglected and abused children, mostly black I might add, demographics being what they are in Atlanta, at the expense of her emotional equilibrium. I couldn't do that job. You sure I can't buy you a piece of chicken?"

"Pepper," Sergeant Fellows said.

"No, Sarge. This young gentleman"—he clasped his hand on the young man's shoulder—"has come to our fair city for an education." He turned his face to make eye contact with the guy. "Where you from, young man?"

"Boston," he said quietly.

"Anyway, I'd like to be a part of that education," Pepper continued with what seemed like genuine goodwill.

Finally, even his victim smiled. "You got me, man." He looked back at his friends. "They know. I can be an asshole sometimes."

His companions nodded their assent. "I know that's right," one said.

The kid reached for a biscuit from the basket on the cops' table. "May I?" he asked Pepper.

"Please."

They delayed going out into the cold as long as possible, sitting around the tables at the Busy Bee, drinking after-lunch coffees, fortifying for the long night ahead. The food—Salt had eaten a bit of baked chicken and greens—had helped a little, but she felt an unease, like she'd forgotten something.

When Lil D'd left Latonya's apartment and gone out to get in his old car it had sputtered, gray exhaust flooding the air in the parking lot, then died. No amount of tinkering, none of the tricks he usually tried to get it going, worked. He went in, told Latonya, called Man, grabbed his jacket, and went out to the nearest bus stop. Even in the air outside he could smell the old Homes apartment in the orange quilted jacket—Danny T, Latonya, his own funk, and maybe, maybe, it was the smell of those red bricks that had always been the smell of The Homes to him. He zipped the jacket against the cold and tucked the fresh white towel around his neck, covering the birthmark he rarely thought about anymore but habitually hid.

Man had said he'd pick him up at the Five Points station. He wanted to work with Man in the club and all, move up from street dealing, but he needed money now. *I don't know how to make money last*, he thought. *It just goes. And now the car.* Being Man's right hand was the only job he'd ever known. He couldn't believe Man wouldn't tell him if he knew anything about who'd killed Mary. The pleasurable fantasy of new shoes for Latonya drifted by. He checked his phone for the time and willed the bus to come, hoping the DNA place wouldn't close before he got there.

Finally the almost empty bus lumbered and hissed to the stop. Riding the bus almost always made him think of his mother and sometimes Mary—remembering the safe closeness when his mother would pull him against her on the seat, sometimes Mary on her other side.

Cold night was fast overtaking the gray afternoon. The crowd was swelling. Groups of students, unsmiling, grim, solemn, packed the streets, forced to walk close to the cops who lined the sidewalks toward Woodruff Park, where the young women had been shot. "Don't cops have more important things to do, like catching the white men who gunned down our sisters?" The squad stood respectfully silent, absorbing the angry looks of the protesters.

Then it seemed school had let out; the marchers were joined by younger teens, certainly some from school, others, young gang members who'd likely rolled out of bed on the lookout for the day's opportunities; many of the youths wore looks of disaffection, discontent, or unfocused anger. Some disembarked from city buses, others rose from the lower level of the Five Points transit station. Some came, four and five deep, in battered or pimped-out ghetto cars, vibrating bass drowning out the amplified voices of the protest organizers.

"Lord. Lord. Lord," Pepper said, standing at parade rest beside Salt. They were on Peachtree Street across from the southern end of the park. A beer can, heavy and slinging foam, flew past the rookie's unhelmeted, ducking head, splashing beer on his shoulders and the officers near him.

The sun had not so much set as it was blotted out by dark night clouds. Rush hour became a gridlocked nightmare, snarled to honking cacophony; all of them, students, cops, dope boys in lowriders, trapped alongside suburban commuters as night fell.

The green, hard plastic chair in the lab's waiting area reminded Lil D of school. He shifted against the uncomfortable seat. Jacket unzipped in the warm room, he inhaled that Homes smell again—his first memory of his grandmother's, his father's mother's, apartment in The Homes, where she'd sold shots of liquor and single cigarettes and kept a card game going. When he'd make a little money slinging dope, she'd make him give it to her. He didn't want to, but he remembered that was the first time he came to know Officer Salt, when he'd fought his grandmother and somebody called 911. Salt had said she could get him away from his grandmother's apartment if he wanted. But she didn't, or couldn't. He didn't know which. He winced, clicked his cheek, and tried to rein in his wishing for, for what? And Mary, stuck with their mom's mom, as bad as Granny M in the other way; wouldn't let Mary hardly breathe she was so hard on her. He didn't know who to blame for any of it. Now he was here, the last of his family, here to give his DNA for Mary.

The man behind the window called out another number. He looked at the ticket in his hand and stood.

When Lil D came out of the lab building, the sidewalks were packed and overflowing. He'd heard about the white boys being flexed in Man and Johnny C's trap. He'd heard about and seen on TV those college girls being shot. But his whole life, it seemed, he spent worrying more about what was fucked up in his and Latonya's life and how he and Man were trying to make it. Now as he shouldered his way, crossways, through the crowds, unable to see much since he was short, it just felt like this was part of that. *How would he hook up with Man in all this?* he thought. Finally he backed against a wall and punched Man's number on his phone.

Stone answered. "We trapped."

"Gimme that," Man said in the background. "Yeah, this traffic ain't goin' nowhere," he said.

"Where you at?" Lil D asked.

"Whoa!" Man said, his voice rising. "This some serious shit. Dude just took a bat and smashed the blues on a police car. Man!"

Then it sounded to Lil D like Man had dropped the phone. His voice came at a distance from the mic. "Take it easy," he said. Then he was back on. "I didn't know all this shit goin' on. I would tole you take MARTA. And Stone be needin' somethin'. His medicine ain't workin' right. He . . ."

"Man?"

"Hole on. Got damn! Stone done got out. He can't take no crowds and carryin' on." Man's voice had lost its cool.

Across the street at the south end of the park streetlights shone through the bare limbs of the trees. To their right, in the triangle of the intersection, was an abstract steel sculpture rising thirty feet, reminiscent of rail tracks, trusses for water towers, girders, and ladders.

"Some of them seem so angry," Salt said as another group passed, yelling, "Cops don't care. Cops don't care." She shifted her weight from one foot to the other in order to lessen the ache from the hard sidewalk and the cold.

"They want us to solve the sisters' murders, but instead we're representing here." Pepper was tired, too. He'd told her his boys were acting up with him being gone long hours. They needed his energy. They needed him to bring them to the aikido lessons at Salt's.

"You ever think we're on the wrong side sometimes?" Salt said. "I agree with them—we should be out there finding who shot those girls. We should be working to solve Mary Marie's murder. You could be closing the dope trap where those Confederate-flag-flying boys got flexed."

Sodium-vapor streetlights spotted the streets in burnt-yellow auroras that in the cold night seemed to offer false warmth. Exhaust from thousands of vehicles and the noise of horns polluted the air and set nerves on edge. And the cold continued to seep from the sidewalk concrete through Salt's boots and wool socks.

"We don't get to pick and choose," one of the other guys said, having listened in on part of their back and forth.

"What about all the times cops were on the wrong side? Civil rights marches, freedom riders, Vietnam?" Salt said.

"Cops weren't the problem then, either," Pepper weighed in.

"Some cops were. Some made reconciliation more difficult," she said. "And now—Tamir Rice, Michael Brown, Trayvon Martin, Eric Garner. Are you saying those incidents are all no-fault on the part of the police?"

"Cops have become symbols of the problems," Pepper argued. "Those incidents didn't start when cops came in contact with those black men. The incidents had their roots in slavery, Jim Crow, and the legacies of poverty and systemic racism. If the outrage becomes only about police reform, then the system will not change, only the cops."

"Officer down! Officer down!" The radios on their shoulders burst in broken, garbled transmissions. They turned their backs to the street and leaned their ears close to the receivers on their shoulders, looking up at one another with pained and worried eyes, trying to sort out the radio traffic.

"Hold your traffic. Radio, what units are transmitting the 'officer down'?" the commander ordered.

"Alpha units at Auburn and Courtland," reported radio. "Ambulance and Fire Rescue are already at the scene."

Blood rushed from Salt's head. Her mouth went dry. She pleaded with the universe for Wills' safety, bargaining for it to be one of the others in Alpha squad. She looked at Pepper and he put his arm around her shoulder. "Sarge, can you get command channel?" he asked Fellows.

They gathered close. All of them knew someone in Alpha. Fellows already had the radio in her hands twisting the channel knobs, ear pressed to the mic, hand held up for silence. "It's Big Fuzzy," she said, lifting her shoulder to press the radio receiver tighter against her ear. Most of them knew him. Salt and Pepper had worked alongside the big cop in their former assignments. "Head injury. Already at Grady ER," Fellows relayed. "They're not reporting his condition over the radio." Media would be monitoring all the channels and the PD had learned the hard way not to give out officers' conditions so that their next of kin didn't hear it on TV or radio. So every family member of every cop began to suffer until they heard from their loved one. "Homicide is at the scene." Homicide would handle any serious assault on an officer, so it didn't necessarily mean his injury was fatal. But they were reminded, and each of them brought out their phones to call home and let their families know they were okay. Salt tried to call Wills, but of course he wasn't answering, probably because he was the "Homicide" working the scene in Alpha squad. She left a message.

"Listen up," Fellows said. "We're still on post. We'll do our jobs. Squad! On line!" she called them to attend their positions. Faces ashen and grim, they turned back to face the people.

Salt's phone vibrated. Startled, she answered without looking at the ID, thinking it was Wills.

"This is Jim Britton."

"Mr. Britton. Sorry, I'm on a detail now. Can I call you back?"

"Where?"

"Downtown. I'm sorry—"

"In that protest? I thought you were a detective? The news says the police department has lost control, that traffic is at a standstill, and that an officer has been injured."

Salt took a breath, then another, willing herself to be patient. "What's up, Mr. Britton?"

"I thought of something, about the quarry."

"You know that's Detective Felton's case?"

"Yes, but you and I—we already talked. I told you about my family, my great-grandfather."

Salt kept quiet again, listening for what was behind Jim Britton's words.

"The mayor," he said.

"Your ancestor," she prompted.

"No, our current mayor. He came to the quarry one day with some people, that rap music guy, the one in the news. He's from here. Jones?"

"Flash Daddy?"

"I think so. It's not unusual for movie people; all sorts of entertainment people use the quarry for filming. But here's what was off— Flash Daddy?"

"Yeah."

"He got there before the mayor and let himself and his assistant in. They already had the access code. Everybody before had to be admitted and accompanied by city employees."

A fraternity in purple hoodies with gold symbols shouted their Greek letters in unison. Fists raised, they stomped by, boots keeping time.

"Hold on. I can't hear," she said.

Heavy glass shattered on concrete somewhere nearby, around the corner or down the street. The crowd parted as a group of teens ran through, high-tops slapping the pavement.

"Are you in danger?" were the last words she heard from Britton before the phone was knocked from her hand as the marchers mushroomed, pushing onto the sidewalk, jostling each other and pushing into the cops. Salt grabbed the phone off the ground before they began to move the line back.

Pepper, Fellows, all of them wore faces lined with worry for Big Fuzzy, a big, simple, loving guy, always there for his friends. He and another friend came to the Homicide Unit last year to warn her about rumors of threats to her safety. He had a wife, son, and daughter and regularly came to work in uniforms and shoes that were worn. Salt squeezed her eyes and swiped her hand across her cheeks. Then she remembered the phone call and put the phone to her ear, but of course there was no connection. "Call ended" read the screen.

Lil D started walking toward where Man told him he was stuck in traffic two or three blocks south. He walked crosscurrent to the crowd that was headed toward the park nearby, in the other direction. Guys bigger than his thin frame bumped into him, going the other way. They all seemed in a hurry. In the street, traffic was stopped, going nowhere, so drivers blew their horns, faces red and white, and pounded their steering wheels. Young people sat on hoods, trunks, and the tops of some of the stopped cars, their bass beats booming. The smell of weed crisscrossed the air. The sound of glass breaking came from several directions.

"I don't like it," Sergeant Fellows said to Salt and Pepper, "but they need to get this traffic unblocked and want me to send two of our squad to one of the intersections, Decatur and Peachtree Center." She nodded east. "Switch to channel four to coordinate with motors units."

Salt and Pepper shrugged at each other and took off toward their new assignment. Wind picked up between the buildings as they turned the corner. The red awning of the shoe store, famous for catering to professional athletes, was flapping and snapping. The crowd passing the store surged, billowing out while a smaller group pushed inward toward the sound of shattering glass. She and Pepper turned sideways to wedge their way through the packed people struggling to get away.

"Can you see?" she asked Pepper, who was taller than most of the crowd.

Craning his neck, raising himself on his toes to see over the heads of the people, Pepper said, "Can't say for sure, but I'm guessing they're looting Walter's." He held the mic on his shoulder. "Radio, suspected looting at Decatur and Peachtree Center," he reported as they continued to shoulder forward. They emerged from the crowd, broken glass on the sidewalk crunching under their boots, and into a scrum of looters battering the already broken windows of the store. Ignoring the shards of glass that hung precariously at the top of one window, young males kicked their way through, jumping over displays and into the dark interior. Standing on the sidewalk right in front of the store, in the midst of the melee, was Stone, his red-brown round face and head like a troubled moon, wearing an expression of frozen glee as he watched the back-and-forth looters going through the missing plate-glass windows and through the broken glass door, tossing boxes and running away with armloads of shoes. Without clothing from his waist up, chest bare, he tightly held a six-inch shard of glass close to his heart.

"Negative on a response to looting. Hold your position. Do not confront looters. Maintain traffic control," said the voice of command from their radios.

Adding to the already surreal scene, Lil D, in his orange jacket, appeared from around the far corner.

Pepper drew his gun. "Drop it, Stone. Drop the glass now," he shouted.

Salt fought through the scattering crowd and running teens, circling, canister of pepper spray held close to her leg, low ready.

Lil D turned the corner and there was Stone in front of the shoe place, holding a big piece of glass close to his chest, naked from the waist up, rolling his crazy-ass eyes to the sky, blind-like, in the middle of people breaking out the store windows. People had broken the door and were jumping through it and the windows, glass flying and falling, and all the shoes. Shoes lying in broken glass on the sidewalk, shoes thrown by the people inside to outside. Shoes in boxes and out, all kinds and colors of the good shoes. Salt was there, too, coming 'round to Stone while Pepper held a gun on him, yelling for him to drop the glass. Lil D didn't care 'bout Stone. He watched out for him; Man had some reason for keeping him around.

He'd looked in the window of Walter's lots of times. Now he looked down on the sidewalk at a pair of shoes the color he'd been thinking of for Latonya. He squatted to look at the shoes, like in some dream—he didn't care what happened to Stone. And here was Salt. *She'd* told him to come downtown for the DNA for Mary, killed and left to rot. He wanted the shoes. He didn't care about any of the rest.

Like he was hit by a plank, Stone fell from the blast of CS spray Salt aimed directly into his face. Flinging the glass shard from his hand, he grabbed at his eyes, screaming and writhing on the broken-glass-strewn sidewalk. While Pepper covered, Salt rolled Stone facedown to get him cuffed from behind. Pepper holstered and got on the radio to call for an ambulance for Stone while trying to block Salt and Stone from people jumping in and out of the store, throwing boxes and shoes. Right beside her Lil D bent down and picked up a shoe, a single green shoe. "You need to get out of here," she told him while she struggled to get glass from under Stone, who was screaming and squeezing his running eyes shut, then opening them wide, trying to clear the capsicum.

"You tole me to come for the DNA." Lil D looked over the scattered, broken-open boxes and reached for a box, like he was shopping for just the right shoe. "All these . . ." he said.

Salt laid a hand on his as he picked up another box. Pepper was on the radio loudly clarifying their location for the ambulance. Lil D looked at the people coming and going. He looked at Salt, shook off her hand, went over and ducked under the door bar into the dark interior of the store, returning in half a minute with a box under one arm just as Salt stood, both of them jostled by another youth coming out right behind Lil D. The box fell from his hands. Salt bent down to lift Stone out of the glass, but picked up the box first and without thinking handed it up to Lil D. And he took it as if he were a person who'd paid and sprinted down the street through the gridlocked cars.

DAWN

OVERCAST, THE SUN DIDN'T APPEAR ON THE HORIZON; RATHER, the streets and buildings emerged from the gray dawn. Everywhere was litter and detritus from the conflagration of the night and early morning: partially burned wet paper, garbage, bottles and cans rolling toward gutters, soggy bits of food. Sergeant Fellows' team—Salt, Pepper, and the rest—had been held over until the streets cleared of people. They stood by in Woodruff Park monitoring the barricades that blocked Peachtree Street. Pigeons flew at the last second from their pickings in front of the street sweepers as they whirred south from Auburn Avenue.

Big Fuzzy was going to be all right. Part of his left ear was severed by the falling bullet; it missed his brain by a few millimeters and lodged in the upper part of his fortunately meaty back.

Stench from the garbage trucks soaked the air. Salt had that staying-up-too-late stomach, sour and jittery from too much caffeine and junk food. Waiting for the van that would take them back to the academy, they stood around stomping their cold feet at the base of the phoenix rising statue, its female figure holding the bird's legs as it took flight, symbolically pulling her from the ashes of Atlanta.

"That bird's gonna shit right on her face," observed Pepper.

Salt, mobile phone to her ear, walked a little ways from the group. "'Lo," Felton answered, sounding the same as Salt felt.

"You know how they say most crime is committed by the same small percentage of criminals?" she said.

"Hold on. I just walked in the door."

Salt, too tired to stand and too chilled to sit on the cold, hard curb, leaned against the base of the statue, waiting for Felton to come back to the phone. Just as she began to think he'd forgotten her, he came on the line. "Home at last," he said exhaling. "Should I drink wine or coffee? Never mind, I've already got a pinot. Now, you called with a sociology question?"

"We may be partnered, like it or not," she said.

"You're full of riddles this morning."

"It's 'cause my brain is riddled. In the middle of a riot last night, Big Fuzzy's condition unknown, burning cars, looting, traffic gridlock . . ."

"I was there," Felton said.

"Jim Britton called me."

"What?"

"I reminded him that it's your case, but I think his calling me has something to do with my being from here—our roots. He thinks I understand about his ancestors, or something."

"Salt."

"I'm getting to it. He said Flash Daddy Jones had the access code for the quarry and that he'd seen the mayor there with him."

There was silence on his end.

"I'm really tired," she said. "Close call for Big Fuzz."

"Salt?"

"Yeah."

"We're partnered on this one because it looks like our cases are linked, but I'd like to make it permanent."

"Partners?" she asked, listening close to what sounded like him taking a sip of his pinot. "That may be the wine talking, and you're tired."

"No, I'd been thinking about it. What say you?"

The sky had gone to a slightly lighter gray. "That would be—um . . ." she began.

"Weird? Queer? Gay?" he joked.

"Awesome," she said.

In the parking lot behind Dr. Marshall's office Salt took off her loaded gear belt: gun, CS gas, baton, radio. It weighed forty or more pounds. She'd been wearing it now for more than fourteen hours, and for the last four it had been digging into and pinching her skin, chafing its way to her hip bones. She threw on an old fleece zip-up and carried the belt in with her.

The hour was early and Marshall himself was waiting behind the receptionist's counter. "You look tired," he said, leading her down the hall. "Coffee?"

"No, I don't need caffeine. I need to sleep."

"You smell like smoke," he said, wrinkling his nose as he sat down at his desk. "That's one way to share your experience."

"I'm not sure I even know what I'm saying. I am physically exhausted—out all night on the demonstration. I'm also worried, really worried, about a young woman who may be in danger."

"Yet here you are."

"Did I have a choice?" she asked.

"You could have rescheduled. Are you angry?"

Here in Dr. Marshall's clean citrus-smelling office, the chemical and burning garbage odor of smoke coming from her uniform, hair, and skin rose to prominence. The fleece that she'd put on had been in her trunk and smelled of engine oil and car exhaust. She exhaled slowly. "Last night—no, night before last"—she shook her head—"Wills and I went up into the attic. He helped me break the lock on an old steamer trunk that had been there, unopened, since before I can remember."

"Were you looking for something in particular?"

"I don't even know why I told you that." She turned toward the window. "It's not related to my fitness for duty."

"Salt"—Marshall leaned forward—"at this point in my evaluation, I'll tell you, I'm not at all worried about whether or not you're overeager to pull the trigger, which is what the department is really worried about—liability. What concerns me is that you keep getting yourself in situations where you have to defend yourself with deadly force."

"I have a duty . . ." Her voice trailed off, the thought unfinished.

"To what? To Whom? Sarah, to whom do you feel you have a duty at the expense of your own safety?"

She shook her head. "I don't know. I'm too damn tired."

"And undefended. Listen. Here's another concern: I worry that in a confrontation with one of these folks that you feel so much empathy for, you'll hesitate or make a move that puts you in harm's way."

"I think it's hard for citizens to understand. Even feeling how I do—feeling what they feel—I can still kill them if they put me in that position." She did not break eye contact. She wanted him to know.

They sat back in silence.

"I needed to go into that steamer trunk because I'm going to leave the house." She felt like that was what she'd come here to say, that she was going to leave the place that she'd grown up in, her father's family home. She put her hand to her throat.

"I would guess that wasn't an easy decision," Marshall said softly.

She hadn't even said that to Wills. Determined not to cry here, she couldn't say more about leaving the house. After a painful silence, she said, "Last night, a friend came close to being killed by a stray bullet. We'd been ordered to the line without helmets."

Marshall said, "Let's call it a wrap for today. You're tired. That's enough, Salt."

SHOES FOR LATONYA

LIL D HAD FOUND MAN IN HIS SUV STUCK IN TRAFFIC GRIDLOCK
like everyone else, on one of the side streets not too many blocks from
the shoe store. "Man, Stone done lost it. He's going to jail," he told
Man as he climbed in the passenger seat.

"You go shopping?" Man asked, nodding at the shoebox in Lil
D's lap.

"Naw, man, these for Latonya." He laid the box on the floor.
"Them boys broke open Walter's. Stone in front of the store, all crazy,
no shirt or coat, holdin' a big piece of glass on his chest. Pepper might
had to shoot him, but Salt, she done spray gas in his face."

Man leaned his head back on the headrest, turning to look out his
side window, quiet, like he didn't want to try to say anything, like he
was tired.

"He be all right," Lil D said.

"Yeah, maybe Salt send him to Grady. He'll be back out in a day."

Man just grabbed the gearshift and bullied his way into the big intersection, where they sat with all the other cars, trapped for hours until
the cops untangled the streets.

Lil D wished he had birthday paper to wrap the shoes in, but he
didn't want to ask Man to stop. JoJo being there, it worried him that
Man might want to come in the apartment. But Man just let him off
like always.

He held the box behind his back as he unlocked the door. Latonya
was in the kitchen putting some of their little stuff in the empty cabinets. Danny T was sleeping in one of the beanbag chairs. JoJo, always
on the lookout for Man, especially when Lil D was due home, was
not in the kitchen or living room in case Man might decide to come
in. He set the box down out of sight behind one of the unpacked bags
near the door. "How you doin', La?"

Tall enough to reach the top shelves, Latonya came down off her
toes, cheeks rounded from the smile she gave him. The light on her
buttery skin always reminded him of fresh-out-of-the-oven browned
yeast rolls. He came on in the kitchen and put his arms around her
skinny body, pulling her close. "You still sad?" he asked. She let him
hold her for a minute, then pulled him closer, hanging her arms over
his shoulders, laying one cheek on the top of his head. "I got something," he said, his lips close to her breastbone.

"What you got, Lil D?" She laughed, relaxed, happy swaying
there, just the two of them.

"Lemme go," he said.

"Naw."

"Come on, girl. You gone like what I got."

She put her lips, warm, soft, and smooth on his neck, right where
his birthmark was darkest. When they were kids, the first time she

did that, he'd squirmed away, ashamed of the mark. But now and for a long time he'd gotten used to her doing it. "I already like what you got, Lil D." She giggled.

"Not that." He took her hand and led her to the back bedroom where there was only a mattress. Latonya had found the mismatched sheets and pillows and put them, still smelling of the old place, on the mattress. He sat her down and, leaving his jacket on the floor, made her wait while he went back and got the shoes.

When he came back, he closed the door of the bedroom before she could get a look at the box, before she squealed with her hand covering her mouth, eyes turned up and wide with surprise.

PAYBACK

THE TAG OF THE SUSPECTS' VEHICLE WAS TRACED BACK TO A sort of recluse who turned out to be the uncle of two cousins, Paul Locklear and Lawrence "Larry" Owens. Then, shortly after the tag registration came back, Sugarman called and confirmed the uncle's name and presence at the supremacists' meetings, all too late to have satisfied one of the chief complaints of the protesters, an arrest of the suspects, but not late enough to accuse the group of conspiracy.

When Wills called, the uncle immediately professed eagerness to come in and give a statement. And as soon as he was seated in the interview room and Wills prompted, "You must know the guys who had your truck pretty well," the uncle unloaded. "Them boys' daddies just took off when the Ford plant shut down," he quickly volunteered.

"How are you related?"

"They daddies are my brothers. We didn't have no dad, either, so I was kinda like one."

"What are their full names?"

"Paul Locklear and Lawrence, he's called Larry, Owens."

Wills wrote the names on his legal pad, tore off the sheet, and handed it to Huff out in the hall.

The uncle kept talking. "I bought the truck last year, added the flag and bumper sticker them rights' group boys give me. Larry and Paul went with me to meeting a few times. But they'd got into meth or something, talked nuts, said they was gonna pull a Charleston. They all the time listening to some radio guy talked about Mexicans. They was always kinda slow. Nothing ever worked out. Never could hold no job." He hung his head and looked down at his hands twisting together. That night he'd left the assault rifle in the truck.

Probable cause had been established with the fuzzy video from the building across from the park, the uncle's statement that he let the two men use the truck that night, and the phone trace from Paul Locklear to one of the flex kids.

Paul and Larry were brought in by a lawyer. In their early twenties and not bad-looking, they were, as the uncle had said, slow, like whatever they were hearing and seeing took them two beats longer than normal to process. Otherwise they seemed average; Locklear was five nine with medium-brown hair already thinning, and Owens was five ten with the same brown hair, buzz cut. Both were thin, likely because of the meth and crack.

Huff had asked the task force FBI agents to conduct the lineup, to escort the witnesses and document the results. It was a "double blind," a procedure in which the agents wouldn't know which of the men in the lineup were suspects and therefore couldn't, overtly or covertly, transmit the desired outcome to the witnesses.

Salt waited in the reception area for Man and the teen dealers.

Rosie was at her desk, her first week back post-surgery. "They're still pretty sensitive." She looked down at her prominent cleavage. "Thank you for the camellias." The buzzer for the double entrance announced Man and the boys. Rosie hit the lock release.

Man, smooth-walking his bowleg side-to-side glide, was followed by the two teens, wary and hitching their crotches. Salt recognized them as two of the boys that had been running the trap for Johnny C at the Chicken Shack corner. "How long this gone take?" Man asked without preliminary greeting, not even a nod of his head.

"Shouldn't be more than an hour," Salt said. "But if you're in a hurry I can bring them back to Sam's."

"Nah, I'll wait." He slumped down into one of the upholstered chairs against the wall, as did both boys, one on either side of him.

"Here's how it works." Salt began explaining that each of the boys would view the lineup separately. "And I need you to fill out these forms." She handed them clipboards. "Are your parents or guardians available to give their consent?" she asked, not expecting an answer, but in order for them to make formal statements, possibly incriminating themselves, she had to ask the question, required by juvenile law.

Man took the clipboard from the smaller of the boys and began checking the boxes, then pointed to where the boy should sign.

"Revved up by haters. Then shat on by black kids," Gardner said, shaking his head. "They were looking for a target."

Salt, sitting next to the window in their booth at the Cuban place, said to herself, "Shame."

"What?" Felton said.

Six blocks up from the office, on "The River Ponce," as the avenue was known, just the four of them were having their lunch after having a successful finish to the lineup.

"That whole Confederate flag thing—guys want to think they are the descendants of some noble cause. It's pathetic," Wills said. "Two groups of have-nots fuckin' each other."

They all went silent when the waiter brought their sandwiches, beans, and plantains. All of them hungry, it was a while before anyone said anything. But the cousins were on their minds. "Not enough education, an economy that no longer rewards physical skills. That flag is what they fall back on for self-esteem." Gardner couldn't let it go.

"Not that different from the boys who sold them the flex," Salt said.

"Those two kids were jam up, though. No question they both picked them right off. Once again our girl comes through. Here's to Salt." Wills lifted his glass and the others followed. Wills touched her foot under the table.

Felton laughed. "Stop it, you two."

Rosie followed Felton and Salt into the break room, and while they pushed back a table and turned chairs to face the muted TV, she unpacked a compartmentalized aqua Tupperware lunch box and set out matching utensils and a napkin on the table next to theirs. "I don't understand why you're not there," Rosie said with an offended tone, nodding at the TV and snapping her napkin before placing it in her lap.

Felton sat down and stretched. "That's what I told her."

The omnipresent burnt microwave popcorn smell of the break room seemed more intense than usual, making Salt queasy as she leaned over to turn up the volume on the old tube TV.

"Would you like an apple slice?" Rosie offered.

Salt winced. "Blech! I've lost my appetite lately. My mouth tastes like copper."

On the screen the press conference was beginning. The FBI, the mayor, the fire chief, two PD deputy chiefs, the major over Homicide, and two lieutenants stood flanking the podium at City Hall, with Chatterjee, barely visible, looking uncomfortable behind them. The mayor stepped up to the bank of microphones. "Today we're gratified to announce the arrest . . ." Chatterjee looked tired, the whites of his eyes prominent between the shoulder-to-shoulder commanders, his usually hangdog look made more so by his having to come in early for the press conference. His droopy blue blazer hung on his slender frame.

"I'm glad I'm not there," Salt said.

"You need to think about the long term, career-wise," Rosie lectured.

"Cochise doesn't look too happy," said Felton.

"Well, he's not as photogenic as Salt."

"Our teamwork . . ." one of the deputy chiefs was saying ". . . the arrest of Paul Locklear and Larry Owens . . ."

"They're taking credit. Why shouldn't you?" asked Rosie.

"They didn't ask me," Salt said.

BIRDS OF A FEATHER

SHE BEGAN MAKING THE ROUNDS, GOING TO THE CLUBS LATE enough to catch most of the dancers: Magic Girls, Gold String, back to Toy Dolls, even to the Royal Peacock. She went to the top-drawer places and the bottom-of-the-line places.

The Peacock wasn't strictly a strip joint, but they occasionally had burlesque shows harkening back to the club's glory days as the most elegant black club in the city. A bird, formerly outlined in neon, having displayed a colorful tail, had lost its glow and now appeared on the marquee above the door, tail feathers stick-like. It was the only peacock around and, with no color at all, could easily be mistaken for some other fowl.

"You should have seen it in its day. Aretha tore this place down!" Leaning just inside the door, an old, heavyset uniformed cop, dark skin, circles under his eyes, and lower lids that drooped, revealing red rims, spoke from out of the shadow.

"You're Peachtree Harrison," she said.

"And you're James Alt's kid." He pushed himself upright.

The Plexiglas display case to the right of the door announced in crooked magnetic letters that Sunday night, tonight, was free ladies' night. Auburn Avenue was cold and empty, its hoped-for revival slow to catch on.

"You're probably wondering why a place so poorly attended needs an extra-job cop." Harrison motioned her inside from the cold.

"Actually I'm speechless. You're the only person who's ever, by way of introduction, identified me as my father's daughter."

"Your dad and I joined the PD at the same time, right after we came home from Vietnam. We didn't serve in country together, but we were both First Cav."

"This is kind of amazing." Salt's thoughts were a jumble. She was too surprised to begin asking questions.

"Why?" He bent his head to one side.

"Well, I've seen you around the department. Your name stands out. You're got quite a reputation. But I didn't know you knew my dad."

"Come on up." He motioned her toward the wide stairs. She followed as he used the handrail to slowly hoist his weight up the rickety steps. At the landing he stopped to catch his breath. "You might also wonder why I'm still on the job and why I work this extra job." Buddha-like, he posed questions.

"If you want to tell me." She loosened the belt of her coat and took off the fedora.

"Always admired those hats," he said, turning to go down the hallway that ran the length of the grand ballroom. Salt got a quick glimpse of the big red-and-black-tiled room as they passed.

"You know this place goes back to my parents' and grandparents' day—when Auburn Avenue was one of the best places in America for black folks." He opened a door marked OFFICE.

"I know a little, but not much." She was sure he wanted to tell her.

"Nobody cares much, either," he said as if he'd tried to tell the history before. He fell into a green leatherette couch and motioned her to the swivel chair behind the desk. "He didn't care much about bullshit."

"My dad?"

He nodded. "Me, either. How come you here tonight?"

She got out the photo of the three girls. "I'm looking for her." She pointed to JoJo. "I'm worried. The other two were shot and killed."

Harrison shook his head, took his time looking at the picture. "I guess I've been around too long—young girl like you on the trail of somebody who killed these babies. I'm old school. Now don't take offense. I'm liable to say something chauvinistic. I am going to retire soon. Lemme look at these girls some more." He shook his head again, slowly. "Maybe. Can I keep this?"

"Yes, of course. I appreciate any help."

"There's one of the managers here, a woman who knows the dance scene, knows quite a few of the girls, burlesque and strippers."

"I doubt these girls were real dancers, not like the professionals." Salt pointed to the posters of elaborately costumed women on the office walls.

"Yeah, it used to be something." He looked around at the beautiful women. "Black was beautiful back then."

"You better be careful who hears you say that kind of thing." She held back a grin until finally the corners of her mouth turned up.

"Told you." He laughed. "I see you're just like your dad. He had that same good in his eyes."

Salt looked down.

"I say something?" The couch crackled as he moved.

"I have a lot of questions about him," she said, looking at her hand minus Wills' ring.

"He was the real deal, born to be a poleese—an artist, a priest, a preacher, a rabbi. He was what they call a 'savant.' He knew way more about people than they knew about themselves. I saw him work. He and I were in a sector car together for a few years, then we were on the old STRIKE Team—we stayed in hot water." He chuckled and wiped an eye.

With barely enough air in her lungs, she asked, "Would you say you were close? Friends?"

"You mean did we pal around outside of work? Naw." Harrison's mouth turned down at the corners. "Back then there was drinking after the shift. Guys would meet up somewhere and drink themselves stupid—fights, whores. You could get away with DUI. But your dad never did that. I didn't much. He was a mystery to us—living so far out in that old house. Talk was his family had money, that the house was haunted. People say all kinds of things. You know cops love to gossip."

"I still have the house. I wish I'd known before now that you knew him."

"There were lots of times I meant to reach out to you. I thought a lot of your dad."

"Maybe I would have been a disappointment."

"Maybe. I mean you being a female. I'm a relic. I never believed in women on the job. I was wrong—slow to learn, I guess." He hitched up his heavy shoulders and shrugged.

"Did you know he was sick?"

"You mean the PTSD or whatever they call it? I never saw that in him. He'd be out for a week or two sometimes, but then again"—Harrison shrugged—"it was the times. Men didn't pry, or cry." He rubbed his hands, fingering large, swollen knuckles.

"You're the only person on the job I've ever talked to who said they knew him—except Lieutenant Shepherd, and she said she only talked to him once."

Harrison passed his hand over the top of his close-cut gray hair. "Let me think—I guess there's hardly anyone on the job longer than me. I'll give it some thought." He looked again at the photo of Mary and the girls. "Tell me about her."

"It's a long story, long story. I've known her family almost since I came on the job twelve years ago."

"Has it been that long? You worked The Homes? Right?"

"I did, almost ten years."

"You know that was our, his, sector? Back when there were only sectors, not yet broken up into beats."

"I knew just about that much. There's an old woman—"

"Sister Connelly?"

"Yeah."

"She still around? She was old when I worked there."

"She's going strong."

"Well, I'll be. Give her my regards." Harrison stood. "Come on, let me give you the five-cent tour." He led her out and down the hall. "Auburn Avenue—we're so used to saying it we don't think about the meaning. Auburn is a reddish-brown color and white people named it that before it was black, a black neighborhood. Strikes me as funny."

They stood in the entrance to the main ballroom. "If, as they say, these walls could talk." The room was from another era: royal red walls north and south, red brick east and west, red-and-black highly polished tile floors, red-carpeted stage, red Naugahyde booths and eight support columns, red on two sides, burnished metal on the other sides.

"What happened to the peacock?" she asked.

"Peacocks went out of fashion. But this place in its time helped to start the careers of a lot of the greats: Little Richard, Jerry Butler, Otis, Sam Cooke, Howlin' Wolf, Fats, Muddy, B.B. I could give you a list a mile long. Now look at it—empty."

It wasn't exactly true: there was the bartender at the long bar along one wall, a couple in a booth, and a DJ sorting records at a spin table to the left of the stage.

"Dancers don't dress up in feathers. No money in that sort of thing. Now they twerk, shake, and show everything. Where's the romance, the anticipation? I remember a time when there was more passion in a little kiss than in all this shake-your-booty stuff." He took out the photo Salt had given him. "These young ladies will never know the sweetness of a little kiss." The old cop wiped his red-rimmed eyes. "Damn shame."

Harrison again held on to the handrail as they went down the rubber-matted wide stairs. The wall of the building across the street was crumbling, taking with it the mosaic mural of what looked like it once might have been the city's symbol, the phoenix, having risen but now literally falling into actual rubble, or it could have been a depiction of another of the peacocks, plumage molting. Salt gave Harrison one of her city-issued business cards, which itself had a tiny phoenix rising from the ashes.

She was making people in the Magic Girls Club uncomfortable, harshing their high. Like a chaperone at the prom, in her trench coat and fedora she stood out like she'd just stepped out of the 1940s. The tables were packed with high rollers around which swarmed the wannabes, strivers looking to catch a ride on the glitter train. Lights arced, glinting off gold and diamond rings, watches, teeth, and oiled bodies. Money fluttered everywhere, thrown into the air toward the women.

Onstage the dancers cut their eyes in her direction, modifying their most ardent displays. They danced but without enthusiasm. Most of the dancers were beautiful, some thick, some slim, but all had significant hip-to-waist ratios. Their skin glowed with youth, sweat, and lotions, all washed in pink light, swinging their expensive hair as they mounted the poles with unbelievable athleticism. There was minimal costuming. Tattoos proliferated, decorating almost every strong thigh. Loose bills, mostly ones, littered the stage.

Wondering if she was strong enough to do those moves, Salt tried to imagine what it would feel like to put her body on display like that. It might be affirming—for a minute. Then she thought about what that would have been like at Mary's age, selling a caricature of sex, just playing. A manager came over. "You crushing the brothers' dreams here, Detective. Can I assist you so you can leave ASAP?" He spread his manicured hands, rings twinkling on every finger.

The music's beat transmitted vibrations through the floor. The walls pulsed. She leaned close. "I'd like to go backstage."

"We don't do that. You'll have to make an appointment."

"I don't do that, Mr. Stokes. So could I get a seltzer water while you make arrangements?"

"Ah, so you remember my name." He sat down, smiling, folding his hands on the table. He held up a finger for a sequined waitress.

"You beat a woman to death. Not a thing I'd forget." Five years ago Salt had arrested Stokes on a homicide warrant. The detectives had asked her to keep an eye out for him. He'd resisted.

The DJ segued into another rhythm and two more dancers advanced to the front-stage positions.

"Self-defense."

"Jury got you on manslaughter only and here you are." She smiled, scanning the room. They grinned at each other as the waitress took the order for Salt's water.

After the waitress had gone, Stokes asked, "What is it you need to talk to my ladies about?"

Salt handed him a copy of the photo. "I'm looking for these women, dancers." She nodded at the stage. "They may have information about a murder."

In the low light he made a show of squinting at the picture, but not for long. "Hard to tell." He folded it and stuck it inside his jacket.

"You're welcome to keep it," she said.

"For the boss. Maybe he'll know them."

"Which boss? He got a name? Does he know many of the employees?"

"Not really."

The waitress delivered Salt's water to Stokes, whispered in his ear, and left. The tables around them had emptied. He nodded at someone across the room. "I'll see about getting you backstage. Call first next time." He smoothed his cornrows, turned, and made his way through the crowd.

A few minutes later a young woman, hobbled by high-heel boots, stood teetering at Salt's table. "I'm supposed to take you back."

Salt left her drink untouched and followed the wobbly woman along the wall to a door to the right of the stage. Her escort only went so far as the door. "You on you own." From the dark, neon-splashed main room a short alcove provided an abrupt transition through to the dressing room, causing Salt to feel a little disoriented. The room bustled with women lit by bright, harsh overhead lights that tore away illusions. The walls were a light, sickly beige, as were the hard-plastic lockers across from more lights, ones that lit the mirrors in front of dressing tables where dancers affixed lashes that resembled mustaches, where sequins were being glued to eyelids and brows, where makeup the viscosity of oil paint was applied to their faces, mouths were outlined in black and filled in with glossy colors. She tried not to stare, but who could not? All large in some way, even the smallest had a thickness of muscle that drew her skin taut and smooth. Some had thighs like Olympic weight lifters. They were fearsome and vivid, most in their twenties, a few thirtysomethings. Their lush bodies covered in tattoos, they must have become accustomed to being stared at.

Two dancers roughly swept by Salt, G-strings shining between enormous butt cheeks. She had to step back to avoid contact. All the women in the room seemed to be transmitting aggression with their hypersexualized bodies and bold movements. Pretending not to notice or care, they pointedly ignored her. Maybe they thought she'd be intimidated as she stood there—a tall white woman in a trench coat, holding a fedora.

They bent toward the mirrors, applying another layer, buttocks bared in her direction. Salt sat down on a couch, part of a conversation area, in the center of the room and waited.

"Honey, you smell something funny in here?" said a large light-skinned woman to the smaller bronzed colleague sharing her dressing table.

"You mean that smell like a white girl?" her friend responded.

Salt, having been acknowledged, smiled at their reflections in their mirror.

Over her shoulder the first woman said, "Like what you see?"

Salt got out some flyers, stood and walked over to the women, and laid them on the dressing table. "I may not be in your club, but I'm on your side," she said.

Both of the dancers at the mirror, now seated, took a flyer, looked at the photo closely, then at each other. The pulsing bass of the music rattled the mirror in front of them, their images quivering. "They ain't work here," said the smaller girl, checking her friend's reflection.

"Why you axin' here? They wearin' Toy Doll shirts." She pointed to the logos on the shirts of the girls in the photo.

"They haven't shown up at Toy Dolls in a while, at least not when I've been there. I was hoping to find someone who knows how to get in touch with them. The little girl in the middle is dead. I'm trying to find out who killed her," Salt told them. She kept Glory's death out of it.

"Aw." They studied the photos more intently, looked at each other, and nodded. The bigger girl leaned close to Salt and said softly, "Them two"—she pointed at JoJo and Glory—"come in with Flash Daddy couple of times; been a while though."

Four dancers came back from the stage, glancing at Salt as they went to their lockers.

"Look, we all kinda look out for each other—to a point. We get hired and fired by whoever, men. We don't know who owns the clubs—just 'somebody' in the business. There's all kinds of talk going 'round. One day this producer own the club, next day some Japanese guy owns it. Word always that Flash Daddy own a big piece of the businesses all over town."

"I get it," Salt said.

They handed the flyers back.

"I'm going to leave some of these out on the table." Salt motioned toward the conversation area. "My number's on them."

Back at the office she fired up the desktop computer, and as the monitor woke up, Salt hung up her coat, which smelled of cigar smoke.

A couple of hours later, having tried every database she could access, she'd been unable to peel back enough layers to find out who the actual owners of any of the clubs were. They were all listed under limited liability corporations with names similar to numerous national and international conglomerates. Her search for information on Flash Daddy Jones, though, yielded addresses of record for his driver's license and vehicle registration and photos of the mogul with the mayor at a ribbon cutting for a music studio in the city's underdeveloped south side. Tax incentives had facilitated the project. In the photo the mayor beamed at Flash Daddy, both of them wearing identical black suits, Mr. Jones basking in the glow of legitimacy, while Mr. Mayor seemed to be enjoying the cachet of cool.

FLASH

FLASH DADDY LIVED IN THE SOUTHERNMOST SPRAWL OF THE
city. Salt's appointment with him was for three p.m. Atlanta, a city of
hills and trees, is more akin to Appalachia than the shaking earth of
the Okefenokee at the bottom of the state. But the land begins to flat-
ten almost right at the southern city limits. Scrub pines start to creep
in and strangle the hardwoods, and the topsoil of fecund black earth
thins to baked, cracked red clay. Even when rain is plentiful, the counties south of the city still have a parched feel. On the same interstate
she usually took for her own home, she passed her exit, once again
reminded that the city was coming ever closer to what had been country. A flutter in her stomach reminded her that she was entering unfa-
miliar territory. She could have waited until Felton was able to go with
her but was too anxious about JoJo. Time was precious and she didn't
know when she'd be back on the protest detail.

Farther south she turned off at the exit for a two-lane highway.

Fences and driveways for new, large houses with acres of lawn lined the road. The architecture of many of these new homes seemed ill defined. Brass numbers on one of the red brick columns, into which was set a security gate, confirmed the address. She turned off the road and pulled up to a call box. When she pushed the button, a voice answered, "Yo."

"Detective Alt to see Mr. Jones."

The gate began a jerky, halting retraction, opening to a black-asphalt single-lane drive through a field of brown grass that had been mown too close to survive. Tall, skinny, fast-growing cypress bordered the perimeter of chain-link fencing that surrounded the property. The house, on a slight rise, was made of angled sections, each having a façade in a different shade of rock. She drove up and stopped beneath an arched portico, where a very tall man who looked familiar—maybe a former athlete—wearing a warm-up suit stood in the doorway of the house. "He's at the pool house. I'll take you. Just leave your car here," he said, his voice a match for the one answering the gate box.

The ballroom-size foyer was all brass and glass and mirrors. Salt followed the tall man past a fountain, scaled for a large bank, trickling into a pool of intense blue water, and out the other side of the house, where they got into a golf cart. Another asphalt drive half circled the back of the house. At the farthest end they stopped in front of a tall arch-windowed indoor poolroom. Palm trees on the inside of the windows blocked the view. Her escort waited while she got out and went to a set of French doors and turned the lever handle. But the glass-paned doors stuck. "Push on the top," her driver said. "Here, let me." He got out and pounded his fist at the top of the double doors. When they popped open, Flash Daddy Jones, large cigar in his mouth, stood facing them, frowning. "I told Maya to get that thing fixed." Mr. NBA shrugged and went back to the cart.

"Don't many people get to see my place," said Flash. "What do you think?" He waved his cigar over the room. Shaded umbrellas, beach tables, and lounge chairs surrounded the money-sign-shaped swimming pool. At one of the far tables two bikini-clad women chatted while a third ate a burger from a take-out bag.

"Impressive," she said.

In the tropical warmth and humidity of the nouveau-Hefner, climate-controlled pool house, Salt took off her fedora and loosened her coat.

"Punkin'," he yelled. One of the girls jumped up and teetered over, high heels clacking on the tiles. "Tell Maya to get this damn door fixed." The girl tapped toward an inner door to the house. "Can't get nobody who takes responsibility these days," he said. "You want something to eat or drink? These girls work for me. They my personal assistants, you might say." He smiled, showing his famous diamond tooth.

"I'm good," she said, removing her coat. "Can we sit?"

He led her to a pair of low lounge chairs under one of the umbrellas. Flash sat down and stretched his legs out on one of the lightweight and insubstantial chairs, which threatened to tip at the slightest unbalance. Salt sat sideways in another lounge chair, knees higher than her waist. Looking uncomfortable, and testing the wobbling aluminum frame, he said, "Let's get to business. You lookin' for that dancer, JoJo? Right?" He grinned as if he'd surprised her.

"You're on top of things, I see, Mr. Jones."

"I got my nose close to a lot in this city."

"I'm sure you do." She gave him a gentle, almost friendly smile. "So it'll be easy, I'm sure, for you to get in touch with those girls and assist me with arrangements to interview them," Salt said, her voice mildly flattering.

He canted his head, chin forward, and made one-eye contact. "You smart, I see." His eyes narrowed, mouth tightened, he nodded at her.

"I like to think I'm talking to the right people."

"See, you did that again." He leaned back in the chair. "That good-girl trick," he said, grinning, tapping cigar ashes on the tile floor. "I like that." He smiled out at the room.

"I am talking to the right person?"

"Yeah, maybe." He looked at the girls around the room, then at the cigar in his hand and took a puff. "How 'bout I call you? See, you could have saved yourself the trouble and asked your favor over the phone and not had to come all the way out here."

"I'd appreciate that, Mr. Jones. The sooner the better." She unbent from her mantis-like posture. "I didn't mind the trip—wouldn't have wanted to miss seeing all this."

A woman wearing tailored slacks and a long-sleeve black silk shirt came from the inner door to the house.

"Maya! Be right there," Flash shouted as he stood. "I'll get her to take you out."

Salt followed him to where the woman waited. "She leavin'," he said, gesturing at Salt. "Why all the doors in this mansion I got don't work right? They all hard to open. Handles be breakin'."

"I believe we had this same discussion about the plumbing," Maya said, her expression as flat as her voice.

"Yeah, well, I ain't happy. I paid a shitload of green for this place. You think you at least could open the goddamn doors."

Maya looked at Salt. "If you'll follow me." She turned and went through the door to the rest of the house.

"I'll be expecting your call, Mr. Jones," Salt said over her shoulder as she followed Maya's tapping heels on the faux-marbled-floor hall.

They walked past an exercise room, a game room with a bar and pool table, bedrooms with canopied beds, and back to the blue-water fountain in the foyer.

"Must be a job, looking after a place this big. Have you worked for Mr. Jones long?"

"You might say that." Maya stood at the main door, waiting for Salt.

Salt reached in her pocket. "Sometimes I find myself giving these out in my dreams," she told Maya, handing her the flyer of JoJo, Mary, and Glory. "I'm Detective Alt, Atlanta Homicide. I'm looking for these two women," she said, once again pointing at JoJo and Glory.

Maya did not once change expression or tone of voice; her eyes were dull. Beneath flawless, matte-beige skin Salt detected anger in her tightened jaw and slight downturn of her eyes and mouth. "What did he tell you?" Maya asked.

"He said he'll call."

"I will encourage him to do that." Maya folded the flyer and led Salt out.

As Salt drove out of the gate she whispered under her breath, "He didn't mention Glory, only JoJo."

Salt had never before had a conversation with the deputy chief, any deputy chief for that matter, but here he stood, white shirt gleaming, brass shining, beside her flimsy, leaning-walled cubicle. "Hi," he said.

She pushed back her rolling chair from the desk. "Chief," she said, struggling to sit at some kind of semi-attention.

"What are you working on?" He repositioned himself so he could look at the monitor on her desk.

"The girl found over at Fox Street."

"Oh," he said uncertainly.

"She was dead three or four months before her body was found? That one."

He looked around her cubicle as if looking for a clue.

"Can I help you, Chief?" Huff skidded to a stop beside the deputy chief. All around the office, heads appeared over the tops of cubicles.

"No," said the deputy chief, turning to look over the room. Heads ducked. "Just wanted to see how the move was progressing."

Eyes bugging and giving Salt a what-did-you-do look, Huff asked the deputy chief, "Coffee?"

"Might as well," the deputy chief said, turning to Huff.

PRESSURE

"CLOSE THE DOOR," HUFF SAID, HIS TONE OF VOICE UNUSUALLY flat. He lifted a stack of murder books from the chair in front of his desk. "They gave me a direct order and said if I didn't carry it out, someone else would."

"That bad?" she said mechanically. Knees going weak, she dropped into the chair and folded her hands in her lap, trying to prepare for whatever the bad news was.

He massaged his forehead with one hand. "I'm inactivating your McCloud case. You're back in rotation. Next body is yours."

"Okay," she said, remaining still, waiting for him to continue.

"Okay? You're not going to argue with me?"

"No, I figured you'd tell me why."

"I'm serious as a heart attack, Salt. I got called to the deputy chief's office. And—now, this is between you and me—if they find out I told you, I'll be back pounding a foot beat in The Bluff."

"Let me guess—Flash Daddy Jones?"

"They want you to quit 'harassing' him." Huff's air quotes again.

"Not sure how interviewing someone once is harassment, but okay, I won't try to get anything more from him. That doesn't seem to be a reason to inactivate the case." She was beginning to feel the blood come back to her face. She'd thought he was going to tell her something worse.

"Salt, there is more." Huff stood and turned his back to her. "God, I hate this job!"

"Sarge, you're scaring me."

He turned around and put his hands on the back of his chair, as if propping himself up. "They asked me—"

"Who's they?"

"I'm just saying it was discussed. They'd gotten wind of a rumor and they want your fitness-for-duty results."

"What rumor?"

"You and Wills."

Salt sat staring, thinking, *Why all this now? It sounded like they were out to get anything on her.*

Huff went on. "There's also a new complaint." He waited.

Salt lifted her eyes to his.

"They showed me a video from a surveillance camera. It was the looting at Walter's."

"Sarge, they ordered us not to confront the looters."

"Roger that. But Salt, what they have—a surveillance video that shows you abetting one of the looters. You could be charged with party to a crime. You gave some guy shoes from the store. They said you could be arrested and fired. It's possible you could be convicted of a misdemeanor theft. Even if you managed to keep your job you'd be assigned to some position where you couldn't work cases or make arrests. You'd never be able to testify in court. Your value as a witness would be compromised."

Salt's mouth went dry. The room went out of focus and Huff's voice sounded muffled behind the sound of her heart beating. She became aware of the rise and fall of her chest. She smelled gunpowder.

"Salt? Salt?"

She blinked. "What do they want?"

"They want the McCloud case inactivated so you won't have any reason for harassing Jones."

"Or what?"

"They were playing it like they didn't know if bringing criminal charges would be necessary, like whether the video was clear enough—if it was a case of your giving the guy the shoes or if you just handed them to him so you could deal with the perp you'd cuffed."

She tried to think. "So they're holding it over my head?"

Huff said nothing, just shook his head slowly side to side.

"I'd like to leave early," Salt said. A numbness had come over her, except for her skin, which felt on fire, like pinpricks along her arms and legs.

"Stay here," Huff said. "I'm going to get Wills . . ."

"I can—"

"Not an option, an order. You don't look good." Huff shut the door behind him, leaving her staring dumbly in the direction of the wall behind his desk. He quickly returned with Wills and shut the door again.

"What's going on?" Wills asked. "Salt? Sarge?"

"I gave her some bad news. She can tell you. I'm not letting her go home alone," Huff said.

"Salt?" Wills said, coming around to face her.

"I'm okay." She stood.

"At least drive her home."

She led the way to her cubicle; Wills grabbed his coat as he passed his desk. She pulled her coat tight and covered her head with the fedora.

"This is scaring me," Wills said in the elevator. "I've seen that look on your face." But of course, here on the city's property, even in the parking lot or in his truck, he wouldn't risk holding her; they were still being cautious about their relationship, especially now. Wills, impatient, drove to the nearest side street, put the truck in park, leaving the engine running like they were teenage lovers, turned, and took her hands in his. "Salt, whatever this is it is not going to make a difference in the long run. Nothing can ruin the life you and I have and will have. It may be a bump, a hill, or a mountain, but we will get over it. Now tell me."

For the third or fourth time in as many days, Salt wept, Wills tightly holding her shaking body.

"I don't like no carpet—too hard to keep clean with kids," Latonya said, tearing greens for their supper. But she didn't sound unhappy. She said it with her chin up, smiling.

"It look real nice, La," JoJo said, doing her part to keep the good mood going. "Jes get you a vacuum, thass all."

Latonya had unpacked all the plastic bags, hung their clothes. Everything was neat and clean. It even looked all right with just the TV, beanbag chairs, and mattresses in the bedrooms. Danny T could run and fall and not hurt himself. Latonya's new shoes in the box were beside her GED book on top of the counter between the kitchen and living room.

Lil D was watching the cartoon channel, sitting in one of the bag chairs with Danny T in his lap, when his phone vibrated. "Yo. Hole on." He sat Danny in the chair and went to the back bedroom. "Wass up?"

"You comin' to the club tonight?" Man asked.

"I ain't got a ride. Piece-a-shit car still not workin'. Man, I ain't got no money to get it fixed." Lil D clicked his cheek in disgust.

"A'ight. I come get you."

"Naw."

"Why you don't want me to come there?"

"It ain't that." Lil D worried he'd screwed up.

"'Bout ten." Man hung up.

Lil D sat, legs crossed Indian-style, on the edge of the mattress, trying to decide if he needed to ask JoJo about Mary. He didn't know how Man would take it if he found out JoJo was staying with Latonya and him. Man was all about Flash Daddy these days; showed Lil D pictures from the paper of Flash and the mayor.

The bedroom door opened and JoJo stuck her head in. "La say your food's ready." She turned to go.

"Who you so scared of, Bit?"

She came back and stood in the open door, respecting Latonya, not coming in the room alone with Lil D, even though they all knew how tight he and Latonya were.

"Who would kill Glory? Why?" he asked her.

"You ain't got to know, Lil D," she said. "And I best not speculate."

"Do it have to do with my sister?"

"Don't go axin' me no questions."

"You gone hide forever?" he asked.

"I don' know, D."

"I ain't gone be able to keep hidin' shit from Man."

"What am I gone do? I got no place away from the 'hood."

"That poleese, Salt, been lookin' for you." He watched JoJo's reaction. Looking back down, he pulled at the new carpet. "She straight," he told her.

"She gonna protect me from the mayor, Lil D?" She started to tear up. "You seen pictures of him and Flash Daddy."

"Naw, come on." He stood. "Come on, less eat. I'll think on it."

JoJo wiped her eyes with the hem of her oversized T-shirt, which had a "Thug Life" logo over an image of guns and money.

Wills' Rotties, Pansy and Violet, lay on the kitchen floor with Wonder, snoots on their paws, looking up with mournful eyes.

"I can't live that way. I can't work waiting for the ax to fall," Salt told Wills. Wonder began pacing, back and forth, staring out the door, then back to Salt's side, wanting her to let him out to the sheep. The Rotties' eyes darted between him and Wills and Salt.

"We need to sort this out. Right now we don't know who's pulling the strings." Wills poured them each a finger of whiskey.

"I don't want you tainted, Wills."

"You insult me by saying that. I don't give a damn about anything they do. Yes, I like, love, working homicides, but what we'll have, Salt, at the end, will be that we did good work, acted with integrity, and cared for our family, you and me."

She took a sip of the whiskey, felt it sliding down, immediately blurring the sharp edges. "Integrity," she repeated.

"No matter what, we, you and I, will come through this righteous." Wills put his whiskey down and pulled her to standing, holding her at arm's length, forcing her to look into his honest brown eyes. "What you cannot do is isolate yourself. You've done that before. We'll figure this out. We're a team. Tomorrow we'll sit down and come up with a plan."

"Isolate." Salt listened to the word reverberate in her thoughts.

"Salt?"

"You're right," she told him. Her eyes fell on her coat hanging on the hook by the door and the fedora.

The next morning, Salt sat at the table, head in her hands. She pushed back the tangle of hair from her forehead, rubbing the scar with two fingers. Wills was at the stove putting egg-soaked bread into the cast-iron pan and pouring water into the filter for their drip coffee.

"Eat," Wills said, setting a plate of French toast, buttered, dusted with powdery sugar, in front of her. He put maple syrup and a platter of bacon and soysage in the middle of the table and a cup of coffee in front of Salt. He sat down with his own plate and coffee, leaned over to the counter, and grabbed a legal pad and pen. "We have to get to the source of this." He tapped the pad with a finger, forking a bite of toast. "Somebody is feeling threatened. Why?"

"Whoever killed Mary."

"That's a reasonable leap. But we need to be careful about jumping to conclusions. Maybe instead of Mary it has to do with the other two girls? JoJo?"

Salt nodded.

"And the girl from the quarry."

"Glory." Salt took a sip of the strong coffee. "Jim Britton, the environmentalist from the quarry, said the mayor, or someone high up in the city, gave Flash Daddy Jones the access code for the gate. Britton said he saw Flash there and that he entered before the mayor got there."

"And just because they take you off Mary's case doesn't mean you can't work it, Salt."

"But if they find out . . ."

"What are your options?"

She shrugged. "Quit? Work under their thumb?"

"Or cut off the hand that's biting you."

"I think you mixed a metaphor or four." Salt gave him a grim smile. "If they want, they'll not just fire me but they can charge me criminally. It's possible I could go to jail." She dropped the fork and pushed back from the table.

"Come on, girl," Wills said to her back as she left the table, walked out and down the hall to the library. She closed herself in, pulling the pocket doors together and leaning back against them. *What if he gives up on me?* she thought.

Her eyes fell on the album and ledgers she and Wills had brought down from the attic. "Good Lord," she said softly. She walked over, sat down on the floor next to the bottom shelf, and pulled out the album of old photos. A faded burgundy cord was threaded through heavy black pages and tied to the dingy, embossed faux-leather cover. The first photos were small portraits of people she believed to be distant relatives, all unidentified. One solemn man wore on his simple, plain suit what appeared to be a law enforcement star.

Salt gently turned the pages, edges frayed and crumbling. The next page also held small portraits of formal and unsmiling men and women and families. She turned to scenes of people in front of meager, unpainted houses with exposed brick or rock pier-and-timber foundations. Children, faces pinched, cheeks hollowed out, sat with their legs over the edges of porches. The adults posed in open doorways.

She heard Wills in the kitchen banging pots and pans, and the occasional scuffling and barks of the dogs.

Toward the back of the album she began to recognize some of the faces: her grandfather alongside other men in uniform from World War II, studio portraits, hazy-edged, pink-tinted cheeks, women in pastel sweaters and dashing men, hair oiled and tamed.

Wills pushed the doors apart. "Hey."

Salt patted the floor beside her, drew in her knees, leaned back against the bookshelf, the closed album in her lap.

Wills sat down. "I thought you might need a minute to yourself."

"You?"

"Just gathering my thoughts, trying to find the best way for us to do this," he said. "What did you find?" He nodded at the album.

Salt lowered her knees, letting the album fall open. She turned a few pages. "I don't know who most of these people are, relatives, I suppose. A few I recognize." She turned to the back. "My grandfather." She pointed to the photo of him standing alone, tall and lean.

"Go back," Wills said. He leaned over. "One more back. There." He touched the page under a photo. "Is this . . . ?"

Salt looked closely. In the foreground were three white men in suits, one of them the man who'd posed for the studio photo with the star affixed to his suit. In this photo the star was barely visible, the photo out of focus where he stood. Also in the photo were two black men in overalls seated in the field to the right of the men standing. The photo appeared to have been taken from where the road was now, facing the slight rise up to where the foundation and frame of a house was under construction, this house. "This house." Salt held the album, looking at the photo, turning the pages, trying to match faces, and then back again. "Is it inference or deduction?" she said, coldly eyeing the men in the photo, imagining their relationship.

Wills took the album from her, closed it, and put it back on the shelf. "You do need to leave this house." He pulled her to standing. "Let's go take the dogs for a walk and figure out a plan to outflank these motherfuckers."

LYING LOW

IF THERE WAS A WAY TO FEEL PALE, AS IF HER BLOOD HAD BEEN drained, that was how Salt felt. At her desk she completed the deactivation e-form and added it to the electronic file for Mary's case. She printed the hard copy and added it to the red-cover murder book— red being the color for this year's cases. Everywhere you looked were fire-engine-red books. She closed the file and rested her hand on its cover.

She and Wills were together now only when they could meet without risking someone from the department finding out. A couple of times he'd caught a ride to her house with Pepper and his boys when they were coming for aikido. They had no way of knowing if their houses were being watched or if they were being followed. Someone in the department, high up, was eager to get her out of the way.

She was frightened, not only about being fired, charged, and found guilty of a crime. It was everything: getting married, being reassigned if she wasn't fired, leaving her home, even worrying whether Wonder would be all right without his sheep. And Mary. What about justice for Mary?

"Let's go." Felton stood beside her desk, fedora in hand, coat slung around his shoulders.

Salt rolled her chair back, silent, the muscles of her throat so tight she couldn't speak. She got her hat and coat and followed Felton through the office and out to the reception area. Rosie beckoned with a long pink fingernail. "This too shall pass," she said in a low voice, covering Salt's hand with hers. Salt turned up her mouth in what she hoped was a grateful smile.

In Felton's unmarked they rode in silence, Salt becoming more and more self-conscious about her anxiety, which made it worse. She wondered if this was what it was like for her father. Staring out the window at the passing night, her vision began to tunnel, until finally in desperation she said, "I've lost my voice."

Felton steered into the empty parking lot of a church and put the car in park. "You know, all these years I've been in Homicide I never had a partner. The reason is because I had what old folks called 'spells.' Not about physical danger." He turned to face her.

Salt nodded.

"I asked you to partner with me, Salt, because if . . . no, *when* my next 'spell' comes, you are the one person I trust to understand."

"Till the spell is broken," she said.

"There's little anyone can say that helps." He put the car in gear. "Now let's go eat."

After their meal Felton drove them to the Narcotics offices. He'd been eager to join Wills and Pepper in finding the source, the person putting on pressure to get Salt out of the way and why. Besides, it was his case, the quarry, that was being muddied. He had been pursuing what he now realized was the perfect smoke screen, gathering the lists of city employees who officially had access to the quarry. And Salt as his now official partner acted as if she were only marking time waiting for her next case.

Formerly an elementary school, the Narcotics building was surrounded by a high fence topped by razor wire. Felton entered the code for the gate and drove through. They parked, walked through the covered walkway, and pressed the buzzer for admittance. Pepper appeared from down the lit hall and came to let them in. "Ain't nobody here but us chickens."

Salt was already in debt to his commander, Mary Shepherd. She'd helped, above the call of duty, when Salt needed it last year. The seasoned lieutenant had fondly recalled a kindness Salt's father had shown her when she was a rookie, and she took helping Salt as an opportunity to return his favor. "LT is on board and covering for me for as long as it takes," Pepper said.

Wills was waiting in one of the former classrooms. When the three of them came in, he took Salt's coat, lightly touching her shoulder with his fingertips, careful not to treat her as if she were fragile but reminding her of his support. They circled some teachers' chairs rounded up from other rooms.

Pepper began, "I was telling Wills, my oldest boy plays basketball with Jarvis McPhee's boy. Jarvis is a family guy, divorced now, but not a playa. His boy is all to him. He and I are not like everyday-of-the-week buddies, but we connect. He's said nice things about appreciating cops, my job."

"Basketball player?" Wills asked.

The rest of them looked at him without saying anything.

"Okay, okay. So I don't know sports." Wills ducked into his shirt collar.

"McPhee has said stuff from time to time—I never followed up—that he didn't like some of the 'action,' was the way he put it, that professional athletes here are offered from time to time in some places."

"You think he could get you an introduction?" Felton asked.

Pepper leaned in. "Right to the source, baby. Right into the playpen."

It was one of those bright winter days with the sun high in a blue-white sky. There was a chill wind, but when it slacked, the sun's warmth felt like a gift. It was just her, Wonder, and the sheep in front of the house, in the half acre that she and Wills, Ann and Pepper, and Mr. Gooden had fenced with posts and lumber, now whitewashed.

Pepper and his boys were on the way, but she had time to put Wonder through his paces. "Away." She gave the command at conversational volume, his hearing keen, sending him wide along the fence. His outrun, circling the little flock, was flawless. "Stand." He froze, staring at the five sheep, now huddling. "Walk up." He slowly put one paw in front of the other, pushing the sheep to her.

Pepper's minivan threw up dust as he turned off the highway to her drive. The boys waved wildly from the back passenger window.

"That'll do," she said to the dog, then knelt to wrap her arms around his shining black fur, warm from the sun. "What will you do without sheep?"

Salt trod the old wide-plank floors, listening to the familiar creaks and groans, mindful that these days might be some of the last, that every day brought her closer to leaving, to letting the house go. She inhaled the unique smells in each corner mixed with the overriding cedar from the shelves in the library.

The boys slammed through the porch and kitchen doors. Pepper, hauling their gear bag, called out, "Hold your horses. Both of you get back out here and go in like you have manners." Wonder danced around the boys, his energy a match for theirs.

"You guys need something to drink?" she asked.

"I'm amped enough. Water's fine. Both of you go outside and run some of that energy off," Pepper said. The boys yelped with joy and once again slammed out of the house.

"Here you go." Salt handed him a glass and they stood watching the boys, now at her tree, climbing the wood rungs nailed up the trunk. Wonder barked below as they climbed out of reach.

"How's Ann?" she asked.

"Better now that I'm not on twelve-hour shifts. I also cut back on the extra job hours."

"That's good."

"The boys will just have to make do with more of me and less electronics." He unzipped the gear bag and shook out the black hakama and the boys' white gis.

She went to the bedroom, changed, then went up the stairs to the dojo and sat seiza waiting for Pepper and the boys. The boys' shouts and laughter surrounded the house and filtered through the walls. She could feel the bark of the tree, the smell that surrounded the limb where she'd been sitting when she was a ten-year-old and heard the shot that killed her father. She sat on the mat, underneath which she imagined were still the faint stains of her father's blood. As she turned from lighting the candle on the altar, Pepper and the boys bowed in.

Theirs was mostly a silent practice. Pepper led by demonstrating what they should do and began their warm-up with rolls and falls; the only sounds were from their exertions and the swishing of Pepper's thick hakama.

The sun's rays pitched deep into the room, lighting the bamboo wall opposite the windows halfway up. They practiced in pairs, mostly the boys as a pair and she and Pepper as another. Today Pepper was struggling to counter her, Salt making up in speed and ferocity what she lacked in skill and technique. He wore an expression of joy, eyes matching the curve of his smile, each time she showed her mastery. He let the practice go on longer than usual. An hour and a half later their faces dripped sweat as they ended their session sitting seiza. Salt's face in the mirrored wall had gone from pale to bright pink. The scar along the side of Pepper's face stood out in contrast to his dark, now slick skin. They each bowed to one another, then to the sensei's picture on the altar shelf.

The boys tumbled down the stairs, throwing belts and gi jackets as they went, Salt and Pepper picking up behind them. "That was a good practice," Pepper said as they watched the boys run outside. He straightened his hakama. "I think it's time you found an advanced practice. You're ready to learn from another sensei."

PARTNERS

HAND-LETTERED IN BLUE MARKER ON PINK POSTER BOARD, THE sign read AME CHURCH ANNUAL YARD SALE. Salt turned the Taurus on to the small street and stopped at the old stone church. The cold month had continued sunny, allowing the church folks to set up tables in the parking lot. People milled, neighborhood hangers-about, church members, mostly older women, and Saturday-morning kids. She spotted Sister Connelly at the linens table and parked along the ditch that paralleled the asphalt street. Greeting a few people as she got out, she made her way to Sister.

"Remember Wednesday nights when you'd come by here in your patrol car?" Sister said without any preliminary greeting.

"In the summer the church windows would be open and I could listen to you and the choir practice."

"Always knew you were up to no good." Sister grinned while fingering a crocheted tablecloth.

Each window of the church depicted one of Jesus' disciples. In one, St. Peter wore a cardboard patch. Alongside Peter were the windows of John, the beloved disciple, hands over his heart, and Judas, leading lambs to slaughter. Salt pictured the other windows around the building, Simon, Matthew, and James. This had been Salt's place, where she'd come to finish paperwork or to meet up with Pepper— those days of fearlessness.

"So, what's got you?" The old woman asked. "That old man said you was going to leave your house."

"You and Mr. Gooden seem to have struck up a friendship." Several times Salt had seen her neighbor and Sister out in back of his house, in the garden or with his chickens or cows.

"He gives me manure for my garden." Sister looked down at the embroidered pillowcase edge between her thumb and finger. "We went in his woods and found some mushrooms I'd told him to look for."

"You don't have to explain."

"Ain't." Sister walked off to a table of lamps and glassware.

Following, Salt said, "I'm going to marry Wills."

Sister picked up a fluted pink bud vase and turned it over to look at the bottom. "You need to get out that haunting anyway."

The weight on Salt's chest let up some. "It's been my home."

"No, it ain't." Sister put the vase down and turned to face her. Age had taken a few of the tall woman's inches, so that now she was just a few inches above eye to eye with Salt.

In preparation for the unit's move, Felton had cleared his desk and cubicle of everything: files, personal items, a rainbow flag, and the photo he'd thrown in the trash. The surfaces and fabric walls were all a monochromatic gray, which made the only object on his desk stand out dramatically: Glory's red murder book. He'd kept it updated with the log sheets and lists of people who'd had access to the quarry; all of the documentation was to show anyone, especially Huff, that he was getting nowhere. The "King of Clearance" finally had a whodunit he didn't seem able to crack.

Salt sat in the vacant cubicle across from him. "This is ruining your reputation. You partner with me and immediately your clearance rate takes a dive."

He flipped the top page of one of the lists. "I'm enjoying the misdirection." He unfastened the bottom button of the black vest he always wore and leaned over the file. "Any time I can bring bullies to justice, it's a win. Imagine how it was—a gay kid named Manfred Felton."

A FINE BALANCE

"SHE GIVE ME THEM SHOES," LIL D SAID.

JoJo, worry all over her face, was on the beige-carpeted floor scooting one of Danny T's trucks alongside the boy. "I don't know, D."

"She ain't like just any cop." He stood at the door ready to go out to catch the bus. "I know La like you here helpin' with Danny T an' all." He nodded at his son, who had picked up one of the books Man had given him and was turning the pages for himself. "Man my homes. I ain't gone lie to him." Man had ways of finding out everything anyway. He didn't know what Man would think, or do, when he found out JoJo had been staying with them. He didn't know or want to know why JoJo was so scared, or who was scaring her. Maybe she didn't even know. Maybe it was cops. "Salt always been straight. She even owe me." Last year he came across Salt about to get shot. 'Course, he might owe *her*. He started thinking about his dad, Big D. "I'm gone." He bent over, bumped fists with his son, kissed him with a loud smack, and was out of the apartment.

Wonder, snout on his paws, lay stretched out a few yards from where Salt was shoveling dirt from the spot she and Wills had chosen for the cedar tree. Wills was inside making a late breakfast. The dog's eyes went back and forth between what she was doing and the goings-on of the sidewalk and street below Wills' house. She rested her foot on the shovel. "Think you could be happy here without your sheep?" she asked the dog.

"What will the neighbors think?" Wills came out on the porch. "My girl does the yard work and talks to the animals."

"Come on." She motioned to him. "Let's do this." Wills came down the steps and over to her. "Hole look about right?"

"Looks like a hole to me." He separated the little cedar from its container and stood holding it aloft. Clearing his throat, he said, "One of us has to be the sentimentalist. So, Sarah Diana Alt, with this tree I thee wed." He plunked the root ball into the hole.

Salt hefted a shovelful of earth. "And we shall be like a tree planted by the rivers of water, that brings forth fruit in our season; our leaves will not wither." She dumped the dirt over the roots. "And whatsoever we do," she said, adding more dirt, "will prosper."

Wills put his hand on hers and they threw the next shovelful together. "What was that you were quoting?"

Wonder came over and began furiously digging in the freshly turned ground.

"Psalms. I guess you can take the girl out the church, but you can't take the church out the girl."

"Meal's ready." He put his arm around her shoulders. "It's good to have you back," he said, acknowledging her return to verbalization.

"It is good to have myself back," she said as they walked up the steps. "Now that we have a plan of action, I don't feel so trapped."

As they entered the kitchen, Wills said, "Or as Popeye says, 'I've had all I can stands and I can't stands no more.'" He went over and uncovered a skillet and gave her a one-eyed glare.

"Is that a spinach omelet?"

Although he would never say it, Lil D hated Magic Girls. He wanted it to make him feel like he was big-time, but it did just the opposite. He wasn't about to throw cash at the strippers like the big-money guys did. Most of the time he just stood against the wall—too short to see over the shoulders of all the men in the packed room. He decided to wait out in the parking lot in Man's SUV.

They'd parked next to Flash Daddy's Bentley. Lil D sat there a while, eyes adjusting to the dim light of the parking lot. He looked over at the tinted windows of the Bentley. There inside in the backseat was a white girl's face. She dropped her head to her chest and her long, straight, dark hair fell like curtains over her face and hid her whiteness in the dark of the car. He went over and tapped on the window beside her. Slowly she raised her head and blinked as if she were trying to focus. She fumbled at the door and window, but wasn't able to get either the window down or the door unlocked. He tried the doors and found them all locked. Shielding his eyes with his hand so he could cut through the glare, he peered closer in the window. She had tattoos on her really white arms and, even sleepy looking, she was pretty. He opened the door of Man's ride and sat down with the door open so the girl could see him. He raised his hand palm up and lifted his chin to her, trying to let her know he was cool, that he was there and would be looking out for her.

.   .   .

Across the street from Magic Girls in a vacant four-story building, Salt and Felton watched from either side of one of the large wood-frame windows of a dark room on the top floor. The man-size neon letters of the Magic Girls marquee threw pink and gold rectangles on the wood floor. The marquee also illuminated the sky above for miles. Below, a single light lit the entrance of the club. As men came and went through the double doors, a pink glow escaped from within, along with the sound of heavy bass beats.

"Your kid there, Lil D? Doesn't seem to have much of a taste for the club." Felton lowered the binoculars.

"I wish we could see what's all that interesting to him inside Flash Daddy's car."

"Maybe I should go take a look."

"Hold on." Salt fished for her phone vibrating in her coat pocket.

"This is Maya," the woman's voice said.

"Maya," Salt repeated, taking a second before it registered that she was speaking to Flash Daddy Jones' housekeeper.

"He's losing control," the woman said.

"Flash?"

"He's got people looking for one girl called JoJo. And he's got some drugged, really young white girl he's carrying around with him."

"Why are you telling me this?"

"Because he's coming undone. And I don't want to be anywhere near him when he goes down. I'm taking the children and going to California, as far away as I can get."

"Children," Salt repeated.

"I don't want my children to know or hear anything about or from their father."

"How can I reach you?" Salt asked.

"Saundra and Otis Wilson, Mill Valley. My parents, I'll tell them you are the only one to trust with my whereabouts."

Below, the doors of the club opened. Two men, not Flash or Man, came tumbling out laughing. Salt took a breath. "I hope things go well. I didn't see you as his wife."

"Thank you," Maya said, and the phone went off.

"There's a girl in Flash's car," Salt said, already headed for the stairwell.

"Wait," Felton said, following on her heels. "If they think you're involved, they're sure to release the video and charge you."

"I'm not going to sit up here while you go down there alone," she told him.

"Call Wills and Pepper," Felton said, heading for the hallway.

Wills answered on the first ring.

"Are you with Pepper?" she asked, moving back to the window, breathless as if she were with Felton. "How quick can you get to Magic Girls?" Felton's footsteps echoed from the far end of the hall. The doors to the club opened again, discharging several men. "Flash has a young girl, in his car."

"On the way." Wills hung up.

Felton crossed the street below into the poorly lit parking lot. Salt shifted her weight back and forth as if readying for a sprint, torn between watching and going after him. The men who'd just come out left, their car kicking up a cloud of dust that rolled over the Bentley. In those moments the doors of the club once again opened and Flash Daddy and Man came out. Salt ran for the exit. The stairwell door banged against the brick wall, the sound reverberating as she flew down the four flights and out the side door of the building. She rounded the corner just as Felton, Man, and Flash, followed by two burly associates, converged near the Bentley. The two muscle men moved in on Felton before he came within conversation distance of Flash.

Salt reached Felton's side just as Man stepped forward. "Oh, it's the fairy detective," he said, stopping in front of Felton.

Flash glowered at Salt from under his brows, eyes narrowed, mouth set tight. One of his guys bumped his chest into Felton. Salt made the briefest eye contact with Lil D as he came out of the open door of Man's SUV parked on the other side of the Bentley. In that second he widened his eyes and cut them to the interior of Flash Daddy's car. Salt moved forward as if to pass the guy threatening Felton. As she hoped, he turned from Felton and grabbed her by the upper arm with both his meaty hands. She sissy-slapped him with her left hand, moved forward, pulling him off balance, circled his wrist with her right hand and, gaining leverage, brought him to his knees just as Pepper and Wills' Taurus collided with the gravel of the parking lot. They moved from the car amid the rising dust, fedoras at jaunty angles. Salt stepped around the kneeling goon to the other side of the Bentley, next to Lil D at the door of Man's SUV.

The tinting on the windows of the Bentley was dark, and the glare off the overhead marquee made it doubly hard to see inside. But just barely Salt made out the shape of a female slumped in the backseat: dark hair obscured her face; white hands, almost disembodied, ghostlike in the dark interior, confirmed her corporeality. Salt rapped lightly on the window.

Flash came up beside her, his face set to hard. "You got no right, no warrant, nothing."

Salt withdrew the asp baton from her back, swung it high, and brought it down, shattering the front passenger window, safety glass spraying and falling in and out of the Bentley. Flash averted his face, covering it with his hands. She reached in, unlocked the back door, leaned in, and lifted the young girl out.

"You gone pay for this, bitch," Flash said.

Flash Daddy's story, backed by Stokes, was that the girl, a minor, had tried to come into the club, and because they could see she was high, they refused her but she wouldn't leave. So they put her in the car until she could sober up and tell them where she lived.

Fellows called from the hospital. The girl and her mother wouldn't say anything about Flash or Stokes or the club.

They had no basis for charging Flash. He was released.

It was actually easier than waiting for it—almost a relief—although seeing herself handing Lil D the shoes, on loop, over and over on TV in the bright lights of the Homicide break room, with everyone coming and going, stopping, watching for a minute, standing by her chair, was bad. Salt saw herself kneeling over Stone, shoebox in her hands, handing the box up and into his hands. Even she couldn't tell whether she was just getting them out of her way or whether her intent had been to give them to Lil D.

Huff put his hand on her shoulder. She looked up. He nodded. She got up and followed him to his office. "City of Atlanta police detective caught on video surveillance . . . looting . . ." The voiceover followed her as she went to be officially suspended and charged for abetting the crime of theft, for giving the looted shoes to Lil D.

Lil D could see himself plainly on the TV and Salt handing him the shoes. While he watched it over and over, he thought back to that second, the news people saying she was suspended and charged with theft. There would be a warrant for his arrest by now. Or would there be? He didn't know how that would work. If she gave him the shoes, which she was being accused of, then how could he be guilty of stealing the shoes? She had put the box in his hands. Salt and Pepper had to tell that she knew him. The down-looking spy camera didn't catch any of their eyes. She did hand him the shoes. Stone, bare-chested and handcuffed, lay in all the glass. He'd been yelling. Salt had offhanded him the shoes so she could get Stone out of the glass that was cutting him. That's what Lil D thought. But then he wasn't sure. There had been less than a second when maybe she realized what she was doing, handing the box that she'd just taken from him back to him. The camera got him holding the box and running out of view. TV was making a big thing of it like she or he was stealing the shoes. They were saying she was going to be fired because cops can't testify if they ever had done any dishonest thing.

Danny T grabbed the remote out of his hands and punched the off button. Lil D grabbed him and nuzzled his neck, blowing raspberries. "You a smart guy! Ain't you?" His son laughed and laughed, kicking his feet, pulling at Lil D's head. "I'm gone give you a big spot like mine," he teased, pointing to the birthmark on his own neck. "Come here." He lunged for the boy, but instead of trying to get away, Danny grabbed Lil D and tucked his little fat neck up against Lil D's mark.

"You two stop now." Latonya came around the counter from the kitchen. The shoes weren't there on the counter anymore. He didn't ask. Ever since it came on TV, she'd been acting like a zombie or something, her eyes not ever looking into his. She didn't laugh or get mad—nothing, Danny watching her close.

"Supper's ready. JoJo!" Latonya yelled toward the bedrooms.

JoJo came out of Danny's room, where she was staying most of the time, got her plate, and went back. La and Danny sat down in one of the bag chairs, sharing a plate, and Lil D sat in the other. He left the TV off.

"Man gone front you bail?" La asked, not looking at him, just looking at Danny, giving him little bites.

"I don't see why they gone arrest me. She give me them shoes."

Latonya cut her eyes at him, hard. He flung his fork on his plate, stood, and went in the kitchen.

"Eat some a them greens," La said to Danny like she was mad at the kid.

"You don't got to be like that," Lil D shouted. "It ain't his fault."

JoJo came out, her plate hardly touched. "Why, D? Why did she give you the shoes? That ain't no cop thing to do. You told me she straight, that I should trust her. Why she gone give you them looted shoes?" JoJo came into the kitchen and scraped her leftovers back in the pots. "You gone answer?" she asked, not mad or judging.

"I don't know why. She know me. I got her out of a couple of bad things. She try to help me with my daddy before he died. I ain't gone say no more 'bout this shit." He slammed his plate beside the stove and went to the back bedroom.

JoJo in her bare feet and big T-shirt came and stood in the doorway again. "She off the poleese?" she asked him.

"I guess." He kept his back to her.

"How I'm gone call her then, she off the poleese?"

"You ready to do that?" He turned to face her.

JoJo shrugged, a corner of her mouth pulled tight. "I got to, Lil D. Ain't no other way."

She had been staying at Wills' house since a news truck had shown up in front of her house. Felton and Pepper stopped by from time to time. Wills was home just barely long enough to sleep because he was working his cases and helping Felton and Pep. She had time. She'd set her phone to go directly to messages and was just getting around to scrolling through them, notepad and pen beside her coffee at Wills' kitchen table. One was from her brother; he'd seen a news story on the Internet. There were some messages of support, one from recovering Big Fuzz, whom she called back. She came to an unidentified number and listened to the message.

"I'm shamed is part a why I ain't tell what happen. I ran away from my mama thinkin' I was all that." JoJo eyed the Rotties and Wonder, each lying at an entrance to Wills' kitchen. "You sure them dogs not gonna come after me?" A plastic garbage bag, her only luggage, spread itself on the floor beside her. She looked very different from the way she'd looked at the club. Not a spot of makeup, her hair in a ponytail, like before, but without the glitter or sequins. She was wearing a "Thug Life" oversized T-shirt, gray sweatpants, and pink sneakers.

"Do you want something to eat? I'm not much of a cook, but I can make a mean sandwich. How 'bout it? Something to drink? Tea? Coffee? Cola?"

"I hate to put you to trouble."

"Really, what sounds good?"

"I like peanut butter."

"Aha!" Salt said when she opened the refrigerator and saw the jar of no-sugar-added organic peanut butter. "Peanut butter." She held the jar aloft to show JoJo. "Jelly?"

The girl nodded, then watched as Salt got out the whole-grain loaf and bread knife and sliced through the dark bread. Salt had to stir the peanut butter. "I can put it on," said JoJo, reaching for the cutting board and bread. "I like milk, too. But you don't got to make it or nothin', do you?"

Salt smiled to herself and took the organic hormone-free milk in its returnable bottle from the fridge. "Wills is kind of particular when it comes to food." She poured the milk and sat down across the table with a cup of coffee.

"Latonya and Lil D good to let me stay with them. I tried not to eat so much since I ain't bringing any money 'cause I too scared to work." The whole-grain slices crumbled as the girl slathered on the peanut butter. "This ain't no regular kind of bread," she said. Eventually she got the slices together and took a bite, closing her eyes as she chewed. Mouth still full, she said, "This good, though."

"How old are you really, JoJo?"

"I lied to get my permit for the clubs." As she drank, she looked at Salt over the rim of her glass of milk.

"No one is going to charge you for faking your age."

"I'm fifteen."

"Why were you hiding? All I'm trying to do is find out who-ever killed Mary. Do you know anything about who would want her dead?"

"I ain't seen Glory since not too long after you came around to the club. Man come tell us Flash Daddy got some party he want us to work, like we used to." JoJo put her sandwich down. "I don't truss Flash. He think me and Glory gone snitch to you 'cause you lookin' for Mary. He know you was at the club."

"I'm sorry I have to bring all this up to you," Salt said.

Pansy got up from the floor, her droopy eyelids and heavy jowls expressing concern about the sadness she heard in Salt's voice. She put her big head in Salt's lap.

"Why that dog sad?"

"She hears how my voice sounds. She's a pack animal, so anything that worries me she worries about." Salt rubbed the furrows of Pansy's brow.

"How come them other two ain't worried?"

"Look at their eyes. See how they're watching? JoJo, I'm so sorry. We found Glory. She's dead. Somebody shot her and dumped her body in the quarry on the west side."

JoJo held the sandwich, focused on it, and put it in her mouth. She took another bite, then another until it was gone, then washed it down with gulp after gulp of milk until the glass was empty.

Salt waited, rubbing and rubbing at the wrinkles above Pansy's eyes. She looked up at the girl. "You want more?"

JoJo shrugged. Shoulders slumped, she looked around at Wills' in-progress renovations, the lath-and-plaster walls, partially stripped trim and doors propped against a wall. "How come you ain't have no nice place to live? Poleese make good money."

"My . . . Wills likes to fix up things. The way houses were built a long time ago, they used really good wood, built things sturdy, to last. So he tears things down to get back to the good stuff."

"It don't look good."

"It will someday."

"I can't ever think about someday. I jess always have to think about today." She put her head down on her crossed arms on top of the table.

"I'll be right back, JoJo," Salt said. "I'm going to go make some calls. Get you a safe place to stay." Salt called the dogs as she went out to the front porch.

Sergeant Fellows answered. "You get my message?"

"I appreciate your support."

"Command ordered us not to interfere with the looting. The way I saw that scene is you were freeing your hands to deal with the perp on the pavement. People have no idea what it's like, situations like that."

"Thanks, Sarge. But the reason I'm calling is I need a safe place for a victim/witness, a fifteen-year-old girl who I suspect has been sexually exploited."

"Call you right back." Fellows hung up.

The dogs on Salt's heels followed her back in. From the hall Salt saw JoJo standing close to the kitchen wall, touching the plaster and lath with her fingertips. "There's something looks like hair in this stuff between the wood pieces."

"You'd make a good detective, noticing details like that. You're right. Back in those days they mixed hog hair or cow hair in with the plaster to make it stronger, make it hold together better."

"Really?" JoJo kept going over the wall, looking closely.

Salt put the dishes in the sink.

"Can I touch that littler dog, the all-black one?" asked JoJo.

"Sure. Sit back down. His name is Wonder. I found him over in The Bluff." Salt called to her dog, "Heel." Then she led him in front of JoJo sitting in the kitchen chair, sideways to the table. The dog looked up, anticipating a command. "That'll do," she said, releasing the dog to do what he wanted. "Just sit there. No need to do anything," she said to the girl.

Wonder relaxed, circled Salt, then wagging his tail came up to JoJo.

"Okay. Bring your hand up, palm side down. Let him sniff the top of your hand."

Wonder sniffed, then moved closer, going between JoJo's knees to her lap.

"He wants you to scratch under his chin," Salt said.

JoJo turned her fingers up, hovering beneath Wonder's mouth. "He won't bite me?"

The dog's whole back end was wagging.

"He wants a scratch."

JoJo tickled him, barely touching his fur. He turned his chin up, giving her access.

"Harder," Salt told her.

Smiling now, JoJo continued rubbing Wonder until he laid his chin on her knee. "He's so shiny." She smoothed her hand all down the back of his head to his flanks. "He don't smell like other dogs." She flung a little fur from her fingers. "Flash Daddy"—she patted and petted—"he had these parties, for guys who like—he call us 'fresh girls.'" Wonder turned around so JoJo could scratch his back, right above his tail. "Me and Mary—he broke me in before he did her."

Salt held her breath. She was scared she'd make a false move or say something wrong or judgmental.

"You think I can come visit this dog again?"

"Sure." Salt slowly exhaled. "You can come back. I hope you do."

ACCOUNTING

THE ATTIC WAS EVEN COLDER THAN THE REST OF THE HOUSE; wind mewled in the rafters. Salt tugged on the light pull chain, made her way to the trunk, hung the lantern, and opened the lid. She filled the bag with the letters, carried it over to the attic opening, then went back to the trunk. After lifting the tray out, she removed the silverware box and the remaining ledgers and photos, put the tray back, and closed the lid. She went back and forth taking the trunk contents to the ladder and then brought them down to the hall.

She'd warmed the house a little but still wore her jacket as she cleared the dishes and sat down at the table piled high with the dusty trunk contents. She took a first sip of coffee, considered where to begin, and finally picked up the smallest ledger that lay atop the rest. Leather-bound, it had an embossed "Ledger" in fading gold script. With fountain-pen-cursive flourishes, the inside cover page was inscribed "Marion Henry Alt, Cloud, Georgia, Feb. 24, 1861." Each subsequent page had the month and year on top of the page. Down the sides of the pages were the days of entry, "Oct. 1, harness repair," and the amount of money spent or taken in, "$.75," "Six pecan bushels, $1.40." Salt turned the pages, not so much yellowed but tanned with age, ink turned brown. "Dec. 23, female negra Mary, $300." Salt shut the ledger, dropped it on the floor beside her, and sat there. *"$300, Mary."* She pulled the photo album she'd previously gone through from the stack, opened it, and turned the pages until she came to the photo.

When Wonder didn't bark at the knock, she knew it had to be Mr. Gooden. "Saw your light on. Thought you might could use a piece of pie." He stood in the doorway holding a paper plate covered in plastic wrap.

"I see two pieces on that plate. I hope you're planning on eating it with me. Coffee?" she asked. "You're becoming the master at pecan pie."

"Don't mind if I do, even if it is late. This is cause for a little celebration. I've missed seeing the lights, and you and this cur." He patted Wonder's back, right above the dog's tail, causing Wonder to back up to him for more.

"What's all this?" he asked, setting the pie on the counter and nodding at the piles from the attic.

She began clearing the table and putting the trunk contents on the counter beside the laundry room. "Cleaning out the attic. Trying to make good use of my time," she said.

Mr. Gooden came over and put his hand on her shoulder. "I wish there was something I could say to make you feel better. And while it is true that time heals and that one day you'll look back on this as just a bump in the road, still it's little comfort right now. Sarah, those of us who know you, well, let me speak personally—I'm very proud of you." He patted her back.

Bowing her head, she covered his hand with hers.

Mr. Gooden cleared his throat. "So, what have you got here?" He looked down at the album still open on the table. "These people look familiar." He touched his finger to a figure in one of the group photos. "This boy might be your grandfather. He's in some old pictures we, I, have." He peered closely at the picture.

"Do you know anyone in this one?" She turned the page back to an older photo, one with the girl.

"Looks to be taken of the property before this house was built, maybe right after the Civil War." He leaned over the album for a closer look. "They look like your kin, but I couldn't tell you who's who." He straightened and pulled out a chair. "Let's have that pie," he said and sat down. "Not many folks your age are that interested in old family histories and pictures. What got you curious?"

Salt put the water on again. "It's a long story, but the short version is that I was going through the albums and found this photo." She nodded at the page. "The girl in that looked familiar to me, at least her features do."

Mr. Gooden turned several pages of the album.

Salt went in her jacket pocket and brought out one of the copies of the picture of the trio of girls. She pointed to Mary. "Now turn back." She reached and turned the page herself. Holding the flyer next to the album, she pointed to the woman and then to Mary.

Mr. Gooden leaned close again. "I can't . . ." He pulled back. "Maybe one of your criminal scientists could tell, but all I can say is that those two, the girl and the woman, look alike. This photo"—he tapped the album—"is old. And they're different ages."

"Here's the thing." Salt picked up the ledger off the counter. "Just now, going through this." She held the book. "I found an entry for the purchase of a slave named Mary. This woman"—she touched the photo again—"would have been about the right age. This girl"—Salt picked up the flyer—"her name is Mary. I'm trying to find out how she died and who killed her."

"I don't understand," said Mr. Gooden. "What's the connection? What do they have to do with each other?"

"The woman, her braids, her nose, mouth," Salt said. "And this girl"—she pointed to Mary—"her grandmother's name is McCloud. Sister Connelly told me that the McClouds came to Atlanta from around here, and I know that some slaves when they were freed took the name of where they came from, the town or plantation."

"Cloud," said Mr. Gooden, repeating the name of the town whose address they shared. "What does it matter?"

"Maybe nothing." Salt put their pie and coffee on the table. "Or maybe it matters a lot."

"I'm old," said Mr. Gooden. "My generation didn't talk about this kind of thing, not in so many words. We've got all kinds of debts."

"Sister quoted the Bible, said that God loves his children, but that they still have to deal with the 'sins of their fathers to the third and fourth generation.'"

They finished the pie and coffee, and as they were putting things away, Mr. Gooden asked, "You ever think you take things too serious, too literally?"

"I'll give it some thought," she said, turning out the lights and locking the door.

IN THE PAN

TWO OF FLASH'S POSSE OPENED THE DOORS TO FLASH'S HOUSE and led them down some stairs. As much as Lil D hated the Magic Girls Club, he instantly hated this more. It smelled bad, a stale odor of cigarettes and spilled beer coming from hard gray carpeting. The walls were gray, lit from above by purple wall lights. Three steps down a level from the bar along the far wall there was a half circle of dark gray sofas surrounding a long coffee table. The room, with its own stripper pole, was almost as big as the main room of the Toy Dolls Club, but it was empty except for Flash smoking his nasty cigar, a glass of something blue on ice at his elbow. Stokes played bartender. Flash and Man gave dap.

Lil D wandered, stepping down to the sofas away from Flash and his cigar. He didn't know why he and Man were here. Flash said something, "Salt . . . ," as Lil D sat down out of earshot of their conversation.

Stokes got Man a beer, then came out and down to Lil D. "You want something? Bar's open."

"Naw, I'm good," Lil D told him. Lil D was the only one in the room in street clothes, a pair of jeans and the old Homes-smelling jacket. Man and Flash were wearing suits, jackets and matching pants. Stokes wore a black T-shirt tucked in black suit pants.

On the low table, which looked like it was made of some kind of fake wood, in front of the sofas were big ring binders arranged by colors, real pale white, regular white, light pink, pink, all the way to a red so dark it was almost black. Lil D got antsy and stood back up, then went up the steps to the bar.

"She got mojo," Man was saying to Flash. "You ain't gonna keep her down. 'Sides she ain't your real problem anyway." Man lit and puffed on his own cigar. "Your girls done broke rank."

"Ain't but one," Stokes said.

"Shut up!" Flash glared at his manager.

Lil D caught Man's eye for a second.

Man said, "It was bad luck Detective Salt got Mary's case. She ain't never let go nothin'. I know you told me you ran Mary off just like I did, but then she got herself killed and that picture turned up with her and the other two."

Lil D didn't like the talk of his sister. He went back to the lower level of the room, sat down again, and, for something to do, opened the white binder.

"She ain't supposed to be here," said Huff.

"She's not, Sarge."

"What do you . . . oh." He raised his fingers in air quotes. "Not here. I get it."

Standing in Lieutenant Shepherd's large office, the former class-room, were Salt, who because she was suspended wasn't supposed to be there, Huff, Pepper, Wills, Felton, and Sergeant Fellows, who had a copy of the CD of JoJo's forensic interview.

"Here you go." Fellows handed the CD to Lieutenant Shepherd. "I've seen it once. I'll be taking notes for the warrant." She sat down in one of the chairs arranged in a circle around the computer monitor on Shepherd's desk.

"How is it that the Narcotics Unit is involved in a sex trafficking case and a homicide case?" Huff asked. "Not that I give a shit, but for the record."

"Let me worry about that, Sergeant," said Shepherd. "PD's all one team, right? We'll call it a task force. Homicide is here because of the girls being murdered. Obviously, SVU is involved because of the age of some of the victims. And Narcotics has the surveillance equipment and allegations that drug money is being laundered out of Magic Girls. Of course the real reason is—off the record—they've pissed me the hell off fucking with Salt."

"Right," they all, except Huff, answered in unison. He gave them a skeptical mouth-turned-down glare.

The CD slid in, the monitor lit up, and without any preliminaries there was JoJo on the screen and a woman at a table across from her. The lieutenant turned the sound up. ". . . and I'm Sally Sims. Today is February nineteenth . . ." Ms. Sims began, and explained to JoJo she was with the Georgia Center for Child Advocacy. Her tone was mild, neutral, but kind and matter-of-fact as she established JoJo's particulars: age, date of birth, competency, as well as JoJo's under-standing of the truth versus a lie. Then, "I've been told that recently some things have happened to you."

Rather than the "Thug Life" T-shirt she'd worn when Salt last saw her, JoJo was wearing a pastel green V-neck T-shirt that was tight across her breasts. JoJo kept looking down at her cleavage and tugging the V up. Salt saw how a jury might see her: full-breasted, a history as a runaway, stripping. JoJo kept her head down.

Felton, Wills, Pepper, and Huff shifted uncomfortably in their chairs.

Holding the end of her ponytail, JoJo said in a barely audible voice, "You mean the reason I been hidin'?"

"Tell me what happened," Ms. Sims said.

The short history of JoJo's life, while terribly familiar, was torture to listen to in specific. The details were heartbreaking. Repeatedly molested by an uncle and a "play" brother, she'd been a poor student. Her mother's home was chaotic: too many kids, too many of her mother's boyfriends. JoJo had run away several times before being taken up by a young drug dealer and brought to William Stokes, whom she knew as "Money," the manager at Magic Girls. "I already weren't no little girl," she told Sims.

"I was told there were other girls," Sims prompted.

"Yeah, at first we was just like roommates. Me and Glory, then later Mary. And it was all good. They give us new clothes, regular jeans, and kicks and stuff like kids wear—all the good stuff."

"What do you remember most clearly?"

"I just black out the first stuff," JoJo said, looking away from Sims and off to the side. "It weren't so bad like with Flash Daddy, him being famous an' all. I thought, I thought I was maybe—maybe I was special."

The detectives, Felton, Wills, and Pepper, didn't seem to be breathing. Salt lowered her head, praying that she could somehow avoid having to hear what was coming.

Sims was tough. She said, "Tell me about that."

"He did it in my bootie and then my mouth and he had Mary there so she know what to do."

Pepper stood up. "Can you turn that off, LT? I need a break." He walked out of the office-classroom. They could hear him going down the hall, hitting the lockers as he went.

"I don't know how you do this day after day," Lieutenant Shepherd said to Sergeant Fellows, who'd remained bent over her notepad. When she looked up, there were tears streaming down her cheeks.

By the end of the hour-long interview JoJo had given descriptions of herself, Glory, and Mary having been coerced to perform at private parties where they were sexually assaulted by multiple men while other men watched. It was excruciating to hear. "I was told that you were afraid and that was why you were hiding," Sims added, coming to the end of the hour.

"Mary run away and she got kilt anyway. Now Glory dead, too."

"I was told you may know something about that."

Salt could not imagine the strength it must take for Sims to remain as calm as she appeared.

"I don't know for sure." JoJo chewed the end of her braid. "I think Mary weren't killed by Flash Daddy's people 'cause she run away from him. But when Detective Salt come 'round with that picture, with me and Glory and Mary—Flash don't want us talkin' 'bout what we do workin' for him. That's what started him off."

PLAN OF ACTION

"THERE'S NO WAY WE CAN MAKE THIS CASE SOLELY ON HER TES-
timony. Not only would we not be able to get a conviction, it would be
cruel to put her through a trial with that much pressure." Sergeant
Fellows leaned back, tapping her pen on the notes she'd been taking.

"So, what's the next step?" Huff was all in now after watching Jo-
Jo's interview.

"Go for the low-hanging fruit," Pepper said. "Stokes."

"That worm will definitely turn," Salt said. "He cut a deal on his
previous arrest. He's a violent motherfucker, though, but once he's
had, he'll roll. It's taking him down that will be hairy."

Felton had a friend. So did Rosie. They divvied up Sergeant Fellows
between the two of them. There had to be some fun to being a super-
hero. Salt got to play sidekick watching the "average" Fellows turned

into a celebrity-whore Cinderella. Her resulting appearance turned out to be not so average; instead, Fellows was a perfect canvas for the nightlife glitter. Sean, Rosie's friend, had picked out a red dress that somehow curved under the sergeant's butt, which was revealed also to be a not-so-average derriere and, in fact, was an astounding asset. "Who knew?" said Rosie as she escorted Fellows hobbling into the Narcotics office on strappy heels. "Practice, honey," Rosie said, patting Fellows' hand as they walked. Fellows seemed more concerned about the shoes than the scene she'd be walking into. "I worked Vice details" was her answer to the expressed concerns of the rest of the team. Her lipstick, thick and shiny, was the same red as the dress. But what made her almost completely unrecognizable was that her shoulder-length brown hair had been dyed cobalt black with streaks of crimson, piled and lacquered to her head like a sculpture, adding even more height to the extra five inches from the heels.

Lieutenant Shepherd wolf-whistled. Wills and Felton stood up from their chairs. "My God!" exclaimed Wills.

"Hold your horses, big boy," Salt warned.

"Yeah, well, I just wish these shoes had some kind of quick-release mechanism." Fellows looked down at her precarious ankles.

"I'd feel naked not being armed," said Shepherd.

"Oh, I'm carryin'," Fellows said, reaching under the dress to the top of a lacy garter on her inside left thigh and drawing out a five-shot pistol.

"Show your badge, Sarge," Salt said.

Fellows folded back the low-cut V-neck of the red dress to reveal her brass badge pinned to the underside. "I'm ready except for the damn shoes. Where's my date? I love McPhee. I'm a huge fan. Imagine, me on an actual date with Jarvis McPhee!" She grinned and tapped her feet in a kind of dance.

"Speak of the devil," Pepper said, coming in the classroom door followed by McPhee ducking under the door frame. "Jeez," McPhee said, looking around the room, scanning the detectives.

Struck starry-eyed, Fellows wobbled toward McPhee, who reached for her arm just as she began to topple. "Whoa," he said, catching her elbow.

"Rebound!" said Pepper.

McPhee was handsome. Six foot nine inches of caramel slim. One could sense the muscularity under the dark suit fitted to perfection. "I sure hope you're my date," he said as he righted the sergeant. "Jarvis McPhee." He extended his considerable hand to Fellows, his voice warm and genuine.

"Laurel," Fellows replied, holding his hand and staring up at his face.

"Hands off the talent," Pepper said, inserting himself between them, removing Fellows' hand from McPhee's. "You two, this is not some romantic TV or movie shit escapade. Where's the bug?"

"Got it," Felton said. "The intelligence guys tested it and said it's ready. Sit." He pointed Fellows to a chair, where he began fastening the tiny device under a wave of hair.

McPhee turned to acknowledge the rest of the team as they were introduced but kept cutting his eyes back to Fellows. "I thought women police were only good-looking on TV," he said, shaking hands with Salt. "Golly, this is an honor. I admire what you do. It's a privilege for me to be able to help you guys."

"Have a seat," said Lieutenant Shepherd, getting up from the desk and waving McPhee to a table the right height for him to lean against. "There will be no heroes tonight. This is intelligence gathering only." Shepherd's dark features were stern.

"Jarvis has met Stokes before, LT," said Pepper.

"I don't really go to the clubs that much," McPhee said, looking at

Fellows again. "But right after my divorce two years ago I went to Magic Girls with some of the guys. It wasn't my thing and I stopped going after a couple of times."

"What was it that you didn't like?" Fellows asked, coming out of her trance.

"Well, for one thing, the manager there—Stokes? He was a creep. Kept asking me how I liked my pussy. Excuse my language. Then he would ask how old I liked it. One night one of my pals got really drunk and went to one of the VIP rooms, where he said he saw some really young-looking girls. Even as drunk as he was, he got the hell out of there."

"You think Stokes will give you the VIP treatment, even with a chick at your side?" Pepper asked the question on everyone's mind.

"I've seen men with their dates going everywhere in Magic Girls, including up to the VIP rooms," McPhee said.

"Okay, folks, I'm satisfied," said Shepherd. "Lock and load. Let's do this."

It was midnight when Pepper stopped the surveillance van in a dark service alley between two old businesses a block from Magic Girls. McPhee drove with Fellows in his Jaguar.

Inside the van, Felton swiveled his chair to the bank of monitoring equipment, switched on the recorder, and turned up the volume on the speaker for the wire Fellows was wearing. Most of what they heard were car noises and little conversation. Fellows would be aware of being monitored, plus she had still seemed starstruck and almost speechless when McPhee had opened the Jag's door for her. Once they were en route he asked if she'd done this before.

They heard her answer. "Something like this but not so dressed up. I did Vice details—you know—posing as a street prostitute."

"So what do you do now?" he asked. "What's your regular assignment?"

"I work Special Victims, crimes against children."

He didn't respond.

"That's usually a conversation stopper," she said, voice low, like she might have said it to herself or to her colleagues in the van.

The next sound they heard was the crunch of tires on gravel, signaling McPhee's arrival in the Magic Girls parking lot. With the engine off, they heard McPhee say, "It's probably because people don't know how to respond." The car door opened. "It makes everything else seem frivolous. Hold on to my arm. You don't want to hurt yourself in those shoes."

The next thing they heard was music blasting. Felton grabbed at the control to turn down the volume. Then all they could hear was the occasional word shouted over music.

Lieutenant Shepherd, in the van's driver's seat, and Salt, in the front passenger seat, turned toward the interior of the van, where Pepper, Felton, and Wills sat in mounted captain's chairs in front of counters on either wall. Above them was other equipment—headphones, recorders, and receivers lit by low LED track lights that would be invisible from the outside of the van's dark-tinted, blackout-curtained windows. They concentrated as if watching a movie, only their focus was on the images produced in their mind's eye by the sounds coming from the speaker.

". . . Man . . ." Stokes shouted. "Bitches is . . ."

A woman's voice shouted for drink orders. "G 'n' T," said Fellows. "Vodka," said McPhee. Then for half an hour all they heard was the heavy bass music and glasses clinking.

The cops in the van slumped against their seats, settling in to the familiar boredom of surveillance.

"Party?" It was McPhee's voice.

Stokes' voice was mostly unintelligible: ". . . up . . ." he said, ". . . cool . . ."

"I like girls," said Fellows. From the sound of it she was moving.

A heavy door closed, as if sealing a vacuum, the music becoming only a faint muffled beat.

"Man, this is some VIP setup." McPhee's voice was clear.

"Sit there. Take a look at the pictures in the books on the table. G 'n' T and vodka coming up." Stokes' voice was from across a large room.

After a stretch of small sounds, Fellows said, "This one here. She available?"

"Which one?" Stokes' voice was close. Ice clinked in glasses. "Oh, yeah. Yeah, Jarvis, your girl like some tight puss, huh?"

"Sure," said McPhee, his voice lower, flat.

"What's the matter, man?" Stokes asked. "Girls like to have some fresh, too!"

"Ah, um. Yeah," McPhee stammered.

"But she in her crib tonight—that one. But look here . . ." Stokes paused. "This one. She waitin' on somebody." There was a grin in his voice, a greasy smacking of words.

"I want her," said Fellows. "Hello, baby! How old?"

"Get 'em before the first bleed I always say . . ." Stokes' voice drifted from the bug. A door sucked open and muffled closed.

"Shush," Fellows whispered, probably in McPhee's ear, warning him not to talk. Even though they were alone, Fellows would be aware the room was likely bugged.

The door opened again. "Glad to see you weren't waiting." Stokes was back. "This is May May."

"Whew!" exclaimed Fellows. "Come over here, baby."

McPhee seemed dangerously quiet, too quiet. "Say something," Salt whispered. Wills cut his eyes to her.

"Smile at the people, May May," said Stokes.

"No, no, no," said McPhee.

"No," said Fellows, jumping in. "We like to see them dressed first—little girl dresses."

"Git," said Stokes, after which was the sound of the door opening and closing again.

Pepper dialed McPhee's phone. They heard him answer over the monitor. "Yeah."

"Say 'Naw,'" Pepper told him.

"Naw," repeated McPhee.

"Mad like, Naw!"

"Naw!"

"Repeat 'The fuck!'"

"The fuck!"

"Now hang up and tell Stokes your other bitch comin' in the club. Then you and Fellows get up and leave."

"Sorry," McPhee said into his coffee cup.

Back at the Narcotics office at four o'clock in the a.m. they all held their coffees tight.

"I am not cut out for this kind of thing. You see stuff on TV and think you could be a detective." He shook his head. "I could hardly hold myself from shaking. Horrible," he said.

"You were fine," Fellows reassured him.

But McPhee didn't look at her.

"We got what we need," said Lieutenant Shepherd. "Thank you, Jarvis."

"Come on, man," said Pepper. "I'll see you out. These guys have the boring paperwork left to do and a warrant to draw up."

McPhee stood. "I don't understand how you do it, be so . . ." he said in Fellows' direction, his voice weak. He turned and left with Pepper.

Once they left, Fellows shrugged. "My shot, my one shot." Her shoes were off and lay on their sides, the straps tangled. Hair wilting, she stripped the Velcro closure for the pistol on her thigh.

But by morning the warrant was signed by the judge.

LAWYERED UP

HOW HARD COULD IT BE TO INCLUDE "SISTERHOOD" IN THE NAME?
Salt thought as she drove to the offices of the International Brotherhood of Police Officers, the IBPO. The stand-alone three-story cinder-block building was surrounded by vacant lots, businesses on all sides having been torn down. Parking was in the open so that even in this very sketchy cheap-rent part of town it would be hard to perpetrate without being seen. And after all, the staff and patrons were mostly cops or former cops. The front door of reinforced glass led to a vestibule with no access to anything but an elevator. There were cinder blocks of a different texture where doors to the first-floor offices had been.

Salt pushed the button for the elevator and waggled her fingers at the dark lens of an overhead camera trained on the spot where she stood. The elevator pinged as the doors opened. When the doors reopened on the third floor, she was met by the union lawyer. She'd seen him around the department but never had reason to meet him. "Jack Lawson," he said, grabbing her hand, pumping it. "Come on back." He waved her down the narrow hall. "I knew we'd see you around here sooner or later. I just thought it would be sooner." He grinned. "Don't take that the wrong way." Small offices on either side were crowded with old desks, file cabinets, and computer components, some working and some obviously not, giving the space a hoarder's feel. Spares of everything were stacked on top of and under all surfaces.

"Welcome to our fortress." Lawson stopped at the open door to a glass-front office and held his arm out for her to go in. "I just got our copy of the surveillance video yesterday." He turned the monitor on his desk toward two chairs. There was little legroom. "I've watched it a couple of times. You okay? You haven't said anything." He smiled, a lot, his mouth full of long teeth and missing molars. There was a Gulf War ball cap hanging on a wall hook.

"This must be how perps feel," she said, hoping not to sound ungrateful.

"Oh, come now. You don't have to worry." He leaned over, maneuvering the computer mouse. "Here we go. Say stop at any time."

It was the same footage that had been played over and over on the news: Salt kneeling over Stone; Lil D coming out of the shoe store, box under his arm; she stands; Lil D bumps into her and drops the box; she kneels over Stone again and hands the box to Lil D, who pauses a half second and then runs out of camera view.

Lawson pressed the stop. "Now, this is only a preliminary hearing and, as I'm sure you know, is only to determine if there is probable cause to charge you. And while the video does seem prima facie sufficient, if we can prove a lack of intent, which I think we can, then the judge will have to dismiss."

"I don't know how you can prove what I was thinking, my intent." Salt sounded like her own prosecutor.

"The first question the prosecutor is likely to ask is did you or do you know Darrell Mobley."

"I've known him, Lil D, for more than ten years."

Lawson's lips closed over his teeth. "Oh."

"He lived in The Homes. It was my beat for years. His mother was murdered and I caught the recent murder of his sister. The reason he was downtown that day was because I had asked him to provide DNA to establish the identity of his sister's body."

"Whoa, hold on." He got up from the chair beside her and went to sit behind the desk. "Salt, you've been charged with party to the crime of theft. Now a case could be more likely made for lack of intent if you didn't know Mobley or if we could establish that you had no reason to give him shoes you knew to be stolen. Did you intentionally give him the shoes?"

"I was in the middle of a riot. I was trying to prevent further injury to a mentally ill man I'd just pepper sprayed and taken into custody. I didn't take time to develop an intention. I needed to get the shoes out of my way." Her knees bumped the metal desk, a sound like a kick drum.

Lawson flinched. "Hey, it's not me that's accused you. I'm on your side."

Salt stood, stepped over to the closed door, and looked out the glass to the empty hall. "I don't know how you stand being this closed in. There's hardly room to move."

Lawson was leaning back in his chair as far as it would swivel and looking up at her. "They brought Mobley in. I don't know if he was arrested or has come forward voluntarily as a witness."

"Really?" She leaned forward. "I get it. They want Lil D to testify that he thought I was giving him the shoes. If he says that on the stand, he won't be charged. If he says I was distracted attending to Stone . . ." She shrugged.

Lawson stood and looked like he was trying to smile again. "I think we'll be all right." He came out from behind the desk and reached for the doorknob. "I always thought you'd be tough."

Halfway through the door she looked at him. "And?"

Lawson followed her through the door. "You are. But in a different way than I expected."

"Not what you'd hoped for?"

"You got some scary about you."

"Thanks," she said.

"See you in court." He waved as she turned to call the elevator.

COURT

NORMALLY COPS SAT ON THE OTHER SIDE OF THE COURTROOM
gallery. But when Salt came in with Lawson, they stood as one, led by
Wills, Pepper, Felton, and Big Fuzzy dressed in their dark navy uniforms, and moved to the other side behind the defendant's table.

"Impressive," grumbled Judge Barrett sarcastically into the microphone on the bench.

Salt had decided not to wear her uniform in case the judge ruled
for sufficient probable cause and she had to be processed through the
jail. So she wore her navy wool jacket over a white shirt and navy
slacks. It was as close to the uniform as she could get, but the waistband of her slacks put an uncomfortable pressure at the most sensitive
place; she was sick to her stomach, as if she might throw up at the
slightest turn. She sipped a bottle of water, afraid to drink more than
her stomach could handle.

The press was confined to the right side of the room, closer to the prosecutor's table. A video screen had been pulled down on the left front wall; a projector was on a stand in the center of the bar area, halfway between the prosecutor's and the defendant's tables, toward the screen.

The courtroom was in full hum. Clerks came and went, addressing the mechanics of justice, papers being signed, dockets being approved, and rolls being checked for the necessary parties. Chatter from the spectators rose to a din, muffled slightly by the sound panels and industrial-grade royal crimson carpet.

Ruddy complexioned with white flyaway hair, Judge Barrett placed his hand on the microphone, his ring clinking loudly, accompanied by feedback, as he leaned toward this or that clerk vying for his attention. Salt had presented cases before him and had always found him affable, if diffident, but generally no-nonsense. He would occasionally get a bee in his bonnet over some seemingly arcane issue driving both the prosecutors and defense lawyers to scratch their heads.

Salt also knew the prosecutor, Lyndon Smith. Usually she and Smith would be conferring, heads together at the other table. He was thin, almost gaunt, his skin bordering on gray-brown depending on the kind of day he was having. He sat at the prosecutor's table adjusting a laptop that Salt presumed would transmit the video. Smith kept glancing over his shoulder toward the gallery, as did Salt, looking for Lil D.

"I'm going to ask Pepper to testify first," Lawson said to her as he sat down at the table beside her. "He'll set the scene, describe the traffic nightmare and the looting."

"Is Lil D here?" she asked.

"I don't know. I wouldn't know him. The judge seems to be waiting for something."

The screen on the wall bloomed to an image of the computer

desktop. News cameras whirred. Photographers focused their cameras. Smith turned again to the back of the room and nodded as Lil D, ever-present towel around his neck, carrying a small gym bag, came up the courtroom aisle to the front row of seats behind Smith. Lil D lifted his chin in an upward nod to Salt.

She nodded in return, but he was bending to sit down and she wasn't sure he'd seen her acknowledgment. Their karma, their fates—her Calvinist ancestors might have used the word "predestined"—were bound by threads, such that when a thread was pulled by one, the other was moved.

The judge banged his gavel. The bailiff shouted, "Hear ye, hear ye. The court will come to order. The court calls all parties in the *State vs. Sarah Diana Alt*, a hearing to determine probable cause for the charge of party to the crime of theft." Barrett leaned into the microphone. "Is the State ready? If so, please read the charges and present your evidence."

Smith glanced at Salt as he stood, mouth tight, grim but determined. "Your Honor, the defendant is charged with party to the crime of theft. The evidence will show that Detective Alt, while working in her capacity as a law enforcement officer, did with intent abet the crime of theft. I request that this video"—he held up a CD—"be entered into the record as prima facie evidence of the abetment." Smith moved to stand beside the projector.

"Well, now, Mr. Prosecutor, I doubt that there's a person in this room, heck, in the entire city, including yours truly, who hasn't seen this video. But, for the record, please proceed." Barrett fell back in his old chair, its increasing tilt over the years made precarious, and folded his hands on his chest. "Any objection, Mr. Lawson?" he asked, voice distant from the microphone.

"None, Your Honor."

The ceiling lights dimmed as the blurry images on the screen wiggled and shook into recognizable forms. Once again there she was in black and white, arm extended toward Stone just the second his head jerked in reaction to the stream of pepper spray coming from the canister in Salt's hand, like a puff of sorcerer's powder. Smith had chosen well to begin the video at that point—Salt, as her own agent, in control of a large, barely clothed man in distress, the shard of glass almost invisible in his right hand. Jerky frame by jerky frame the video from the surveillance camera proceeded until that precise moment when Salt held the box of shoes, looked up at Lil D, expression on her face unreadable, and handed him the box. The video ended. The courtroom was silent. A camera in the press gallery whirred, a shutter clicked, and there was a stirring among the spectators. Salt blinked as the lights rose.

"Your Honor," said Smith, "the State believes that this video is sufficient probable cause and at this time will rest, although reserving the right to present further evidence depending on the evidence put forth by the defense."

Lawson leaned into her. "Why didn't Smith call Lil D?" he asked, barely whispering before rising and buttoning his jacket. "The defense has no objection."

"Very well. Happy to see this moving along," Barrett said. "Present your evidence, Mr. Lawson."

"We call to the stand Detective Wesley Greer."

Pepper, tall and handsome, groomed to glowing, having once again sacrificed his undercover beard, passed her, the air stirring slightly on his way to the stand. Sworn in by the bailiff, he, as a veteran of the courtroom, made eye contact confidently, alternating between the judge and Lawson.

"Please state your name, place of employment, and your assignment on the night of January third of this year," Lawson requested.

Pepper was, and always had been, a star. He was every justice system official's ideal of what a law enforcement representative should be: handsome, educated, well spoken, battle scarred, forthright but with a self-deprecating sense of humor, and he was a minority in this minority/majority city.

Friendship hardly described how she and Pepper felt about each other; they'd been drawn to each other, lost count of whose ass had saved whose, partly because the lines were blurred in many of those incidents. He'd come to the hospital when she'd been injured still in a sky-blue pajama shirt printed with white clouds. And here he was, once again on her side. She closed her eyes and lowered her head so the tears dropped unseen into her lap.

"Detective Alt and I were assigned to crowd management and traffic control in the downtown area near the center of the demonstrations," Pepper told the courtroom.

"Might you say the resources of the police department were strained?" Lawson asked.

"That would be putting it mildly," Pepper understated. Salt was certain Barrett knew they'd been working under extreme pressures and tension.

"Our colleague had been shot. At the time we didn't know how badly," Pepper continued.

"Your Honor," Smith said, standing in objection to the lengthy, sympathetic lead-in to the specific incident. "We know all police work under certain pressure."

Barrett raised his eyebrows, looking over his glasses at Lawson.

"Your Honor, I think context is important . . ." Lawson pled.

"This is a preliminary hearing, Counselor," Barrett said. "I've been around long enough to understand the circumstances. They were up to their asses in alligators." There were guffaws from the gallery.

"Detective Greer, please tell us how you happened to be at the corner of Marietta Street and Central Avenue in front of Walter's Shoes, and what occurred when you and Detective Alt arrived at that location."

Pepper had always had a gift for storytelling. He told just the right details, the little specifics—their glimpse above the crowd of Stone's hand holding the glass; being jostled by the cross flow of the tightly packed groups, looters going one way, demonstrators another; Salt making her way through to Stone; and Pepper momentarily losing sight of her.

Smith stood. "Detective Greer, did either you or Detective Alt recognize or personally know any of the individuals in front of Walter's that evening?"

"We both knew two of the individuals we encountered," Pepper answered.

"How would you characterize your relationship with those two people?" Smith pressed.

"We had known both Curtis Stone and Darrell Mobley, Lil D, from when we worked patrol. They were from The Homes, which was Salt's, Detective Alt's, beat. I worked the adjacent beat."

"For how long?"

Pepper leaned into the microphone. "Ten years." His voice gave weight to those two words.

"So it's safe to say that Detective Alt knew both of those men well?"

"It is safe to say that, yes." Pepper was starting to sound uncharacteristically irritated. Salt understood his reluctance to reduce their interactions with Stone and Lil D to a courtroom testimony description; good as he was at getting to the heart of a story, it would be challenging to explain the years of day-in-and-day-out witnessing of events and interventions in the lives of Lil D and Stone.

There was a noise from the gallery behind and to the right of Salt. The judge looked up. Smith and Lawson turned as Lil D, carrying a bag, tripped and stumbled, hitching up his baggy khaki pants while holding on to the towel and swinging open the gate to the front of the court. "This bullshit." He held a challenging gaze on Judge Barrett. The bailiff moved forward, all others taken aback by a surprisingly assertive Lil D.

"Naw, man." Lil D held up his hand and stopped in the center of the room directly in front of Barrett on the bench above. "It ain't got to be like that," he said to the bailiff and then turned, appealing to the judge.

"Young man, are you somehow involved in this case? If so, you need to have a seat and wait to be called." Barrett was practiced at unconventional interruptions in his courtroom.

But so was Lil D practiced in courtroom appearances. And for one who'd so often seemed voiceless, he was manifesting an awkward but determined presence. "Your Honor, you ain't got to sit here through all this." He waved his hand at Pepper, Lawson, and Smith. "I got someplace I got to be, too."

One or two people in the audience made a noise as if they were suppressing a laugh disguised as a cough. A frown from Barrett quickly discouraged similar outbursts. The bailiff moved closer to Lil D, but Barrett stopped him with a shake of his head.

Lil D said, "You ain't got to look no farther. That was me." He pointed to the video screen now paused on fuzzy lines. "I'm the one got the shoes from Officer Salt."

"Objection," Lawson and Smith said in unison.

"Now hold up, gentlemen." Barrett raised a quieting hand.

Lil D turned to both attorneys.

Barrett said, "While I don't ordinarily entertain breaks in courtroom procedure, I think this unusual case calls for some discretion and I'm going to hear what this young man has to say. He may, like he says, help us cut to the chase. Swear him in, Mr. Bailiff. You may step down, Detective." Pepper left the stand, Lawson and Smith went to their respective tables.

Lil D hitched his pants, which had puddled over his shoes, and street-strolled to the witness stand. Holding tightly to the towel around his neck, not the slightest bit of the birthmark on his neck visible, and the bag in the other hand, he dropped into the chair like a boxer into his corner.

Barrett himself conducted the questioning. "Now, Mr. Mobley, first tell us how you know Detective Alt—I believe you call her Salt."

"She our poleese since I can remember."

"Would you describe your relationship with her as friendly?" asked the judge.

Lil D shrugged. "She all right."

"Mr. Mobley, you have volunteered to give testimony in this case. Now you need to be forthcoming, to explain fully when you are asked. Do I make myself clear?" Barrett peered over the bench at Lil D.

"She straight," Lil D said emphatically. "Know I'm sayin'? She do her poleese thing and we . . ." He hesitated as if searching for a phrase. "We doin' Homes' bidness." He looked Barrett in the eye.

"Thank you," said Barrett. "Your eloquence and honesty are refreshing. Now tell us please how you encountered Salt in front of Walter's Shoes."

Lil D seemed to settle back. "I ain't gone go back over all the times Officer Salt done have some call with my family but"—Lil D slid his eyes briefly over in Salt's direction—"when she come ax me to do the DNA for my sister who they found kilt, I know she ain't axin' just to be axin'. Know I'm sayin'?" He looked up at Barrett, who nodded. "An' I know once she take a case she gone keep at it 'cause she done that for my mama's case and she did it lookin' for my daddy, too. So I know I might as well go on down to the place where they do the DNA, downtown. I wasn't thinkin' 'bout no crowds or them girls that was shot marching. Truth is I got enough to think about. I just want to do this one thing for my sister, the last of my family. I got my own family now. I'm gone make it good. So I give my DNA and come out and there's all this crowds and when I come 'round a corner there's Stone. He all actin' crazy like he do sometimes with a big long piece of glass from Walter's store window, I guess. There was people jumpin' in and out of Walter's, shoes flying everywhere." Here he paused, took a breath, and seemed to gather himself. Salt reflected that the length of Lil D's soliloquy here surely exceeded any previous conversations in his life.

"Them shoes just like some I'd thought about for my girl, and I just went in like everybody else was doin' and got some her size and come back out 'bout the time Salt done got down dealin' with crazy Stone, who was rollin' around in glass, and she got run into by people and I got hit and drop La's shoes near Salt and she hand them back to me. Waddin' no she give me them or me take them. It wasn't either one." Lil D sat back in the witness chair. "It wasn't like they sayin' on TV." He crossed his arms over his chest, momentarily letting the towel hang loose.

The only sounds in the courtroom were the whirrs and clicks of the cameras until Smith pushed himself up from the prosecutor's table. "Your Honor, if I may, I have a few questions for the witness."

"Go ahead, Mr. Smith," Barrett said.

"Mr. Mobley, you say Detective Salt handed you the box. What did you think she meant for you to do with the shoes?"

"Objection, Your Honor." Lawson rose. "There's no way the witness can know the intent in the mind of the accused. He is being asked to speculate."

"Don't get your feathers all ruffled, Mr. Lawson. I know he's being asked to speculate and I'll keep that in mind. But more for my own curiosity I'd like to hear what he thought. I'll be sure to weigh his answer accordingly." He leaned over to Lil D. "Now, young man, I want you to answer two questions for me."

"This gone take long?" Lil D shifted side to side, his hands on the witness stand in front of him.

Judge Barrett's eyes shone with an indulgent glimmer while he tightened his lips over a repressed smile. "No, Mr. Mobley, I don't think anyone wants this convergence to keep us keepin' on any longer than is necessary. So, I'll make it short. First, what was your reason, what made you show up today for this court proceeding?"

Lil D pulled the towel taut. "I guess I don't know." He tightened his mouth and leaned forward, inadvertently too close to the microphone. "I know they might get a warrant on me for stealin' shoes—I could just wait till they find me. But I'm tired of being always under what somebody else gone do or not do. So I come to deal with it." He leaned down to the bag beside him and from it lifted a shoebox, then handed it to the judge.

Salt realized she'd been holding her breath as time seemed to have both stopped and flown, like a vortex that swept her back to the steps of Lil D's grandmother's when he was twelve and she was a rookie, as if miraculously they'd been taken up in a maelstrom that had landed them here, both of them having survived. She drew air into her lungs in a deep, long inhale, and she became aware of the courtroom and the silence.

Judge Barrett lifted the lid on the box and looked in. He turned to Lil D and with a voice genuine and straightforward that dared anyone to speak or even think otherwise, he said, "I admire that quality in a person, Mr. Mobley—taking things into your own hands and, well, I don't know what to call it but courage."

Lil D looked up with a raised, questioning eyebrow as if checking out Barrett for signs of disingenuousness. "You said there was two questions."

Fitting the lid back on the box, Barrett said, "Indeed, and now that I'm convinced of your sincerity I'll know how to weigh your answer. I want you to think back to that moment when Detective Alt, Salt, put the box in your hands. Did she look up while she was giving, sorry, when she was handing you the shoes? What was her expression?"

Already leaning forward, Lil D looked over at Salt as if to remind himself of her expression. He kept his eyes on hers as he answered. "She just look like she always look—straight."

There had been in Salt's life occasional moments, mostly in the street, when from nowhere would come a feeling of transcendence, like this. She closed her eyes just to focus on the lightness of her heart and then opened them. She looked at the judge and was no longer anxious, no longer fearful of what the ruling might be.

"You may be excused," Barrett said to Lil D, who stepped down from the witness stand. With his head lowered, he made his way to the doors of the courtroom. The judge pounded his gavel. "Officer Alt, in this case I find that you acted without intent to commit a theft."

The gallery noise began, hands clapping, a whoop, someone saying, "All right!"

Judge Barrett's voice rose. "Detective, while you may have meant for Mr. Mobley to take the shoes, you had no intent for him to steal them. Case dismissed."

VOICES FROM THE FIRE

BARRETT SIGNED THE ARREST WARRANT FOR STOKES, BUT THE feds had stepped in. Oh, they wanted Stokes, but they wanted him as an informant, no matter that he was also a co-conspirator in murder. Salt supposed, hoped, that there was a bigger picture. So they had to formulate a plan for a low-profile arrest. Obviously it couldn't take place at the club. They began surveillance, and once again took the detail in eight-hour shifts, partnering up two at a time.

At the planning meeting, Lieutenant Shepherd said, "I want to take a shift."

"LT, you don't have to," Huff said. "See, if you do, then how does that look for me?"

The lieutenant made the sign of the cross. "Go, my son. I absolve you of your penance. Really, I want to, and because I'm a lieutenant, I get to pick my shift and my partner. How 'bout it, Salt? You up for midnights?"

Since her reinstatement Salt's colleagues had been deferential. The hearing was fresh in their minds and the fit-for-duty evaluation had been further grist for the blue rumor mill. Even those with whom she worked most closely, the Homicide guys, were being careful with her, more out of cautious concern than doubt, she hoped. Wills was the same, but she and Wills had not yet worked out the barriers to their marriage. Wills seemed to be waiting, giving her space and time. Only Pepper was his usual self and intent on pushing her to find an additional aikido practice under another sensei.

So Lieutenant Shepherd's offer was welcome, even if it was an order. "Sure LT, that would work." Salt wouldn't mind the midnight to eight a.m. hours when there were fewer cops and supervisors around.

Shepherd, naturally reserved with a flat, neutral manner, looked up at Salt and leaned forward, folding her hands on the center of her desk. "So tomorrow night, then. See you here."

"Caught you," Salt said, letting herself in the back door of Mr. Gooden's house. "Together. My two favorite geezers."

Sister Connelly stood at the counter next to the door. Beside her Mr. Gooden was putting eggs into a recycled carton. "Yep, here we are, solving the world's problems one organic egg at a time." Sister handed an egg to Mr. Gooden from the apron tied at her waist. He put it in, closed the carton, and walked over to Salt. "I haven't gotten to see you since the court hearing." He grabbed her in a hug. "I don't get how the news people got all that so wrong." He pushed back, holding her at arm's length. "I sure get tired of worrying about you."

"Old man, haven't you figured out by now that this blue-eyed girl got seven kinds of mojo workin'?" Sister wiped her hands on the apron.

"Naw, you don't even believe that yourself." He laughed. "You just like to scare people with that black magic act."

"I'm telling you. For real," she said, putting her hand to her mouth, barely covering her grin.

Wonder scratched at the door and Mr. Gooden reached to let him in. "Come on now, dog," he said as Wonder wiggled happily to Salt's side.

"See what I tell you?" Sister said. "She even got her black dog, her spirit guide." Sister Connelly was full-bore intent on putting them on.

Salt rubbed at the scar on her forehead. "You go on—have fun at my expense." But she was laughing, too. "Really"—she dropped her hand to the dog's head—"I came to ask you to keep an eye on the place. I've got a detail over several nights and I'll be staying with Wills."

"How 'bout the mutt?" Mr. Gooden reached down and ruffled Wonder's fur.

"I don't know. I'm trying to acclimate him to life in the city, to wean him off the sheep, but . . ."

Mr. Gooden turned and walked to the other side of his kitchen to the sink, where he pulled off a paper towel from the roll and, with his back turned to them, dabbed at his face. Clearing his throat, he said, "Why don't you let him have a few more days, a few more runs with his sheep? Let him stay with me. That way I can keep up with you. You'll have to check in with me if I'm keeping him."

Sister went over to the wall-mounted coatrack and pulled down her coat. "Lettuces ain't gone put they selves in the ground."

"Hold up. I'm comin'." Mr. Gooden turned and crossed to her, holding her coat while she slipped her arms into the sleeves.

With the three of them in close proximity, Salt was struck by a sudden awareness of their height. She was used to being the tall woman in a group, but Mr. Gooden and Sister were both right at six feet tall, taller than she. It was somehow comforting.

"Come on." Mr. Gooden grabbed for the door. "We got work to do."

"Looks like he's gonna be closing." Salt sat back from the surveillance van's periscope.

Lieutenant Shepherd, in the captain's chair bolted to the floor beside Salt's, blew across a full cup of coffee. The van, on loan from the feds, had its own coffeemaker, as well as lots of other bells and whistles. "Figures, since he came in at seven p.m. Pepper said he always drives the black Mercedes parked over there by the entrance."

They'd gotten to the block above the club around one a.m. and had been waiting for Stokes. There'd been long stretches of silence; Shepherd being as much the quiet type as Salt, it had seemed a little awkward at first.

"I ran into Peachtree Harrison the other day," Salt said.

"Aha."

"He knew my dad." Salt leaned up and peered into the scope. The club parking lot was beginning to clear.

"Peachtree still working that EJ at the Peacock?" Shepherd glanced at Salt over the top of her coffee.

"Yeah, he gave me the tour—pretty amazing place."

"I'm sure it was in its day. Probably still jumping when he and your dad came on the PD."

"He's the only person I've met in the department that said he knew my dad well."

"Funny the ways you get paid working this job," Shepherd said.

The lights of the club marquee went out, leaving only the streetlights and the funnel light above the entrance glowing with cold halos.

"Paid?" Salt widened her eyes, refocusing in the darkness of the van in order to see Shepherd.

"Cops like you, you don't work the way you do, so close to the street, just for the paycheck." Shepherd set the cup on the dash and leaned toward Salt. "You work it because it teaches you things you'd never be able to learn any other way—about the city, about yourself."

"I hadn't thought about it that way. Pepper and I used to say to each other, 'You know more than you think.'"

"That's some of it," Shepherd said, "learning to pay attention."

"Sounds like the voice of experience, LT."

"See, some folks look at Peachtree Harrison and all they see is a worn-out old beat cop who never rose above patrol. It's like people look at this city and see its surfaces—the glitter and lights or maybe all they see is the grit and grime." She shrugged. "But if you work investigations, if you really police, you get to the interesting, good stuff about Atlanta."

There were only two cars left at the club, Stokes' Benz and an older-model pimped-out sedan. "I don't know if it did my dad any good."

"Interesting that your dad and Peachtree were close."

The door to the club opened and three people came out, one of whom was Stokes. "Here we go," Salt said.

Shepherd stepped over her and into the driver's seat. The two others with Stokes were a man, large, looked like muscle, and a female, who walked between the men. It was hard to see the female's face or to determine her age. The muscle man escorted the female to the passenger side of Stokes' car and held the door as she got in, and then waited until Stokes was behind the wheel before going over and getting in the pimped sedan.

The lieutenant drove parallel with Stokes for a while, then let the

GPS tracker take over, allowing them to follow at a distance. After thirty minutes of northbound streets and no sign of the pimped sedan, they caught up with the Mercedes again and followed its taillights first into a newer cul-de-sac neighborhood, then past the driveway where Stokes' car sat billowing exhaust in front of a two-car garage door that was slowly opening.

Over the next two nights Shepherd and Salt watched from the van as Stokes pulled into the same driveway at the same time each night, confirming his residence at that location. His house was similar to all the others in the ten-year-old subdivision: red brick, one or two stories with white trim, and short drives that led to either front- or side-entry garages. The neighborhood had a theme: all the streets were named for either a character or location in *Gone with the Wind*: Rhett Butler Way, Tara Trail, Ashley Avenue. Stokes lived on Belle View.

The team, all seven of them, sat shoulder to shoulder in the close quarters of the van idling several blocks away on Prissy Path, ready to serve the warrant. Huff looked at Felton. "Wasn't Belle the madam in *Gone with the Wind*?

"What makes you think I'd know the answer to that?" Felton glared at the sergeant.

"I don't know. You, anybody. I wasn't just asking you."

"You were looking at me."

Shepherd, using her most maternal voice, said, "Now children, we're almost ready, almost there. Charlie, quit looking at Manfred."

They could take Stokes down in his car before he got out of the cul-de-sac on his way to work, but they wanted to get inside the house; they wanted to know who else lived there. They'd seen him go in with at least one female. Lieutenant Shepherd decided the seven of them would be sufficient to execute the warrant safely, but they also called several marked cars to stand by at the entrance to the subdivision. At noon exactly Pepper slowly drove them to the house—no flashing lights, no sirens, nothing about the van that even remotely resembled law enforcement.

There was no running as they each quietly slipped from the van. They were dressed as they normally would be except that on top of their clothes they each wore their protective vest with the word "PO-LICE" in bold letters on each side. Salt and Pepper walked briskly around the right side of the house, Huff and Felton to the left, and Lieutenant Shepherd, Wills, and Sergeant Fellows, forming a triangle, positioned themselves at the front door.

There was a brisk wind. The sun was bright. The neighborhood at lunch hour was quiet. At the back of the house Salt heard Wills' aggressive, loud knock and announcement at the front door. "Police. Open up!" *Thwack. Whap.* He graduated to his retractable baton, rapping on the door, and again, "Police. Open the door!" Unintelligible staccato voices came from inside the house, then noises like furniture being overturned and bumping and running sounds. Salt put her ear close to the back patio glass doors. Curtains obscured their view of the inside. Still unable to discern words, she heard a man's voice and a responding high-pitched female voice.

Fellows, having been on a field team and trained in warrant serves, had been assigned to handle the breaching tool; eight seconds was her record, she'd told them. Pepper had positioned himself at the back corner so he could see the side of the house as well as Salt and Huff at the back. Felton was in corresponding position on the other side of the back. Salt and Huff, guns at low ready, stood on either side of the sliding door.

The screech of wood splintering was followed half a minute later by Wills' shout, this time from the inside, "Police!"

"Clear!" yelled Lieutenant Shepherd from the inside.

"Clear," called Fellows from somewhere closer to the back door.

"Don't move. Do not move," commanded Wills from a more distant place in the house.

Shepherd lifted the back-door curtain. It seemed to take an eternity for her to disengage the door lock.

"Out! Out! Show me your hands," yelled Fellows at yet another location in the house. As soon as Shepherd got the door open, Huff bounded toward the sound of Fellows' voice.

"On your knees," Wills ordered from toward the front of the house. "Keep your hands where I can see them."

Salt strode past Shepherd toward the sound of Wills' voice.

"LT, back here," called Fellows.

Salt rounded the corner hallway entrance to a cathedral-ceilinged great room where Wills, pistol drawn, was twelve feet from Stokes, who stood facing the wall behind a long red sectional sofa. "Climb the wall and spread your arms," said Wills. Salt holstered, pulled out her handcuffs, moved forward to Stokes, and with a satisfying ratcheting of the cuffs' teeth, clamped them on one wrist then the other.

"This is not my house" were the first words Stokes spoke.

"Dude." Wills winced as he caught sight of Stokes' animal-print briefs and quickly reached to belt Stokes' hotel-logoed bathrobe.

"Those probably aren't your pants, either," Wills said, referring to the ubiquitous denial of ownership of pants in which illegal substances or contraband were found.

"Huh?" said Stokes. Some of his cornrows were less than tidy.

"Salt," Pepper called from another part of the house.

Down a hall, past three small bedrooms, Salt walked into a larger bedroom at the end of the hall where Pepper, Fellows, and Shepherd were standing over three young girls sitting on a king-size bed. They appeared to be naked except for the bedspread they were jointly using to cover themselves. They looked up at the cops surrounding them, the whites of their eyes revealing fear. "You're safe," Sergeant Fellows said.

Glory, JoJo, and the three girls they found at Stokes' were only the tip of the iceberg, according to the feds. They needed Stokes first, and then once they had used him to inform and get Flash on a wire, they'd turn Flash. The aim was to find and arrest sex traffickers at both the national and international level. This solved Salt and Wills' dilemma about where she would be reassigned. She and Pepper were being transferred to the joint task force with the feds. And she and Wills could make their engagement public.

Stokes did roll on Flash regarding Glory; he'd been at the quarry, he said, when Flash had shot her. But he said that Mary had gotten away from them. He believed she'd made it back to her old neighborhood, which confirmed what JoJo had told them, leaving Mary's murder still a mystery.

LAST SESSION

DR. MARSHALL STOOD WITH ONE FOOT ON A RAIL OF THE SHEEP paddock. He'd called early and said he wanted to come down, asking for directions to her place.

Salt opened the paddock gate to let Wonder in, steadying him behind the sheep as he pushed the flock out and into the orchard. "That'll do," she called to him. They watched the sheep disperse throughout the pecan trees. "How is your daughter?" she asked.

"Right now we're hopeful. We found another residential program." He shook his head. "I can't imagine what it must be like for parents who don't have the resources my wife and I do. Even with everything we know and have access to, having an adult child with a chronic mental illness . . . we often are at the end of our rope. You recognized pretty quickly how ill she is."

"Cops end up wrangling those neglected souls all the time. It's frustrating." She called Wonder to heel as they walked from the orchard to the back porch. "There's also my personal experience, my father."

Marshall stood at the bottom of the steps. "When people think about cops, I don't think they imagine anything like this." He looked at the house and back out to the sheep.

"Come on in." She opened the screen door and led him to the kitchen. "I'll fix us some special cop sandwiches. Vegetarian, okay?"

Standing and watching while Salt put out a fresh loaf of the heavy, dark bread, a brick of Swiss cheese, avocado, and condiments, Marshall did most of the talking this time. "You must be wondering why I'm breaking protocol—coming down to your home." Marshall started building his sandwich.

Salt brought glasses and a pitcher of water to the kitchen table. "Have a seat."

"Sarah, the reason I wanted to come here today is to do what therapists are not supposed to do. I want to advise you. The fit-for-duty evaluation is done. But evaluations are not therapy." He took a large bite of his sandwich, chewing and mumbling, "Mmm." He swallowed. "I was hungry. The fresh air maybe."

They ate in silence. "Advice?" she prompted.

Finishing his sandwich, he nodded at her hand. "I see you're wearing your ring. That's good."

Salt got up to start coffee. "Is that the advice?"

"No, no." He laughed. "That was a great sandwich!"

"Another?"

"No, that was perfect. How about we have coffee in a bit. I'd like to see the rest of this fascinating house." He looked up at the overhead light set in a plaster medallion, then over to the deep porcelain sink.

"Not much has been changed from when it was built, just a few upgrades. The wiring needs to be replaced next. Come on." She went to the hall. There was something vaguely paternal in the ease with which Marshall carried himself—in the set of his shoulders? Salt tried to figure out what it was while she was showing him through the downstairs dining room and bedroom and into the library. When she pulled back the pocket doors, Marshall didn't hesitate. He went directly to the shelf where her father's books on mental illness were. He touched a few of the book spines, then went around the room looking at the rest of the books. "How different this is from TV images of cops." He held his arms out, indicating the room.

"Images," Salt repeated, thinking to herself, *He is the father of a mentally ill daughter and I am the daughter of a mentally ill father.* "I'll show you where he died," she said, and led him through the living room and up the stairs.

As they walked up the stairs, Salt asked, "My evaluation?"

"Sorry, I don't mean to keep you in suspense," Marshall said.

She gave him a cursory tour of the upstairs, waved him at last to the door of the dojo, and took off her shoes. He followed her lead, removing his shoes and entering the room with her. He went to the center of the room, where he stood quietly for a few seconds and then began turning to each wall. "It's beautiful—the light, the weathered wood and bamboo, the white mat."

Salt knelt in front of the sensei altar.

"Your father." Marshall sat down cross-legged beside her and pointed to the photo.

"This was their bedroom, where I found him." She lit the candle.

Marshall faced the photo while he talked. "Salt, as beautiful as the place is, as much as you've transformed this room, and even with all the positives you've brought to the property with the sheep and Wonder, the improvements"—he turned to her—"I still don't see how it can be healthy for you to be reminded, day in and day out, of that day. And it's not just that day. My suspicion is that this house holds a history that contributed to his depression." He nodded at her father. "Sure, it's likely he was predisposed, as is my daughter. And he might have felt the stigma, being a cop and all. But he failed to find help. Why do you think you would want to stay?"

"I guess I was hoping to come to some understanding."

"Is that true? Or is it that you want to recover something lost and you're hoping that it's here?"

The candle's flickering light reflected on the photo, lighting her father's eyes. His face was composed, serious, without either the sadness or the joy Salt remembered. His uniform, same as the one hanging in Salt's downstairs closet, was sharp, spotless, the badge and name tag shining, the patent leather of his hat brim gleaming. Sitting seiza, Salt bowed, touching her forehead to the floor in front of the altar.

Marshall put his hand on her shoulder. "I came here today to tell you in person—that, of course, I've found you fit for duty."

Salt sat upright and turned toward him.

"With your engagement to Wills, you have some decisions to make—where you'll be living and other changes you mentioned, work related. As I said, it's not the job of a therapist to advise people, but this evaluation is time limited and not therapy. So I'm cutting straight through to advice: find your father in the memories, the better memories, when he was able to love you into becoming the person you are. You should leave this bloody house." Marshall stood and walked to the door of the room. Salt leaned over and blew out the candle.

CERTAINTY

SALT DROVE THROUGH THE STREETS OF HER OLD BEAT, THE Homes, and the shabby little houses and businesses surrounding it. The sounds of the bulldozers, excavators, and jackhammers seemed to come from all directions. She'd come back to where she often had, to Sister's old stone church, which sat almost dead center of the beat.

This morning she'd woken early; a loud bird perched on a limb right outside the window where she and Wills lay. When the sun was up in the country, that had never bothered her. But here in the city the singular call of that one bird had brought her out of a dream. Wills snorted softly, rolled over on his side, and began sleep breathing again. She got up, dressed without riling the still sleepy dogs, and left a note on the coffeepot.

There had been only a couple of cars in the neighborhood pharmacy parking lot when she'd pulled up. It hadn't taken five minutes for her to find the testing kit, pay for it, and ask for the restroom. She should have gone home, home now being Wills' house, their place, to tell her soon-to-be husband. But instead she was here at the old stone church staring at the pink double lines on the little test "stick," as it was called. She thought of it as more of a wand. She had a positive wand, something to keep to herself at least until she figured out how she felt about it. She knew what Wills' reaction would be; he'd been hinting about having a child.

Up the street from where Salt sat in the church parking lot, a mid-level sedan was parked outside a small house. A man dressed in slacks and a windbreaker and carrying a briefcase came out, got in the car, and drove a block to another little house. The insurance man. Salt realized she'd seen him around for years, always in the background, and had never really noticed. She'd heard people talk about their paid-up or not-paid-up funeral insurance. *Gill? Gill? Gilligan*, she remembered his name as she drove the Taurus the short distance, parked behind his car, and waited for him to come out of the next house.

When he came out, she was standing at his car. He raised his hand and smiled at her in recognition. "Officer Salt, good to see you again. How are you? Haven't see you around lately."

"Mr. Gilligan, right?"

"Yep." He nodded. He was what they called "paper-bag brown," affable as one would want in an insurance salesman. She guessed he sold some measure of peace.

"Tell me, sir, how does confidentiality apply to your line of work?" Salt propped one foot on the front of the Taurus.

Gilligan smiled again. His fifty-something face was permanently creased with that oft-used expression of, if not happiness, at least satisfaction. "Well now, it depends," he said. "Nothing really in the law about it, but I wouldn't be in business long if I went around gossiping about whose funeral was paid for and whose wasn't—who had insurance and who didn't. But I'm not bound by anything." He laid his briefcase on the hood of his sedan, seemingly in no hurry, either.

"Thank you, sir. Do you by any chance know Mrs. McCloud? Lives a couple blocks south of here on Jonesboro."

"Sure," he said. "Funny you should ask. I just had a reconciliation with her. It did seem odd, not that it hasn't happened before, but she took out a policy, a little life policy, on her granddaughter just a month or so before the girl was shot to death. These policies are small. Life is short in this neighborhood. Maybe she had a premonition or something." He shook his head. "But it's not my money so I don't mind a bit."

"Do you have a record of the date she took out the policy?"

"'Course." He opened his case. It was full, but he confidently thumbed through the files and papers. "I'm kind of a one-man operation. Keep all my office business right here. No computers for me—too old. Here it is." He handed a two-page policy to Salt. It was signed on August 15, five days before Mrs. McCloud had reported Mary missing, approximately three weeks after the medical examiner had estimated Mary's time of death and three months before her body was found. It was too close, but she knew. Salt put a hand to her belly.

"I never much cared for that old woman. Been dealing with her for years. First her husband—I guess he was her husband. Then you know her daughter was killed, too. There's something not right there, you know?" Mr. Gilligan shut his case.

Salt put out her hand. "I do know. Thank you."

Driving from Sister's church to God's World, Salt reflected on the Flannery O'Connor quote "While the South is hardly Christ-centered, it is most certainly Christ-haunted." It seemed she was forever in front of, beside, in back of, going to, or coming from one of Atlanta's churches, there being one almost every other block or so. Didn't seem to do much for the crime rate, though.

Given God's World's seven-day-a-week schedule and it being close to spring, the glass-front door was open for business. Sitting in the parking lot, Salt considered whether or not her child should have a religious education and if so what flavor. The childhood prayer returned.

> *Jesus, tender shepherd, lead me*
> *Through the darkness be thou near me*
> *Guide thy little lamb tonight*
> *Wake me with the morning bright.*

Her phone vibrated—Wills. "Hey," she answered.

"I got your note," he said. "Where are you now?"

"God's World."

"Yeah." He laughed. "But where exactly?"

"Really, I'm at the church." Before he could protest, she added, "You still at home? I'll come by in a few. I've got some news." She tucked the test wand in her jacket inside pocket.

"Sure," he said. "I was just going over the floor plans again. We could still squeeze in a small workout area. I hate that you're having to give up that great dojo."

Man came to the open door of the church, saw her, and leaned against the doorjamb.

"Uh, you might want to wait for me and we'll look at the plans together."

"Deal," he said. "I'll make us lunch and we can negotiate while we eat." His voice was eager, his speech rapid, as if wanting to get going. He paused. "By the way, what are you doing down there? I thought we agreed you'd wait for your partner to go out—after all, you've only got a week before the new assignment."

Stone appeared in the doorway beside Man.

"Loose ends," she said. "Just clearing up a few for my own satisfaction. I'm okay, Wills, really. I've got lots of reasons to be careful." She touched the St. Michael's pendant between her breasts. "I'll see you in about an hour. Okay?"

"Bye, babe."

Salt pocketed the phone, got out of the car, and said hello to her old nemeses.

"I guess we done owe you," Man said. "Stone coulda gone back to state custody if you hadn't got him to the hospital instead of jail." He tapped Stone's arm with a finger. "Say something, Curtis."

Curtis? She couldn't remember the last time she'd heard anyone call Stone by his first name.

Stone did his best impression of a smile, drawing his lips back and chomping his too-white dentures together. "They give me some new pills and a shot. My head quiet." He rubbed his palm over his round scalp.

"That's good," she said. "Really, no one's happier than me that the docs are doing you some good."

"Man, happy." Stone's eyes narrowed. He stood to his full height, challenging, fists tightening.

"Sorry, I didn't mean that . . ."

"Naw, man, chill," Man said to Stone. "She mean she real happy, too."

"I came by hoping to see you, Stone. I'm being reassigned, so I might not get a chance to get down here any time soon and I wanted to clear up something."

Stone was waggling his hands, loosening his fingers from their tight-fist position, rolling his shoulders.

"Can you remember the last time you saw Lil D's sister? If she said where she was going?"

Stone's eyes began to lose focus. "Yeah, I remember 'cause she had that look."

Salt knew, and she suspected Man also knew, the hazards in Stone's losing awareness of the present.

"Like she on empty and give up," said Stone. "She say she goin' back to her grandmaw. That the last I seen of her."

"I sure hope an even disposition is a dominant gene," Salt said, entering the kitchen, dogs swirling around her legs.

"What?" Wills asked, distracted, taking the lid off a pot on the stovetop. The kitchen smelled warm, something to do with garlic, onions, and maybe faux-bacon grease?

"Disposition," she repeated, stepping through the dogs. She held out the little test wand to Wills.

He looked at it. "Is that . . . ?" He looked up with wide eyes.

Salt lifted her brows, an expression of what-can-I-say. "We seem to have a convergence."

He took the wand and stared at the double bars.

"It's positive. We're pregnant," she said.

ABOUT MARY

ALTHOUGH SHE'D KNOWN THE ANSWER, SALT HAD ASKED THE DA anyway. Despite the insurance Mrs. McCloud had taken out after Mary had gone missing, and Stone's assertion that the last time he saw her she was returning to her grandmother, they didn't have enough to bring charges.

So with little hope Salt had taken her last afternoon in Homicide and returned to the house on Jonesboro where both Mary and her murdered mother were raised. It was the last thing Salt wanted to do, to go back to that house. She could still see Mary getting off the bus at the corner, pulling at the heels of her socks while the cool kids, the carefree kids, skipped past.

Mary's image accompanied her up the steep steps. In her mind's eye she could see Mary trudging up the steps with her heavy book bag. Salt knocked and waited. When Mrs. McCloud opened the door and saw Salt she tried to close the door but Salt stuck her foot out.

"God knows I don't want to be here any more than you want me to be here," she said. "But aren't you just a little bit curious, or concerned, about what I have to say? Maybe there's new evidence. Most people would want to know how a case of their murdered loved one is progressing."

Mrs. McCloud stepped out and looked to the right and to the left. "I don't want you standin' on my porch."

"That's right. What will people think? What will they say? Of course, they recognize the Taurus. How about I come in?" Salt pushed past the now unresisting woman.

The floors gleamed with polish. Mrs. McCloud looked down at Salt's shoes.

"My shoes stay on," Salt said.

Mrs. McCloud walked away and down the hall, her slippers making a swishing noise. Salt followed her to the kitchen at the back of the house, the memory of Mary still with her. Salt remembered the girl's rigid posture and her anguished cry—how she'd wished for some way to have been able to shelter her.

Although Mrs. McCloud always remained stout, as before there were no signs that food had ever been either consumed or prepared in the kitchen, every surface spotless. Like a dated advertisement, sunlight reflected off the old appliances. It was disconcertingly incongruous. The sun shone from the back window, also highlighting the perfect blond chignon at the back of Mrs. McCloud's head. Mrs. McCloud grabbed and held on to the back of the kitchen chair on the opposite side of the table from Salt.

"Oh, that's right. You want to get to the new evidence."

"Get to it. I'm not about playing games with you." The old woman tightened her hold on the chair back.

"I see." Salt tucked her chin to her chest. Looking back up, she said, "I expect we come from the same place, you and I. You cannot escape shame. It's partly what made you shoot and kill your grand-daughter. And here I was carrying around the motive all along—the photo of Mary and the other two girls, the dancers. When someone sent you the photo—after that, that shame, you killed her."

Mrs. McCloud opened her mouth wide and laughed. Still grinning, she said, "You got nothing. If you did, you wouldn't be all talk. You'd be here with a warrant and some more cops to put me in handcuffs. But here you are—all talk."

"It began to make sense when I thought about it, asked myself who had the most to lose by Mary being alive? It wasn't the men who had used and abused her. They weren't threatened by Mary's escape. They were threatened by her death and the investigation, but not her escape. They knew she wouldn't, couldn't, do anything to them. So who had something to lose by Mary being alive?" Salt took off her hat and dropped it on the table. "You are partly right. I don't have enough evidence to convict you in a court of law. This is one murder for which there'll be no conventional resolution."

"Get out of my house." Mrs. McCloud's voice was loud, but she didn't move.

Salt went around the table and stood too close to Mary's murderer. "She was desperate for shelter. You killed her mostly because you were ashamed, and then there was the premeditated aspect—the insur-ance. She was a living testimony to your failure. I just wanted to let you know that at least I, one person, am witness to that. You took her to that field—it would have been the very end of blackberry season—and shot her right through the heart." Salt reached out and put the tips of her fingers in the middle of Mrs. McCloud's chest.

Mrs. McCloud backed away, went around Salt and back down the hall to the front door.

Salt blinked and opened her eyes in the too-bright light. *That will have to do, Salt*, she said to herself. *That'll do.*

THE PAST IS NOW

THERE WAS ONLY ONE BOX; SALT HADN'T BEEN IN HOMICIDE long enough to accumulate a lot of personal artifacts and memorabilia. Not only was she leaving, on loan to the FBI task force, at least until the baby arrived, but this was also the last week of the unit inhabiting the old building. Mary's file, all the other cases she'd worked, all the colored-by-year books had been transferred to storage. Mary's file, because it was still open, would go with the unit. The rest, the solved cases, would go to a climate-controlled remote facility. Salt leaned into the aisle down which she could see into Huff's office, where he stood rubbing his head amidst the stacks and piles of case folders.

Her landline gave off its staticky death-rattle ring. "Honey, you have a visitor," Rosie said. "A Mr. Jim Britton."

"Oh?"

"He said he doesn't have an appointment but was hoping to catch you."

"I'll come out." Salt dropped the handset into its cracked cradle.

When Salt came out to the waiting room, Britton was standing facing the command staff photographs on the wall. He strode to her, extending his hand. "Thank you for seeing me. I should have called, but this was somewhat of an impulse."

"Sure, no problem. Come on back." Salt held the door for him. Britton not being a member of their usual visitor demographic, Rosie registered her curiosity by arching her eyebrows.

"Pardon our mess," Salt said as they walked through the unit, passing boxes on boxes and cubicles dreary and bereft of their curiosities, mementos, and departmental reminders. "I'm going to a new assignment and the unit is also moving."

"Ah, yes, I heard about the new headquarters," he said.

Salt grabbed a chair from the empty cubicle across from her. They sat. Britton looked around. Salt waited, then finally said, "What can I do for you today, Mr. Britton?"

"Sorry to keep bothering you." On his windbreaker was the logo of the environmental group he worked with, the same jacket he had worn before. "This might seem trivial to you, what with all this." He pointed at the files on her desk, a stack of eight-by-ten crime-scene photos, the boxes and files on nearby work spaces. "But I'd like to know whether or not the information I gave you about seeing Flash Daddy Jones at the quarry was helpful to the investigation." His voice trailed off as he looked down at his lap.

"It was. It certainly was. One thing I've learned in this job is you never know when some small detail will be the piece that solves the mystery or gives enough information to complete the picture." She was still struggling to find hope and peace about Mary's case.

"I didn't see anything in the media about an arrest," he said.

"Without saying too much, let's just say there's an even bigger picture that's being considered in regard to Mr. Jones."

Britton sighed and leaned back. "Like the butterfly effect."

"Are you talking about the weather—that thing, something about the wind from a butterfly's wings causing a tornado somewhere far away?"

"It may not be that dramatic or extreme, but yes, random occurrences have been observed to significantly affect outcomes," he said.

"As humans, though, don't we consciously, knowingly control more of the factors?" Salt asked. "We're not blown about by the wind. We can steady ourselves if we choose."

"Of course, but what I'm talking about, Detective, is the randomness of the conditions to which we are born." Britton stood. "I am, as I'm sure you've suspected, tortured by the legacy of my ancestors' barbarous treatment of the conscripted laborers a century ago, those bodies found at the South River. They were born poor, mostly black, and on whose backs my great-grandfather, grandfather, and even my father built their wealth, my wealth." Awkwardly, he stood.

Salt folded her hands atop her desk, then looked up. "I recently found some records and photographs in my attic. I think there's lots of that stuff rotting away in old houses like mine. My neighbor who's old enough to be my grandfather told me there used to be more, but people were ashamed and got rid of it, burned it, buried it. It's hard to come face-to-face with the past, sins of our fathers and all."

"So what are we to do?" he said, his voice thin.

"Isn't the work you do, trying to reclaim the polluted places, enough? Don't you feel like you're giving back through your work?" she asked, even as she felt a hollowness within her own chest, thinking about what she should do with those old records from her attic.

"I don't know." He winced and squeezed his eyes shut. "I go about my daily pursuits hoping I'm leading an honorable life, and then I'm struck by some particular, some instance where I'm confronted with an example of a life, like the woman in the quarry, those bodies from the river, and it brings me to my knees." Britton rocked forward and back.

"Don't we all have debts? Here in the South we live up close and personal with them, in a very obvious way, confronted daily with legacies of our ancestors. It's an advantage, in a way." Salt stood and took her father's coat from its hanger.

"Inescapable," Britton said.

"Like the air stirred by a butterfly's wings?"

Britton turned to go. "May the wind be always at your back, Detective."

CARRY ON

BY THE TIME THEIR BABY WAS BORN, DANNY T WOULD BE FOUR
years older than their baby; Pepper and Ann's boys, nine and eleven years
older. Maybe there would be still be sheep, certainly dogs.

Lil D and Latonya had walked fifty yards out into the orchard,
which was just beginning to show tiny new yellow-green shoots from
the branches.

Reverend Gray came down the back steps dressed in a sort of cleri-
cal robe, chartreuse with a stole of cerulean blue embroidered with
pink flamingos. He carried a red Bible. When the bagpiper began
tuning, the dogs came running. Wonder lifted his snout and howled.
The Rotties, watching him, halfheartedly woofed. Theo and Miles
skidded around the corner of the house from the front, Danny T
dangling between them.

It was way more commotion than Salt had imagined. There'd
been no invitations; they'd just asked their friends to show up. As the

piper began in earnest, Mr. Gooden, escorting Sister Connelly, swung open the new gate between his place and Salt's.

Wills offered Salt his arm as they descended the steps from the back porch, followed by Ann and Pepper, Felton and Rosie, and Sergeant Huff. They came together with Reverend Gray under Salt's tree. The dogs quieted when the piper came to the final notes of the hymn. The boys held on to Danny T while they waited as Lil D and Latonya joined them, completing the circle.

Lil D and Latonya had been induced to come by Salt, who'd used the prospect of a day in the country for Danny as a way to convince them to be a part of the celebration. The sheep were also a draw.

Reverend Gray began, "Dearly beloved . . ." Salt was wearing her one dress, the crocheted off-white lace that she'd bought last year at the thrift store when she'd been getting clothes for Pearl, the homeless blues singer who was now off the streets and waiting by herself on Salt's back porch.

Wills wore a new dark blue suit that had cost him a paycheck, an expense he justified by pointing out that there would be other occasions, "like the baby's baptism," when he'd be able to wear it. He looked handsome, Salt thought.

"We are gathered today . . ." Gray continued. Salt was surprised that he was using such a traditional liturgy.

Across the circle Pepper smiled, winked at her, then jerked at the closest wiggling son.

Gray asked, "Who gives this woman?" The group in unison, almost shouting, answered, "We all do," and broke out laughing.

Salt had decided to tell her mother and brother after the fact. She would say that she and Wills had kept it simple and didn't want them to have to come down for such a short ceremony. That way when next she was face-to-face with her family, she'd have Wills for backup. The baby would have to know there were ancestors.

Mr. Gooden wore a blue blazer over nice slacks and stood smiling and holding Sister's arm on his. Sister, Ann, and Rosie all wore dresses in shades of spring green.

"Let us pray." Gray bowed his head. From the porch there came a sound, an instrumental sound track, strings, a harp, then Pearl singing "At Last," the iconic Etta James tune. Wills, ever the sentimentalist, had gotten together with Pearl and made sure all the pieces, corny and sweet, were in place.

Lil D and Latonya were dressed as always in Homes wear: athletic pants and jackets, and both wore new green footwear.

Then it was over. The piper broke into a jig. And as if on cue, Theo, having escaped his parents' clutches, opened the sheep paddock. Wonder took that as his call to duty and began rounding up the sheep and drove them to Salt. Danny T shrieked and jumped up for his mama. Lil D grabbed him and put him on one of the rungs of the tree ladder. Miles and Theo ran between the dogs and the sheep. And while the piper vigorously piped, there was a gay jostling movement of the wedding party toward the house.

"Go on," Salt told Wills. "I'll get the sheep penned and be right in." Wills whistled for the Rotties.

Lil D and Latonya walked toward the orchard again, but Danny T broke away, screeching at the sheep bunched around Salt, Latonya chasing after him.

"I'm glad you could come," Salt said to Lil D. "He's having a good time." Boys don't bother the sheep." Miles and Theo played a made-up tag game as they ran through the flock.

"He been to the zoo, but he don't get to run around like this," said Lil D, making his way, trying not to touch the animals or to let them rub against him.

Danny eluded Latonya, running from the tree to the sheep pen, where he began climbing the rails. Lil D started toward them.

"He can't hurt anything," Salt told him. "Besides, there's something I want to ask you about."

Lil D looked at the house, the fields and orchard. "You raised up here?"

"My family owned the place."

Latonya scooped up Danny and sat him on the top rail so he could watch the five sheep rustling around Salt and Lil D.

"She likes this for him," said Lil D, nodding at his family.

"She's a good mother."

Lil D, shrugging, looked down at his feet.

"I'll be leaving here. I'm going to be living with Wills now that we're married." Salt turned to face Lil D. "I'm going to need someone to stay here and take care of the place—a caretaker."

"Big place. I guess you do."

"What if you, Latonya, and Danny lived here?"

Lil D looked up at her, tucking back his chin, squinting. "What? We don't know nothin' 'bout no country shit."

She waited, watching Latonya and Danny. "I'd come and help you for a while, on my off days. Mr. Gooden lives right over there." She pointed across the field. "Anything you need right away he'd help you. It would solve problems for both of us. You'd have it free in exchange for taking care of the place and the sheep. Just think about it. You and Latonya talk it over."

"I ain't . . ." As he shook his head, his voice trailed off.

"D, we've never talked about it. You've saved my life twice now, and your testimony last month—I worried about Man's reaction, if he might feel different about you."

Lil D, twisting his mouth, made a click sound. "He ain't straight over Flash yet."

"What future can you have with Man? What future can you give Danny T if you're working for Man?"

"Me and him, we be kids together, come up together in The Homes."

"I've known you both for about half that time, more than ten years. But The Homes is gone, torn down. And you've got Latonya and Danny T now."

"I don't know." Walking toward his family, he said it like there was much he didn't know.

Pepper called the boys. Lil D and his family followed them into the house.

Salt gave Wonder the old Gaelic command, "Come by." And the dog rounded the small flock, causing them to bunch up and follow her to the pen, where she opened the gate and put Wonder at a stand. The sheep trampled in. "That'll do," she said to Wonder, realizing that if Lil D decided against their moving here, this was maybe one of the last times Wonder would have this, the job he was born to do. She touched the dog's head and he turned with her toward the door, where Wills stood watching and waiting for them.

The piper was long gone, as were Reverend Gray and the guests. Lil D, Latonya, and Danny T were staying with Mr. Gooden, who would take them back to the city tomorrow when he drove Sister back. Ann, Sister, and Rosie had done their best to set the house back to normal, plates washed, leftovers wrapped and stored.

"That turned out to be quite a party," said Wills, sprawled on the living room sofa.

Salt sat on the rug beside him with the dogs. "It was kind of magical." She looked up at him and smiled. "Thank you. I wouldn't have thought of all those details."

Wills sat up and held her hand. "We'll make good partners."

"You think Lil D and Latonya had a good time?" she asked. "They seemed a little overwhelmed."

"Danny T wasn't. He was having the time of his life." Wills nudged her with his knee. "What's up with that? You seemed intent on Lil D and his family being here."

Salt stood and pulled at Wills. "Come on. This is our wedding night." She held his hand, tugging him toward the bedroom. "This might be my last night in this house. I'd like to leave it with a good memory."

They bid the dogs settle in the hall outside their bedroom door. The spring wind picked up and howled in the attic rafters.

ACKNOWLEDGMENTS

I am very grateful to Sara Minnich Blackburn, my editor, and Katie McKee, my publicist, and to all the team at G. P. Putnam's Sons. Nat Sobel, my agent, is a mensch, and my thanks go out to him and all those at Sobel Weber Associates. Bless you, first reader Lorna Gentry. I'm ever thankful for the support of my family, Noah, Viki, Gabriel, and Sadira, and my ground control, Rick Saylor.